I0707599

# THE GATES OF HELL
## AND THE DEMONS
### THAT PROTECT IT

FOR MOM

This story is based on actual events that took place in 2003, in and around Sallisaw, Ok. Only, the names of the people involved have been changed to protect their identity.

The Devil is real, Demons do exist, and darkness is everywhere. We just have to find the light to help us find our way through.

- Jason Walker.

# CONTENTS

# One

## NOT JUST FOLKLORE

I settled into the cozy backseat of the car, excitement bubbled within me. Today was going to be a fantastic day, I could feel it. My mom, Anna, took her place behind the wheel with a confident smile, ready to navigate the winding roads ahead. Her friend Julia joined her in the front seat. As we drove, her long hair flowed in the wind, creating a mesmerizing Bronte-esque effect.

We set off on our adventure, and the countryside unfolded before us like a painting came to life. The open windows allowed the gentle breeze to dance through the car, ruffling our hair and bringing a sense of freedom and joy. Mom and Julia, immersed in conversation, shared laughter and exchanged stories, their voices blending harmoniously with the rustling of trees outside.

I watched them from the backseat as their infectious laughter and animated gestures drew me into their world. Their jokes and banter filled the air, creating a warm atmosphere that enveloped us all. It was a sight that made my heart swell with happiness, knowing that these two incredible women were part of my life.

Beside me was Jordan, my younger brother who was immersed in his own little world of imagination. With his action figures in hand, he created epic battles and daring rescues, lost in a world of adventure that only he could see. I smiled at his excitement, and joined him in the epic battle going on with his action figures. Together, we were a team, ready to conquer any challenge that came our way.

The countryside rolled by, showcasing its natural beauty with every passing moment. Endless green hills stretched out like a vast carpet, speckled with vibrant wildflowers that added splashes of color to the landscape. The sun played hide-and-seek with the clouds, casting ethereal beams of light that danced upon the fields, creating an enchanting scene.

As we continued our drive through the countryside, I couldn't help but be captivated by the breathtaking scenery that surrounded us. The quaint town of Sallisaw unfolded before our eyes, revealing a picturesque landscape that seemed straight out of a postcard.

The road stretched out ahead, lined with towering trees that formed a natural canopy, filtering the sunlight and casting intricate patterns on the asphalt below. Their leaves rustled in the wind, creating a soothing melody that accompanied our journey.

The countryside of Sallisaw was a patchwork of vibrant colors. As we passed through open fields, we were greeted by a sea of golden wheat swaying in the breeze. The sight was mesmerizing, as waves of grain undulated like an ocean, stretching out as far as the eye could see.

Occasionally, we would catch glimpses of charming farmhouses nestled amidst the fields, their roofs adorned with weathered terracotta tiles. The scent of freshly cut grass wafted through the air, mingling with the sweet aroma of blooming flowers that lined the fences.

The countryside was dotted with picturesque ponds and lakes, their glassy surfaces reflecting the clear blue sky above. Ducks and swans gracefully glided across the water, creating ripples that expanded outward, like nature's own abstract art. The sight was serene, evoking a sense of tranquility and peace.

As we ventured deeper into Sallisaw, rolling hills emerged, covered in a tapestry of lush greenery. Tall grasses swayed in the wind, creating a gentle undulating motion that resembled the ebb and flow of the ocean. The hills seemed to roll on forever, as if nature itself was putting on a grand display of its majesty.

Every turn in the road offered a new vista, each one more breathtaking than the last. We passed through dense forests, where sunlight filtered through the canopy, casting a warm glow on the moss-covered ground. The air was cool and refreshing, carrying the scent of pine needles and earth, reminding us of the beauty of untouched wilderness.

Wildflowers adorned the sides of the road, their vibrant hues adding a burst of color to the landscape. Daisies, buttercups, and poppies danced in the wind, creating a vibrant mosaic that contrasted beautifully against the lush green backdrop. It was as if the countryside had painted its own masterpiece just for us.

Above all, it was the open road that beckoned us the most. There was something amazing about the feeling of freedom as the car carried us further into the countryside, away from the noise and bustle of the city.

As the hours passed, the road seemed to stretch endlessly before us, and yet, it felt like time was slipping through our fingers, leaving behind a trail of happiness in its wake.

The countryside was our playground, and I and my brother reveled in its beauty. Rolling down the windows, we embraced the smells and sounds of nature. The scent of freshly mown grass and blooming flowers infused the air, filling our senses with a tranquility that only the countryside could provide.

Eventually, the sun began to dip below the horizon, but we kept moving as we had an eventful evening ahead of us. Today was no ordinary day; as we were venturing into uncharted territory—a forbidden graveyard located far away from town. The idea had always lingered in the minds of both my mom, Anna, and her friend Julia, but today, they had made the bold decision to finally commit to the journey.

With each passing mile, the scenery began to change subtly. The fields of golden wheat and rolling hills gradually gave way to a darker and more mysterious landscape. Thick forests loomed on either side of the road, their branches intertwining like gnarled fingers, creating a natural canopy that darkened the path ahead.

I glanced at Mom and Julia in the front seats, their faces alight with both excitement and a touch of apprehension. Their determination to explore the forbidden graveyard was contagious, and I couldn't help but share in their sense of adventure. Julia's long hair whipped wildly in the wind, creating an ethereal aura around her, while Mom's eyes sparkled with a mix of curiosity and excitement.

Jordan and I, huddled in the backseat with our action figures, exchanged furtive glances. We were too young to fully understand the implications of our destination, but we could sense that this was no ordinary outing.

Anna and Julia had grown up hearing captivating legends and tales about this mystical place. These stories had woven their way into their childhood, leaving an indelible mark on their curious minds.

The legends spoke of restless spirits that roamed the graveyard, ancient curses that held the land captive, and evil people that lay buried beneath the tombstones. These tales fascinated Anna and Julia, igniting a sense of wonder and curiosity that couldn't be satiated by mere stories alone. They yearned to unravel the mysteries that enveloped the forbidden graveyard and to explore its secrets firsthand.

As time passed, the legends became a part of their shared history, a bond that deepened their friendship. They would spend countless hours discussing the graveyard while having coffee in our home, their imaginations running wild with vivid imagery and untold possibilities.

Their desire to experience the truth behind the legends grew stronger with each passing year.

Finally, the day had arrived when their thirst for adventure overpowered their trepidation. They had made the daring decision to venture into the forbidden graveyard, and in a moment of spontaneity, they invited Jordan and I to join them on this expedition. It was a chance for us to create our own memories, to immerse ourselves in the tales that had captivated their imaginations for so long.

As we journeyed towards the graveyard, the anticipation in the car was thick in the air. Mom and Julia's eyes sparkled with excitement, their shared childhood memories adding an extra layer of magic to the experience. The legends that had shaped their lives were about to become the backdrop of our own adventure.

Sitting in the backseat with Jordan, I couldn't help but feel a mixture of nervousness and exhilaration. We were young and impressionable, drawn into the captivating allure of the forbidden graveyard by the enthusiasm and determination of our mother.

The drive through the countryside seemed to heighten the sense of anticipation. The changing scenery mirrored our own transformation, from curious onlookers to intrepid explorers. The fading daylight added an air of mystery to the landscape, as if nature itself was conspiring to add a touch of enchantment to our adventure.

We veered off the main road onto a narrow, winding path, the atmosphere grew thicker with secrets. The trees seemed to close in around us, their branches almost forming a protective barrier as if warning us to turn back. The forbidden graveyard was not for the faint of heart, and we were about to find out why.

The wind carried whispers of the past, tales of lost souls and haunted memories that had made this place off-limits to the townspeople. Yet, Mom and Julia had always been drawn to the mystique of the graveyard, fascinated by the stories that had been passed down through generations.

As we approached our destination, the air seemed to grow heavy with an eerie silence. The car's engine hummed softly, the only sound breaking the stillness. The trees loomed taller and darker, casting long shadows that seemed to dance along the ground. Goosebumps prickled on my skin, a mixture of excitement and fear coursing through my veins.

As I looked up to the sky, a sense of awe washed over me. Evening was settling in, casting a golden hue across the horizon. The once vibrant and colorful scenery that had accompanied us on our drive was beginning to lose its brilliance. The fields of golden wheat that shimmered in the sunlight were now bathed in a soft, warm glow, as if bidding farewell to the day.

The trees, once dressed in vibrant shades of green, now took on a more somber appearance. Their leaves seemed to reflect the fading light, turning a deeper shade of emerald before eventually succumbing to the coolness of dusk. Shadows grew longer, stretching across the landscape like fingers reaching out to touch the edges of the road.

As the evening progressed, a subtle change swept through the air. The warm breeze that had caressed our faces earlier gradually grew colder, carrying with it a hint of the approaching night. I could feel a chill seeping into my bones, causing me to pull my jacket a little tighter around me.

The countryside, once bursting with life and vibrant colors, now seemed to be wrapped in a serene stillness. The wildflowers that had danced in the wind earlier had closed their petals, preparing for their own slumber. The landscape, now cloaked in shades of dusky blues and muted purples, exuded a sense of calm and tranquility.

The chirping of birds began to fade, replaced by the distant calls of nocturnal creatures waking from their daytime slumber. The symphony of nature changed its tune, as if orchestrating a peaceful lullaby to accompany us on our journey through the twilight.

The fading light painted a melancholic beauty over the countryside, as if nature itself was bidding farewell to the day. Shadows deepened, enveloping the landscape in an air of mystery. The silhouettes of trees stood tall against the darkening sky, their branches reaching out like gnarled fingers, casting elongated shadows on the road.

Jordan and I huddled closer in the backseat, seeking warmth and comfort in each other's presence. The chill in the air sent a shiver down our spines, but we found solace in knowing that we were on this journey together, surrounded by the love and warmth of our family.

The car drove on and the day slowly gave way to the evening. The sky transformed into a vast canvas, splashed with hues of deep blues and fiery oranges, as the last remnants of daylight faded away. Stars began to twinkle overhead, painting a celestial spectacle above us.

I leaned back in my seat, taking one last glance at the changing landscape. The warm air had given way to a cool breeze, carrying with it the bloated promise of a peaceful evening. The countryside, now shrouded in the tranquility of twilight, held an otherworldly charm that would forever be etched in my memory.

As we got closer and closer to the forbidden graveyard, our path took an unexpected turn. The road ahead twisted and turned, leading us onto a narrow and desolate path that seemed to have been swallowed by darkness. It was as if the very atmosphere shifted, and an eerie stillness settled around us.

The car's headlights cut through the gloom, casting long shadows that danced along the trees. The silence was deafening, broken only by the soft hum of the engine and the distant hoot of an owl. A sense of unease began to permeate the air, wrapping its tendrils around my brother Jordan and me.

Sitting in the backseat, we exchanged worried glances. The once-exciting adventure now seemed to take on a foreboding tone. The hair on the back of my neck stood on end, and a chill ran down my spine. We both felt the weight of the graveyard's history and the legends that had fueled our curiosity.

As I glanced at Mom and Julia in the front seats, I noticed something remarkable. They appeared unfazed by the creeping unease that enveloped Jordan and me. Their faces radiated excitement and determination, their eyes sparkling with an insatiable curiosity. It was as if their thirst for knowledge and their deep-rooted friendship shielded them from any feelings of fear.

Yet, despite the mounting unease, Mom and Julia remained resolute. Their laughter and whispered conversations filled the car, punctuating the silence with a sense of familiarity and comfort.

Soon, our car rumbled along a rough and dirty road that snaked its way through the eerie landscape. The wheels kicked up clouds of dust, creating a hazy atmosphere that added to the sense of mystery and anticipation. The uneasiness between my brother Jordan and me began to intensify, casting a shadow over our excitement.

The bumpy ride rattled our nerves, and the dusty air filled our lungs. The once vibrant and colorful countryside scenery had given way to a more desolate and haunting landscape. The trees along the road stood tall and gnarled, their branches reaching out like skeletal fingers, adding to the eerie ambiance.

As I glanced at Jordan, I could see his apprehension mirrored in his eyes. The unfamiliar surroundings and the legends we had heard whispered in our ears made the atmosphere even more unsettling.

I looked towards the front seats again, observing Mom and Julia conversing animatedly. Their laughter broke through the tension, filling the car with a sense of lightness. Their hair, previously blowing freely in the wind, now carried traces of dust. Their excitement seemed to grow with every passing mile, their curiosity propelling them forward.

Perhaps this was their way of convincing themselves not to be afraid and go on on this eerie road. I had no idea. But their unease was a huge source of comfort to me and my brother. Despite the chill in the air and the fading daylight, their spirits remained unphased.

As the car continued along the dusty road, the colors of the surrounding scenery seemed to blend together, losing their vibrancy. The warm air gradually gave way to a slight chill, reminding us that the evening was settling in. The fading light cast long shadows, and the silence became more pronounced.

As we approached the forbidden graveyard, the sight that greeted us sent shivers down our spines. The imposing presence of big, broad iron gates loomed ahead, their cold, metallic structure casting an air of foreboding over the entire scene.

Barbed wire, twisted and menacing, encircled the perimeter of the graveyard. Its sharp edges glinted in the fading light, serving as a stark reminder of the solemnity and isolation that permeated this hallowed ground. The wire seemed to form a symbolic boundary, discouraging all but the most determined from venturing further.

As we approached the rusted iron gate that guarded the entrance to the graveyard, a mixture of excitement and trepidation flooded our souls. This was the moment we had all been waiting for. The stories, the legends, and the tales would no longer be confined to our imaginations. We were about to step into a world where reality intertwined with folklore.

Anna and Julia pushed open the heavy iron gates, the rusty hinges creaked in protest, adding to the eerie ambiance of the graveyard. The gates swung open, revealing the solemn expanse of the burial ground beyond. Without hesitation, the two friends stepped inside, their footsteps resolute and determined.

With hesitant but determined steps, we followed them through the iron gate, leaving behind the safety of the car and entering a realm shrouded in mystery. Our hearts beat in sync, the sound echoing in the stillness of the graveyard. The moon cast an ethereal glow over the tombstones, casting elongated shadows on the ground.

As we ventured deeper into the graveyard, our senses were heightened. Every rustle of leaves, every creak of a weathered tombstone, seemed to carry whispers from the past. The atmosphere was heavy with the weight of history, a symphony of emotions and stories that tugged at our hearts.

The old gravestones, weathered by time and etched with the names of those long gone, stood as silent witnesses to the passage of centuries. They formed a haunting labyrinth, a maze of forgotten souls.

In the center of the graveyard, a large burn pit stood as a grim focal point. Its charred edges hinted at past rituals or perhaps even darker secrets. It was a place that seemed to hold a history of its own, fueling our curiosity and sparking our imaginations. The burn pit emanated an aura of mystery and unease.

To the right of the graveyard, a narrow dirt road wound its way around the backside of the burial ground. The road, worn and barely visible, beckoned with an eerie invitation. It seemed to lead to the unknown, its destination shrouded in shadows.

Just off the road, a river flowed quietly, its gentle current reflecting the fading hues of the twilight sky. The river, in its tranquil demeanor, stood as a stark contrast to the mysterious atmosphere of the graveyard.

The wind whispered through the gravestones, carrying echoes of forgotten voices and stirring the fallen leaves. The atmosphere was thick with a blend of solemnity and anticipation. We stood at the threshold of the forbidden graveyard, aware of the risks and challenges that lay ahead, yet driven by an insatiable curiosity to uncover the truth that lay buried within its depths.

However, as I and Jordan looked upon the scene before us, fear gripped our hearts. The gravestones seemed to loom ominously, and the dark shadows cast by the fading light made the place feel even more forbidding. The sight of the burn pit at the center of the graveyard sent shivers down our spines, and the barbed wire surrounding the area served as a stark reminder of the graveyard's isolation.

Trepidation held us in its grip, and we hesitated, unsure if we could summon the courage to go on. Sensing our fear, Anna turned back to us with her face filled with understanding and compassion.

"It's okay, my darlings," Anna said gently, reaching out to hold her sons' trembling hands. "I know it looks intimidating, but we're here together. There's nothing to be afraid of. This is just a place filled with history and stories from the past. We'll stay close and keep each other safe."

Her reassuring words melted some of the fear in my heart, and I took a deep breath, finding strength in my mother's presence.

As we walked among the ancient gravestones, Anna shared snippets of history and stories she had heard from the legends. Her voice was soothing, weaving a tapestry of the lives that once were, painting portraits of the souls that rested there. Slowly, the fear that had gripped I and Jordan began to ebb away, replaced by a growing fascination for the past.

Anna's words carried a sense of respect for the resting souls and the significance of the graveyard. Her reverence infused the atmosphere with a feeling of tranquility and contemplation. With her guidance, we started to view the place with new eyes, appreciating the beauty of the aged gravestones and the legacy left by those who had come before.

At this point I and Jordan had snatched our hands from hers and wanted to play on our own.

As we walked through the graveyard, my eyes scanned the surroundings, taking in the eerie scene before me. To the left of the burial ground, a vast open field stretched out, reaching as far as my eyes could see. The field seemed to hold an air of desolation, its emptiness contrasting with the somber presence of the graveyard itself.

Beyond the field, a line of trees stood like guardians, separating the graveyard from a dark and foreboding forest. The dense foliage cast long shadows, and the gnarled branches seemed to intertwine, forming a barrier that whispered of mystery and danger. The woods exuded an ominous aura, and I couldn't help but feel a shiver crawl up my spine as I glanced in that direction.

The contrast between the open field and the menacing woods intensified the sense of isolation and vulnerability that surrounded us. It was as if the graveyard stood at the crossroads of different worlds—the peaceful rest of the departed on one side and the unknown darkness of the woods on the other.

The wind rustled through the trees, sending a chill down my spine. The leaves whispered secrets I couldn't decipher, heightening the mystery of the woods. My gaze lingered on the tree line, my imagination running wild with stories of what might lurk within those sinister shadows. The thought of venturing into the woods sent a shiver of apprehension through my body.

The fading light cast long shadows, creating an atmosphere of both tranquility and unease. I couldn't help but glance towards the dark woods, their enigmatic allure still beckoning to me.

As I and Jordan played in the graveyard, I kept a watchful eye on the tree line. The legends and tales whispered throughout the town flooded my mind, filling me with a mix of fascination and fear. The woods held a deep, dark secret that had been part of the local lore for generations, dating back to the 1800s.

According to the stories, hidden deep within the dense thicket of trees lay a hidden Satanic church. Its existence was shrouded in mystery, accessible only to those who dared venture into the woods at specific times. The tales spoke of strange rituals, haunting chants, and inexplicable occurrences that took place within the sinister walls of the hidden church.

The legends had been passed down from one generation to another, their details growing more embellished with each telling. People spoke of eerie lights emanating from the heart of the woods during certain moonlit nights, and whispers of eerie hymns carrying on the wind. It was said that only the brave or the foolish would dare to seek out the hidden church, for its secrets were rumored to be both mesmerizing and terrifying.

As I looked into the depths of the woods, my imagination conjured images of flickering candlelight illuminating the darkened sanctuary, sinister symbols etched upon the walls, and an atmosphere charged with an otherworldly energy. The thought of such a place existing sent a chill down my spine, yet it also ignited a spark of curiosity within me.

But amidst the allure of the legend, a wariness also lingered. The woods seemed to hold an energy, an ancient presence that whispered caution. It was as if the very trees themselves warned of the dangers that lay hidden within. I couldn't help but wonder if these tales were simply the product of vivid imaginations or if there was an element of truth buried within the layers of folklore.

Julia brought out her small camera, eager to capture the essence of the place that held such mystique. The camera, though old and worn, had a certain charm to it. Julia adjusted the settings, attempting to capture the scene before us.

"These pictures are turning out quite blurry," Julia complained, her brows furrowing with disappointment. "The lighting isn't ideal, and it's making it difficult to capture the details."

At first, I thought the camera was blurry because of the dimming light of the evening casting long shadows across the field.

However, Julia continued to snap pictures of both Anna and us. Our faces illuminated by the soft glow of the camera's flash. The fading light added an ethereal quality to the photographs, giving them an old-world charm. The soft hues and muted tones mirrored the atmosphere of the graveyard, capturing its somber beauty. Each image was a fragment of the stories we had heard, frozen in time and etched onto film.

As we took pictures, I ran to Julia to check them out and couldn't help but feel a mixture of awe and trepidation. The blurred edges and the subtle distortions seemed to reflect the enigmatic nature of the place we stood. It was as if the camera itself struggled to capture the essence of this hidden realm.

Julia soon got disappointed at the blurry images and carefully tucked away the camera.

As we wrapped up our exploration of the graveyard field, a subtle realization began to creep into my consciousness. The fading light of the evening had gradually given way to the encroaching darkness. The once vibrant colors of the landscape now appeared muted, and the shadows lengthened, stretching like tendrils across the ground.

A shiver ran down my spine as I glanced around, noticing how the familiar landmarks had taken on an eerie and unfamiliar aura. The gravestones that had earlier stood as stoic sentinels now appeared more ominous, their shapes merging with the encroaching darkness. The field, once a place of curiosity and intrigue, now held an air of uncertainty.

I felt a knot tighten in my stomach, a flicker of unease dancing within me. It was as if the fading light had taken with it a sense of security, leaving us exposed to the unknown that now surrounded us. The distant sounds of nocturnal creatures and the whispering wind carried a sense of foreboding.

Anna noticed the change in atmosphere and gathered us close. Her reassuring touch on my shoulder offered some solace amidst the encroaching darkness. I could see concern etched on her face, mirroring the unease I felt within myself.

The realization that darkness had fallen upon us in the graveyard field awakened a sense of urgency within me. The legends and tales of the hidden church, the mysteries of the woods, and the encroaching night all merged into a tapestry of uncertainty.

We soon began to make our way back, back towards the iron gates. Each footfall echoed through the silence. The air grew colder, and the sounds of the nocturnal world enveloped us, adding to the mystique of our surroundings.

A sudden movement caught Anna's keen eye. She stopped abruptly, her gaze fixed on something in the distance. Her sharp intake of breath drew my attention, and I followed her line of sight, squinting into the growing shadows.

Straining my eyes, I struggled to discern the source of the movement. My heart quickened with anticipation and a hint of apprehension. It felt as if time itself held its breath, waiting to reveal the secrets concealed within the darkness.

At first, my vision failed me, the contours of the landscape blurring in the fading light. But as my eyes adjusted, I caught a flickering glow across the field. A flicker that danced and swayed with an otherworldly rhythm. My breath caught in my throat as the realization washed over me—it was fire.

Fire, like a distant beacon, cast an eerie glow against the night. Its warm, flickering light contrasted sharply with the encroaching darkness, illuminating the hidden corners of the field. It seemed to sway and dance in the wind, casting long shadows that stretched and twisted across the ground.

I strained my eyes, attempting to make out the details of this mysterious fire. My gaze darted back and forth, trying to discern its origin and purpose. But the distance and the encroaching darkness played tricks on my vision, obscuring the true nature of the fire's source.

My mind raced with questions. Was it a bonfire, casting its glow from a gathering of people? Or was it something more sinister, fueled by the legends that surrounded this place?

As I squinted, the fire seemed to take on a life of its own. Shadows danced and twisted in its glow, playing tricks on my senses. I strained my ears, hoping to catch the distant sound of laughter or the echo of voices carried on the wind. But all I could perceive was the crackle and hiss of the fire, a mysterious symphony in the night.

I turned to look at my mom, Anna, and her friend, Julia, only to find their expressions contorted with fear and panic. It was a sight I had never witnessed before—a raw, unfiltered fear etched on my mom's face.

Anna's eyes widened, her normally composed demeanor shattered by the unsettling scene before us. Her hand instinctively tightened its grip on mine, her fingers trembling ever so slightly. Julia, usually quick-witted and bold, stood frozen, her face drained of color.

In that moment, their fear transmitted to me, infecting my own thoughts and emotions. My heart raced, and a knot formed in my stomach, as a sense of impending danger washed over us like a menacing tide.

"M-Mom, what's wrong?" I stammered, my voice betraying my own unease.

Anna struggled to find her words, her voice quivering with a mixture of terror and disbelief. "There's an unsettling presence here, something beyond what we can comprehend."

Her words sent a shiver down my spine, confirming the gravity of the situation. I looked to Julia, hoping for some guidance or reassurance.

But her eyes, once filled with a sense of adventure and curiosity, were now filled with a deep-seated fear that mirrored our own. Her lips trembled, but no words escaped them.

The silence that enveloped us felt deafening, punctuated only by the crackling of the distant fire and the pounding of our hearts. Time seemed to stretch, suspended in the grip of uncertainty.

Anna, her voice steadying slightly, managed to break the silence. "We need to leave. Now. This place... it's not what we anticipated."

Her urgency resonated within me, dispelling any hesitation that lingered in my mind. I nodded, understanding the gravity of the situation. Together, we turned away from the haunting glow of the fire, retreating from the graveyard field.

The sense of fear and panic that gripped us grew stronger with each step, the echoes of our own racing footsteps amplifying our unease. The once-familiar surroundings of the graveyard now felt like a labyrinth of shadows and foreboding.

As we hurriedly made our way towards the car, confusion and a growing sense of unease enveloped me. I glanced around, desperately searching for any signs or clues as to what had stirred up such fear in my mom and Julia. But there was nothing, no visible threat, no tangible danger that I could discern.

The air hung heavy with tension, as if invisible forces were at play, taunting us from the shadows. It felt as though we were being watched, scrutinized by eyes that remained hidden from our view. The unease gnawed at my insides, a relentless reminder that something was terribly amiss.

Anna's voice, filled with urgency and a hint of desperation, pierced through the darkness. "Jason! Jordan! Get in the car now! We need to leave!"

Her words were a jolt, snapping me out of my thoughts and propelling me into action. The tone in her voice left no room for hesitation or questions. It was the voice of a mother driven by instinct, fueled by a need to protect her children from an imminent threat.

Jordan, my younger brother, sensed the urgency in Anna's voice too. Fear etched across his face, mirroring my own, he darted towards the car, his small figure a blur of movement in the dimly lit surroundings.

My heart pounded in my chest as I raced to catch up with Jordan, the gravity of the situation weighing heavily upon me. The car, our refuge from the unknown, stood illuminated by the faint glow of the moon.

As I approached the vehicle, Anna stood by the open door, her eyes scanning the surroundings, her body tense with apprehension. She urged us on, her voice laced with a mix of fear and determination. "Hurry! We can't waste any more time!"

Without hesitation, Jordan and I leapt into the car, the familiar scent of leather and the comforting warmth of the interior offering a brief respite from the unsettling atmosphere outside. The engine roared to life, drowning out the haunting whispers that seemed to echo in the air.

As Anna slid into the driver's seat, her hands trembling slightly, I stole a glance at her face. The lines of worry etched deep into her features, her eyes reflecting a mixture of fear and fierce determination. It was a side of her I had rarely seen before.

The tires screeched as Anna accelerated, the car lurching forward, propelling us away from the graveyard and its enigmatic secrets. The wind whipped through the open windows, carrying with it a sense of both relief and lingering dread. We left behind the graveyard and the mysteries it held, retreating from the unknown with a renewed sense of caution.

As the car sped along the winding road, a veil of uncertainty remained, leaving us with unanswered questions and a lingering unease. Who or what had stirred up such fear within our hearts? Were we being targeted by some invisible force, or were we simply victims of an overactive imagination?

As we sped away from the graveyard, the adrenaline coursing through my veins, I couldn't shake off the feeling of being watched. I took a final glance back at the graveyard, catching glimpses of the retreating silhouette of the cemetery. But what caught my attention, and sent a shiver down my spine, were the figures emerging from the dark woods.

In the fading light, I strained my eyes, trying to make sense of the scene unfolding behind us. My heart pounded in my chest as I realized that the darkness that had settled upon the graveyard was now being infiltrated by an eerie procession. Eight to ten figures clad in dark robes, their faces concealed by hoods, moved with an unsettling purpose, their torches casting flickering shadows upon the ground.

Fear gripped me once more, and I leaned forward, my voice trembling as I called out to Anna. "Mom! Look! They're coming from the woods!"

Anna's eyes widened, her grip on the steering wheel tightening as she stole a glance in the rearview mirror. Her breath caught in her throat, mirroring the mix of disbelief and apprehension that washed over me. "What... what is happening?"

Julia, sitting in the passenger seat, turned her head, her eyes widening in shock as she too caught sight of the approaching figures. "Oh my God... who are they? What are they doing?"

The questions hung in the air, unanswered, as we watched the robed figures draw closer to the graveyard. Their movements were deliberate, their presence casting an even darker shadow over the already ominous atmosphere.

An unsettling silence settled within the vehicle, punctuated only by the hum of the engine and the distant crackling of the torches. Each passing moment seemed to stretch, as if time itself held its breath, frozen in anticipation of what was to come.

As the figures neared the graveyard gates, a chilling realization washed over me. The legends and stories we had heard, the rumors of a hidden satanic church deep within these woods, suddenly seemed more than just folklore. It appeared that we had stumbled upon something far more sinister, something that now stood on the precipice of unveiling itself.

As the car lurching further and further into the distance Anna and Julia's terrified screams pierced the air, filling the vehicle with an overwhelming sense of panic. The fear that had settled upon us in the graveyard now intensified, fueled by the haunting images that had unfolded before our eyes.

Anna's hands gripped the steering wheel tightly, her knuckles turning white as she navigated the treacherous road with unwavering determination. The headlights cut through the inky blackness, casting fleeting glimmers of light upon the dense foliage that lined the narrow path.

With each turn, each swerve, the terror in Anna's voice grew louder, her words intertwining with Julia's panicked pleas. "Faster! We need to get away! We have to leave this place!"

The urgency in their voices echoed the tumultuous rhythm of our pounding hearts. Adrenaline surged through our veins, propelling us forward as we sought refuge from the nightmarish scene that had unfolded in the graveyard.

Outside the confines of the car, the darkness seemed to close in on us, casting long shadows that danced menacingly in the periphery of our vision. The countryside, once a tranquil landscape, now felt like a labyrinth of fear, with each passing moment intensifying our desperate need to escape.

As we hurtled down the road, the engine roared with a deafening crescendo, almost drowning out the cacophony of our terrified cries. The car jolted over uneven terrain, its tires gripping the road with a fervor matched only by our determination to outrun whatever unseen terror lurked in the night.

Through the rearview mirror, I caught glimpses of Anna's face, etched with a mix of fear, determination, and an unwavering motherly instinct to protect us at any cost. Her eyes darted from the road to the mirror, scanning the darkness behind us, as if expecting an imminent threat to emerge from the shadows.

Julia, her breath ragged and frantic, clutched at her chest, her voice strained with desperation. "Don't look back! Just keep driving, Anna! We can't let them catch us!"

I nodded in silent agreement, my gaze fixed on the road ahead, my heart pounding in my ears. The car seemed to be an island of fleeting safety in a sea of encroaching darkness, a lifeline that we desperately clung to as we pushed its limits.

The night air rushed past us, carrying with it a chilling reminder of the events that had unfolded just moments before. The wind whispered eerie secrets, amplifying our fears and pushing us further into a state of relentless panic.

Time seemed to blur as we barreled through the night, our minds consumed by thoughts of escape and survival. The country roads stretched out endlessly, an unforgiving path that offered no respite from the terrors that pursued us.

With each passing mile, the grip of fear began to loosen its hold, replaced by a lingering sense of unease and the solemn realization that we had narrowly escaped a fate that remained shrouded in darkness. The car's engine gradually settled into a steady hum, the intensity of our cries giving way to heavy breathing and subdued whispers.

The car glided down the once vibrant country road, its tires rolling over the asphalt with a muted whisper. A heavy silence settled within the vehicle, each of us lost in our own thoughts, the weight of the recent events hanging heavily in the air.

The once cheerful and colorful landscape now wore a somber cloak, shrouded in shadow and darkness. The moon, hidden behind a thick layer of clouds, offered only sporadic glimpses of its pale light, casting an eerie glow upon the desolate scenery. The vibrant hues that had adorned the countryside during the daylight hours had faded into muted shades, as if drained of life itself.

The wind that brushed against the car's windows carried with it a chill that seemed to seep into our bones, intensifying the unsettling atmosphere. It whispered through the trees, rustling the leaves that had lost their luster, and carried with it a mournful melody that mirrored our own somber moods.

The once bustling sounds of nature had surrendered to an eerie stillness. The nocturnal creatures that typically filled the night air with their symphony of chirps and calls had fallen silent, as if sensing the residual tension that clung to the surroundings.

Inside the car, no one uttered a word. The weight of our shared experience hung heavily upon us, rendering even simple conversation a daunting task. Each of us was lost in our own thoughts, grappling with the aftermath of what we had witnessed and the lingering fear that refused to dissipate.

The headlights of the car illuminated the road ahead, their beams cutting through the darkness, revealing fleeting glimpses of the once familiar landmarks. Shadows danced along the edges of our vision, casting an unsettling presence upon the surroundings.

Through the window, I caught sight of the trees that lined the road, their branches reaching out like skeletal fingers, seemingly contorted in an eternal grasp. The foliage that had once swayed with life and vitality now appeared as a sea of dark silhouettes, their leaves rustling with a ghostly whisper.

As we drove deeper into the night, the landscape took on an otherworldly quality. The absence of vibrant colors and the hushed stillness magnified the sense of isolation and desolation. The road stretched out before us, a ribbon of gray cutting through the encroaching darkness, seemingly leading us further into the unknown.

The silence within the car became a tangible presence, its weight pressing upon us, magnifying the intensity of our emotions. It was as if each of us, lost in our own thoughts, feared that breaking the silence would shatter the fragile semblance of normalcy that remained.

The once lively countryside had transformed into a place of shadows and secrets, its allure replaced by an unsettling and ominous aura. The journey that had begun with excitement and curiosity had now morphed into a haunting reminder of the darkness that can lurk just beyond the surface of our perceived reality.

As the car continued to glide along the desolate road, I couldn't help but long for the return of the vibrant colors, the joyful sounds, and the sense of security that had been stolen from us. But in this moment, as the chilling breeze whispered its mournful melody and the landscape draped itself in shadows, we were left to navigate the uncharted path of our own thoughts and emotions.

As we finally reached the outskirts of town, the comforting glow of streetlights illuminated our path, casting a fragile shield against the lingering shadows that clung to our memories. We pulled the car to a halt, our bodies trembling with exhaustion and the weight of the harrowing experience we had just survived.

Anna, her voice now a mere whisper, turned to us with a mixture of relief and lingering fear etched across her face. "We made it... we're safe."

The tension in the vehicle gradually eased, replaced by a mixture of relief and lingering unease. New questions swirled in my mind, demanding answers that seemed elusive and unattainable. Who were those figures? What was their purpose in that desolate graveyard? And what would have happened if we had stayed a moment longer?

Days turned into weeks, and weeks into months, but the memory of that encounter in the graveyard never faded. It served as a constant reminder of the thin veil that separates the known from the unknown, the familiar from the unsettling.

We never spoke of that night in great detail, each of us silently acknowledging the unspoken pact to keep our experience buried deep within ourselves. But the knowledge of what we had witnessed lingered, forever altering our perception of the world and the hidden mysteries.

Twelve years had passed since that fateful night in the graveyard, and life had taken its course. I had grown into a young adult and my once innocent eyes now reflected the wisdom and resilience that had been forged through the trials of my past. And here I was, at a lively party, surrounded by friends, laughter, and the comforting embrace of the present moment.

Tessa and Steven, my trusted companions, stood by my side. We had weathered storms together, celebrating victories and consoling each other through hardships of high school.

The atmosphere took on a mystical and enchanting quality. It was the later end of October and we all got invited to a Halloween celebration. We felt this party was certainly going to beat prom night that had been strictly monitored by our school authorities. This was a chance to unwind, say goodbye to one chapter and embrace a new one.

The room came alive with a kaleidoscope of colors, as people arrived in an array of costumes inspired by their favorite spooky characters. Ghosts, ghouls, witches, and vampires mingled with the crowd, their eerie presence adding an extra layer of excitement to the festivities. From classic horror movie icons to mythical creatures, the costumes showcased a range of influences and personal interpretations. The air buzzed with anticipation as each new guest entered the room, their costumes masterfully crafted to embody the essence of the macabre.

A group of friends arrived dressed as a pack of werewolves, their realistic fursuits and fierce masks giving them an air of primal power. Their commitment to their characters evident in every movement as they howled and prowled.

Not far away, a couple embraced the haunting allure of vampires. Clad in elegant Victorian attire, their porcelain skin contrasting with crimson lips and eyes that seemed to hold secrets of the night, they exude an aura of seduction and mystery.

A group of friends had chosen to pay homage to the realm of fantasy, donning elven costumes complete with ethereal robes, pointed ears, and delicate, intricate face paint. Their graceful movements and whimsical presence transported us to a world of magic and wonder.

Not all the costumes were dark and foreboding. Some guests had embraced the lighter side of Halloween, opting for characters that brought a touch of humor and nostalgia. I spotted a familiar figure dressed as a friendly ghost, his white sheet adorned with a cheeky grin. The infectious laughter that followed him wherever he went spread joy throughout the room.

The music shifted, seamlessly blending eerie melodies with infectious beats that compelled even the most reserved guests to dance. The room became a swirling sea of color and movement, as witches twirled in their flowing black dresses, and zombies shuffled and groaned in time with the rhythm.

The decorations enhanced the ambiance, transforming the space into a haunted wonderland. Spiderwebs adorned every corner, their delicate strands catching the light and casting intricate patterns on the walls. Dimly lit lanterns flickered, casting an eerie glow that added to the otherworldly atmosphere.

Conversations were intertwined with laughter, the revelers sharing stories of Halloween traditions and reminiscing about their favorite spooky moments. The mingling scents of sweet treats and pumpkin spice filled the air, evoking a sense of nostalgia and fond memories.

In the midst of the Halloween revelry, Tessa wore a ghost costume that exuded an ethereal charm. Her flowing white gown billowed around her, giving the illusion of weightlessness as she gracefully moved through the crowd. She wore a translucent veil that concealed her features.

Steven, on the other hand, had taken on a more extraterrestrial persona. Clad in a vibrant alien costume, he stood out among the sea of spooky characters. His silver jumpsuit shimmered under the disco lights, and a pair of large, glossy eyes adorned his mask, making it seem as if he had just landed from another galaxy. I chuckled as I noticed him occasionally holding the mask in his hands to engage in conversations, revealing his infectious smile.

As for myself, I had chosen to don the guise of the Grim Reaper. Cloaked in black from head to toe, the hood of my costume concealed my face, leaving only the glow of my eyes visible. With a scythe in hand, I embraced the theatricality of the character, occasionally playfully pretending to chase after my friends in jest.

Laughter and banter filled the air as we mingled with other partygoers. The room buzzed with a lighthearted energy, as jokes and playful taunts were exchanged between friends and strangers alike. It seemed as though every corner held a new encounter, a shared moment of amusement and connection.

Tessa, in her ghostly attire, glided across the dance floor, her translucent presence weaving through the throng of partygoers. She playfully startled unsuspecting guests, eliciting a mix of surprise and laughter. Her infectious spirit and mischievous antics turned her into the life of the party, drawing smiles from everyone she encountered.

Meanwhile, Steven, with his alien costume, added a touch of whimsy to the festivities. His playful attempts at mimicking extraterrestrial mannerisms and exaggerated gestures earned him amused glances and delighted chuckles from those around him.

As for me, the Grim Reaper, I found myself engaging in witty banter with fellow partygoers. The anonymity provided by the costume allowed me to adopt a slightly mischievous persona, exchanging playful quips and delivering exaggerated gestures in the spirit of the character. Laughter echoed in response, creating a sense of camaraderie and shared joy.

The room pulsed with vibrant energy, music reverberating through the air and adding a lively rhythm to the atmosphere. Conversations danced in harmony with the melodies, filling the spaces with laughter, shared stories, and playful banter. Glasses clinked as we raised toasts, the effervescent liquid within them mirroring the joy and merriment that permeated the room.

We shared memories and we relived the adventures we had embarked upon, reminiscing about the mischievous escapades that had filled our youth. Each tale ignited fits of laughter, momentarily lifting the weight of responsibilities and allowing us to revel in the carefree spirit of the moment.

The room became a sanctuary, where time lost its grip and the worries of the world seemed to fade into the background. We found solace in the company of one another, appreciating the simple pleasure of shared laughter and the unbreakable bond we had cultivated over the years.

Throughout the night, the room echoed with the symphony of laughter and merriment. Funny anecdotes were shared, stories were embellished, and witty comebacks became the currency of the evening. From impromptu dance-offs to hilarious photo sessions, the bonds forged in this spirited gathering transcended the masks we wore. The laughter and banter became the threads that wove us together, creating a tapestry of mirth and celebration.

In this laughter-filled haven, time seemed to suspend. The weight of everyday life lifted, replaced by the carefree abandon of the moment. As we reveled in the hilarity of the night.

What crowned this night was the fact that we were not only celebrating our freedom from our high school. But Tessa received exciting news just before we got to the party. She had been accepted into a prestigious college located in a city far away. We couldn't be prouder of her accomplishments, and this party was a way to honor her success. The air was charged with a mixture of anticipation, nostalgia, and the bittersweet realization that our paths were diverging.

As for myself and Steven, we had decided to take some time before diving into further education. We wanted to savor the freedom and revel in the last moments of carefree youth before venturing into the world of academia. This celebration was our way of embracing the present, living in the moment without the constraints of a structured routine.

We reminisced about our high school years, exchanging stories that ranged from hilarious mishaps to poignant moments of personal growth. The drinks flowed freely, adding a touch of merriment to the already festive atmosphere. It was a night to honor our accomplishments, to toast to the friendships we had cultivated, and to embrace the uncertainty that lay ahead.

Tessa's upcoming adventure brought a sense of excitement and a tinge of wistfulness. We knew that her departure would create a void in our close-knit circle, but we also understood that it was an opportunity for her to explore new horizons and chase her dreams. We shared in her joy, albeit tinged with a hint of longing for the familiarity of our shared hometown.

For now, we were determined to make the most of the time we had together. We laughed, danced, and immersed ourselves in the carefree spirit of the evening. The music pulsed through our veins, infusing us with a sense of liberation and possibility. It was a celebration of our youth, of the friendships that had stood the test of time, and of the uncharted paths that awaited each of us.

As the night wore on, we got together and our conversations grew deeper, transitioning from lighthearted banter to heartfelt discussions about our hopes, fears, and aspirations. We supported one another, sharing words of encouragement and offering reassurance as we navigated the uncertain terrain of adulthood.

As the sky outside darkened, and the stars twinkled overhead, we raised our glasses, toasting to the memories we had made and the adventures that awaited us.

As we sat together, still laughing and sipping on our drinks, Tessa's words hung in the air like a playful challenge, her mischievous smile hinted at the possibility of newfound adventure and her declaration sparked a lively discussion among us.

"You know what, guys?" Tessa began, her eyes alight with excitement. "I've been thinking about it, and honestly, our high school years were fun, but we never really did anything too daring or unforgettable together. This party might be the craziest thing we've done as a group!"

Her bold statement drew curious glances from both Steven and me. It was true; our high school days were filled with memorable moments, but they were mostly of the typical teenage variety. We had not done something too dangerous or that would lead us into much trouble with the authorities.

'Oh I have an idea. How about you finally let go of your virginity. I am willing to assist with that.' Steven said with a smug smile on his face while Tessa glared at him. Steven playfully nudged Tessa with a mischievous grin on his face. "Come on, Tessa," he teased, his voice laced with excitement. "Do something truly reckless tonight. I dare you."

Tessa's eyes sparkled with a mix of amusement and defiance. She leaned back, crossing her arms with a sly smile. "Oh, Steven," she retorted, feigning nonchalance. "Are you sure you're up for the challenge? I don't think you can handle the level of recklessness I'm capable of."

Steven stretched out his hands like he was about to receive an embrace 'Dare me Love.' he said. But Tessa pinched him in his armpit making both of them chuckle in amusement

Their friendly banter filled the air, creating an electric energy within our group. The playful taunting continued as Tessa and Steven exchanged teasing remarks, each trying to one-up the other. It was a dance of wit and confidence, a battle of egos that brought laughter and amusement to all of us.

Tessa's eyes gleamed with a mixture of mischief and curiosity. She leaned in closer to Steven, a challenge evident in her voice. "Alright, Steven, I'll accept your dare," she declared, her tone daring and confident. "But remember, you asked for it. I hope you're prepared for what's coming."

Steven chuckled, accepting the challenge with a twinkle in his eyes. "I wouldn't have it any other way," he replied, his voice filled with anticipation. "Tonight, we'll embark on an adventure that will push our limits and create memories to last a lifetime."

Tessa's excitement soften a little. 'But aren't there better, more daring things in life than sex?' she turned to me. 'I mean, when was the last time we went on a trip and launched ourselves into lakes we had no idea was beneath it? When last did we have real wounds and scars. Not scratches everyone is bragging about nowadays.

Steven grinned at Tessa's words. "You might have a point there, Tessa," he replied, raising his glass. "Maybe it's time we step up our game and go on an epic adventure before college starts. We've got nothing to lose and everything to gain!"

I nodded in agreement, feeling the thrill of the idea taking root in my heart. It was exhilarating to think about the endless possibilities that lay ahead. "You're right," I chimed in. "College will bring its own adventures, but we can make the most of this time together. We could explore new places, try daring activities, and create unforgettable memories!"

Tessa's eyes lit up at the prospect of embarking on a wild journey with her best friends. "Exactly! I don't want to go to college with regrets or the feeling that I missed out on something amazing. We need to challenge ourselves to do something we'll be talking about for years to come!"

Steven's expression turned contemplative, as if he were lost in a distant memory. He took a sip of his drink before clearing his throat, capturing our attention with his story.

"You know, guys, speaking of recklessness" he began, his voice tinged with a mix of intrigue and caution. "There was this one time when I got involved with a girl who I swear was a ghost."

Our eyes widened, intrigued by the mysterious turn the conversation had taken. Steven leaned in closer, his voice lowered as if sharing a closely guarded secret. "It was after a party, just like this one," he continued. "We were both caught up in the buzz of the night, the music, the laughter. But there was something different about her, something ethereal."

He paused for a while and then continued shortly after "As the night progressed, I found myself drawn to her. There was an undeniable connection, a magnetic pull that I couldn't resist. So, I mustered up the courage and pulled her aside, seeking a quiet moment away from the crowd."

Steven's gaze shifted, his eyes focused on an invisible point in the distance. "And that's when things took an eerie turn," he whispered. "As we stood there, hidden away in the shadows, she seemed to... change. It was as if her form became translucent, like a flickering specter. I couldn't believe my eyes."

Steven let out a sigh, his gaze returning to meet ours. "I panicked, to be honest," he admitted, a hint of vulnerability in his tone. "I couldn't comprehend what was happening, and fear gripped me. I stumbled back, my mind racing with thoughts of the supernatural. From that moment on, I decided to steer clear of party girls, afraid of what secrets they might hold."

I and Tessa exchanged knowing glances as Steven finished recounting his eerie encounter. There was a playful skepticism in our eyes.

"Oh, come on, Steven," Tessa finally said and chuckled. There was a playful smirk playing on her lips. "You can't seriously expect us to believe that you saw a ghost, can you? Sounds like you're the one translucent that night with alcohol."

I joined in, unable to contain my laughter. "Yeah, Steven, next you'll be telling us you were abducted by aliens or discovered a hidden treasure map. I definitely think the punch has gone to your head!"

Steven shrugged, his eyes twinkling with a mix of amusement and defiance. "Believe what you want, but I'm telling you, it happened," he insisted, holding his ground. "I can't explain it, but I know what I saw. And let me tell you, it was a once-in-a-lifetime kind of experience."

Tessa raised an eyebrow, her tone dripping with sarcasm. "Well, if ghosts really exist, I hope they throw a party and invite us. It'll be the ultimate adventure!"

We all burst into laughter, the playful banter continuing. We teased Steven about his "ghostly encounter," playfully challenging the validity of his story.

I chuckled some more, nudging Steven playfully. "Maybe it wasn't the girl who was translucent, but you after having one too many drinks! You were probably stumbling around, thinking you were Casper the friendly ghost!"

Tessa joined in, her laughter infectious. "Yeah, Steven, did you check if there was a hidden mirror nearby? Maybe you caught your reflection and mistook it for a ghostly apparition!"

The laughter grew louder, filling the room with a jovial energy. Steven couldn't help but chuckle along.

"You guys are relentless," Steven retorted, rolling his eyes in mock exasperation. "But mark my words, there was something strange happening that night. I know what I saw, even if you don't believe me!"

Tessa playfully nudged him back, her eyes dancing with playful defiance. "Oh, we believe you, Steven," she teased. "We believe that you had an otherworldly experience... of having too much to drink!"

"Hey, Steven, next time you see a ghost, make sure to take a selfie with it, okay?" I joked, pretending to hold up his phone and strike a funny pose.

'I don't know why people in this civilized day and age will still believe in ghosts or gods or spirits. I mean, grow up Steven.' Tessa's voice cuts through the humorous atmosphere with her serious tone.

As Tessa voiced her disbelief in the existence of ghosts and questioned the motives behind beliefs in gods and spirits, I couldn't help but be taken aback. Her words seemed to challenge not only our understanding of the supernatural but also the very foundation of our upbringing.

"But Tessa," I interjected, my voice laced with surprise, "you come from such a strong Christian background. How can you say you don't believe in God?"

Tessa paused for a moment, her expression thoughtful. "I don't discount the possibility of a higher power or a divine presence," she explained. "I just haven't found enough evidence to solidify my beliefs. Throughout history, powerful individuals and institutions have used religion as a means to control and manipulate the masses. That's enough reason to question the true nature of faith and spirituality."

Steven chimed in, his voice tinged with curiosity. "So, you're saying that all these stories of ghosts and gods are just tools to control people? That they're merely fabrications?"

Tessa nodded, a hint of uncertainty in her eyes. "It's possible," she replied. "I think it's important to question everything and seek truth through critical thinking and personal experience. Beliefs should be based on evidence and reason, not blind adherence to traditions or societal expectations."

Her words lingered in the air, causing a moment of introspection among us. It was as if a curtain had been lifted, revealing a deeper layer of skepticism and intellectual inquiry. The conversation took on a more philosophical tone as we delved into the complexities of faith, belief systems, and the search for meaning.

I shared my own thoughts, explaining that while I had my moments of doubt, I still found comfort and guidance in my faith. I mentioned the experiences that had shaped my beliefs and how they provided a sense of purpose and moral compass in my life.

Our conversation continued late into the night, with each of us expressing our perspectives and grappling with the weighty questions that surrounded the nature of belief. Soon silence settled in as it seemed none of us had any other thing to say to each other.

'You know, guys. I think I've seen something worse than a ghost.'

As the silence settled, anticipation hung in the air. I took a deep breath, gathering my thoughts before speaking up. Tessa and Steven turned their attention towards me, their eyes filled with curiosity and a hint of excitement.

"Well," I began, my voice slightly hesitant, "there was this one time when I had an encounter that made me question the existence of things beyond our understanding. It happened when I was just a child, during a visit to a graveyard with my mother, her friend Julia, and my younger brother, Jordan."

Their eyes widened, their attention fully captured by my words. I continued, my voice filled with a mix of nostalgia and awe.

"The graveyard was unlike any I had ever seen before. It had big, broad iron gates that seemed to guard the secrets within. The atmosphere was heavy, almost ominous, and a sense of unease filled the air. But despite the initial apprehension, we ventured inside, driven by our curiosity and a desire to uncover the truth behind the legends that had captured our imaginations."

I paused for a moment, reminiscing about that day and the emotions that had accompanied our exploration. The memories were vivid, as if etched into my mind forever.

"As we walked among the old gravestones, I couldn't shake the feeling that we were being watched. It was as if unseen eyes followed our every move, sending shivers down my spine. The wind whispered eerie melodies through the trees, adding to the eerie ambiance. And then, we saw it."

Their gazes intensified, their anticipation reaching its peak..

"In the distance, through the fading light of the evening, I saw a flickering glow. It was fire, dancing and swirling, casting eerie shadows across the graveyard. At first, I couldn't make out the figures, but as we ran off to the car. They drew closer, I saw them—eight to ten individuals dressed in dark robes, their hoods hiding their faces. They held torches, their flames casting an ethereal glow upon their features."

A hushed silence enveloped us as they absorbed the gravity of my words. I continued, my voice filled with a mix of awe and trepidation.

"The sight sent chills down my spine. It was as if a veil had been lifted, revealing a world beyond our comprehension. I couldn't fully explain what I saw, but in that moment, the possibility of something supernatural, something beyond our understanding, became undeniably real to me."

Tessa and Steven exchanged glances, their expressions a mix of disbelief and wonder. The silence that followed was a testament to the weight of my words. We sat there, each lost in our thoughts, contemplating the mysteries that lie beyond the realms of our comprehension.

As I spoke of my haunting experience at the graveyard, the night embraced us with its full presence. The atmosphere was filled with the sounds of laughter and music, mingling with the clinking of glasses and the rhythmic beat of the party. The vibrant festivities surrounded us, but amidst the revelry, my attention was drawn to the sky.

Above us, the full moon stood in all its majestic glory. It hung in the inky darkness, casting its ethereal light upon the world below. Its radiant glow bathed the surroundings, illuminating the night with an otherworldly brilliance. Its sheer size and luminosity seemed to defy logic, capturing our gaze and demanding our attention.

The moon, usually a symbol of tranquility and beauty, appeared different that night. Its brilliance took on an almost foreboding quality, as if it had transformed into an imposing tyrant ruling over the nocturnal domain. Its light painted the landscape in shades of silver, enhancing the shadows and creating an eerie ambiance that sent shivers down my spines.

Despite the joviality of the party, a sense of unease settled upon me as I stared up at the moon. It was just like the night with mum. The moon seemed to have a power of its own, casting an enchanting yet ominous spell upon the night. Its mesmerizing glow held us captive, as if it possessed secrets and mysteries that were waiting to be unraveled.

The moon's presence intensified the weight of my story, infusing it with an air of mystique and intrigue. The combination of its luminosity and the tales of the supernatural created an atmosphere charged with both excitement and trepidation. It was as if the moon itself was conspiring to make our imaginations run wild, igniting a spark of curiosity and a thirst for the unknown.

Amidst the partying crowd, I could see the glimmers of fascination in the eyes of Tessa and Steven. The moon's radiance reflected in their faces, mirroring the mix of wonder and apprehension that I felt deep within. We were connected not only by our shared experiences but also by the enchanting presence of the celestial body above us.

The music, once lively and carefree, now seemed to echo in the background, its rhythm blending with the distant howl of the wind. The laughter and chatter of the partygoers became distant whispers, drowned out by the profound influence of the moon. It was as if the celestial luminary had cast a spell, enveloping us in a cocoon of contemplation and introspection.

In that moment, as the full moon shone brightly overhead, our conversation took on a newfound depth. We delved further into the realms of the supernatural, exploring the boundaries between reality and imagination. The party atmosphere faded into the background, replaced by an ethereal ambiance that mirrored the enigmatic allure of the moon itself.

We discussed the legends and myths that surrounded the moon, tales of werewolves and witches, of mysterious rituals and hidden powers. The moon, as our silent witness, seemed to encourage our discourse, urging us to embrace the unknown and venture into uncharted territories of thought and belief.

Soon a moment of silence hung in the air, pregnant with anticipation. Tessa and Steven looked at me, their eyes wide with a mixture of curiosity and disbelief. And then, as if released from a tension they had been holding, they burst into laughter.

Their laughter echoed through the night, mingling with the music and the chatter of the partygoers. It was an infectious laughter, contagious in its mirth, and soon I found myself joining in. The weight of the moment dissipated, replaced by the lightness of shared amusement.

Tessa, wiping away tears of laughter, managed to gasp between fits of giggles, "Oh, Jason! You had us going there! I thought you were serious for a moment!" Steven, struggling to catch his breath, chimed in, "Yeah, man! You had me thinking we were in a horror movie or something!"

I couldn't help but laugh along with them, relieved that the tension had been broken. It dawned on me that my tale had indeed been quite outlandish, especially amidst the vibrant and carefree atmosphere of the party. Perhaps I had taken the moment too seriously, allowing the moon's enchantment to weave a web of seriousness around my words.

With a playful grin, Tessa leaned closer and nudged me gently. "You really had us going, Jason. I almost believed you!" she said, her eyes sparkling with amusement. Steven nodded in agreement, adding, "Yeah, dude, that was quite the story. You should consider writing horror novels!"

Steven wiped away the tears of laughter that had pooled in his eyes, his chuckles subsiding into a mischievous grin. He turned to Tessa, a playful twinkle in his eye, and said, "Well, well, Tessa, it seems I'm not the only one with a vivid imagination here! Jason's got some serious storytelling skills!"

Tessa, still giggling, held her stomach as if to contain the laughter bubbling within her. She shook her head, her eyes crinkling with amusement, and said, "Come on, Jason, you can't be serious! That whole story about the graveyard and your mom being scared? It sounds like something straight out of a horror movie!"

I leaned back, a slight smile playing at the corners of my lips, as I met their skeptical gazes. "I know it sounds unbelievable, guys, but I assure you, it's as real as it gets," I said, my voice tinged with a hint of conviction.

The laughter in the air began to subside, replaced by a quiet curiosity. Steven's grin faded into a more serious expression, and Tessa's eyes searched mine for any signs of jest. They could sense the sincerity in my words, even if they found it hard to believe.

"It's true," I continued, my tone earnest. "That night at the graveyard, something happened that I can't explain. I saw fear on my mother's face, a fear I had never seen before. It was as if there was something beyond our comprehension, something that even she, with all her strength, couldn't fully comprehend."

Tessa's laughter gradually faded, replaced by a thoughtful expression. She leaned forward, her gaze fixed on mine, and asked, "Do you really think there's something supernatural out there, something beyond what we can perceive?"

I paused for a moment, reflecting on my own experiences and the enigmatic mysteries that surrounded us. "I can't say for certain," I replied, my voice tinged with a mix of curiosity and uncertainty. "But that night, in that graveyard, something shifted within me. It made me question the boundaries of our understanding and opened my eyes to the possibility of a world beyond our comprehension."

Steven leaned in, his voice laced with a newfound curiosity. "So, you're saying that maybe there's more to this world than what we can see or rationalize?"

I nodded, a flicker of excitement lighting up my eyes. "Exactly. We may never fully understand the extent of what lies beyond, but I think it's in those moments of uncertainty that the true beauty of life resides."

As the conversation continued, the laughter that had once filled the air now mingled with a newfound curiosity. We delved into discussions about the mysteries of the universe, the realms of the supernatural, and the boundless potential of the human imagination. The conversation eventually dissipated into another quiet contemplation of possibilities

"Why don't we go back to that graveyard? It could be the perfect adventure for us before we part ways." Tessa said, breaking the silence.

Steven's eyes lit up at the idea, a mischievous grin spreading across his face. "Theres only one way to find out if this is true or not. I'm in!" he exclaimed.

Tessa and Steven soon began eagerly discussing the logistics of the trip with excitement bubbling within them. Yet, I couldn't shake off the lingering unease that settled in my gut. Memories of that fateful night resurfaced, and a shiver ran down my spine.

"I don't know, guys," I hesitated, my voice filled with skepticism. "That place holds too many unsettling memories for me. It's like stepping back into a nightmare."

Tessa's expression softened as she placed a hand on my arm, her voice laced with empathy. "I understand, Jason. It was a traumatic experience for you. But maybe facing your fears and revisiting that place can help you overcome them."

Steven chimed in, his tone gentle yet persuasive. "Think about it, Jason. This could be our chance to debunk those legends, to prove to ourselves that there's nothing to fear. Besides, it might be our last adventure together before we go our separate ways."

'Look, it's really dangerous out there. It's out of town in the most unsettling place you could ever imagine.' I said.

However, Steven and Tessa continued to push me, their voices laced with genuine concern and a hint of playful persuasion. They insisted that revisiting the graveyard could be an opportunity for me to rid myself of the delusions I had believed in as a kid and confront my deepest fears head-on.

"Come on, Jason," Tessa pleaded, her eyes filled with a mix of determination and empathy. "You've grown so much since then. It's time to let go of those childhood fears and see the truth for yourself."

Steven added, a mischievous glint in his eyes, "Think about the stories we could tell, the memories we could create. This could be the ultimate adventure. I mean, if what you saw was the real Jason then it's huge. These things could be aliens trying to communicate with us. We need to find out!"

Their words resonated with me, stirring a combination of trepidation and curiosity within my soul. A part of me longed to face those fears, to prove to myself that the events of that night had merely been figments of an overactive imagination. Yet, another part of me hesitated, fearing what truths I might uncover in the process.

"I understand what you're saying," I replied, my voice laced with uncertainty. "But look, it's a bad idea. It holds memories that still haunt me, memories that I'm not sure I'm ready to face again."

"Jason, we're not asking you to do this alone. We'll be right there with you every step of the way. We've faced our own fears, and now it's time to face yours together. You're stronger than you think." Tessa said

Steven chimed in, his tone earnest yet playful. "Come on, mate, think of it as an opportunity to prove to yourself that those childhood fears were just stories."

As Tessa and Steven continued to insist on revisiting the graveyard, a seed of doubt began to take root within me. It had been fourteen long years since that fateful night, and with the passage of time, memories can become hazy and susceptible to reinterpretation. Maybe what I had witnessed was not as supernatural as it had seemed at the time. Perhaps it was all just an elaborate prank, a figment of an overactive imagination, or a sinister plot by individuals who derived joy from scaring others away from the graveyard.

The more I pondered on these possibilities, the more I started questioning the authenticity of my own experiences. Could it be that the figures in dark robes were simply party-goers dressed up for some macabre celebration? Could the eerie sights and sounds I had encountered be mere illusions, orchestrated to provoke fear and stir the imagination? And what if my mother's reaction had been an overreaction, fueled by the adrenaline of the moment?

These doubts gnawed at me, making me question the very foundation of what I believed to be true. Had I been living under the shadow of a childhood delusion all these years? Was it possible that the supernatural occurrences I had attributed to that night were nothing more than a fabrication of my own mind?

Tessa spoke with unwavering conviction, her eyes filled with determination. "Jason, it doesn't matter whether it was supernatural or not. What matters is how it affected you, how it shaped your beliefs and perceptions. By revisiting that place, we have a chance to confront our past and find closure, regardless of the nature of what we encounter."

Steven chimed in, his voice earnest and reassuring. "You're not alone in this, mate. We'll face whatever lies ahead together, and no matter what we discover, it will be an opportunity for growth and self-discovery. Our experiences, whether supernatural or not, have shaped us, and it's time to make peace with them."

Their words resonated with me, reminding me that the truth I sought wasn't solely about the existence of the supernatural but rather about my own personal journey. It was an opportunity to confront the past, challenge my beliefs, and ultimately find peace and clarity within myself.

I looked into Tessa's and Steven's eyes, I couldn't help but notice the infectious excitement that radiated from them. It was a glimmer of anticipation mixed with a touch of nervousness, mirroring the emotions bubbling within me. Their unwavering conviction and genuine desire to explore the unknown sparked something deep within me, reigniting the adventurous spirit I had carried as a child.

I took a deep breath and met their gaze, finding solace in the connection we shared. The doubts and uncertainties that had plagued me moments ago seemed to fade into the background as the allure of the unknown beckoned. The prospect of revisiting the graveyard, this time with my friends by my side, felt like an opportunity for redemption, a chance to face my fears and lay to rest the lingering doubts that had haunted me for years.

"I'm in," I said, my voice laced with a newfound determination. "Let's confront the shadows of the past together and uncover the truth, whatever it may be."

Tessa's eyes widened with excitement, a smile spreading across her face. "That's the spirit, Jason! We embrace this adventure with open hearts and open minds."

Steven nodded approvingly as he threw his hands around me and patted me on the back, his playful grin reflecting the thrill of the unknown. "We're in this together, mate."

Without a second thought we threw ourselves into Steven's car and took off to the graveyard. While we drove on the road, the silence settled around us like a heavy cloak.

The country road we traveled on was isolated and desolate, winding through the darkness of the countryside. The only source of light was the beams from our headlights, casting long shadows that danced along the edges of the road.

The chilly breeze seeped through the cracks in the car windows, sending shivers down our spines. Tessa, sitting in the front passenger seat, wrapped herself in a thick jacket, trying to ward off the biting cold. The wind seemed almost stinging to the skin, and it carried with it a sense of anticipation and apprehension.

The full moon hung high above us, bathing the landscape in an eerie, pale light. Its presence was commanding, almost as if it were a voyeuristic tyrant observing our every move. The moon's glow cast an otherworldly aura over the countryside, accentuating the darkness around us and emphasizing the mysterious nature of our journey.

Steven's car sliced through the dark and isolated countryside. The cool breeze that brushed against our faces was laden with a biting chill, making us shiver involuntarily.

The once vibrant and lively countryside now seemed abandoned and forgotten. The towering trees lining the road reached out like gnarled fingers, casting long, haunting shadows that danced with every swerve of the car. The rhythmic hum of the engine was the only sound that broke the silence, punctuated by the occasional hoot of an owl, adding to the nocturnal ambiance.

The darkness seemed to amplify our senses, heightening our awareness of every little detail. The distant hoot of the owl echoed through the night, as if guiding us towards our destination. The pale moonlight filtered through the thick canopy above, casting an ethereal glow on the road ahead. It was a scene straight out of a horror movie, and the tension in the car was palpable.

We exchanged glances, our eyes reflecting a mix of excitement, nervousness, and anticipation. The gravity of our decision to revisit the graveyard weighed heavily on our minds. The stories and legends that had been woven over the years swirled in our thoughts, fueling our imaginations and stirring a potent blend of fear and curiosity within us.

The road stretched out before us, seemingly endless in its desolation. There were no signs of civilization, no comforting glow of distant houses or passing cars. It was just us, the darkened road, and the looming presence of the graveyard in the distance. The atmosphere crackled with an intangible energy, a fusion of adrenaline and uncertainty that pulsed through our veins.

As we pressed on, the car's headlights cut through the darkness, revealing glimpses of the surrounding landscape. The barren fields on either side of the road whispered tales of forgotten memories, lost souls, and untold secrets. The moonlit sky provided little solace, its pale glow casting eerie shadows on the gravestones that dotted the horizon.

The silence in the car grew thicker with every passing mile, each of us lost in our own thoughts as we continued down the winding road. The only sounds were the rumble of the engine and the occasional rustle of leaves as they brushed against the car's exterior. We felt like intruders in the stillness of the night, tiptoeing into a realm that held secrets beyond our imagination.

As we drove, the memories of my past encounter with the graveyard and the fear it had instilled in me resurfaced. The haunting images flashed in my mind, making me question the wisdom of returning to this place.

Tessa glanced at me from the front seat, her eyes filled with a mix of concern and encouragement. "You okay, Jason?" she asked softly.

I nodded, offering her a reassuring smile. "Yeah, I'm good. Just a bit nostalgic, I guess," I replied, trying to downplay the unease that gnawed at me.

Steven, who was focused on the road, chimed in, "We're here to support you, J. Whatever happens, we've got your back."

I appreciated their words, knowing that their presence by my side was the very reason I had mustered the courage to return to this haunting place. We had come a long way from the carefree teenagers we once were, and this night felt like a rite of passage, an opportunity to conquer the shadows that had haunted our past.

As we drew closer, the atmosphere grew heavier, and a sense of foreboding enveloped us. The full moon seemed to cast an even more intense glow on the giant trees we drove through, giving the impression of an impenetrable barrier.

"Are we sure about this?" I questioned hesitantly, feeling a wave of doubt wash over me.

Tessa turned to me, her eyes reflecting a mix of determination and excitement. "We've come this far, Jason. Let's see this through," she urged.

Steven nodded in agreement, his grip tightening on the steering wheel. "We've got each other, remember? We'll be okay."

Steven turned on the radio and slid an audio cassette into its plate. Soon a familiar tune hummed through the radio. And soon its infectious rhythm filled the car, cutting through the tense silence that had enveloped us. The familiar beats and melodies immediately sparked a wave of nostalgia, and before we knew it, our heads were bobbing and our voices joined in unison, singing along to the lyrics.

The music seemed to have a magical effect, lifting our spirits and easing the palpable tension that had built up during our drive. Laughter erupted as we sang at the top of our lungs, the lyrics echoing through the confined space. In that moment, it felt like we were transported back to simpler times, carefree and full of youthful energy.

But even as the car was filled with the sound of laughter and music, the outside world remained shrouded in an ominous stillness. The darkness seemed thicker, as if it held its breath, waiting for something to unfold. The moon's glow, once bright and inviting, now seemed to cast long shadows that danced with a hint of malevolence.

I couldn't help but glance out the window, my eyes drawn to the eerie surroundings. The narrow road loomed in the distance, and I pictured the gate standing as a foreboding entrance to the unknown. However, the playful atmosphere inside the car clashed with the sense of unease that settled upon us, creating a dissonance that sent a chill down my spine.

As the last notes of the song faded away, the silence returned, wrapping around us like a heavy blanket. The laughter ceased, and a somber mood settled over us once more. The reality of our surroundings began to seep back into our consciousness, reminding us of the purpose of our journey.

Tessa, her voice filled with determination, broke the silence. "Let's not forget why we're here," she said, her tone more serious now.

Steven nodded, his eyes meeting mine in the rearview mirror. "We're here to face our fears, to challenge the darkness that has haunted us," he added, his voice resolute.

I swallowed hard, a mix of apprehension and determination coursing through my veins.

The narrow road led us to a dirt path. Unlike my previous visit with mum, this time the road was not shrouded in a cloud of dust but was instead rough and bumpy, making our drive uncomfortable. The tires of the car jostled against the uneven terrain, causing us to grip the seats for stability.

Each bump in the road sent a jolt through our bodies, as if the very ground beneath us was resisting our progress. The car groaned in protest, its suspension straining against the rugged path. The headlights cut through the darkness, revealing the rough edges of the dirt road as it stretched out before us.

The atmosphere inside the car grew tense as the discomfort of the journey settled upon us. Conversations dwindled, replaced by intermittent sighs and muttered expletives as we braced ourselves against the relentless bumps. The once vibrant energy that had filled the car had now given way to a quiet anticipation, a shared understanding that we were entering into unfamiliar territory.

Tessa shifted in her seat, her brows furrowed with concern. "Are you sure this is the right way?" she questioned, her voice betraying a hint of unease.

Steven, gripping the steering wheel tightly, responded with a determined tone. "I dunno, Jason said it is." he said and they both turned to me.

'Yea, we are. The dirt road leads directly to the graveyard.'

I glanced out the window, observing the dark, surrounding landscape that seemed to close in around us. The moon, now partially hidden behind a shroud of clouds, cast an eerie glow that only added to the foreboding atmosphere.

With each passing minute, it became clear that this path had been forgotten by time and neglect. The once-clear track was now marred by potholes and overgrown vegetation. Branches scraped against the sides of the car, leaving faint marks as a reminder of our passage.

Tessa observed the growing apprehension in the car due to the discomfort of driving on the rough dirt road and she felt the need to alleviate the tension. With a mischievous glint in her eyes, she decided to steer the conversation towards the memories of our time in high school, particularly the trouble we had managed to get ourselves into.

A playful smile spread across her face as she began recounting one particularly amusing incident. "Hey, remember that time when we snuck into the school after hours to pull off a prank on the principal?" she asked, her voice brimming with nostalgia.

Steven chuckled, his eyes lighting up with excitement. "Oh, how could I forget? We were like a bunch of sneaky spiders, carefully evading the security cameras and tiptoeing through the hallways."

"And the look on the principal's face the next day! Priceless! He couldn't figure out who was behind it." I added, I couldn't help but join in and chuckle.

As memories flooded back, we shared stories of other misadventures, laughing at our own audacity and youthful folly. We reminisced about the time we organized an impromptu dance party in the school gymnasium, complete with smuggled speakers and disco lights. The image of our teachers attempting to maintain order while secretly tapping their feet to the music brought tears of laughter to our eyes.

Tessa added her own account, revealing how we once managed to sneak out of a school assembly to indulge in an impromptu picnic on the rooftop. The thrill of breaking the rules, even if just for a little while, had bonded us and created lasting memories.

With each shared memory, the mood in the car lightened, and the unease of our journey faded into the background. The discomfort of the dirt road seemed insignificant compared to the joy and camaraderie that resurfaced as we relived those cherished high school memories.

We laughed until our sides hurt. The stories reminded us of a time when our biggest concerns were homework assignments and weekend plans, when our lives were filled with the thrill of exploration and pushing boundaries.

In that moment, as we collectively embraced the nostalgia of our teenage years, the tension dissipated entirely. The car became a time capsule, transporting us back to a time of innocence and carefree rebellion.

As the laughter subsided, Steven's eyes sparkled with a mischievous glint as he interjected with a tale of his own. "Hey, remember that time when Jason here turned into a real-life hero and defended Jeremy from those bullies?"

Tessa's eyes widened with curiosity, and she leaned in closer. "Really? I didn't know about this!"

A hint of a smile played on my lips as I recalled that fateful day. "I noticed Jeremy being cornered by a group of older students near the school gates. They were taunting him, calling him names and making cruel jokes."

Steven nodded, chiming in with excitement. "Yeah, and Jason here swooped in like a guardian angel, standing up for Jeremy and putting those bullies in their place. It was quite the sight!"

I couldn't help but feel a sense of amusement at the memory. High school was quite a rough time.

"I couldn't stand by and watch someone being treated unfairly, especially when they were unable to defend themselves. So, I confronted the bullies demanding that they leave Jeremy alone. And when they didn't I got physical."

Tessa's eyes shimmered with admiration. "That was incredibly brave, Jason."

Steven chuckled, his eyes gleaming with mischief. "But the best part, guys, was the aftermath. It turned out those bullies were losers. They dared not approach Jeremy when we all eventually found out his parents were satanists!"

The car erupted in laughter, the irony of the situation not lost on us. As the laughter subsided, Tessa spoke up, her voice filled with contemplation. "It's fascinating how life has a way of putting us in our place. They never made it to graduation, did they?"

Steven and I nodded no. 'Not even Jeremy did.' I said.

That moment, I couldn't help but feel a pang of melancholy. "You know," I began, my voice tinged with a mix of sadness and reflection, "after that incident, Jeremy never said a word to me. He didn't thank me or even acknowledge my presence. It was as if he carried the weight of the world on his shoulders, silently enduring the torment."

I recall that moment. Back then, I had been unaware of the reasons behind the bullying he endured. He suffered their kicks and punches in silence, and when I finally intervened, he remained silent still.

Jeremy's silence after the incident spoke volumes. He didn't utter a word of gratitude or acknowledgement, choosing instead to keep his thoughts and emotions hidden. I wondered what he must have been feeling in those moments, enduring the pain and humiliation quietly.

It was in the aftermath of that incident that the rumors about Jeremy's family began to circulate more prominently within our school. Whispers of alleged satanic practices grew louder, further isolating him from his peers. The weight of those false accusations took a toll on his already burdened shoulders, exacerbating his feelings of loneliness and alienation.

Regrettably, the rumors persisted and intensified, when one of the bullies went missing, and the remaining two fell gravely ill, with one even becoming paralyzed. It was during this time that rumors circulated rapidly, accusing Jeremy and his parents of being involved in satanic practices. The news spread like wildfire within the school, further isolating Jeremy from his peers.

Eventually driving Jeremy to the point where he felt he had no choice but to leave the school altogether. It became increasingly difficult for him to navigate the halls of the school, as the whispers and stares of judgment grew louder.

Tessa nudged me out of my thoughts 'So, what's up with the graveyard and the legend about it?' her voice filled with curiosity and excitement, 'You know, I've never been to a graveyard before?

I turned to her, a mixture of surprise and curiosity etched across my face. "You've never been to a graveyard before?" I asked, my voice laced with disbelief.

Tessa shook her head, her eyes sparkling with a blend of anticipation and curiosity. "No, never. It's always been a place that intrigued me, but I never had the opportunity or the courage to visit one. I guess I've always been fascinated by the mystery and history they hold."

Steven, chiming in with a hint of excitement, added, "Yeah, same here! This is my first time going to a graveyard as well. It's like stepping into a realm of stories and secrets."

A smile tugged at the corners of my lips as I listened to their words. Suddenly, their eagerness to explore the graveyard made more sense to me. For Tessa and Steven, it was an opportunity to delve into the unknown, to satisfy their curiosity about a place shrouded in history and legends.

I turned to face Tessa and Steven. "Well, tonight we'll get to experience something new together," I said, a touch of excitement in my voice. "We'll face our fears, challenge the stories we've heard, and perhaps find answers to the mysteries that have captivated our curiosity."

'Tell us about these legends and folklore about this forbidden place.' Steven said as he kept his finger pressed on the wheel and his eyes on the road.

"The legends surrounding this graveyard are quite unsettling," I began, my voice laced with a mixture of intrigue and apprehension. "It's said that this place is deliberately unmarked on any map, hidden away from prying eyes and curious souls."

I could feel Tessa and Steven leaning in closer, their expressions eager for the chilling stories that awaited them. "According to the local lore, this graveyard is rumored to have been a site of dark rituals and sinister gatherings. Whispers of a long-forgotten cult, steeped in occult practices and forbidden knowledge, have circulated for centuries."

The moonlight cast eerie shadows across the car, creating an atmosphere of both fascination and unease. My voice lowered even further as I delved deeper into the sinister tales. "It is said that those who venture into the graveyard at night may witness the remnants of ancient ceremonies, haunting specters that roam the grounds seeking solace or retribution."

I paused, allowing the weight of the legends to settle in the silence. The discomfort of the bumpy road now seemed insignificant compared to the foreboding atmosphere that surrounded us.

"There are also whispers of a powerful curse that hangs over this place," I continued, my voice tinged with caution. "Legend has it that anyone who disturbs the peace of the graveyard may suffer dire consequences, their lives forever entwined with darkness and despair."

A shiver ran down my spine as I contemplated the chilling tales I had grown up hearing. The graveyard had become a symbol of fear and the unknown, its very existence instilling a sense of caution and trepidation within the community.

"The stories speak of restless spirits who wander the cemetery, seeking vengeance on those who dare to trespass upon their sacred grounds," I added, my voice carrying a hint of warning. "It is said that the echoes of their cries and the whispers of their anguish can still be heard in the dead of night."

The car fell into an uneasy silence as the weight of the legends hung heavy in the air.

"The woods that surround the graveyard," I continued with my voice steady yet tinged with a hint of unease, "are said to hold a dark secret dating back to the 1800s. Legend has it that deep within the dense foliage, a hidden Satanic church resides, concealed from prying eyes and accessible only at specific times."

The car grew quieter, the weight of the legend settling upon us like a heavy fog. I continued, my voice laden with a mix of fascination and trepidation, "According to the tales passed down through generations, those who stumble upon this hidden church are said to witness eerie rituals and experience a palpable malevolence that permeates the air."

The moon's glow seemed to dim slightly as I spoke, casting elongated shadows across the interior of the car. The air grew thick with anticipation as we imagined the hidden depths of the woods and the secrets they held.

"It's believed that the Satanic church's existence is intertwined with supernatural forces," I added, my voice barely above a whisper. "At certain times, when the veil between our world and the realm of the occult is at its thinnest, the hidden church is said to materialize, revealing itself to those who possess a keen eye and an unwavering resolve."

A sense of reverence and caution enveloped us, as if we were treading upon sacred ground. The legends of the hidden church had woven a tapestry of fear and fascination in the minds of the locals, drawing a clear boundary between curiosity and danger.

"The woods themselves seem to possess an otherworldly aura," I continued, my words carefully chosen. "Many claim to have heard strange whispers carried by the wind, while others have reported glimpses of shadowy figures lurking within the tree line. It's as if the woods hold secrets that defy comprehension, beckoning the brave and daring to unlock their mysteries."

As the car carried us closer to the edge of the woods, the darkness seemed to deepen, engulfing us in an atmosphere of foreboding. The full moon cast an eerie glow through the gaps in the dense canopy, as if illuminating the path to a forbidden realm.

We sat in contemplative silence, the weight of the legends hanging heavily upon us. The stories of the hidden Satanic church and the eerie rituals conducted within its walls heightened our anticipation, mingling with the haunting tales of the graveyard itself.

"You never know," Steven chuckled, his voice carrying a hint of mischief. "Perhaps we'll stumble upon Jeremy playing a role he never anticipated. Maybe he's turned into a devoted usher or an altar boy."

A wave of nervous laughter swept through the car. The tension that had built up within us was momentarily diffused by the lighthearted comment, providing a brief respite from the weight of the legends and mysteries that surrounded us.

Tessa joined in the laughter, her eyes sparkling with a mix of amusement and anticipation. "It would certainly be an unexpected twist," she remarked. "To witness something we've only heard about and seen in movies would be quite the thrill."

I couldn't help but find their humor infectious, allowing myself a momentary break from the somberness that had accompanied our journey. It was as if their playful banter injected a dose of lightness, momentarily dispelling the eerie atmosphere that clung to the night.

Yet, beneath our laughter, a subtle undercurrent of excitement and curiosity lingered. Despite the jests and jesters, we were aware that we were venturing into a realm that held a blend of fascination and trepidation.

The road stretched out before us, its twists and turns a testament to the unknown path we were embarking upon. The full moon loomed above, casting an ethereal light upon our adventure, as if guiding us toward the realms of the unseen.

With each passing mile, the anticipation in the car grew. The legends of the Satanic church and the prospect of witnessing something beyond our comprehension danced in our thoughts, mingling with the lingering echoes of laughter.

As we neared the entrance of the graveyard, the moon casting an ethereal glow upon the rugged path, my gaze caught sight of several signs dotting the dirt road. The bold letters warned us not to trespass and informed us that the road was closed. It was as if the universe was cautioning us to reconsider our decision, urging us to turn back and abandon our venture into the unknown.

However, the infectious laughter and lighthearted banter that filled the car drowned out the warnings. The atmosphere inside was electric, charged with excitement and a sense of camaraderie that seemed to defy any lingering doubts or apprehensions.

Amidst the chorus of laughter, I couldn't help but feel a tinge of unease. The signs were not to be ignored lightly. They served as a reminder of the potential dangers that lay ahead, the unseen perils that could befall those who dared to defy the warnings.

Yet, buoyed by the carefree spirit that enveloped us, we continued on, our curiosity and eagerness overshadowing any sense of caution. The road ahead seemed to stretch endlessly, beckoning us closer to the forbidden grounds that awaited us.

As the car pressed on, the moon's glow cast long shadows that danced alongside us, mirroring the mixture of excitement and trepidation that coursed through our veins. Each sign we passed was a silent plea to reconsider, a message from the unknown begging us to turn back.

The allure of the adventure proved too strong. The laughter and the bonds of friendship that had carried us this far were now our guiding lights, eclipsing any doubts that threatened to dim our spirits.

As the car rattled along the dirt road, the signs became a blur, fading into the periphery of our focus. The warnings were merely remnants of a reality we had chosen to leave behind, swallowed up by the intoxicating energy of our shared journey.

With every passing mile, the air grew heavier with anticipation. The laughter subsided momentarily, replaced by a charged silence that hung in the car. It was as if a collective understanding settled upon us, acknowledging the gravity of our decision and the path we had chosen to tread.

The signs, now mere relics of cautionary tales, failed to dampen our spirits. We forged ahead, propelled by a shared belief that we were meant to explore the forbidden, to challenge the boundaries of our comfort zones, and to unravel the secrets that lay shrouded in the night.

As the car bumped along the dirt road, the vibrant tapestry of laughter and friendship intertwined with the warnings we had left behind. We were on the precipice of the unknown, venturing into a realm where legends and reality merged, where the mundane and the extraordinary converged.

In that moment, the signs and their foreboding message became distant echoes in the recesses of our minds. The road stretched out before us, and we embraced its twists and turns, guided by an unwavering belief that the journey itself was worth the risk.

And so, with every passing sign, we pressed on, our laughter and jesting were shield against the unspoken fears that lingered in the depths of our hearts. We had chosen to venture forth, to dance with the shadows, and to unravel the secrets that the forbidden graveyard held.

That moment, something suddenly leapt in front of the car into the woods, causing us all to startle and Steven to slam on the brakes.

The sudden movement sent a shockwave through the vehicle, and for a moment, silence replaced the jovial atmosphere that had filled the car just moments before. It took us a few heart-pounding seconds to gather our wits and process what had just happened.

"What was that?" Steven's voice broke the silence, his eyes scanning the road ahead as he searched for any sign of the mysterious creature.

'I don't know,' I said, my heart pounding heavily.

Tessa, seemingly unfazed by the unexpected encounter, leaned forward and calmly stated, "It was just a deer. I caught a glimpse of its leg as it leapt away. Probably got spooked by the car's headlights."

Relief washed over us as Tessa's explanation sank in. The tension that had momentarily gripped us began to dissipate, replaced by a mixture of nervous laughter and grateful sighs. We had narrowly avoided a potential collision, thanks to Tessa's quick observation.

With a collective exhale, we resumed our journey, the car's engine revving once again as Steven carefully navigated the road.

As the car continued to propel us forward, the air inside seemed to regain a sense of normalcy, albeit tinged with a lingering unease. Our eyes darted back and forth, scanning the surroundings, half-expecting another unexpected encounter to disrupt the night's tranquility.

In the back of our minds, the deer's intrusion was because of the untamed nature that surrounded us. We thought of nothing else.

Eventually, we got to the graveyard and stepped out of the car. The chill in the air seemed to intensify, sending shivers down my spine. The atmosphere crackled with an unsettling energy, as if the world itself was holding its breath. I glanced at Tessa and Steven, their faces reflecting a mix of courage and uncertainty. We shared a nod, silently acknowledging our shared purpose and the risks we were about to take.

With cautious steps, we made our way towards what we believe to be the entrance of the graveyard. Each creak of the rusty hinges echoed through the night, magnifying the sense of anticipation. The moon, now a pale crescent in the sky, cast an ethereal glow on the tombstones that stretched out before us.

However, I couldn't help but notice that the graveyard appeared different from what I remembered as a child. It seemed as though time had worked its hand on this place, altering its features and erasing some of its haunting elements.

Gone were the big, broad iron gates that once stood as a foreboding entrance, replaced now by more modest, albeit still somber, entrance markers. In their place, stood an unassuming opening, marked only by a weathered sign. The sign declared that this was a family graveyard established in the 1800s. I was very much familiar with this family back home.

The absence of the gates took away the sense of forbiddance that I had associated with this place for so long. The mystery that had once shrouded the graveyard seemed to dissipate, leaving me with a sense of both relief and curiosity.

The central burn pit, a focal point of my childhood memories, was nowhere to be seen. Its absence left a void in the center of the graveyard, as if a piece of its history had been taken away. The burn pit had held an air of mystique, with tales of eerie rituals and inexplicable phenomena surrounding it. Now, all that remained was an empty space, devoid of its enigmatic allure.

The gravestones stood in neat rows, their weathered surfaces bearing witness to the passage of time. Some were moss-covered and worn, while others still retained a semblance of their original luster. The names etched into the stones carried stories and histories of lives once lived, now captured within the confines of this hallowed ground.

We cautiously made our way through the graveyard, our footsteps disturbing the hushed tranquility. The moonlight cast an ethereal glow upon the tombstones, creating eerie shadows that seemed to dance in the pale illumination. The absence of any other presence heightened the eerie atmosphere, as if the souls that resided here were holding their breath, watching our every move.

As I looked around, I couldn't help but feel a mixture of nostalgia and apprehension. Memories flooded my mind, evoking images of my mother, Julia, and my brother Jordan, their faces etched with fear, their eyes wide with disbelief. It was here, in this very place, that I had witnessed fear in its rawest form. The weight of that memory lingered, tugging at the corners of my consciousness.

Tessa and Steven walked alongside me, their expressions a reflection of both excitement and trepidation. They had joined me on this journey, not fully understanding the significance of what awaited us. Their skepticism mingled with curiosity, creating an unspoken bond as we navigated the solemn terrain.

The night air was filled with a sense of anticipation and an underlying energy that seemed to permeate the very fabric of the graveyard. Our footsteps echoed through the stillness, punctuating the silence that hung heavy in the air. The absence of any visible signs of life only intensified the eerie atmosphere, leaving us to wonder what secrets this place still held.

As we reached the center of the graveyard, we paused, our gazes sweeping across the landscape. The moonlight bathed the surroundings in an ethereal glow, casting long, haunting shadows that danced along the ground. The absence of the burn pit, once a focal point of mystery and intrigue, left a void in the heart of the graveyard.

A sense of melancholy washed over me, mingled with a tinge of disappointment. The graveyard had undergone a transformation, shedding its eerie aura in exchange for a more sanitized appearance. Yet, a part of me couldn't help but feel relieved, as if a weight had been lifted from my shoulders.

Since this was not intriguing enough, we decided to venture further and deeper into the graveyard. The atmosphere grew increasingly eerie as we moved further into the heart of the graveyard. The moon's pale glow cast elongated shadows that danced upon the weathered tombstones, adding an ethereal touch to the surroundings.

Our path eventually led us to the backside of the graveyard, where an old gate stood, partially covered by overgrown vegetation. Its iron bars bore the marks of time, rusted and weathered. The gate beckoned us forward, offering a passage into the unknown. With a sense of anticipation, we pushed open the gate, its rusty hinges creaking in protest.

Stepping through the gate, we found ourselves standing at the edge of a vast field. The moonlight illuminated the expanse before us, revealing an eerie beauty. The grass swayed gently in the breeze, casting long, sinuous shadows on the ground. The field seemed to stretch out endlessly, merging with the darkness that enveloped the night.

The air felt charged with a palpable energy, as if the field held its own secrets, waiting to be discovered. It was a stark contrast to the orderly and solemn nature of the graveyard we had just left behind. Here, in the vastness of the field, there was a sense of liberation and boundless possibility.

We exchanged glances, a mixture of excitement and caution reflected in our eyes. It was as if we were standing on the precipice of an adventure, unsure of what lay ahead but determined to face it head-on. The moon, now high in the sky, watched over us like a silent witness, casting its ethereal glow upon our path.

With each step we took into the field, the silence of the night seemed to deepen. The distant sound of nocturnal creatures became faint, drowned out by the weight of our own footsteps. The darkness enveloped us, embracing us in its enigmatic embrace. We felt like explorers in an unknown realm, venturing into the depths of our own fears and curiosities.

The moon continued to cast its watchful gaze upon us, illuminating our path through the field. Shadows danced and swayed, creating an illusionary dance of light and darkness. We moved with caution, mindful of the ground beneath our feet, wary of disturbing the delicate balance of this sacred place.

As we walked deeper into the field, our flashlights cut through the darkness, a strange realization began to settle upon us—there was nothing spooky, supernatural, or eerie. The field remained tranquil, bathed in the soft moonlight, devoid of any visible signs of the paranormal.

Tessa's footsteps crunched lightly on the grass, and Steven's flashlight illuminated the path ahead. We kept our senses on high alert, half-expecting some unearthly encounter or a whisper from the spirits that were said to inhabit this place. Yet, as minutes turned into hours, the silence remained unbroken, save for the occasional rustling of leaves or the distant hoot of an owl.

Doubt began to creep into my mind. Had I been carried away by childhood tales and legends? Were the stories I had heard merely the fabrications of overactive imaginations? The absence of any eerie phenomena challenged the very foundation of my beliefs, leaving me questioning the validity of the tales I had grown up with.

The moon continued to watch over us, its silvery light casting an ethereal glow on the field. We explored every corner, searching for a hint of the supernatural, but found nothing more than the stillness of the night and the gentle whispers of the wind. The absence of any supernatural encounters weighed heavily on our expectations, and a sense of disappointment washed over us.

We paused for a moment, our gazes meeting in silent contemplation. Tessa's voice cut through the quietude. "Could it be that the legends and stories were nothing more than folklore, passed down through generations?" Her words hung in the air, punctuated by the absence of any tangible evidence to the contrary.

Steven chimed in, his voice tinged with both relief and skepticism. "Perhaps this place has been romanticized over the years. People enjoy a good ghost story, after all. But maybe, just maybe, the reality isn't as thrilling as the tales we were told."

I listened to their words, pondering the possibility that my childhood fears had been built upon exaggeration and embellishment. The realization that what I had sought might not exist began to lift the weight of my apprehension. The graveyard had lost its aura of mystery, reduced to a peaceful resting place for those who had come before us.

Still, a part of me couldn't fully let go of the memories and the unexplained experiences of my childhood. The fear I had witnessed in my mother's eyes, the genuine terror etched upon her face, the figures that gathered when we were living, lingered in my mind. I couldn't dismiss those memories entirely, even if the present circumstances didn't align with the stories that had fueled our imagination.

We continued walking through the graveyard, and soon an unexpected realization struck us—we had gone much farther than anticipated. The field stretched out endlessly, and it seemed as if there was no end in sight. A collective decision took hold among us, fueled by a lingering curiosity and the desire to uncover the truth that lay hidden in the depths of this mysterious place.

Without exchanging a word, we veered off the beaten path and crossed the field, our flashlights piercing through the darkness. The tall grass brushed against our legs, creating a whispering symphony that seemed to beckon us further. We felt a mixture of excitement and trepidation as we entered the woods, the canopy of trees swallowing us into their shadows.

The woods were an entirely different realm—a stark contrast to the open field we had just left behind. The air grew cooler, and the sounds of nocturnal creatures filled the space, adding an eerie symphony to the atmosphere. Moonlight filtered through the branches above, casting patches of ethereal light on the forest floor. The silence of the night was broken only by the rustling of leaves under our feet and the occasional hoot of an owl in the distance.

Navigating through the woods became increasingly challenging as the trees grew denser, their branches reaching out like skeletal fingers, as if warning us against proceeding. But our determination fueled our steps, and the allure of uncovering the truth pushed us forward.

As we ventured deeper into the woods, a palpable sense of anticipation hung in the air. The legends that had captivated our imaginations for years echoed in our minds, fueling our resolve. We searched for any signs that would lead us to the supposed satanic church, our flashlights scanning the surroundings for any hint of an elusive path.

Time seemed to warp within the depths of the woods, the minutes stretching into hours as we pressed on, undeterred by the obstacles that crossed our path. Twisted roots snaked across the forest floor, threatening to trip us with every step. Thick underbrush impeded our progress, entangling us in a web of branches and leaves. Yet, our determination remained unyielding.

The woods held an otherworldly ambiance—an amalgamation of fear and excitement intertwined. Shadows danced around us, morphing into elusive figures that seemed to taunt our presence. The rustling of leaves in the wind took on a whispering quality, as if the forest itself held secrets that it dared not reveal.

As we pushed deeper into the woods, we noticed a subtle change in the atmosphere. The air grew heavy with an unfamiliar energy—a sense that we were no longer alone. Whispers seemed to echo through the trees, carried by an unseen force. We exchanged wary glances, the weight of our shared anticipation palpable.

The gravity of our decision to explore this ominous location weighed heavily on our minds, but none of us wanted to be the first to back out. We were determined to unravel the mysteries that lay hidden within these haunting woods.

Each step forward seemed to amplify the eeriness of the surroundings. The dense foliage swallowed the moonlight, casting an impenetrable darkness that obscured our vision. Shadows danced and flickered, playing tricks on our senses. The silence was broken by the rustling of leaves, amplifying the unease that had settled upon us.

Every creak of a branch and every distant noise set our hearts racing. The woods seemed to come alive with a chorus of unsettling sounds—whispers that carried on the wind, the scuttling of unseen creatures, and the occasional cracking of twigs underfoot. The symphony of the night sent shivers down our spines, as if the very woods were whispering secrets that we were not meant to know.

Despite the mounting fear, we pressed on, our determination overriding our instincts for self-preservation. Each passing moment heightened the sense of trepidation, but we found solace in our collective unity. We leaned on each other, drawing strength from the shared experience of venturing into the unknown.

As we continued through the depths of the woods, the trees seemed to close in around us, creating an oppressive atmosphere. The gnarled branches reached out like skeletal fingers, clawing at the edges of our consciousness. Our flashlights struggled to penetrate the thick darkness, casting feeble beams of light that only served to illuminate fragments of the surrounding gloom.

Imaginations ran wild, as every shadow took on a sinister form. Our minds played tricks on us, conjuring images of lurking figures among the trees, unseen eyes watching our every move. It was as if the very essence of the woods conspired to keep its secrets hidden, manipulating our senses to test our resolve.

We forged ahead, though our pace had slowed, cautious of every sound and movement. The woods seemed to have a life of their own, with unseen forces at play. Whispers grew louder, the air grew thicker, and the line between reality and imagination began to blur.

The intensity of the experience weighed heavily on us. Fear, like an invisible barrier, threatened to halt our progress. Yet, we pushed forward, bolstered by a combination of curiosity, stubbornness, and the unwillingness to be overtaken by our own fears.

The symphony of eerie sounds continued to accompany us on our journey. The woods seemed to respond to our presence, the rustling growing more pronounced, the creaking more ominous. Every shadow cast a long, unsettling silhouette, as if the very fabric of the forest had been woven with an air of malevolence.

Despite the growing unease, we remained resolute. We knew that turning back now would forever leave us with unanswered questions and a sense of unfulfilled curiosity. So, we pushed deeper into the woods, clinging to the hope that our determination would be rewarded with answers, or perhaps even a glimpse into the truth that lay veiled within these haunting depths.

We continued to navigate the labyrinthine woods, each step fueled a mixture of anticipation and trepidation. The unknown lay before us, shrouded in darkness and mystery, while the noises and creaking sounds persisted, their origin still eluding us.

The mysterious noise grew louder and closer, our hearts pounded in our chests, this time we couldn't ignore it. The anticipation of what awaited us in the darkness reached its peak, and we instinctively grasped our flashlights tighter, desperately scanning the surroundings for any sign of movement.

But despite our efforts, the beams of light seemed to dissipate into the thick, impenetrable darkness. Shadows danced and twisted, playing tricks on our senses. Our eyes strained to catch even the faintest glimpse of what approached us, but it was as if the darkness itself had swallowed any visual clues.

Each step we took was accompanied by a symphony of fear—a symphony woven from the rustling leaves, the creaking branches, and the pounding of our own hearts. The noise that pursued us seemed to defy comprehension, fluctuating between whispers and distant echoes, making it impossible to discern its origin.

A primal fear gripped us, an instinctual response to the unknown. We huddled closer together, seeking solace and safety in our shared vulnerability. With trembling hands, we adjusted our flashlights, directing their beams in every direction, hoping to catch even the slightest glimpse of what lurked in the shadows.

The darkness remained unyielding, concealing its secrets with a cruel indifference. The closer the noise approached, the more our imaginations ran wild. Unseen shapes and figures materialized in our minds, each more terrifying than the last. The unknown took on a tangible form, playing havoc with our sanity.

In the midst of this unsettling atmosphere, doubts crept into our minds. Had we made a grave mistake by venturing into these woods? Were we being led into a trap? Questions swirled, but answers remained elusive.

As the noise reached its crescendo, we braced ourselves for the unknown. Adrenaline coursed through our veins, sharpening our senses. But just as we prepared for the worst, the noise abruptly ceased, leaving behind an eerie silence that engulfed the forest.

Confusion and relief washed over us in equal measure. We exchanged nervous glances, attempting to process the sudden absence of sound. Had we imagined it? Or had something truly been stalking us in the darkness, only to vanish without a trace?

The uncertainty lingered, casting a shadow of doubt over our collective resolve. We questioned whether to press on or retreat, unsure of what lay ahead. The experience had been a chilling reminder of the forces at play in this haunting realm. Our hearts pounded with a mix of fear and anticipation. Every nerve in our bodies was on high alert, prepared for an encounter with something truly menacing.

And then, in an instant, the source of the noise revealed itself—a small, harmless possum scurrying across the forest floor. Relief washed over us like a wave, and we couldn't help but let out nervous laughter.

In that moment, the intensity of our fright dissipated, replaced by a sense of amusement at our own overactive imaginations. We were both relieved and slightly embarrassed by the sudden realization that we had allowed ourselves to be swept up in our own fears.

This was the point where we should have turned around and called it a night. But, stubbornly, with our hearts still racing and minds clouded by uncertainty, we steeled ourselves and took a collective breath. We were determined to face whatever lay ahead, head-on, ready to embrace the consequences of our decision.

With renewed determination, we continued our journey through the darkness, our flashlights cutting through the murky veil, as we ventured deeper into the heart of the woods, eager to discover the truth that awaited us, yet wary of what it might reveal.

We continued our journey deeper into the woods. The path ahead seemed to beckon us, promising secrets and discoveries that only the darkness could hold. The allure of the unknown drew us further, curiosity overriding any lingering doubts or trepidation.

As we ventured deeper into the woods, the atmosphere shifted. The sounds of nocturnal creatures filled the air, their calls echoing through the trees. Each step we took seemed to immerse us further into an otherworldly realm, where reality blended with the mystical.

The dense foliage above cast intricate patterns of shadow and light upon the forest floor, creating an eerie and ethereal atmosphere. The silence that had once filled the woods was now punctuated by rustling leaves, whispering winds, and the occasional hoot of an owl.

We pressed on, our flashlights illuminating the path before us. The beams of light danced through the underbrush, revealing gnarled tree roots and fallen leaves. Time seemed to lose its meaning as we delved deeper, following an invisible thread of curiosity and the desire to uncover the truth.

As the night wore on, a sense of anticipation hung in the air. The forest whispered its secrets, teasing us with glimpses of hidden wonders. Every shadow, every rustle, held the promise of something extraordinary.

Our fears had transformed into a sense of exhilaration—an intoxicating mix of adrenaline and curiosity. We were now willing to embrace the enigmatic and the supernatural, stepping beyond the boundaries of ordinary existence.

With every step, our anticipation grew. The legends and tales we had heard about the hidden satanic church fueled our curiosity, but as time passed, doubts started to creep into our minds. The darkness enveloped us, casting elongated shadows that danced among the trees. The forest seemed to stretch on endlessly, its dense foliage concealing any signs of civilization.

The excitement that had initially propelled us forward now mingled with a tinge of bewilderment. How could we have gone so deep into the woods without finding any trace of the rumored structure of the Satanic church?

We continued our search, our flashlight beams piercing the darkness and illuminating the path ahead. We scrutinized every nook and cranny, hoping to stumble upon a hidden entrance or a telltale sign that would guide us to the Satanic church.

As minutes turned into hours, frustration began to mingle with our lingering curiosity. We started to question the authenticity of the legends we had heard. Had we been misled by embellished tales and exaggerated accounts? Or perhaps the passage of time had erased any remnants of the rumored church.

While flashing my flashlight around the forest, looking for any semblance of any structure, the beam of my flashlight cut through the darkness, revealing the path ahead.

Suddenly, something caught my gaze in the distance. A flicker of light caught my attention, drawing my focus to a pair of eyes that glowed like embers. Two bright, glowing yellow eyes stared back at me, and a chill ran down my spine. At first, I brushed it off, thinking it could be a deer or some other nocturnal creature. But as I continued to watch, the unsettling realization set in—it couldn't possibly be a deer.

They seemed to pierce through the darkness, radiating an otherworldly intensity, something about those eyes struck me as strange. As the beam of light illuminated the mysterious figure, my heart skipped a beat. The eyes were not where they should be for a deer, deer's eyes are typically closer together, not several feet apart.

The distance between those glowing orbs was too great, suggesting a much larger creature lurking in the shadows. My heart pounded in my chest as I tried to make sense of what I was seeing. They gleamed with an unnatural brightness, as if reflecting a source of light that eluded my flashlight.

That moment a chill ran down my spine as I realized that what I had stumbled upon was something far more extraordinary than a woodland creature. Tessa and Steven, sensing my unease, turned their attention to the peculiar sight ahead.

The forest around us seemed to hold its breath as we stood there, frozen with uncertainty. The air was thick with tension, and the rustling leaves and nocturnal sounds had ceased. It was as if the entire forest had gone eerily quiet, anticipating something unknown.

As we inched closer, our fear gave way to a mix of curiosity and caution. The eyes remained fixed on us, unblinking and unwavering. I couldn't shake the feeling that we were being watched by something ancient and primal

The three of us cautiously approached the source of the glowing eyes as our apprehension built with each step. The air grew still, punctuated only by the distant chirping of nocturnal creatures. The woods seemed to hold its breath, as if aware of the presence of an enigmatic force.

As we drew nearer, the figure began to take shape—a massive silhouette against the backdrop of the night. It stood tall, almost unnaturally so, its form shrouded in the darkness. The glowing eyes seemed to fixate on us, unblinking and filled with an otherworldly intensity.

A mix of curiosity and fear consumed us, yet our determination urged us forward. Our minds raced, attempting to rationalize the sight before us. Was it a trick of the light? An optical illusion? Or something far more extraordinary?

With every step closer, the details became clearer. The figure remained shrouded in darkness, however, its presence was palpable as it possessed a commanding presence, exuding an energy that seemed to permeate the surrounding forest.

We approached within a few feet of the mysterious entity, a surge of adrenaline coursed through our veins. My friends shone their flashlights in the same direction, their beams intersected with mine, revealing the same pair of glowing yellow eyes. The light danced upon the eyes, reflecting an otherworldly luminescence.

There was something uncanny about those eyes, as if they belonged to a being that existed beyond the boundaries of our comprehension. I strained my eyes, hoping to catch a glimpse of the creature behind those piercing orbs, but all I could see was darkness. It was as if the eyes floated disembodied in the night, devoid of a physical form.

My mind raced with questions. How could a pair of eyes exist without a visible body? Was it an illusion, a trick of the light? Or were we truly in the presence of something supernatural?

The silence of the forest became deafening as our collective unease grew. We were acutely aware that we had ventured into a realm where the ordinary rules of nature might not apply. The air seemed charged with an electric energy, prickling our skin and heightening our senses.

Suddenly, as if emerging from the very shadows themselves, we caught sight of movement ahead. Two other enigmatic figures materialized before us, shrouded in darkness so deep it seemed to consume the surrounding night. They stood in a formation, one in the middle flanked by two on either side, like sentinels guarding an ancient secret.

Our hearts skipped a beat as we realized they were no longer just a pair of glowing eyes, but something much more daunting. Three distinct shapes stood before us, with one in the middle and two flanking it on each side.

The sight was unsettling. The figures, blacker than the night itself, were stark contrasts against the backdrop of the moonlit forest. They exude an air of otherworldliness, their silhouettes towering over us at a staggering height of thirteen feet.

Time seemed to stand still as we stared frozen in disbelief, our minds struggling to comprehend the enormity and strangeness of what we were witnessing. Fear and curiosity intertwined within us, an electric current charging the air.

Silence settled upon the woods, broken only by the faint rustling of leaves and the quickened beats of our hearts. We exchanged glances, wordlessly communicating our shared astonishment. This was a moment that would be etched into our memories forever.

As our eyes adjusted to the dim light, we attempted to discern the features of these enigmatic beings. Their forms remained shrouded, as if cloaked in a perpetual shadow. No distinguishable facial features or limbs were visible, only their towering presence, a presence that emanated an aura of eeriness and death itself.

The figures remained motionless, their gaze fixed upon us. The air crackled with a palpable energy, like a tempest about to break free from its confines. It was as if time itself held its breath, awaiting the outcome of our encounter.

A surge of adrenaline coursed through our veins, mingling with a primal instinct to flee. We stood before these towering enigmas, our faces upturned to meet their inscrutable gaze.

Then, in a moment that felt like an eternity compressed into a single heartbeat, the figures began to move. Their movements were slow and deliberate, like the shifting of tectonic plates deep beneath the Earth's surface.

With each step they took, the forest floor trembled beneath them, amplifying the sense of their power. We watched, spellbound, as their towering forms seemed to meld seamlessly with the night, becoming one with the darkness itself.

As the figures drew nearer, we felt a surge of reverence and fear. It was an encounter that transcended the realm of the known, an intersection of our mundane reality and a world unseen. We were in the presence of an enigma, witnessing a convergence of the extraordinary and the everyday.

Steven, usually quick to act, took a step forward, his voice shaking but resolute. "Who...or what are you?" he asked, his words carrying a mixture of wonder and trepidation.

The middle figure seemed to incline its head slightly, as if acknowledging Steven's question. But there was no audible response—only a deep, resonating silence that seemed to envelop us.

Tessa and I exchanged glances, and she whispered, "We should go. This doesn't feel right."

But our feet remained firmly rooted to the ground, as if an invisible force held us captive. There was an inexplicable pull, as though we were trapped to the forest floor.

The figure on the right took a step forward. Its movement was graceful yet powerful, akin to that of a large predator asserting its dominance. The figure on the left mirrored the action, flanking the central entity in a display of symmetry.

As if in response to our unspoken thoughts, a deafening sound suddenly emerged from one of the colossal figures, shattering the stillness of the night. It was a cacophony unlike anything we had ever heard before—an amalgamation of primal forces that seemed to echo through the very fabric of our souls.

The sound began with a hiss of a rattlesnake warning of its presence. It slithered through the air, curling around our senses with an eerie intensity. The hair on the back of our necks stood on end as the hiss intensified, sending chills down our spines.

Then, like a lion's roar reverberating through the vast savannah, the sound crescendo. It was a primal, earth-shattering roar that shook the very ground beneath our feet. Each reverberation seemed to penetrate our bones, rattling our resolve and filling us with an overwhelming sense of awe and terror.

Interwoven within the roar and hiss was a fluttering, like the wings of a thousand bats taking flight. It was a haunting sound, ethereal and disconcerting. The fluttering created an eerie backdrop to the symphony of primal voices, adding a layer of unease that sent shivers down our spines.

The volume of the sound was so overpowering, so immense, that we were compelled to clutch our ears in a desperate attempt to shield ourselves from its deafening force. The pressure built within our skulls, threatening to overwhelm our senses. We staggered, nearly collapsing to the forest floor under the weight of the sound.

That moment it was as if the very fabric of reality had been torn asunder as the overwhelming symphony of sound enveloped me, and I found myself caught in the midst of a surreal experience.

When the sound intensified, I felt my consciousness begin to unravel, as if I were being pulled away from my physical self. My head seemed to expand, the pressure building within it like a balloon on the verge of bursting. It was an excruciating sensation, as if my mind were expanding to grasp the incomprehensible magnitude of the moment.

My body, once strong and agile, betrayed me in this surreal state. I felt my limbs grow heavy and unresponsive, as if shackled by an invisible force. I tried desperately to move, to escape the overwhelming tumult, but it was as if I were trapped in a sleep paralysis, unable to break free.

As the sound continued, the air around me underwent a profound transformation. The once chilly and crisp atmosphere turned oppressively warm, suffocating me with its heat. It was as if I were standing in the midst of a blazing inferno, surrounded by thick liquid darkness that seemed to devour the light.

The contrasting sensations of scorching heat and enveloping darkness created an eerie and disorienting paradox. The hotness clung to my skin, intensifying with each passing second, while the darkness seemed to press in on me from all sides. It was as if I were suspended in a void, where light and darkness merged into an indistinguishable blur.

Fear and confusion gripped my heart, yet there was also a strange allure to this disorienting experience. It was as if the very fabric of reality had been unraveled, revealing a hidden realm beyond human comprehension. I found myself torn between the instinct to flee and an inexplicable fascination with the enigmatic forces that surrounded me.

Time seemed to lose all meaning as I stood there, a mere speck in the vast expanse of this bewildering encounter. I struggled to find my footing, both physically and mentally, as the overwhelming sensations threatened to consume me.

In the intensity of the moment, I glanced at Tessa and Steven, who were standing beside me in this bewildering experience. Their faces mirrored the same mixture of fear, awe, and confusion that I felt within myself. It was evident that they, too, were being consumed by the surreal forces that surrounded us. I could see the distress etched across their faces, their eyes wide with fear and wonder.

Tessa's hair defied gravity, like an ethereal halo. It floated weightlessly in the air as if she were suspended in space. The sight was both mesmerizing and unsettling, as if the very laws of physics had been suspended in this enigmatic realm. Her body remained firmly rooted to the ground, yet her hair danced in an ethereal ballet, defying all logic.

Steven, on the other hand, had succumbed to the overwhelming intensity of the encounter. He lay crumpled on the ground, his hands clutching his head as if trying to shield himself from the onslaught of sensations. The overwhelming cacophony had taken its toll on him, and he seemed to be grappling with the very essence of his existence. I could see the torment in his eyes, the struggle to comprehend the incomprehensible.

Just then, as suddenly as it had begun, the cacophony ceased. The oppressive heat dissipated, replaced by the stinging coolness of the night air. The ethereal darkness receded, leaving me standing in a state of bewilderment and awe.

I took a moment to gather myself, my body and mind slowly regaining their composure. The echoes of that extraordinary experience still resonated within me, leaving an indelible mark on my consciousness.

Quickly, I moved closer to Tessa, my own sense of wonder mingling with concern for my friends. I could feel the invisible energies coursing through the air, electrifying the atmosphere with their enigmatic presence. There was a palpable weight to the darkness in the air.

The sudden cessation of the otherworldly sounds seemed to snap Steven out of whatever trance he had been in. 'Get out guys! Get out!' His urgent scream pierced the air. Without a moment's hesitation, he turned and bolted into the darkness, his flashlight cut through the darkness, revealing his path. His fear was palpable, contagious even, and it propelled us into motion.

Tessa wasted no time and followed suit, abandoning her flashlight in her haste. I grabbed my own flashlight, clutching it tightly, and hurriedly pursued Tessa's retreating figure. The beam of light sliced through the night, illuminating the path ahead, but the shadows danced and flickered ominously on the periphery.

The forest engulfed us in an eerie silence as we raced through the dense undergrowth. The only sounds were the pounding of our footsteps, the rustling of leaves beneath our hurried strides, and the occasional snap of branches as we pushed through the thick foliage.

I could feel the adrenaline coursing through my veins, heightening my senses and sharpening my focus. Fear gnawed at the edges of my mind, but determination fueled my steps. There was a desperate urgency to reach the safety of the car, to escape the unknown horrors that lurked in the depths of the forest.

The flashing of Steven's flashlight in the distance acted as a guiding beacon, leading us through the labyrinthine maze of trees and tangled vegetation. With every step, the forest seemed to grow darker and more foreboding, as if it were conspiring to keep us trapped within its clutches.

As we ran, a sense of isolation and vulnerability pervaded the air. The absence of familiar sounds, replaced only by our rapid breaths and the pounding of our hearts, amplified the feeling of being at the mercy of the unknown.

With each passing moment, the distance between us and the enigmatic creatures grew, but their presence still lingered in our minds. We dared not look back, our focus solely on the path ahead, our thoughts consumed by the need for escape.

As we ran, I noticed I passed Tessa and glanced back to see Tessa following closely behind, her flashlight abandoned in the chaos of the moment. Her face was etched with fear, and her eyes darted around, searching for any sign of danger.

My mind was racing, trying to process everything that had just happened. What were those creatures? Why were they here? And most importantly, were they still pursuing us?

Time seemed to lose all meaning as we ran through the night, the adrenaline fueling our desperate flight. I could feel the exhaustion creeping into my muscles, but the fear kept me going, pushing me to keep moving, to keep running.

As I ran, fear gnawed at my core, intensifying with each passing moment. The adrenaline coursing through my veins propelled me forward, but a sense of déjà vu washed over me, as if I had experienced this nightmarish scenario before. My heart pounded so forcefully that I could almost taste its weight in my mouth.

In the chaos of our escape, the gap between Steven and me widened, and I lost sight of him amidst the engulfing darkness. Panic surged through me as I strained to catch any glimpse of his flashlight or the sound of his footsteps. But there was nothing. He had vanished into the black void, leaving me standing alone, the weight of the silence pressing down upon me.

A shiver ran down my spine as the reality of my solitary situation sank in. Tessa, too, had disappeared into the inky abyss, leaving me to navigate this ominous forest on my own. The once comforting presence of my friends was replaced by an unsettling void, amplifying my vulnerability and isolation.

The forest stood silently, as if holding its breath, hiding its secrets within the impenetrable shadows. Doubt crept into my mind. Should I continue searching for my friends, risking my own safety? Or should I retreat and find my way back to the car?

Fear clung to me like a second skin, urging me to find safety, to escape this haunting place. That moment I felt a nudge, like an invisible force was tapping me from behind to turn around. Like I was controlled by a power beyond my control, I did turn around.

As I turned my gaze back, my heart pounding in my chest, a chilling sight met my eyes. One of the creatures, the one that had stood in the middle, with its ominous presence and piercing yellow eyes, remained rooted to the spot. It seemed to have fixated its attention solely on me, its malevolent aura radiating in the air.

A shiver ran down my spine as I realized that the other two creatures had vanished, leaving only this formidable entity behind. Its very presence exuded a sense of impending doom, and I knew instinctively that I had to escape its reach before it could unleash whatever horrors it held.

Without a moment's hesitation, fueled by a primal instinct for survival, I sprinted forward, my legs propelling me through the tangled undergrowth. Fear propelled me forward, every fiber of my being focused solely on putting as much distance as possible between myself and that malevolent presence.

The forest seemed to blur in my peripheral vision as I ran, my heart racing in my ears. The adrenaline surged through my veins, lending strength to my trembling legs as I weaved through the gnarled trees and leaped over fallen branches. Panic consumed me, amplifying my senses, making every rustle of leaves and every distant sound appear as potential threats.

I dared not look back, afraid of what I might see, afraid that those piercing yellow eyes would still be fixed on me, haunting my every step. My only goal was to escape the clutches of that nightmarish entity, to find safety in the familiarity of the car and leave this twisted realm behind.

The air tore at my lungs as I gasped for breath, my muscles burning with exertion. I could feel the sweat trickling down my forehead, mixing with the tears of fear and desperation. The forest seemed to stretch endlessly, the path ahead illuminated only by the weak beam of my flashlight.

Every now and then, I stumbled, my foot catching on a hidden root or loose rock, threatening to send me crashing to the ground. But sheer determination propelled me forward, my will to survive overpowering the physical strain.

As I sprinted through the dense forest, my heart pounding in my chest, I couldn't help but notice an additional sound accompanying my hurried footsteps. A heavy, rhythmic thudding reverberated through the air, as if someone or something was running in parallel to my frantic pace.

Curiosity mingled with trepidation as the notion settled in that I was not alone in this desperate flight. A glimmer of hope sparked within me, hoping against hope that it was Tessa, desperately trying to catch up and find safety together. With a flicker of hesitation, I turned my head, stealing a quick glance to my side.

The beam of my flashlight swung through the shadows, casting eerie silhouettes on the surrounding trees. In that fleeting moment, I caught a glimpse of a figure, moving with a swift and purposeful stride. Relief surged through me as I recognized the familiar contours of Tessa's form.

A surge of hope propelled my weary legs forward as I veered towards her, the sound of our synchronized footsteps resonating through the stillness of the forest. With each passing stride, the gap between us closed, and the fear that had gripped my heart began to subside.

However, as I closed the distance, hope quickly gave way to horror. The figure that I had initially identified as Tessa suddenly transformed before my eyes, morphing into the towering, thirteen-foot monstrosity. Its once-familiar features distorted into a grotesque visage, and its eyes glowed with a malevolence that sent a chill coursing through my veins.

Shock paralyzed me for a split second, but the primal instinct for self-preservation kicked in, urging me to run as fast as my trembling legs would carry me. But to my dismay, the creature matched my pace effortlessly, its massive form lunging forward with each stride and its heavy, rhythmic thudding reverberated through the air, hardly faltering or slowing down.

The forest around us blurred as I darted through the tangled undergrowth, fear gripping my every step. The creature's relentless pursuit sent waves of terror crashing over me, heightening my senses to the surrounding danger. I could feel its eyes, burning into my back like searing coals, its unwavering gaze fixed solely on me.

My heart pounded in my chest, each beat echoing the desperate rhythm of my escape. Adrenaline surged through my veins, numbing the fatigue that threatened to overwhelm me. No matter how fast I ran, the creature matched my every move.

Every muscle in my body screamed with exhaustion, and yet I pushed myself harder, propelled by a primal fear that bordered on hysteria. The forest became a blur of dark shapes and fleeting shadows, the trees blurring into a whirlwind of motion as I desperately tried to put distance between myself and the relentless pursuer.

Branches lashed against my face, leaving stinging marks and tears in their wake, but I pressed on, determined to outrun this nightmarish predator. Panic gripped me, my breath coming in ragged gasps, and the wild thumping of my heart drowned out all other sounds.

The realization that the creature showed no signs of tiring only fueled my terror. It moved with an unnatural grace, disregarding obstacles in its path, as if consumed by a single-minded focus on capturing me. Every glance I stole over my shoulder confirmed that those menacing eyes remained fixed on me.

Time lost all meaning as the chase seemed to stretch on endlessly. The forest became a twisted maze, each turn only leading to more darkness and uncertainty. My mind raced, desperately searching for an escape, for a way to break free from this nightmarish pursuit.

No matter how fast or how far I ran, the creature remained a haunting presence, its glowing eyes burning into my soul. My legs ached, my lungs burned, and despair threatened to consume me. Yet, I ran, desperately clinging to the hope that somehow, against all odds, I would emerge from this nightmarish ordeal unscathed.

Suddenly, I heard a sharp shrill cry pierce the air. That was Tessa's voice. Immediately I stopped and froze at the spot not minding the eerie force pursuing me. It seems to have stopped from a distance watching me.

'Tessa!' I screamed back in fear and trepidation. A fear that exceeded the nightmare standing and watching me eerily in the distance.

As the deafening sound of my own voice faded into the night, a chilling silence settled over the forest. My desperate cry for Tessa echoed through the trees, the echoes fading into the darkness, leaving me with an unsettling sense of dread.

Time seemed to stand still as I anxiously waited for a response, my ears straining to catch any sign of her presence. The forest enveloped me in its oppressive silence, broken only by the sound of my own heavy breathing. Panic surged within me, threatening to overwhelm my senses as I grappled with the uncertainty of Tessa's fate.

Was she captured by the creature that pursued us? Was she hurt, trapped, or worse? A thousand possibilities raced through my mind, each one more terrifying than the last. I called out her name once again, hoping against hope that she would answer, that her voice would pierce through the thick veil of darkness and bring a glimmer of reassurance.

But all I was met with was an eerie stillness, as if the very air held its breath in anticipation. The creature, too, remained motionless, its glowing eyes fixed upon me with an intensity that sent shivers down my spine. It seemed to revel in the moment, basking in the fear and uncertainty that gripped my soul.

Questions swirled in my mind, each one a dagger of doubt, piercing through my resolve. Had Steven abandoned us in our time of need, leaving us to fend for ourselves in this nightmarish realm? Or was he simply lost in the darkness, fighting his own battle against the unknown?

A mixture of anger and desperation welled up within me, fueling my determination to find Tessa and uncover the truth. I couldn't bear the thought of leaving her behind, at the mercy of this malevolent force that lurked in the shadows. My legs trembled with a renewed sense of purpose as I prepared to venture deeper into the forest, willing to face whatever horror waiting and watching me in the shadows.

Just as I took a step forward, a glimmer of movement caught my eye. It was the creature. It seemed to get bigger and bigger in the darkness and it edged closer to me. We stared at each other eye to eye, like I was defying it to do its worst. No one hurts my friends and gets away with it.

In a split second, haunting groans and gasps started emanating from the creature. Just as loud as earlier. It echoed through the air, sending a chill down my spine. The sound was unlike anything I had ever heard before—a discordant symphony of rasping breaths and low, guttural moans that seemed to vibrate through the very fabric of my being.

Realizing this was beyond me I took a step back. The dark figure before me quivered and convulsed, its silhouette pulsating with an otherworldly energy. It was a sight that defied rational explanation, as if the creature itself was in the midst of a horrifying transformation.

Shadows danced and flickered around its form, lending an eerie, ethereal quality to its presence.

In an instant, the figure split apart, multiplying into seven distinct entities. Each new form bore the same ominous glow, casting an eerie fire-like light that illuminated the surrounding darkness. The air crackled with a sinister energy, as if the very fabric of reality had been torn asunder.

Sensing the imminent danger, I wasted no time. Fear propelled me forward, my feet pounding against the forest floor, desperately seeking an escape. My heart raced, mirroring the rapid rhythm of my footsteps, as the creatures trailed closely behind.

The unsettling groans and gasps followed me, growing louder with each passing moment. It was as if the creatures reveled in their own torment, delighting in the terror they instilled. The sound permeated the stillness of the night, a haunting chorus that sent shivers down my spine.

As I sprinted further into the depths of the forest, the splitting creatures continued their pursuit, their distorted forms shifting and writhing in a macabre dance. Their eerie glow cast eerie shadows on the surrounding trees, creating a nightmarish tableau that heightened my sense of dread.

Driven by sheer survival instinct, I pushed my body to its limits, my mind focused solely on finding a way to elude the creatures' relentless pursuit. Adrenaline surged through my veins, sharpening my senses and lending me a burst of speed that seemed almost superhuman.

With every fiber of my being, I propelled myself forward, my legs burning with exertion as adrenaline surged through my veins. The chilling cries of the creatures echoed behind me, growing louder and more distorted with each passing second. I dared not look back, for fear that their menacing presence would only fuel my terror.

Branches whipped against my face, leaving stinging marks in their wake, while thorny bushes clawed at my arms and legs. The darkness engulfed me, swallowing my vision and heightening the sense of disorientation. Yet, fueled by fear and the desperate need to escape, I pushed through the obstacles that stood in my way.

The rhythmic sound of my pounding footsteps matched the pounding of my heart, both resounding in my ears as a testament to the primal instinct of survival. The forest seemed to stretch on endlessly, a labyrinth of shadows and unknown terrors. Each step I took carried me further into its depths, further away from the safety of familiarity.

But even in the midst of my frantic flight, a small sliver of hope pierced through the darkness. It was the faint glow of moonlight filtering through the canopy above, offering glimpses of the twisted and gnarled trees that surrounded me. It was a reminder that even in the darkest of moments, there was still a flicker of light, a glimmer of possibility.

The creatures pursued relentlessly, their haunting sounds echoing through the night, reverberating in my bones. The ground beneath me seemed to tremble in response to their presence, as if the very earth shared in my fear. Yet, I refused to surrender to despair. I clung to the belief that somewhere within me, there was a reserve of strength and resilience that would carry me through this ordeal.

As I ran, time became distorted, the minutes stretching into eternity. Sweat soaked my brow, mingling with tears of fear and exhaustion. With each passing moment, I willed myself to run faster, to outpace the encroaching darkness that threatened to consume me. The sound of my own breath mingled with the cacophony of groans and gasps, creating a disorienting symphony of fear.

As I dashed deeper into the forest, I could only hope that the creatures would eventually lose interest, their ethereal forms fading into the blackened void.

In an instant it overtook me. I felt something smack me to the floor. Like I had been slapped by a swift, unseen force. The creature stood before me as it watched me try to get up like it was mocking my effort.

The sight before me was beyond comprehension and my heart pounded like a drum, each beat echoing in my ears, as I took in the scene. Seven sinister figures stood before me, bathed in an otherworldly glow that resembled flickering flames dancing in the night and soon they transformed into a terrifying congregation of dark entities. So many I couldn't count the number of glows that surrounded me.

As their dark forms quivered and shook, emitting eerie groans and gasps, I felt a primal fear gripping me like a vice. It was as if the very fabric of reality was unraveling, revealing a realm of nightmares I could never have imagined. Panic surged through my veins, urging me to sprint up and flee again from this malevolent force before it consumed me.

With every ounce of strength left in my body, I sprinted deeper into the forest, desperate to escape the relentless pursuit of these dark entities. My breaths came in ragged gasps, and my legs burned from the exertion, but I pushed myself to go further, to outrun the terrifying manifestations that hunted me.

The forest seemed to blur around me as I ran, the trees passing in a frenzied blur. My flashlight flickered, casting eerie shadows on the path before me. Yet, despite the darkness that surrounded me, I dared not slow down, for the haunting sounds of those creatures still echoed in my mind.

Every fiber of my being screamed for me to keep going, to put as much distance as possible between myself and those otherworldly beings.

Suddenly someone collided with me, causing both of us to tumble to the ground. This time I was too exhausted to get up. It had overtaken me again, I thought as I resumed panicking. I reached out for a branch beside me to ward it off. If I was going to die at least I was going to die fighting.

But as my flashlight illuminated the figure lying beside me, my fear transformed into astonishment and relief. It was Tessa! My trembling hands lowered the makeshift weapon as I let out a breath I didn't realize I was holding.

Frantically, I reached out to touch Tessa, running my fingers over her body to ensure she was unharmed. Relief washed over me as I felt her familiar warmth and heard her whimper softly. "Tessa, are you okay?" I asked, my voice trembling with a mix of concern and relief.

She nodded, her eyes still wide with fear. "I... I thought I lost you," she managed to say, her voice quivering.

"I thought the same," I replied, my voice filled with relief. "We need to find Steven. He ran ahead of us, but we lost sight of him. I don't know where he is."

Tessa's eyes darted around, scanning the surrounding darkness. "We can't just leave him behind. Let's try to find him and get out of here together."

I nodded, gripping Tessa's hand tightly as we rose to our feet. The forest seemed to close in on us, its shadowy depths filled with unknown dangers. But our determination to find our friend fueled our resolve.

With my flashlight leading the way, we cautiously ventured through the tangled woods, calling out Steven's name and not sure what side of the forest we were. The silence that followed our desperate pleas only intensified our sense of unease. The air was thick with an otherworldly stillness, broken only by the rustling

Tessa's voice trembled as she recounted her own encounter with one of the creatures. Tears welled up in her eyes, reflecting the mix of fear and relief that enveloped her. She explained how she had been pursued by one of the dark entities, feeling its presence closing in on her. But to her surprise, just as it seemed poised to capture her, it abruptly changed its course and raced past her, disappearing into the depths of the forest.

Her voice quivered as she shared her realization. "I think it's heading towards the field, where we left our car," Tessa whispered, her words filled with a sense of urgency.

My heart skipped a beat at the revelation. The thought of those malevolent beings reaching our only means of escape filled me with a renewed sense of dread. We couldn't afford to let them get there first. Determination flooded through my veins, overshadowing my fear.

"We have to get to the field before they do. We can't let them reach the car," I said, my voice resolute. Tessa nodded, her eyes shining with a mix of fear and determination.

We turned on our heels, retracing our steps through the treacherous forest. Every rustle of leaves and crack of branches sent shivers down our spines, as if the very forest itself conspired against us. The moon's feeble glow filtered through the dense canopy, casting eerie shadows on the forest floor.

As we neared the field, a sense of urgency consumed us. Our footsteps quickened, our breaths grew shallow, and the air seemed to grow thicker with each passing moment. We knew time was running out, and the fate of our escape rested upon reaching the car before those sinister entities did.

Together, Tessa and I sprinted through the forest, our feet pounding against the forest floor. Fear fueled our every step as we dared not look back, fearing the lurking presence of those enigmatic creatures. Branches whipped against our skin, and our breaths came in ragged gasps, but we pressed on, driven by a desperate need to reach the field.

As we emerged from the dense forest, a sense of relief washed over us. The full moon cast its ethereal glow upon the open field, illuminating our path and creating a stark contrast to the darkness we had just escaped. The moonlight seemed to breathe life into the surrounding landscape, painting it with an eerie yet comforting light.

It was then that we caught sight of a familiar figure darting across the field, heading straight for our parked car. It was Steven. Recognition flashed in our eyes, relief flooding through our weary bodies.

"Steven!" we shouted, our voices laced with a mixture of urgency and hope. "Wait for us!"

Steven, who seemed to be running frantically, halted when he heard our voices. He turned, a mixture of relief and surprise on his face as he recognized us. His pace slowed for a moment, uncertainty flickering in his eyes. But then, understanding dawned, and he gestured for us to hurry.

Tessa and I pushed ourselves forward, our legs propelling us faster. The field stretched out before us, the distance between us and Steven diminishing with every stride. The air crackled with anticipation as our feet pounded against the soft ground, the sound blending with the rush of blood in our ears.

Finally, we reached Steven, our chests heaving with exertion.

"Steven!" Tessa called out, her voice a mix of relief and urgency as she hugged Steven

"Thank goodness you're both safe," he said, gasping for breath.

But before we could take a step toward the car, an unsettling feeling washed over me. The light from the full moon that bathed the field in its glow seemed strangely disconnected from the darkness that lay beyond. And all the dark creatures seem to be nowhere to be found. Why would they pass Tessa if they had no intention of getting to the field or the car before we did?

"Tessa, the moonlight doesn't seem to reach the forest?" I asked, my voice low and filled with apprehension.

Tessa nodded, her eyes darting between the car and the eerie darkness behind us. "It's like there's an invisible barrier keeping the darkness at bay," she replied, her voice trembling.

Steven glanced back, and a shiver ran down his spine. "We can't stay here. We have to get out of this place," he said urgently.

Without further delay, we rushed towards our car, our fear urging us to move faster than ever before. The moonlight acted as our guide, illuminating our path and granting us a small semblance of safety. But as we drew closer to the car, an unsettling feeling of being watched washed over me.

As we sprinted across the field, our ears filled with the thudding of our own footsteps, a chilling realization washed over us. The sound of something else running, something otherworldly, echoed through the woods surrounding us. It seemed as though those enigmatic creatures were still in pursuit, their presence closing in on us with every passing moment.

Gasping for breath, we finally reached the edge of the field, our hearts pounding in our chests. I glanced back, scanning the tree line, and my blood ran cold. There, at the edge of the darkness, one of the creatures came to a sudden halt. Its glowing eyes pierced through the blackness, fixated on us with an intensity that sent shivers down my spine.

But what troubled me most was the absence of the other creature. It had vanished, as if swallowed by the shadows themselves. I strained my ears, hoping to catch any hint of its presence, but the only sound that reached me was the eerie silence that enveloped the field.

As we continued running in desperation, our escape led us to the graveyard. Dread washed over us as we entered the eerie atmosphere, surrounded by crumbling tombstones and the haunting stillness of the night.

Breathing heavily, we navigated through the graveyard, our footsteps hushed, as if afraid to disturb the slumber of the departed. The moon cast a pale glow over the worn headstones, casting long, ominous shadows that seemed to dance in the wind.

It was then, as we made our way through the backside of the graveyard, that I caught a glimpse of something that froze me in my tracks. In the distance, illuminated by the moonlight, stood the creature that had previously pursued Tessa. Its glowing yellow eyes pierced through the darkness, fixated on us with a malevolent intensity.

Fear coursed through my veins, intertwining with the adrenaline that still pulsed within me. I felt my friends tense beside me, their breaths catching in their throats as they too noticed the creature's presence.

The atmosphere grew heavy, a tangible aura of menace enveloping us. We were trapped between the graveyard's cold embrace and the unyielding gaze of this unearthly creature. It felt as though time had slowed, each second stretching out into an eternity of anticipation and terror.

Unable to tear my eyes away from those glowing eyes, I could only imagine the malicious intent lurking within the creature's form.

My friends and I stood rooted to the spot, our bodies trembling with fear and uncertainty. It was as if the world had faded into the background, leaving only the creature and us, locked in a paralyzing standoff.

Time seemed to hang in suspension, the air thick with an impending threat. Each passing moment brought us closer to an unknown fate, held captive by the creature's piercing gaze and the ominous silence that surrounded us.

Summoning all the courage we could muster, we slowly began to back away, keeping our eyes locked on the creature's glowing gaze. Every step was measured, cautious, as if any sudden movement would trigger its wrath.

As we retreated, our minds raced for the car. The graveyard whispered its secrets, the gravestones casting long shadows that seemed to offer both refuge and danger.

Finally, with our lungs burning and our hearts pounding we sighted our car and hurriedly made our way to the car, our footsteps echoing in the stillness of the night. With trembling hands, Steven fumbled for the keys, my heart pounding in my ears. The metallic jingle of the keychain seemed to reverberate through the tense atmosphere.

As the car doors unlocked with a click, a surge of relief washed over us. Without wasting a second, we piled into the vehicle, our bodies trembling with adrenaline and exhaustion. I slammed the door shut and buried myself into the seat like I wanted to disappear from this nightmare immediately..

Steven wasted no time as he slipped behind the steering wheel, his hands trembling with a mix of adrenaline and determination. He inserted the key into the ignition, the familiar sound of the engine roaring to life bringing a glimmer of reassurance.

Without hesitation, Steven shifted into gear, his foot pressing down on the accelerator with a newfound urgency. The car surged forward, its tires gripping the earth as we left the confines of the graveyard behind.

As we peeled away from the field, the headlights pierced through the darkness, illuminating the surroundings in a cone of clarity. We scanned the area, searching for any signs of the creatures that had pursued us relentlessly. But the night held its secrets tightly

As the vehicle tore through the night, a newfound sense of freedom washed over us. The wind whipped through the open windows, carrying away the lingering dread that had clung to our souls. We were leaving the darkness in our wake, moving towards the light of safety and solace.

The car's headlights pierced through the darkness, illuminating the path before us, casting long shadows that danced along the roadside. The engine's roar drowned out the haunting echoes of our ordeal, filling the void with the reassuring symphony of horsepower and mechanics.

As we raced away from the graveyard, my heart still pounded in my chest like a war drum, and my breath came in uneven gasps. The car's engine roared, drowning out the sounds of the night, but I couldn't shake the feeling that we were being pursued. It was like a recurring nightmare, a twisted sense of déjà vu that gripped my mind, leaving me on edge.

Unable to resist the compulsion to look back once more, I stole a quick glance through the rearview mirror. My heart nearly skipped a beat when I saw the creature still standing on top of the grave, its glowing yellow eyes locked onto me, unyielding, unblinking. The creature stood tall and imposing, its silhouette etched against the moonlit sky. It was as if it could see right through my soul, piercing me with an intensity that sent shivers down my spine.

With a mix of dread and determination, I tore my gaze away from those hypnotic eyes, forcing myself to face forward. Fear coursed through my veins, urging me to keep my eyes focused on the road ahead, to never look back. I knew that dwelling on the creature's gaze would only fuel the terror that threatened to consume me.

The car's tires hummed over the road, and the landscape flew by, but I couldn't tear my eyes away from that haunting sight. The image of the creature, perched above the resting place of the dead, filled me with a profound sense of unease. It seemed to be watching us leave, a silent reminder that we were not alone, that the darkness still lingered.

I forced myself to focus on the road ahead. I couldn't let fear consume me, not when we were finally making our escape. We needed to find safety, somewhere far from this cursed place, where the memories of tonight's horrors would hopefully fade away.

Inside the car, tension hung heavy in the air, and no one spoke a word. We were all lost in our thoughts, haunted by what we had just witnessed. The forest now lay far behind us, but its presence seemed to linger, a shadow that refused to be cast away.

As we drove on, the moon sailed across the sky, illuminating the landscape around us with its ethereal glow. The fields and trees that once appeared peaceful now held an eerie quality, their long shadows stretching like fingers trying to reach out and drag us back into the abyss.

I couldn't shake the feeling that we were being followed, that those creatures were still out there, lurking in the darkness, watching, waiting. Every rustle of the leaves, every flicker of movement in the shadows, sent my heart racing, my imagination running wild with terrifying possibilities.

The sound of the tires on the road seemed to merge with the pounding of my heart, creating a cacophony of fear that threatened to consume me. I kept stealing glances out the window, half-expecting to see those glowing eyes, those twisted forms, appear beside us in the dark.

Time seemed to stretch on endlessly as we drove, the miles passing by in slow motion. Each turn, each bend in the road, felt like a step further into the unknown, deeper into a nightmare from which there might be no waking.

As the car raced through the night, I could still sense the creature's presence, its malevolent energy seeping into the very fabric of our surroundings. The moon, once a beacon of tranquility, now cast an eerie glow that seemed to conspire with the darkness. Shadows danced along the roadside, playing tricks on my weary mind.

The passing landscape became a blur of trees and fields, a hazy backdrop to our desperate escape. The wind whispered haunting melodies, carrying fragments of our fears and the lingering echoes of the creature's growls. It felt as if we were racing against time itself, hoping to outrun the shadows that threatened to consume us.

In the safety of the car's interior, I stole glances at my friends, their faces etched with a mix of relief and trepidation.

The image of Tessa's hair floating in the air haunted me, a surreal reminder of the inexplicable and terrifying events of the night. What had those creatures been? Where had they come from? What did they want with us?

My mind was a whirlwind of questions and fears, but I knew there were no answers, at least not yet. We had to focus on escaping this nightmare first, finding our way back to civilization, to safety.

With each passing mile, the creature's presence faded, gradually relinquishing its grip on our consciousness. The road stretched out before us, an open invitation to leave behind the darkness that had plagued us. We were determined to embrace the light, to find solace in the world beyond the graveyard's reach.

As the distant memory of the creature began to fade, a flicker of hope ignited within us. We knew that we had escaped its clutches, that we had defied the odds and emerged from the depths of fear. Our journey had left an indelible mark on our souls.

Finally, after what felt like an eternity, we spotted the distant glow of city lights on the horizon. Hope surged within me, and I felt a sense of relief wash over me. We were almost there, almost back to civilization, back to the safety of the world we knew.

Steven's grip on the steering wheel tightened, his eyes fixated on the road ahead. I could tell he was just as anxious to leave this nightmare

As we neared the city, the weight of the night's events began to lift, replaced by a newfound sense of survival and resilience. We had faced something otherworldly, something inexplicable, and yet, we had made it through.

We pulled into the familiar streets, the bright lights and bustling activity offering a stark contrast to the darkness we had just escaped. The fear and uncertainty slowly began to ebb away, replaced by a feeling of triumph, of having overcome the unimaginable.

The car came to a stop, the engine purring in quiet satisfaction. We sat in silence, still processing what had transpired, each lost in our own thoughts. The night had changed us, left its mark upon our souls, but we were alive, breathing, and that in itself was a victory.

With a collective sigh, we stepped out of the car, our legs shaky but determined. We would carry this experience with us, a reminder of the darkness that exists just beyond the edge of our everyday lives.

# Two

# TOO CLOSE TO HOME

inding myself unexpectedly standing in the middle of the cemetery was the oddest feeling. The same cemetery that my buddies and I had dared one another to explore a few years earlier. But unlike previously, everything seemed muffled and as though I were looking through a layer of fog.

The graveyard was not fully obscured by darkness despite the time of day. The gravestones were obscured by a dusky blue-gray cloud that gave everything a ghostly appearance. There was an oppressive silence and the air was still. There was no wind to stir the leaves, no nighttime chorus of crickets, and no distant sounds from the town that could be heard.

To remember how I got here, I made an effort to go back and retrace my steps. A dream, perhaps? It seemed too vivid and real to be just a fabrication of my imagination. However, the strange silence of the surroundings caused me to doubt everything.

I made the decision to move and find a way out. I could see the entrance gate ahead, its imposing figure casting long shadows on the ground. It had a menacingly gothic design with twisted iron bars that ended in sharp ends that resembled skeleton fingers reaching above. Its center was ornamented with the insignia of a raven with wings outstretched, and it featured elaborate curls and designs. Stone gargoyles guarding its flanks stood watch, their faces permanently frozen in stone with twisted snarls.

I felt relieved despite the strange surroundings. All I had to do was get through the gate, and everything would be fine.

I walked while paying close attention to the gate. The ground beneath my feet was an uneven mixture of gravel and rusty cobblestones that had been worn down over time. I expected the distance to the gate to close and the complex patterns on the gate to become more visible with each step.

However, after what seemed like minutes, then tens of minutes, I started to feel off. With each stride I should have taken, the gate should have gotten closer, yet it seemed to be staying the same distance away. I accelerated my pace, but nothing changed. My chest started to fill with a heavy weight of panic as well as perplexity and terror.

I came to a sudden stop and scantily assessed my surroundings. I had been walking for what seemed like an eternity when I suddenly realized that I was still standing where I had started. The identical worn gravestone is to my left, and the identical old tree is to my right. It appeared as though I was imprisoned in an invisible bubble, unable to move forward while the world around me was in motion.

I felt the grip of desperation. My feet were hammering into the pavement as I attempted to run, but it felt like I was on a treadmill. The environment remained static. I was helpless.

My breathing grew irregular as panic set in. I shouted in the hopes that someone—anyone—would hear me. However, the sound was absorbed by the oppressive quiet, as if a stone were dropped into a deep pit.

I experienced a sense of mental and bodily confinement, as if the cemetery were more than just a location. I then realized why people spoke of this location in hushed tones and with wide eyes. It was more than just a cemetery; it served as a prison for lost souls.

The hairs on the back of my neck stood up as a sudden cold breeze blasted past me. Unintelligible, far-off, yet shiver-inducing whispers permeated the air. I really wanted to shout, struggle, and run as fast as I could. The murmurs, though, became stronger and more forceful as I felt I was held hostage.

The already gloomy surroundings were suddenly and abruptly plunged into complete darkness. The inky abyss engulfed the subdued blue-gray haze. It was night already and the chilly evening air grew colder and colder, as if the darkness had drained away all warmth.

My feet had an odd sensation; they were heavy and burning with a sharp pain. Panic swept through me as I attempted to lift one leg and discovered I couldn't. When I looked down, a scene straight out of a nightmare greeted me. The earth beneath me had changed into quicksand, with a terrible crimson stain covering its surface as though it had been saturated with blood.

My pulse quickened. The pressure on my legs grew with each movement I made. The more I fought, the quicker I slid into the murky blood. The sensation was revolting, like being completely consumed by a breathing, alive creature. The crimson quicksand began to suck me deeper into its clutches as it clung to my legs and climbed.

My voice was raw, and it echoed strangely in the empty space of the cemetery as I screamed. "Help! Please aid me, someone. But no one could hear my frantic shouts. Only the graveyard's silence spoke in response, and it seemed to relish my dread.

Sand covered in blood crept up to my waist and then my chest. I jerked my head back and gasped for air as it got close to my neck. The tightening of the tightness around my chest made each inhale more challenging. The eerily Gothic gate stood in the distance, taunting my attempts to flee as my eyesight clouded and the borders of my field of view grew darker.

My own choking cries were the only thing that could be heard above the graveyard's eerie silence. I came to the terrifying notion that I might never awaken from my nightmare. With its icy grip, the quicksand seemed determined to pull me under, out of the land of the living and into the realm of lost souls.

I was being pulled further into the treacherous quicksand by its persistent draw while I experienced extreme desperation. I scanned the area, looking for some sign of light in the oppressive blackness. I flitted upward, searching for solace in a single star, a tiny dot of light in the great darkness. However, it appeared as though even the heavens had abandoned me; all that remained was a vast expanse of nothingness. Even the most vivid recollections appeared to be transient shadows because everything was hollow, the kind of hollowness that penetrates into one's own core.

The silence that surrounded me was oppressive, pressing on my eardrums and making me aware of how loud my own heartbeat was. It was a silence that I felt as much as heard; it clung to me, enveloping my skin with a chilling shroud.

I noticed movement out of the corner of my eye. I initially believed my mind was playing tricks on me, a desperate delusion, because it was so subtly done. But as I concentrated, I could clearly see them. Mysterious shadowy figures that were darker than the void that encompassed me started to appear. Their shapes were hazy and constantly changing, like seeing smoke rise in an enclosed space without a breeze. Although I couldn't see them, I could feel their eyes as they stood on the edge of my field of vision, all of which were trained on me and keeping vigil as I was engulfed in the bloody muck.

More so than the quicksand ever could, terror held me fast. The weight of my situation's actuality sinking in was almost as oppressive as the sand that was threatening to drag me down. I made an effort to shout and implore the figures for help or mercy. My mouth opened, but nothing came out. It appeared as though my lungs had lost all of their breath. Every time I tried to cry out, it simply made me feel more alone. My voice seemed to be absorbed by the night's oppressive silence, which silenced every frantic scream.

The cool sensation of the blood-soaked sand on my cheek was in sharp contrast to the blazing dread I was feeling inside. I instinctively held my breath because I knew what was going to happen. Until it brushed my lips, it inched painfully closer until it reached me. My senses were assaulted by the metallic flavor of the blood combined with the gritty sand. I tried to grit my teeth, but the draw was too powerful. Sand and blood started to ooze into my mouth, filling each nook and cranny.

The feeling was terrifying. I felt as though I was being filled from within and consumed. The already limited air supply was further reduced as the bloody mixture entered my nose. Uncontrollably, my head began to thrash in an attempt to flee, but the figures just watched, their ethereal presence intensifying the agony. My eyes were covered in sand, which rendered me blind. The motionless, ghostly eyes bearing witness to my gradual disappearance into oblivion were the last thing I saw before darkness robbed me of my vision.

A primitive yearning to breathe, to inhale, and to live rose up in my chest. However, there was no escape or reprieve. The sand's heavy weight weighed heavily on my ears, adding to the already deafening quiet. As my senses were gradually taken away, a peculiar calm started to descend. It appeared as though my thoughts started to separate from the terrifying reality and float away after comprehending the pointlessness of resisting.

Every second felt like an eternity as time seemed to distort and stretch. A jumbled montage of my life's events—happy, tragic, commonplace, and profound—flew across my mind's eye without any specific sequence. It appeared to be a silent film playing out as my life passed me by. The background was a depressing emptiness.

The dark figures appeared to be the watchmen of this liminal region, the line dividing life from what lay beyond, with their unflinching stare. I had a single thought as the last of my consciousness started to fade: "Is this the end, or is this just a new beginning?"

Immediately, I jolted out of the bed. As I sprang awake, the reality came pouring back to me in a murky haze, the primal dread from the dream still echoing in my veins. With each anxious breath, my chest heaved as I tried to tell where a dream ended and reality began. My bedclothes clung to me in a strangling hug because my skin was slippery from perspiration. For a minute, the darkly lit room—its soft glow from a streetlamp seen through the curtains—felt strange.

My phone beeped from the nightstand almost as if on cue, breaking through the deafening calm that had descended in the wake of the nightmare. I made a weak attempt to ground myself while trembling by running a hand through my messy hair. The simple gesture helped me regain some sense of reality. The feel of each strand and the little pull I felt as I tugged on them all screamed promises that I was awake and that the terrifying quicksand and eerie figures were now confined to my dreams.

I reached for the phone as the harsh, bluish light emanating from its screen filled the space. I squinted and saw that Steven had left a number of missed calls. I felt a wave of guilt. I despised the notion that he had been calling me while I was engrossed in a horrible fantasy, ignorant to his calls.

I hesitated before I even opened his most recent text. "We are commemorating Theo's sixth month," it said. "Come if you want to. I don't give a fuck. Tessa insisted." The bluntness of the message was so Steven – a mix of indifference and brutal honesty, masking a deeper care.

Now that I was completely upright, I made an effort to get the dream out of my head. It weighed heavily on me and was almost physically oppressive. As I struggled to come up with a response for Steven, my fingers lingered over the phone's display. I wanted to be present for Theo's achievement, but the dread from the nightmare was still with me, making even the smallest movement and thought difficult.

I took a deep breath and started to type, "Hey, sorry I missed your calls," while attempting to drive away the residual shadows. "Just awoke from a nightmare. I'll be there. Give me some time to prepare."

I put the phone down and stretched out over the side of the bed. As a result of the dream's vividness, every movement felt planned. I needed something to totally reassert myself in the live world, like a spray of water on my face. So i got up and walked to the restroom.

I saw myself in the mirror as I was making my way to the restroom. Dark bags beneath my eyes and a pale complexion were signs of the toll the dream had caused. Each drop of the cool water grounded me and helped me to struggle free from the nightmare's frightening grasp.

I walked back from the bathroom and walked back to the room.

Another message's piercing buzz interrupted my train of thought. Once more reaching for the phone, I saw another message from Steven on the screen. "Party's on the weekend. Don't forget," The words were so straightforward, but they were surrounded by a whirlwind of memories that threatened to suffocate me once more.

I threw the phone to the bed, it bounced quietly to the pillow, and relaxed my legs, feeling the cool hardwood under my soles. I let out a heavy sigh while seated there with my head in my hands, letting it fill the empty space. The weight of the past seemed inescapable.

Tessa and Steven. We three used to be inseparable, bound by friendship ties that appeared impenetrable. However, they now had each other and had created a life with their small boy. And me? I was still entrapped and bound to that tragic evening in the cemetery.

It was annoying. As Tessa and Steven celebrated important life events, I was stuck in a cycle, unable to break free of the bonds of the past. I had the impression that the world was moving around me while I was standing motionless. All of these events—their union, Theo's birth, and now his six-month anniversary—serve as frequent reminders of how divergent our paths had turned out to be.

As I ran my fingers through my hair, the sweat-induced moisture brought back memories of my most recent nightmare. How did it get to this point? Why was it just me who was troubled by that night? Why couldn't I do it as others did and find a way to go on?

I was shocked to realize that, despite the efforts of my friends to nudge me into the present, I was the only one who could let go of the past. I needed to face my anxieties, my darkness, and find a way to heal.

I tried to push the memories away, but they came back.

The recollections of what happened following that night started to play out in vivid detail. The terrifying grasp of what we saw at the cemetery had not just dissipated with the daylight, but had instead deeply embedded itself within me and turned into an obsession I was unable to overcome.

I can still feel the rush of adrenaline coursing through our blood as we fled that location and those eerie individuals. We pulled out our phones and dialed 911 once we felt comfortable enough to do so, our voices quivering as we attempted to describe the peculiar encounter. The idea of three mature adults telling a ghost story must have seemed ludicrous. Instead of three terrified adults truly fearing for their lives, they presumably anticipated to find a few drunken teenagers doing practical jokes.

That evening, when the police arrived at the cemetery, they were not welcomed by the horrifying sights we had described, but rather a strange silence. No eerie figures. No weird occurrences. There were only endless rows of gravestones, silently recording the passing of time. Their flashlights' powerful beams pierced the night, but they didn't see anything unusual.

I can still picture the officers' skepticism as they listened to our story a second time. They probably thought it sounded like a story made up after a few too many drinks. They seemed to think we were either lying or had hallucinated the entire thing based on the subtle, patronizing tones in their voices and the subdued roll of their eyes.

As would be expected, nothing unexpected was stated in the official report. And within a week, our case had been discarded as an absurd claim—possibly even a practical joke. The rest of the world changed, but I couldn't. I discovered myself entangling more deeply in the mystery as Tessa and Steven turned to each other for solace while attempting to forget the encounter.

I have made an effort to learn the truth about that evening. examining historic municipal records to contacting purported paranormal authorities. I had spoken to older residents in the area in the hopes of finding related anecdotes or hints. Every night I would search online discussion boards for anyone who might have gone through a similar situation or knew anything about the past of the cemetery. On certain evenings, I would even return to the cemetery with a flashlight in my hand, looking for a sight or an explanation.

It was frustrating. I was obsessed by the need to confirm our experience. I had to show that it wasn't a figment of our collective imagination and that we hadn't just dreamed it. I wanted to prove to the world that we were right and that our fear was justified.

But as time went on, I had less and fewer answers. The town had a lengthy history, but the personalities we saw were not mentioned. Some townsfolk thought of the cemetery as just another location where the dead were laid to rest; a few mentioned hazy folklore or ghost stories that every town undoubtedly has, but nothing specific. Each lead eventually came to a halt.

Despite the obstacles, I continued out of a need that I couldn't quite put my finger on. Perhaps it was the overwhelming skepticism of people around us, or perhaps it was the raw horror from that particular night. Whatever it was, it had rooted itself firmly within me and compelled me to pursue the truth at all costs.

One insight that came to me when I thought more about that night. Even if the police's official attitude was one of skepticism and apathy, there was a tension I hadn't seen. I recall how Officer Mitchell avoided making eye contact with us and how, while collecting our statement, his voice quavered just a little bit. Sure, there was skepticism, but there was also an undercurrent of... recognition? Fear? maybe even both.

There was also noticeable change in the atmosphere as I moved around town in the days that followed the event in the cemetery. As I passed, people would interrupt their talks and give me quick glances. Although no one openly mentioned that night, whispers spread like wildfire, and their weight hovered in the air. Everyone was aware, but nobody wanted to talk about it.

I attempted to discuss it with a few close friends, but each time I did so, they either swiftly changed the conversation or pretended not to hear me. It was frustrating. It was as though the entire community had made a tacit decision to conceal the graveyard's secrets.

At the neighborhood cafe one evening, I overheard an older couple conversing in low tones about "the old legends." Their discourse was hazy, but I had a feeling it had something to do with what we had witnessed. However, when I approached them in an effort to learn more, they retreated and gave me a look that made it apparent they had no interest in helping me in my search for information.

These were the times when I felt the most alone. My resolve was only strengthened by the town's quiet and their deliberate avoidance of the subject. I was determined to uncover the mystery that lay here—a secret tucked away in the town's past. My search for solutions had expanded to include every other local resident who had chosen to remain silent.

It was my duty to make the town aware of anything that might be hiding in that cemetery and that they were too terrified to confront. I wouldn't stand by and watch like everyone else. I had witnessed improper behavior, and now I was determined to comprehend it.

As the gap between myself and my closest friends widened, the burden of my lonesome pursuit pushed down heavily on my shoulders. Tessa and Steven, who had previously accompanied me on all of my adventures, now appeared distant. There was a noticeable tension every time I brought up that terrible night. They would abruptly shift the subject or, in Steven's case, simply ignore my questions. When I brought up the graves, Tessa's once-curious eyes suddenly bore an imploring expression, as if pleading with me to drop the subject.

I recognized their need for normalcy and their need to bury the past deeply in order to go on. The world had carried on as usual, unmoved by our terrifying ordeal. Tessa and Steven had found solace in their small family, which had become a source of joy for them. At times, I envied their capacity to overcome fear and accept life's basic pleasures.

But I couldn't just tuck the past away; it was a part of me. I was troubled by the eerie figures we had seen that night every time I woke up. I couldn't help but be drawn in by the unsolved puzzles and cemetery mysteries. It wasn't just about getting revenge or showing the town we weren't lying; now, it was also about comprehending and wanting to know why.

I then ventured off by myself to delve further into the graveyard's mystery and that of its spectral occupants. As I buried myself in study, poring over old papers, and traveled into the graveyard under the cover of darkness, seeking answers, days passed into nights.

The hardest part of the trip was how lonely it felt. The solitude I experienced overwhelmed every action I took and every discovery I made. Friends who were once only a phone call away felt far away. The town only made me feel more alone with its hushed gossip and sideways glances. The weight of solitude threatened to overwhelm me on numerous occasions as I sat by myself with my notes and theories. It was extremely different from the earlier times when Tessa, Steven, and I would openly discuss our fears, joys, and secrets.

But something inside of me kept me going—a burning need for knowledge. I clung to the hope that discovering the truth would not only make me happy but also possibly heal the chasm that had grown between me and my friends. Maybe, just maybe, we could get back together if I could solve the puzzles of that evening.

The journey went on as the days became weeks, then weeks into months. Months turned to years. I got a little bit smarter about mysterious folks and what their motives might be, every piece of information, and every encounter in the cemetery. But it was still nothing tangible. Solid fragments of facts diluted with fiction and the supernatural

Comparing the graveyard during the day to the eerie expanse I had seen at night revealed a vastly different landscape. The weathered gravestones were given mottled patterns by the sun as it peaked through the forest canopy. A light breeze rustled the foliage while birds sang. Any observer would have simply seen a serene, albeit slightly neglected, ultimate resting place.

But every time I entered that space, I was flooded with flashbacks of that terrifying night. No matter how bright the sun shone, my heart would beat a little faster and a feeling of dread would come over me.

I repeatedly went to the cemetery, frequently during the day, in the hopes that the security of the light would give me a chance to run into the mysterious figure once more, but this time on my terms. I would often find myself spending hours sitting on a weathered stone bench not far from where we had originally spotted them. I would close my eyes and use my senses to try to detect any indication of their presence or any change in the energy surrounding me.

I secretly thought that these ghosts or beings—whatever they were— had something important to say. There are legends about ghosts that roam the earth with unfinished business or tales to tell in every culture. Perhaps they weren't evil. Maybe they were only attempting to communicate because they were disoriented, and our unexpected encounter had surprised them just as much as it did us.

With each visit, the desire to communicate with them got stronger. I created a wide range of scenarios. How would I respond? How may they react? Do they even comprehend? My curiosity was tinged with a little bit of terror, but my need to learn and comprehend took precedence over anything else.

There were times when I'd think, This is it, especially when the wind would kick up or a sudden chilly spot would form near me. They are present. I would prepare myself while mentally practicing the questions I had planned out, watching for a sign. The anticipation would eventually give way to disappointment as the seconds grew into minutes and nothing else out of the usual happened.

I never clearly encountered them throughout the day despite the endless hours and several visits. But occasionally, something would occur—a whisper in the trees, a fleeting shadow at the edge of my field of vision—that would confirm my conviction. They were there, observing.

Aside from my curious and genuine interest in these beings, sometimes, there was a weight that seemed to surround me every time I entered the cemetery. Even in broad daylight, with the outside world bustling and alive, the interior of those iron gates was devoid of sound. My skin felt as though it were being crawled over by an energy that was thick and charged with the air and gave me goosebumps.

I tried to convince myself on occasion that it was all in my imagination and a result of the trauma I had experienced that evening. But deep inside, I had a basic instinct that sensed danger and the unknown and knew better. The air wasn't simply heavy; it was also attentive. The silence wasn't dead; rather, it was expectant.

I had the impression that I was being watched and evaluated as I moved. I constantly felt as though eyes were on me and that there were observers lurking just out of sight. Frequently, when I quickly spun around to look for my spectator, all I saw were gravestones bearing silent witness.

The most unnerving aspect was that I continued to feel as though someone was watching me after I left the cemetery. Even on a bright day, it stuck to me like a second shadow. I would still sense it when I was moving through the town, passing by recognizable landmarks and daily routines. The hairs on the back of my neck would occasionally stand on edge, or I would get a shiver down my spine. When I turned around, there was nothing even though I could see brief motions in my peripheral vision or feel a presence close by.

Nighttime was awful. The line separating dreams and reality appeared to be porous. My heart would race as I would awaken from a night nightmare, convinced that a ghost had been watching me in the confines of my room. My current experiences and the eerie recollections of that evening started to blend together. Was it just the tragedy playing over in my head, or were they actually trying to reach out to me outside of the cemetery?

In a web of anxiety and uncertainty, I felt entrapped. Conversations with friends got more difficult since I would frequently become distracted while sensing that presence all around me and wondered if they felt it as well. However, nobody seemed to notice anything was off. It appeared as though the strange creatures had chosen me out and were tying me to them in a terrifying dance that I was powerless to leave.

It all started to weigh heavily on me. Friends commented on how drained I appeared and how distant I had grown. How, yet, am I to explain? How could I describe the constant sense of being tracked down and watched, even in the most secure environments? My personal horror that threatened to swallow me had evolved into the quest to learn the truth about the graveyard. I was however resolved to learn the truth in order to rid myself of this ominous presence once and for all, despite my fears and the constant observers.

I started to feel alone in the world because of the overwhelming feeling that I was always being observed and that someone or something was following my every move. Even among large crowds, I felt alone and on edge, waiting for a chill to run down the back of my neck or the sense of being watched from just out of sight.

My once-vital relationships started to suffer. I found myself looking over my shoulder or pausing abruptly during conversations as I struggled to get rid of the nagging feeling that I was being watched. I frequently changed arrangements at the last minute because I preferred the seclusion of my home and believed that it would allow me to take a break from my constant watchfulness. However, even there, within the walls that ought to have been my haven, I never truly felt alone.

Once the cornerstones of my life, Tessa and Steven started to fade away. Their efforts to comprehend and support me were rebuffed by my erratic conduct and growing seclusion. Then came the important events that I simply couldn't bring myself to attend because of the haunting presence that was always there.

Being unable to attend Tessa and Steven's wedding was a serious setback. When Steven had called, seeking an explanation, I could still make out the hurt and perplexity in his voice. "Jason, how could you? He had stated, "This was our day, and you weren't there," in an emotional tone of voice. The distance between us only grew as I tried to explain and communicate the gravity of my experiences using words that were insufficient.

Our relationship was really tested to the limit when I was unable to attend their child's christening, though. It was a sacred moment, a celebration of new life, and I wasn't there. This wasn't just any occasion. The resulting outrage in Steven was evident. He had never shown displeasure or anger to me, and they were piercing and severe. He believed that I had put my infatuation before our friendship, and that there was no justification for this developing gulf between us.

Tessa, who was always the peacemaker, sought to keep the peace. She reached out and made an effort to comprehend, constantly recommending therapists or spiritual mentors who could be helpful. But every time we met, there was a hidden rebuke in her eyes, a sign that she, too, was upset.

Seeing our relationship fall down was really heartbreaking. These were the folks who had stuck by me through good times and bad, and I felt terrible for having abandoned them when they most needed me. However, the constant watchfulness and unseen presence made me feel alone and stuck in a paranoid cycle.

The struggle for solutions versus the cost of my interpersonal relationships had turned my existence into a never-ending conflict. It was a price that threatened to rob me of everything I previously treasured and that appeared to get steeper with each passing day.

The days grew shorter and more lonely, but amid this wide sea of loneliness, my mother and her friend Julia shone like beacons of hope. They stood out not only for their unshakeable faith in me, but also for their sincere desire to learn about and solve the puzzles of the cemetery.

Mom, with her instinctive empathy, could always tell when things weren't right. She had been my pillar through all of my bumps and bruises, from childhood mishaps to deeper adult struggles. She remained unwavering even in the face of the gossip in the community and the separation from my closest friends. She would frequently spend hours sitting by my side as I talked about my worries or my most recent discoveries.

Julia, on the other hand, offered a distinct form of assistance. She knew all about the mythology and history of the place. Her insatiable interest and depth of knowledge were priceless. Many evenings were spent reading through old town records and untold stories in search of some hint or information about the enigmatic characters. Julia frequently discussed energies, places that held memories, and the possibility of memories that are so intense that they appear. Her advice gave me a new perspective and opened up possibilities I hadn't thought of before.

The voyage was a little bit easier to endure since they were by my side, encouraging me to keep going and be determined. When nearly everyone else had given up on me, their belief in me was the lifeline I clung to.

Despite this, my heart was torn up by Steven's broken relationship. A continual reminder of what I had lost was the memory of our shared experiences, our joy, our dreams, and even our anxieties. Whether right or wrong, the idea that I was to blame for the rift just added to my expanding list of burdens.

Theo's six-month anniversary glowed brightly in the distance. It was also a chance at forgiveness. Despite its flaws, Steven's message was an olive branch, and I knew I couldn't and wouldn't let this chance pass me by.

I silently made a commitment to myself. I would be there despite the graveyard's draw and the weight of the unseen gaze. I had to make amends and get back in touch with the family I had chosen. This was for myself as well as Steven, Tessa, and Theo. a step in the direction of taking back the aspects of my life that had been sullied by the eerie ghosts of the past.

I woke up to the early sun shining through the blinds, creating patterns of light on the walls. Although it was warm, I felt a chill come over me as memories of last night's dream played back in my head. Even though it was all too familiar, the eerie figures, the engulfing quicksand, and the deafening silence were still horrifying.

I required clarity and a break from the never-ending loop of fears and dreams. I hurriedly got dressed and went to my mother's house. I had always considered her house to be a haven, a place where the weight of the world seemed to be a little bit less.

The familiar aroma of her garden welcomed me as I got closer. The scent of roses, lavender, and a trace of jasmine drifted through the air, instantly calming me. But even in this peacefulness, my heart raced and anxiety began to rise as I considered telling someone about the specifics of my most recent dream.

As I entered Mom's house, the tantalizing aroma of roasted chicken wafted through the air, mingled with the buttery scent of mashed potatoes. My stomach immediately growled in response. "Mom?" I called out, following the delicious smells into the kitchen.

There she was, standing by the stove, her apron smeared with bits of gravy and potato, her face bright with a mischievous smile. "Well, look who's come visiting! Just in time, too." She motioned to the dishes on the counter.

Chuckling, I asked, "What's the occasion? Expecting the queen?"

She gave me a playful swat with her kitchen towel. "Funny, you. No occasion needed to cook a good meal. Besides, you look like you could use some good healthy home-cooking."

Pulling her into a tight hug, I felt the familiar comfort of her embrace. "Always," I murmured, breathing in her familiar scent, a mix of lavender and the kitchen's comforting aromas.

Pulling away, she tilted her head, giving me a once-over. "You know, Jason, Julia mentioned you're growing quite the potbelly. She said you might soon need a bra if you're not careful!"

I gasped in mock horror, clutching my stomach dramatically. "Traitor! I knew I shouldn't have had that second helping of pie last time I visited her."

Mom laughed, her eyes twinkling. "Well, you know Julia. She's never been one to mince words. But maybe, just maybe, she has a point. How's the gym membership going? Or did you forget where the gym is?"

I groaned, feigning defeat. "Alright, alright! Point taken. I'll hit the gym. But only after I feast on this delicious meal you've prepared."

We shared a moment of laughter before settling into the cozy kitchen nook. The conversation flowed effortlessly, as it always did with Mom. We chatted about everything and nothing – from the latest town gossip to plans for the upcoming weekend. The familiarity of it all, the gentle teasing, and our shared memories wrapped around me like a warm blanket, pushing away the shadows, if only for a little while.

Settling into the familiar plush cushions of the couch near the kitchen, I watched Mom as she gracefully moved around, adding a pinch of this and a dash of that to her dishes. The comforting hum of the oven and the sizzle from the stove created a soothing background rhythm.

As Mom stirred the gravy, she began sharing the latest town updates. "You know, Mrs. Patterson's cat went missing again. Third time this month. She's convinced it's the Henderson boy, but I think that old cat just has a taste for adventure."

I chuckled. "Mr. Whiskers always was a curious one."

Mom nodded, smiling. "And remember Mrs. Green from the bakery? She's decided to retire. Wants to spend more time with her grandkids. So the bakery's up for sale."

My eyebrows raised in surprise. "Really? That's the end of an era. Her raspberry tarts are legendary."

She sighed in agreement. "Oh, they are. I do hope whoever takes over can live up to her standards."

There was a brief pause as Mom took a tasting spoon to the gravy, nodding in approval at her culinary skills. Then, her tone shifted, becoming a tad more serious. "On a less cheerful note, there's been some talk around town about Tessa's baby, Theo."

I sat up straighter, instantly alert. "What about him?"

Mom hesitated, searching for the right words. "Well, it seems some folks are a bit... concerned. They've noticed that he's a little different. Little Emily from next door said he has a way of looking at things, like he sees more than the average baby. And Mrs. Johnston, you remember her, the one with the loud parrot? She mentioned that Theo didn't cry or fuss, even when he was just born."

I frowned, trying to understand the implications. "So what? Every child is unique. Why are they making a fuss about it?"

Mom sighed deeply, her gaze focused on the simmering pot before her. "You know how it is, Jason. In small towns like ours, anything slightly out of the ordinary becomes fodder for gossip. And after what you three experienced in the graveyard... I think people are just connecting dots, whether it makes sense or not."

I exhaled slowly, trying to contain my rising worry. "It's just idle talk, Mom, right? It'll pass."

She looked at me, her eyes filled with a mix of sadness and understanding. "I hope so, dear. But people talk…especially when they don't understand something. All we can do is support Tessa and Steven and hope this blows over soon

Mom paused for a moment, as if choosing her words carefully. "It's not exactly about his behavior, Jason. It's something…physical."

"Go on."

She took a deep breath. "People have noticed a peculiar rash on Theo. Around his neck and hands. It's... it's not like any rash I've seen before."

Intrigued and anxious, I pressed on. "What does it look like?"

Mom looked uneasy, her usual composed demeanor slightly ruffled. "It's greenish, almost luminescent. The edges of the rash seem to shimmer in a way. Mrs. Davis from the pharmacy said she'd never seen anything like it in all her years. From what I know, It's not spreading, and it doesn't seem to bother Theo, but it's…unnerving."

My mind raced, trying to process the information. Theo, innocent and unaware, had somehow become the center of town gossip because of a strange rash? It seemed absurd, yet knowing the history and the superstitious nature of our town, it wasn't entirely surprising.

"Have they taken him to a doctor? Surely there's a medical explanation for this."

Mom nodded. "Yes, they saw Dr. Allen last week. He's equally puzzled. He took some samples and said he'd consult with some colleagues from the city. For now, he's advised them to keep the areas clean and moisturized."

I raked a hand through my hair, feeling overwhelmed. The thought of little Theo being the subject of hushed whispers and pointed fingers was unbearable. "This is ridiculous. They're just trying to live their lives. Why can't the town just leave them be?"

Mom gave a sympathetic smile, reaching out to hold my hand. "You know how people are, love. Fear of the unknown, combined with the past incidents, makes them conjure up all sorts of tales. All we can do is stand by Tessa and Steven."

I nodded, taking a deep breath. "Of course, Mom. I just... I wish they didn't have to go through this."

She squeezed my hand gently. "Life throws challenges our way, Jason. It's how we face them that defines us. And remember, they have us. We'll get through this together."

Despite the weight of the situation, Mom's words brought a measure of comfort.

"Poor Tessa looks worn out, more than any new mother should," Mom sighed, stirring her sauce absently. "The bags under her eyes, the fatigue evident in her posture... It breaks my heart. Every time I see her in town, she looks like she's barely holding it together. And when folks ask her about it, all she talks about is Theo keeping her up."

I frowned, leaning forward. "Keeping her up? Why?"

Mom sighed deeply, her fingers playing with the edge of the kitchen towel. "It's not just any regular baby fussiness. Tessa confided in me the other day. She said Theo doesn't sleep much during the night. He wakes up at midnight, crying inconsolably, and nothing seems to soothe him. And the oddest part? As soon as the first hint of daylight peeks, he stops and falls into a deep sleep."

A chill ran down my spine. The pattern was too unusual, too specific to be mere coincidence. "Every night?" I inquired, trying to wrap my head around the situation.

"Every night," Mom confirmed. "It's like clockwork. Tessa says she's tried everything – from lullabies to rocking him, even those old remedies our grandmothers swore by. But nothing seems to soothe him. By morning, she's a complete wreck."

I leaned back on the couch, my mind racing. The strange rash, the peculiar sleep pattern, the crying only at night – it all painted a very unsettling picture. The logical part of me wanted to believe there was a reasonable explanation, perhaps a medical one. But given everything I'd experienced and the ongoing mysteries surrounding the graveyard, I couldn't help but wonder if there was more to it than met the eye.

"That's really strange, Mom," I finally murmured, my gaze distant.

She nodded in agreement. "It is. And with the town's whispers and speculations, it's only adding to their stress. I wish there was more we could do to help. But, they're trying to handle it discreetly."

Mom seemed to sense the growing tension in the room. A glint of mischief sparkled in her eyes as she let out a soft chuckle, attempting to shift the mood. "You know how folks in this town are. Half of them are already telling Tessa it's just 'normal baby stuff' and that Theo will grow out of it. The other half... Well, they have their superstitions and tales."

I raised an eyebrow, appreciating her attempt to bring some lightness to the conversation. "And which half do you belong to, Mom?"

She smirked, playfully wagging her finger at me. "Now, now, I'm staying neutral. But I did tell Tessa to hang in there. Babies have their phases. Maybe it's just a tough one for Theo."

I nodded slowly, though the weight of concern still lingered. "I hope you're right."

With a swift, motherly motion, Mom placed a plate overflowing with chicken and mashed potatoes in front of me. The sight and smell instantly made my mouth water. "Eat up," she instructed, her voice filled with warmth.

Before I could dive in, she leaned in with a teasing glint in her eyes. "But remember, every bite adds to that growing potbelly of yours."

I laughed, the earlier tension dissipating for a moment. "Thanks, Mom. First, it's Julia, now you? I'm surrounded by critics!"

She chuckled, patting my hand. "All in good fun, dear. But seriously, you need to go to Theo's six-month commemoration. Tessa and Steven are not happy with you. You really need to do better with those two."

I smiled, taking her words to heart. "I will, Mom. Thanks for everything."

As we settled into a more comfortable rhythm, sharing the meal and indulging in lighthearted banter, I felt grateful for these moments with Mom. Amidst all the uncertainties, they were my anchor, grounding me and reminding me of the love and warmth that still existed in the world.

The night was cool, and an eerie silence blanketed the graveyard. The silver glow of the moonlight cut through the dense fog, casting long, shifting shadows on the ground. I recognized the place instantly – it was the same haunting terrain that had plagued my dreams so many times before. But this dream felt different, more vivid, more real.

As I tread cautiously, the muffled sound of shovels digging into the earth reached my ears. I followed the noise, each step heavy with dread. My heart raced, a primal fear threatening to take over, but an inexplicable pull drew me closer to the source of the sound.

In a clearing, bathed in the moon's ethereal glow, stood shadowy figures, cloaked in darkness. Their movements were precise, synchronized, as they worked tirelessly, digging a small grave. But what truly froze my blood was the sight of another figure, distinct from the rest, holding a baby.

The infant's cries were loud, piercing the stillness of the night. As the baby wailed, the figures continued their task, seemingly unperturbed. Drawn to the sound, I tried to get a clearer view, and as I inched closer, the baby's features became more discernible under the dim light.

Covering the baby's tender skin was a distinct green rash, shimmering and pulsating as if it had a life of its own.

A surge of panic welled up within me. What were they planning to do with the baby? My mind raced, grappling with the horrifying scene before me, trying to find a way to intervene, to save the child.

But before I could act, one of the cloaked figures turned its gaze towards me. Though its face remained obscured, I could feel the intensity of its stare, a coldness that seemed to seep right into my soul. The air grew colder, the baby's cries echoing louder and more desperate.

Paralyzed with fear, I could only watch in sheer horror, praying for a way out, praying that this was just a dream and not a portent of things to come.

The cloaked figures, with their deliberate movements, gently placed the wailing baby into the freshly dug grave. The infant's cries pierced the cold air, a desperate lament that tugged at the very core of my being.

Every instinct in me screamed to intervene, to rush forward and snatch the baby away from this horrifying fate. And so, I found myself bolting towards the scene, my heart pounding loudly in my chest, echoing the baby's desperate cries.

However, as I raced forward, an unexpected obstacle appeared before me. The fog, previously a mere atmospheric presence, seemed to thicken and coalesce, becoming almost tangible. It twisted and curled, wrapping itself around my legs like a pair of ethereal shackles, slowing my pace.

I tried to fight through it, to push forward with all my might, but the more I struggled, the more ensnared I became. My foot caught on something unseen, perhaps an old tombstone hidden beneath the fog, and I stumbled, crashing heavily to the ground.

The impact was jarring. As I tried to gather myself, lifting my head, the world spun around me. From my fallen vantage point, I could still see the cloaked figures, their giant shovel raised, poised to cover the crying child with earth. Desperation welled up inside me, a scream building in my throat.

"No!" The word tore from my lips, a raw plea echoing into the night.

But the cloak-clad entities continued their task, oblivious or indifferent to my cries. The baby's wails grew more distant, more muffled, as the first shovelful of dirt landed atop the grave.

The weight of hopelessness pressed down on me, my chest constricting as the darkness of the dream threatened to consume me entirely.

Immediately I jolted out of my dream, still screaming "No!"

I woke up with the dream's eerie echoes still fresh in my thoughts as the morning sun shone brilliantly through the drapes. I inhaled deeply, trying to get rid of the residual dread. Being Saturday, I had a commitment to keep today.

I carefully choose an outfit while in front of my closet that was both attractive and not too formal. I recalled the easy times when I would just put on a shirt and pants, go visit Steven and Tessa, and we would speak, laugh, and share stories for hours. Although things had changed, this was a chance to go back to those earlier days.

I chose a nice, fluffy teddy bear with lovely brown eyes that I had bought for Theo and wrapped it. I hoped it would give the baby some solace. I moved to my car while holding onto the present and felt a sense of resolve coming over me.

Each of our town's well-known sites passed by as I was driving, evoking memories and providing a glimpse into our common past. The cafe where we would frequently get late-night snacks, the park where we would spend endless afternoons relaxing, and the ancient bridge where we would often make future promises. But the journey today was different; it was tinged with both eagerness and trepidation.

I hadn't traveled this way to Steven and Tessa's house in such a long time. Even though the path was well-known to me, it felt unfamiliar, as though I were seeing it through a lens that had been distorted by time and events. The anxiety knot in my stomach grew tighter as I got closer.

I felt relieved by the soothing hum of the car motor and the breathtaking scenery outside. I had an unending view of the broad road, which was peppered with trees and colorful wildflowers. I had never actually seen Theo before, I realized as I was driving. I felt a surge of curiosity come over me and a twinge of regret for being so distant.

I made an effort to visualize him. Would he possess Tessa's sparkling eyes or Steven's sly grin? I was genuinely excited about meeting this new life, which was a combination of two of my dearest friends. It was enjoyable to have something to look forward to and to get a brief respite from the gloom that had been enveloping me.

The land below was bathed in a gentle glow as the sun painted the sky in warm tones of gold and orange. Birds flew freely, their carefree tunes highlighting the peaceful atmosphere. The burden of the previous night's dream temporarily vanished, to be replaced with a sense of lightness I hadn't experienced in a while.

I noticed that when I was lost in thought, I was visualizing a different existence for myself. A life free from secrets and the ghosts of the past. I imagined a warm house full of love and laughter, perhaps even a child of my own. I imagined what it may be like to go through the ups and downs of fatherhood, to have a small hand grab my finger, and to hear my child's coos and giggles. It was a brief vision, but it made me feel warm within.

I felt tantalizingly near to a future where I could settle down, be surrounded by family, and discover basic bliss. For the first time, I did not reject or doubt the concept but instead allowed myself to relish it.

A little sense of comfort gradually grew upon me as I traveled further. The drive seemed like a journey towards hope and rejuvenation because of the reunion with Tessa and Steven, the eagerness to meet Theo, and the possibility of rekindling past ties.

Even as I approached Steven and Tessa's house, I could sense the joyous atmosphere. Numerous blue and white balloons, anchored to the ground and floating beautifully, were strung out in their front yard and danced to the sound of the wind. The hues evoked a sense of surprise and purity that was appropriate for the celebration of a young life.

I inhaled deeply to calm my anxiety before walking up to the door. After missing so many significant occasions, I had mentally prepared for a potentially uncomfortable reunion. I felt burdened by my previous absences and half-expected a cold welcome.

But as soon as I walked inside, Amidst all the guests, Tessa's face was the first one I saw, and all of my worries vanished. Her always-expressive eyes shone with unrestrained excitement and love. Pure, sincere delight prevailed, with no sign of bitterness or dissatisfaction. She looked even more excited when she saw me, and I experienced an emotional uplift.

Tessa immediately covered the gap between us and embraced me with her arms tightly around me before I could say anything. The cozy embrace and the comforting aroma of her were soothing.

She said softly, "I'm so glad you made it," her voice full of passion.

A knot in my throat appeared as I gave her another hug. "Tess, I'm so sorry I missed out on so much. But I'm here now."

She smiled as she drew back, tears of happiness sparkling in her eyes. "That's all that counts. Come on, I want you to meet this person."

She then guided me through the crowd, as we moved deeper into the home and the center of the party.

I just felt weightless for a moment when Tessa was holding me. It was a warm bubble of relief from the gnawing guilt I felt. I was brought back to reality by Steven's voice. The familiar tone of Steven's voice, tinged with a mixture of surprise and lingering frustration, made my heart drop. Turning around, I was met with Steven's piercing gaze.

His eyes, always so expressive, seemed to be having an internal battle. On one hand, there was the unmistakable glint of happiness at seeing an old friend, but on the other, there was a clear shadow of disappointment. It was evident; Steven had not completely let go of the past.

"Jason," he stated, more of an acknowledgment than a greeting.

Taking a deep breath, I approached him, searching for the right words. "Hey, Steven. It's been a while."

He crossed his arms, his posture guarded. "It sure has."

I winced at the underlying reproach in his voice. "I know, Steven. I'm genuinely sorry."

For a moment, we just stood there, two old friends, separated by past mistakes and circumstances, trying to bridge the distance that had grown between us. The atmosphere was thick with unsaid words, memories, and regrets.

Facing Steven, I hesitated for a split second, desperately hoping to find that familiar glint of camaraderie in his eyes, that old playful smirk we'd shared after countless inside jokes. I thought I glimpsed it, a brief flash, but it vanished almost instantly.

Instead, Steven's eyes bore into mine, cold and distant. The nod he gave was formal, almost curt. Without uttering a word, he turned on his heel and walked away, leaving a chilling void in his wake.

His unspoken disapproval hit me like a sledgehammer. The fleeting moment of warmth and acceptance I'd felt with Tessa was suddenly overshadowed by a thick cloud of guilt and regret. Every missed call, every unattended event, every moment of absence – they all weighed heavily on me as I watched Steven's retreating figure.

The jovial ambiance of the party, the cheerful chatter, and laughter all seemed to blur into the background. I was anchored in that moment, grappling with the reality of the rift between Steven and me.

Tessa, sensing the weight of the moment, stepped in gracefully. "Give him some time, Jason," she whispered softly, her gaze sympathetic. "Steven has his walls, but they'll come down. He's just...protective, especially now with Theo."

Grateful for the distraction, I let her guide me to a quieter corner of the room. We found a cozy spot, away from the heart of the celebration.

As we settled down, the years seemed to melt away, and we were back to being those carefree souls, sharing stories and jokes like we used to.

However, amidst the warmth of our reunion, I remembered the little one. "Speaking of Theo," I began, looking around, "Where is the young man? I brought him something." I held up the wrapped teddy bear, shaking it playfully.

Tessa's face, previously lit up with joy, shifted to a more coy expression. She smiled sheepishly, a blush coloring her cheeks. "Ah, Theo," she began, her voice filled with a mother's adoration mixed with a hint of exasperation, "He's a bit...unconventional."

Curiosity piqued, I raised an eyebrow. "Unconventional?"

She laughed softly, her eyes dancing with mirth. "Let's just say he has his own little quirks. But you'll see for yourself soon enough."

The mysterious tone in her voice only deepened my intrigue. I was now even more eager to meet this 'unusual' little fellow who seemed to be the talk of the town and the heart of this celebration.

Tessa stood up and left the room. Later she returned with a baby wrapped in a red cloak.

Tessa, with the grace of a mother, carried the baby with such tenderness. She gently approached me, her face radiating maternal pride. "Here's the star of the day, Jason," she announced, holding out baby Theo for me to see.

As my eyes settled on the child, an icy jolt of recognition shot through me. Every feature was painfully familiar: the ginger hair, those piercing blue eyes, even the little fingers clutching a red coat. The very same coat that, in my dream, was wrapped around the baby in the grave.

The air around me felt like it thickened, my surroundings blurring as my focus remained locked onto Theo. A knot of dread tightened in my stomach, making it hard to breathe. The dream had felt so real, so vivid, and now with Theo in front of me, looking exactly as he did in the nightmare, the boundaries of dream and reality seemed perilously thin.

For a split second, I wondered if I was still dreaming, but the noises of the party, the distant laughter, and chatter, grounded me back to the present.

My gaze must have betrayed my shock because Tessa's cheerful demeanor changed to one of concern. "Jason? What's wrong?" she inquired, her voice laced with worry.

I swallowed hard, trying to find the right words, but they seemed to evade me. "He... he looks just like... I mean, I had this dream," I stammered, my voice barely above a whisper.

Tessa frowned slightly, clutching Theo a little tighter. "What dream?" she pressed, her gaze searching mine.

The gravity of the situation weighed on me. How could I explain the dream without causing undue alarm? Would she think I was crazy? Regardless of the consequences, I knew I had to share the haunting vision with her. After all, it was about her child.

I inhaled deeply and started to describe the terrifying dreams that had kept me up at night. Tessa's face turned progressively paler as I described the burial, the eerie figures, the green rash, and more. Her apparent discomfort was cast in a palpable shadow as the weight of my words seemed to press down on her.

After I was done, there was a long silence between us that was only broken by Theo's croons. Tessa turned to face me, her eyes a mix of terror and understanding. "I've had the same dreams, Jason," she muttered, her voice shaking.

This revelation gave me the chills.

Tessa abruptly turned, holding Theo close to her breast, without saying anything else. She moved more quickly as she searched the house for Steven. I followed closely as I tried to make sense of the growing repercussions of our shared dreams.

Tessa found Steven talking to some visitors in the backyard and made a purposeful move to get closer to him. "Steven," she said, sounding frantic, "Jason and I... we had the identical dreams. concerning Theo. And those figures in the grave."

Steven's expression changed from mild irritation to shock after being interrupted. In an effort to determine the seriousness of our statements, his gaze alternated between Tessa and myself. The three of us were united by a common fear as we struggled to understand the enigmatic force that appeared to be entering into our lives. Suddenly, the party's festive atmosphere seemed out of place.

Feeling the weight of the situation, and driven by an innate desire to find answers, I put forth my suggestion, "Maybe... maybe we should go back to the graveyard. See if we can find any answers there."

Steven's reaction was immediate and intense. His face darkened, eyes narrowing at me with a mix of anger and disbelief. "Go back? Are you serious, Jason? After everything? We're not obsessing over old haunts like you. We have a life now, responsibilities."

I flinched at his words, especially the term "obsessing." It stung. I had hoped that our shared experiences, the eerie dreams, and Theo's condition would bridge the gap that had grown between us. But Steven's reaction made it evident that mending this relationship would be an uphill battle.

Trying to control the rising frustration, I persisted, "Steven, I know it sounds crazy, but think about it. We both experienced the same thing. And now, both Tessa and I are having these dreams. There might be answers at the graveyard, something that might explain what's happening to Theo."

But Steven's stance was unyielding. He took a step closer, his voice firm, "Nothing is 'haunting' our son, Jason. We've got specialists looking into Theo's condition. They'll figure it out." He paused, taking a deep breath, his eyes still fixed intently on mine. "And I'd appreciate it if you'd keep your theories and your past obsessions away from my family."

I could feel the gap widening, the chasm between Steven's life and my own becoming more evident. The longing for the old days, when the bond between us was unbreakable, gripped me. But faced with his staunch resistance, I felt more isolated than ever.

"Steven," I began, trying to keep my voice calm, "I know it sounds mad, but there's something we missed that night at the graveyard. Something that might explain these dreams, and maybe even Theo's condition."

Steven scoffed, "You're always on about that graveyard, Jason. It's been years! Move on."

"Steve, please," I implored, the desperation in my voice evident. "You, Tessa, and I all experienced something that night. We can't just ignore it. Especially now, with Theo."

Steven's face contorted with a mix of frustration and disbelief. "You're really trying to drag my son into your wild fantasies now? Every day, you're proving the town right about how unhinged you're becoming."

His words stung, but I pressed on. "It's not a fantasy, Steve! I wouldn't be so insistent if I didn't believe that it could help Theo."

Throwing his hands up in exasperation, Steven retorted, "Help Theo? By dragging him into the same dark rabbit hole you've been diving into? No way, Jason. We're getting real help for him, not chasing ghosts."

I could feel the eyes of the guests on us. Their whispers, though muted, added to the oppressive atmosphere. "Steve, I'm not 'chasing ghosts'. I'm trying to find answers. Real answers. And I need you with me on this." i whispered

Steven took a deep breath, his eyes hardening. "Look, Jason, you were my best friend, and a part of me still wants to believe in you. But right now? You're sounding more and more like one of those crazy conspiracy nuts from the online forums."

"It's not a conspiracy, Steve," I shot back, my patience wearing thin. "It's our shared past. We both know what we saw that night. It's Theo's present. We owe it to him, at least, to explore every possibility."

He shook his head, the finality in his voice unmistakable. "I've had enough of this. If you want to go on another one of your wild chases, be my guest. But leave my family out of it."

The intensity of the argument between Steven and me had reached such a level that I almost missed Tessa's soft voice when she finally intervened. She stood there, baby Theo cradled close to her chest, her usually bright eyes now clouded with emotion.

"He's right, Jason," she began, her gaze meeting mine, "We do have responsibilities." The gravity of her words made my heart sink. I was preparing myself for another round of rejection. But then she shifted her focus to Steven. "Responsibilities to our son, Steven. To protect him, to keep him safe."

I watched, taken aback, as Tessa's demeanor changed from her usual gentle self to something fiercer, more determined. "If that means going back to the graveyard, then so be it. I'll do it."

Steven looked at her, his expression a mix of shock and confusion. "Tess, what are you saying?"

She took a deep breath, her grip on Theo tightening. "I've watched our baby suffer every single day, Steve. The specialists are doing what they can, but it's not enough. The rash... it's spreading, moving closer to his heart. Every night I hear his cries, see the pain in his eyes. It's tearing me apart." She paused, trying to hold back the tears that threatened to spill. "If there's even a slight chance that going back there can help, then I'm willing to try. For him."

The air seemed to stand still for a moment, the weight of Tessa's words pressing down on all of us. Steven looked from Tessa to Theo, his face a storm of emotions. I could see the internal battle he was waging, torn between skepticism and the undeniable love he held for his family.

Steven's silence was thick, an almost tangible cloud hanging over the three of us. The weight of Tessa's plea, combined with the mounting pressure of the unknown, seemed to be too much for him. After what felt like an eternity, he finally bowed his head, conceding to the urgency of the situation.

"Alright," he murmured, his voice barely above a whisper. The resignation was clear, yet underlying it was a hint of the old Steven - the brave, adventurous soul who had once been my partner in every wild endeavor.

But as he lifted his gaze to meet ours, a flash of caution darkened his eyes. "Just remember," he began, his voice carrying a steely edge, "if this turns out to be another wild goose chase, or worse, if we end up facing those...things again, and they decide to finish what they started, don't say I didn't warn you."

With that final statement, laden with a mixture of dread and determination, Steven turned on his heel and walked away. His stride was heavy, weighed down by the enormity of the decision he'd just made, and the potential consequences that lay ahead. The air felt colder in his absence, the lingering tension a testament to the gravity of our impending journey.

It was clear that the cemetery had altered as soon as we pulled up to it. There was no sign of the gate, that once-dominant Gothic building that had tormented my dreams. The early evening colors produced a picture of the entire environment that was at once strangely similar and familiar.

Before getting out of the car, Tessa and I exchanged a quick, apprehensive glance. Only the distant tweeting of evening birds and the rustling of branches in the breeze disturbed the eerie calm of the graveyard as it greeted us. We paused for a time to allow the reality of our surroundings to set in while the pressure of our previous experience here weighed heavily on our memories.

Steven, though, resisted more. From where I was standing, I could hear him taking a big breath as he mustered up the confidence to leave. He eventually did, but he continued to walk a few steps behind us, his gaze darting all over as he likely struggled with the memories of that terrifying night.

We cautiously started our walking while listening closely for any strange noises. Our main attention was on the last place where we had seen that dark, threatening figure. But when we got closer, we were only faced with the recognizable scene of graves, gravestones, and old trees. There was no sign of recent movement on the leaf-covered ground.

The terrain was covered in lengthy shadows as the three of us stood there in the waning light of the evening. None of us spoke for a while. In contrast to our frenetic memories of the location, the silence seemed almost strange. It was as though the cemetery, with all of its mysteries, was making fun of our quest for answers.

But we were unable to get rid of the underlying fear that the solutions to our questions lay just out of grasp, hidden deep within.

The tall and twisted forms of the trees that made up the canopy loomed ahead, creating an almost impenetrable wall of darkness. We walked from the open cemetery towards the forest. The dense tangle of trees above had almost completely blocked up the evening sun, which had previously cast long shadows across the tombstones.

Steven came to a stop, his eyes uncomfortably darting to the thick forest. "Look, guys," he began, his voice tinged with genuine apprehension, "I'm just going to stay here. There's no way I'm going back in there." He stood resolutely in place, crossing his arms in a stubborn manner.

I could understand Steven's hesitation. My thoughts kept returning to our last foray into those dark woods. I still got the creepy sensation of being watched and being pursued. I paused as an internal conflict flared up. Should we proceed or is this a foolish endeavor?

But before either Steven or I could raise any further objections, Tessa took a decisive step forward without even looking at us. She entered the ominous woods without turning around, the darkness slowly enveloping her as she moved.

I looked at Steven with wide eyes. There wasn't much we could do. We didn't want to go in, and we didn't want to leave Tessa on her own to face whatever might be there.

We hurriedly followed Tessa, treading cautiously on the thick mat of fallen leaves as we sighed together in resignation. We were surrounded by the oppressive solitude of the forest, which served as a strong reminder of the potential hazards that lay ahead.

The evening was rather unremarkable in many ways. The initial unease gave way to a peculiar peace as we walked further into the wooded region. The ambiance was not what you would anticipate from a location with such a horrific past. There was a startling sense of normalcy in place of the eerie silence or unpleasant vibe.

Although the air was cool and served as a gentle reminder of the impending night, it wasn't bone-chilling cold. There wasn't the usual heaviness in the air that makes you feel watched or pursued. It was only impartial.

When we looked up, the trees towered over us, their branches extending like long fingers towards the setting sun. But rather than seeming overbearing, they appeared to be merely sentinels, quietly observing our passing without opinion or hostility. The often ominous silence of such a place was missing, and in its stead were the delicate noises of nature, such as our own footsteps and the light crunching of leaves underfoot, as well as the distant owl's call.

For a moment, as we moved side by side, it appeared as though we had left the haunting graveyard and entered a normal forest on a tranquil evening. I nearly laughed out loud at the concept because it made me feel as though the evil entities who haunted this location had left for the day and were taking a much-needed break.

The lingering memories of our earlier interactions here served as a constant reminder to be watchful beneath the surface of this seeming tranquility. But for the time being, the world felt surprisingly calm and... average.

Tessa's voice pierced the quiet evening, echoing through the dense woods and vast expanse of the graveyard. "Hello!" she called out, her hands cupped around her mouth, amplifying her voice. "Hello! Is anyone here?"

Each call was desperate, laden with the weight of a mother's worry. The forest seemed to absorb her pleas, only to return them as haunting echoes that eventually faded into nothingness.

"We need your help!" she continued, her voice quivering with a mix of determination and fear. "My baby... he's suffering. Please, whatever you're doing to him, stop. We beg you. Hello!"

Her pleas, so raw and vulnerable, echoed back to us, making the stillness even more pronounced. It felt as though the very fabric of the evening had stilled, as if the trees, the wind, and even the distant creatures of the night were holding their breath, waiting for a response.

I stood there, heart pounding, straining to hear any sound, any sign that her calls were being acknowledged. But there was only silence. A heavy, oppressive silence that seemed to amplify our isolation in this vast, eerie place.

Tears welled up in Tessa's eyes as the reality of our situation began to weigh down on her. Her voice, once strong and defiant, now broke with emotion. "Please," she whispered, more to herself than to the unseen forces we hoped to communicate with, "Please help us."

The stillness that followed was almost tangible, a thick blanket of quiet that seemed to press down on us, emphasizing our vulnerability and the gravity of our mission. We stood there, three figures in the vastness of the night, united in our shared sense of desperation and hope.

Steven's usually tough demeanor broke down as he approached her, exhibiting a depth of emotion I hadn't seen in him in a long time. It was heartbreaking to see Tessa cry in front of him. He drew Tessa close and encircled her in his arms, giving her the solace and assistance she so sorely required.

Tessa, who is typically a tower of fortitude and resilience, turned into Steven's hug and entirely let down her guard. She let out a loud wail that was racked with agony and desperation. Each expressed how much they feared and felt powerless for their son.

A knot started to form in my stomach as I watched the event take place. I could hear the pain in Tessa's sobbing and feel the weight of her misery in my bones.

The vastness of the trees surrounding us appeared to vanish, and was replaced by the couple's tremendous, almost palpable feelings.

Tessa's heartbreaking sobs seemed to stand in stark contrast to the graveyard's oppressive silence. In that instant, all I could offer was my silent support and our shared drive to find solutions. I wished there was more I could do to lessen their suffering.

All of us were feeling the effects of the events of the evening, but the accusing glance Steven cast my way was enough to pierce my heart. His eyes conveyed a lot. The silent statement: "This was a mistake. That icy, steely glare echoed, "I knew we shouldn't have listened to you.

Tessa was still snuggled in Steven's hug as he started guiding her away from the forested area's dark interior.

As I observed them, I was overcome with sentiments of regret, sadness, and guilt. The couple's palpable raw emotions served as a mirror to my own internal conflict. I felt the pressure of responsibility bear down on me. The toll it was having on Tessa was clear because I had brought them back to this eerie location in my search for answers.

My sense of pessimism seemed to be amplified by the desolation of the graveyard and woodland. Perhaps Steven was correct. Maybe this isn't the place for us to find the answers. The environment's utter silence appeared to belittle our efforts.

I stood by myself among the gravestones and soaring trees as their silhouettes dwindled away, wrestling with my own sorrows and pondering whether we would ever be freed from the shadows of that fatal night.

The switch from the preceding scene's deep emotions to the this seemed abrupt and bizarre. At first, I was confused and felt as though I had been thrown into another world. My feet no longer felt like they were on solid ground; instead, I had the impression that I was suspended in the air.

The earth below was a sea of green, with trees' constantly extending leaves. They made a tranquil lullaby that stood in stark contrast to the upheaval of the night by gently rustling in the breeze. I suddenly became aware that I was towering over everything, equal in height as the trees that surrounded the cemetery as my eyes turned downward.

I attempted to move while covered in a lengthy, ominous cloak that seemed to go on forever, but in vain. My legs appeared to be firmly fixed into the ground, like they were an extension of the planet. I was able to feel the land's own pulse, a constant rhythmic beat that echoed the passing of time.

The night was alive with sounds, including an owl hooting in the distance, delicate leaf rustling, and wind whispering in the distance.

Nevertheless, despite all of its beauty, I was overcome by a strong sense of loneliness. I was a lone figure, stuck in place in this huge space, unable to move or speak.

I experienced a sense of being imprisoned within my own body, watching the world from a high perch but unable to engage with it.

I breathed in, feeling the crisp air fill my lungs with an energizing freshness as the deep calm of the night engulfed me. However, just as swiftly, a harrowing, uncanny feeling of darkness and boldness swept through me. I had the impression that a force had gripped my whole soul from the inside.

An unexplainable impulse to laugh, not just a mild chuckle but a deep, booming laugh that would reverberate all night, welled up within me. The chuckle was one of assurance and power, as if I owned the entire world in the palm of my hand.

This abrupt change astonished me, and my thoughts were racing to figure it out. Was this a possession of some kind? Had a ghost from the cemetery seized my body as its vessel? Or was this a posthumous version of me that I was experiencing, since I was dead?

My internal laughing was so strong that it almost threatened to burst forth. But even as I experienced this strange emotion, a part of me—the real Jason—fought to maintain control. In the midst of this tumultuous storm of emotions, I made an effort to fight back against this intruding force and reclaim my sense of self.

A strange atmosphere was produced by the dramatic contrast between the peaceful beauty of the night and the internal fight. I found myself fighting an internal force as the world around me stood by, ignorant to my struggle. I was locked in this bizarre, surreal condition and felt more alone than ever since the gentle whispers of the night stood in stark contrast to the deafening turbulence inside.

One moment I felt enormous, but then my head tipped down and my eyes were drawn to the well-known graveyard's expanse. But what I witnessed was equally familiar and horrifying. We were it. As we had earlier in the evening, Tessa, Steve, and I were moving. And i was watching them from above

I was horrified as I watched in silence, yet this was not a scene from a movie. It was a repetition of our words, feelings, and deeds. Uncanny accuracy was used to mimic every movement and look.

Tessa's scream broke the stillness and echoed in the darkness, becoming even more eerie from this distance. Every aspect was emphasized, making the experience even more disturbing. Her sobs, Steve's protective posture, and the icy, hard stare he shot me. I saw it all from above.

I was getting more and more anxious as I began to feel immobile and anchored. I was watching what was happening from above, but I had no ability to stop it or even speak out. No matter how hard I tried, it appeared as though my voice was stuck inside and wouldn't let out any sound.

There was nothing like this experience I had when I was outside of my body. It was difficult to reconcile the dissonance caused by the contrast between my towering form and the recapitulation of the previous night's activities. I had the impression of being a quiet observer who was both emotionally distant from and linked to the reality being reflected in a way that was both vivid and horrifying. This unsettling vantage point heightened the evening's feelings of guilt, stress, and terror, which all erupted once more. No matter how much I tried, I was unable to awaken from the bizarre and frightening experience.

The sight of myself striding amid the tree from my eminent vantage point was both unnerving and interesting. It resembled viewing a scale model of the world with tiny moving figures, a miniature representation of the real world. Despite the fact that the person below me appeared to be so small from above, I felt incredibly alienated and remote from him.

I then attempted to raise my hand as a fresh sense of curiosity took hold. To my surprise, it replied by slowly rising in front of me. The same gloomy, dark cloak that encircled my entire form also surrounded it. The material appeared hazy, swaying and whirling as if it were composed of smoke or mist.

My body began to shiver. That hand wasn't mine. My body wasn't mine. All other feelings were drowned out by a wave of panic. A scream burst from deep within when I suddenly found my voice, resonating throughout the size of the dream world. It was an utterly terrified, bewildered, and desperate wail.

I sprang awake, struggling for air and feeling my heart race. The recognizable shapes of my bed and room's walls brought me back to consciousness as the shadows inched closer to me. The dream's unsettling feelings clung to me, but my immediate surroundings gave me confidence that it was done. I had returned to my own universe and body. However, the shadow created by that terrifying experience would continue to loom over the security and comfort of the waking world.

I felt compelled out of a sense of urgency to touch my own face, noticing the wetness of my still wide-eyed eyes, the shape of my nose, and the familiar roughness of my mustache. In a desperate attempt to feel the comforting solidity of my own body, my fingers slid through my hair and traced the contours of my hands. The remnants of the dreamworld lingered to the margins of my perception, making the space around me feel both familiar and alien.

I ran to the mirror, nearly anticipated seeing that ominous, shadowy image staring back at me when I stumbled to the mirror. However, it was only me, my unkempt hair, pale skin, and eyes still reflecting the nightmare's fear. I spent a considerable amount of time examining my mirror as I looked for any indication of that supernatural presence. But it was only Jason, albeit a frightened and shaken Jason.

Then I came to my senses. It wasn't me observing from some bizarre, dream-induced perspective from that vantage point, the aerial vision. It was Them . That creature. They had demonstrated to me how they had watched discreetly from the shadows while we were unaware of their presence. It was terrible to think that we were under constant surveillance, especially during such a sensitive occasion.

I felt exposed and helpless. My skin pricked with cold sweat, and every hair on my body stood on edge. It felt as though there was no longer a clear distinction between the real world and the dream, and that there was no way to hide from their constant surveillance.

I stepped back as I nervously cast one more anxious glimpse in the mirror, half expecting those eyes to emerge behind me. The weight of the knowledge was oppressive, settling deep within me as a mixture of dread and horror. There was now no turning back because the lines separating the mundane world from the paranormal had been crossed.

My heart leaped into my throat as I heard my phone's piercing ringtone in the stressful environment. I briefly became paralyzed as the abrupt roar added to my sense of panic. I swiftly moved to the bedside table, where my phone was eagerly buzzing, shaking off the shock of panic.

In the midst of the night's unsettling occurrences, Tessa's name flashed on the screen, and her contact photo offered a tiny bit of normalcy. My gaze quickly landed on the time on my phone: 2:50 a.m. Why on earth would she call at such a godforsaken hour?

I felt a wave of anxiety come over me. All of the things that happened in the dream, the unsettling conclusion, and the sudden call felt like parts of a puzzle that I wasn't sure I wanted to put together.

I inhaled deeply to calm my anxieties before answering the phone with a swipe of the screen.

"Tessa?" My voice was tinged with worry as I asked, wondering what she may say next.

The abrupt piercing intensity of Tessa's cry sent a wave of panic surging through me. Every hair on my body stood on end, and a cold dread settled in the pit of my stomach. "Theo! It's Theo!" She repeated, her voice breaking with every word.

I tried to process what was happening, to make sense of her panicked cries, but my mind raced faster than I could form coherent thoughts. I could hear the desperation in Tessa's voice, and the muffled sounds of Steven trying to console her in the background, his own voice thick with emotion.

"What happened to Theo?!" I found myself shouting, my voice echoing with a mix of fear and urgency. I strained to hear any coherent words amidst the cries and sobs, hoping for some explanation, some clarity amidst the chaos.

"Tessa! Tessa, talk to me!" I implored, trying to pierce through her anguish. The few seconds of silence that followed felt like an eternity, punctuated only by her intermittent sobs and Steven's attempts to soothe her. The weight of the unknown bore down on me, and I gripped the phone tighter, praying for an answer.

He's gone! He vanished! " My world briefly appeared to spin out of control as Tessa's words rang in my ears. She spoke with such bare-boned desperation that it chilled me to the core.

Gone? Disappeared? My thoughts were racing as I tried to piece together this difficult conundrum.

As I searched for the perfect words to provide some consolation or help, my heart hammered ominously in my chest. I spoke, trying to be as cool as I could, "Tessa, calm down," Give me the full story. starting at the start. How did this occur?

Steven's voice could be heard in the background humming sweet consoling words as the line was filled with her labored breathing and sporadic cries. My willpower was in danger of crumbling under the pressure of the situation and the horrifying images from my earlier-in-the-night dream.

By putting all of my attention on Tessa's voice and any information she could supply, I attempted to fight off the dread that was slowly enveloping me.

Steve's voice soon steadied the line, "He is gone, Jason" steven said, there was a quiet crack in voice. A crack I had never had never heard from Steve before.

"Steve, what are you saying?" I stammered, my head spinning as I tried to grasp what I'd just heard. The firm, confident voice I'd always associated with Steven seemed to have diminished to a whisper of its former self. His voice was laden with despair, each word punctuated by pain.

"He... he was just at the babysitter's. She... she said she woke up to a weird feeling in the room, and then... Theo was gone," Steven repeated, the disbelief evident in his voice. "Just... vanished. No trace of him, nothing."

I struggled to take it all in. The concept was nearly impossible to wrap my mind around. How could a baby simply disappear, leaving no trace? The chilling memories of the graveyard and the dream seemed to close in on me, intensifying the feeling of dread that weighed heavily on my chest.

The line remained silent for a moment, save for the sound of our heavy breaths, filled with shock and despair. Every logical explanation I tried to summon seemed to crumble under the weight of the absurdity of the situation.

"Have you called the police?" I finally managed to ask, my voice shaky.

"Yes," Steven responded, his tone sounding defeated. "They're on their way, but... but I don't know, Jason. This... this doesn't feel right. It doesn't feel... normal."

His words echoed my own thoughts.

The cacophony of emotions pouring through the line was deafening. Steven's crushed spirit and Tessa's inconsolable anguish resonated through every fiber of my being. For a few seconds, the weight of the situation bore down on me, threatening to pull me into a pit of despair. But then, the dream — that horrific, twisted vision of the creatures burying Theo alive — flashed before my eyes.

Suddenly, something within me snapped.

A fierce heat rushed through my body, as though a dormant volcano had erupted, churning up waves of determination and fury. The previously cold air of my room felt stifling, thick with the weight of the injustice done to Theo and the pain it caused my friends.

Gone were the feelings of helplessness and fear. In their place, a newfound resolve took root. My hands clenched into fists, nails biting into my palms. I wouldn't — couldn't — let those abominations succeed in whatever vile plan they had for Theo.

I had stood on the sidelines for too long, consumed by fear and plagued by nightmares. But no more. My love for my friends and their child, combined with the seething anger at the entities that had dared to disrupt our lives, propelled me into action.

"They took him, Steve. They took him to the graveyard." I said to Steve before I hung up.

I swiftly grabbed a shirt, put on a jacket and went to get my dependable old flashlight, making sure it was in good working order. A glimmer of optimism appeared when a beam of light pierced the gloom in my room. I went through a locket and took out my grandfather's shotgun.

With every step toward the door, my determination grew. I wasn't the same man who had fled the graveyard in terror. I was driven by a mission now, and I would see it through, come what may. Those entities had taken something precious from my friends, from all of us, and I would move heaven and earth to set things right.

There was no room for fear in my heart anymore. Only a burning desire for retribution and justice. The night was still young, and as I stepped out into the cool air, I made a silent vow to Theo, to Steven, to Tessa, and to myself.

I was going to bring Theo back, no matter the cost. And woe betide any creature that stood in my way.

I left my house without stopping, the night air hitting my face as though to startle me back to reality. However, there was no going back. My entire being was tuned to a single objective.

The truck's engine came to life, mirroring my own increased level of awareness with its sound. As I rushed through the deserted streets, the world outside blurred, my headlights creating lengthy shadows that oddly swirled with every turn. I had a firm grasp on the steering wheel, and the cool metal felt almost comforting next to my skin.

My adrenaline and sense of urgency made the typically long drive to the cemetery seem unusually quick. In the distance, the cemetery's imposing wrought trees could be seen, its silhouette lit by the dim moonlight. More than ever, it appeared to be a doorway to another universe.

As I parked the truck, I took a moment to collect myself as my heart was racing. There it was. the vanishing point. I wasn't stupid. I was aware of the dangers. However, a life was on the line—that of an innocent child who deserved none of this. To make sure he was secure, I had to take action in some way.

I entered the cemetery with the flashlight in my hand, the graveyard's well-known environs taking on a more ominous edge in the pitch-blackness. But the predominant feeling was no longer fear. Determination and a ferocious drive for protection took its place.

Each shade and rustling leaf served as a terrifying reminder of our previous meetings in this location, bringing up recollections that we had previously had. But I persisted because of a fire inside of me that wouldn't go out.

I was prepared to take on the evil and to resist the forces that had kidnapped Theo. I wasn't just Jason at that time, the man troubled by guilt and nightmares. I was a ray of hope, a parent willing to battle valiantly for a child's life. Nothing was going to get in my way, either.

I felt as though each step I took increased the volume of the echo. In the murky light, the well-known gravestones appeared to be smirking at me, generating unsettling shadows that twisted and turned as my flashlight's beam passed over them.

My stomach began to heave with a sickening sensation that I was being observed. The graveyard was surrounded by a deafening silence as the temperature dropped. It was the kind of silence where every little sound seemed to be exaggerated and where you could hear your own heartbeat.

By taking deep, deliberate breaths, I attempted to slow down my racing heart, but it was ineffective. Unease grew more intense, nearly stifling. Being constantly aware of predators hiding in the shadows made me feel like a prey animal.

I forced a hard swallow and continued, scouring the area with my torch to check for any indication of activity. My instincts shouted for me to flee from this evil location. But without Theo, I was unable to.

I suddenly felt as though there were a thousand eyes on me, sending a chill down my spine. I carefully circled around while illuminating the area with my torch. Then I sensed it: a huge, menacing figure coming from farther into the cemetery.

I moved cautiously in the direction of the source of this strong feeling. All of one's senses were acutely alert, straining to pick up even the slightest sound or movement. Then, like the sound of wind or the rustle of leaves, I heard it: a soft, nearly inaudible whisper. But neither of those were it. Something else, something alive, was there.

I kept moving forward because I was lured to that gentle voice even though every fiber in my body was screaming at me to run. I felt as though I were stepping right into the teeth of death, but I had to find out what was going on. To save Theo, I had to.

The voices got louder and more distinct as I went deeper. They appeared to circle me and come at me from all sides but not in any particular order. It seemed as though the earth itself was attempting to warn me or maybe even draw me in.

"Come out and face me!" I yelled, my voice trembling from a combination of anger and fear.

My words erupted from my throat with a vehemence I had never felt before, driven by a flood of rage, despair, and desperation. I could taste the acrid tang of the adrenaline.

My remarks seemed to be swallowed by the graveyard's vastness, which only offered the suffocating calm in reply. The weight of that quiet pressed down on me, stifling me and making me feel cramped, with each passing second. As though I were trying to breathe underwater, the air itself felt heavy. My racing heart was the only sound in the eerie silence, hammering wildly in my chest.

My nails dug into my hands as I clenched my fists. My hold on the torchlight shook, generating restless shadows that swirled and tricked my sight. I hardly noticed the bite of the night air in my face. My entire attention was on the oppressive quiet that was surrounding me, testing me, and mocking me.

"Is this a game to you?!" With my voice cracking, I yelled. "You steal a child, haunt my nightmares, and then you hide? What would you like?

Nothing was said in return, and the eerie silence persisted. It was frustrating. Everything appeared to be done to make me aware of my own insignificance and the utter audacity of my challenge to the forces that were hidden from view, including the size of the cemetery and the seemingly endless length of night.

But there was tension and a tangible sense of expectancy hidden beneath that cloak of stillness. It appeared as though the ground itself was holding its breath while waiting for a sign or signal.

I felt alone, as though I were sealed inside a soundproof bubble. I was surrounded by grave monuments, which added to the poignancy of the isolating, lonely feeling I was experiencing.

I yearned for a reaction, a sign, anything, with all of my being. I was on the verge of breaking because I was waiting and not knowing. Whatever was there appeared intent on straining my willpower and pushing me to my limits.

I felt more alone and exposed than ever before as the eerie nothingness appeared to swallow my cries and leave an echo that echoed back to me. As I paced, growing more and more frustrated with each passing second, the only things I could hear were my heart beating and the rustle of the leaves beneath my feet.

I wanted to see them, confront them, and make them come clean about their intentions at all costs. But they remained elusive, shadows that only ever hinted at the borders of my awareness.

I had the impression that they, whoever or whatever they were, had the cards and I was enmeshed in some macabre game. The evil and darkness seemed to penetrate the very earth I was standing on, and I could feel them. It was also frustrating.

"Enough!" I yelled, and the echoing of my voice was defiant. "Stop blending in the background! I'm here for a battle if that's what you want.

I was ready for anything as I waited, every muscle tensed. Silence stretched for what seemed like hours. It was a teasing stillness that was content to let all of my fears spiral inside of me. It seemed as though everything around me was making fun of me, testing my brashness, and daring me to do something.

I struggled to keep my cool as my fear started to rise. I knew deep down that this was about more than just dealing with an outside force. This was about facing my own anxieties, guilt, and past.

I made an effort to control my breathing in an effort to control the warring emotions inside of me. The impulse to find Theo, to defend him, and the desire to atone for guilt, fear and paralyzing feeling of helplessness all whirled about inside of me, threatening to overwhelm me. But I was unable to and would not permit them.

As I moved my touch around the night, suddenly my touch stumbled upon a giant bat-like creature that hissed, jumped on me and pushed me.

As the creature's weight knocked me to the ground, fear flooded every cell in my body. Only the lingering odor of decay and the piercing, chilly sensation of night air on my skin were left behind when its icy, leathery wings briefly touched my face. In an effort to make sense of the quick-paced, terrifying experience, my thoughts raced.

My back was scraped by the burial path's coarse gravel, which served as a constant reminder of the serious danger I was in. Every instinct screamed at me to get up, run, and go as far away as possible.

I lay there for a brief period of time, startled and confused, trying to absorb what had just transpired. The creature's bulk, its icy, leathery skin, and the piercing hiss were still vivid in my thoughts.

I quickly leapt to my feet after gathering my wits and frantically reached for the shotgun I always carried. My fingers formed a tight seal around its icy, comforting hold. My other hand searched the area for the dropped flashlight, whose beam was casting inconsistent light due to the ground's unevenness.

My frantic gasps of breath filled the frigid night air as I pointed the shotgun into the distance. The graveyard became ten times more eerie. Every shade and rustling leaf seemed to pose a danger. The gloom appeared to be alive and pulsing with malice.

I continued to strain my ears, listening for any noise that would provide a clue as to where the thing might be. But there was nothing but silence, save for my own labored breathing and the faint, far-off sounds of the night.

"Come back!" I roared, fusing challenge and desperation in my tone. My voice, which was harsh and tinged with fear, pierced the silence like a razor. My nerves were on fire from the terrifying experience with the beast, but I was also filled with a fiery drive.

As I hastily aimed the shotgun in all directions, sweat beaded on my forehead and trickled down my temples. The shotgun's weight was both a comfort and a burden. Every darkness and smallest movement turned into a possible danger. My ears strained to hear anything, be it a whisper, a rustle, or a breath. But the graveyard didn't say anything; it just remained silent.

I tightened my hold on the torch as it flickered, its beam piercing the darkness to reveal nothing but trees and gravestones. The silence weighed heavily and each passing second seemed to last forever.

Was the beast still lurking in the shadows, keeping watch for a chance to attack? Or did it withdraw after feeling content with the fear it had caused in me?

As I stood there, shotgun lifted, waiting for something to happen, every second seemed to last forever. The gnawing unease and sense of being on the prowl were nearly intolerable.

"Why are you hiding?" I yelled, my voice trembling. "What do you want?"

The silence that followed my comments only made the dread that had already crept up into the pit of my stomach grow more. My loud breathing and the sporadic cricket chirping in the distance broke up the night's silence.

But despite the dread engulfing me, I was also driven by a deep need to face this monster head-on. to learn more. to keep Theo safe. This was no longer just about me.

I wrangled my wits together and made an effort to overcome the crippling fear before advancing further into the darkness. Even though I couldn't see them, I could feel the weight of countless eyes following me with each stride. But despite my fears, I persisted because of a higher goal. No matter the cost, I had to save that child.

Immediately there was a loud noise, from the distance of the wood. My heart was thumping loudly in my ears along with that eerie cacophony as I stood still and stuck to the spot. My hold on the shotgun became more firm as the icy metal appeared to sink into my bones. My body begged me to run and escape that sound, but my feet felt heavy and reluctant to move.

An unpleasant frost descended upon the place as the sounds grew closer. In front of me, I could see small puffs of air created by my breath. The flashlight's beam shook as my hand shook, casting shadows across the tombstones and adding to the ominousness of the image.

When Steven, Tessa, and I first entered this cemetery and came face to face with those repugnant beings, memories of that tragic night came flooding back. The rumbling that preceded the appearance of those menacing entities was the same sound I heard this moment.

Every breath I took while trying to control my breathing tasted of the chilly, moist air of the cemetery. The roar was followed by an eerie quiet that was almost more unsettling. The entire world appeared to be holding its breath while waiting for something to happen or for the other shoe to drop.

I moved cautiously towards the direction of the noise, mustering all the confidence I could muster as I did so, my flashlight's beam piercing the darkness like a dagger. The stillness echoed back to me with every step as the leaves beneath my feet crunched and every rustle appeared to be ten times louder.

I had a sneaking suspicion that I was stepping into a trap since I was lured to the very threat I was trying to avoid. but I had to be aware. I wanted solutions. For Tessa, Steven, Theo, and myself. I was prepared to take on whatever challenges lay ahead of me in those forests.

With adrenaline pumping through my veins, I pushed further into the woods, my voice raw and filled with a mixture of fear and anger.

"Show yourself, you godforsaken shadow!" I spat, my every word laced with venom. The dense underbrush crunched and snapped beneath my boots, echoing my agitated state. "I'm not afraid of you!"

"You think hiding makes you powerful? You coward!" My voice echoed eerily in the thick woods, but I pressed on, refusing to let the creature think it had the upper hand. "Come out and face me, you damned phantom!"

Every darkened hollow and shadowed crevice seemed like a potential hiding spot for the creature. My torchlight darted around wildly, always trying to catch a glimpse of the elusive being. "You think you can terrorize a child and just hide in the shadows?!" I yelled, my voice quivering with rage. "Come out, you damned beast!"

The woods around me seemed to close in, the trees towering ominously, their branches swaying in the gentle night breeze. But I refused to be deterred. "Where are you, you spineless wretch?!" I shouted, my voice growing hoarser. "If you have any guts, any at all, show yourself!"

Every ounce of fear I had felt earlier had transformed into sheer determination and rage. I was not going to be played with any longer. This creature, whatever it was, was going to face me, and I was going to get answers, no matter what.

My entire existence shouted at me, pleading with me to turn around and run away so that I could go back to the security of the familiar. However, there I was, mired in a darkness so dense it felt like I was swimming in ink, deep within the woods. With their lofty shadows scarcely discernible against the pitch-black sky, the trees appeared to be closing in on me.

My heart beat quickly, its beat resonating loudly in my ears and seemed to time with the occasional rustling of leaves or the distant owl's hoot. My fingers were tightly gripping the cold metal of my shotgun as I was on high alert for any tiny movement in the nearby bushes.

The wind picked up and began to weave among the tree limbs, whispering secrets. My acute senses were heightened by the rustling of the leaves and the eerie background created by their whispered discourse. I could sense the weight of all the unseen beings, presences, and eyes that were watching, waiting, and hiding in the shadows.

I forced a hard swallow as I attempted to relight my torch, but it would not burn, leaving me adrift in a sea of darkness. As it tried to overwhelm me, the fear was so harsh and biting that I could taste it. Jason, you've faced worse than the dark, I repeated under my breath, pleading with myself to remain composed.

However, the truth was that this wasn't any old darkness. This was a live, breathing creature that suffocated any sense of time and place while consuming light and sound. The absence of my torch's illuminating light caused the woods to transform into a labyrinth, where each tree appeared identical, each road led to nothing, and each step may result in a loop.

I made an effort to remember my route, the turns I made, and the distinctive features. However, every recollection started to blend together into an unrecognizable jumble. I felt panic rising inside of me, and I could feel the cold fingers of despair around my heart.

I suddenly became aware of a far-off sound. A pleasant humming that reverberates through the trees. It was both reassuring and unsettling. I'm being drawn in by the sound of a siren. I didn't give it much thought as I started to go in the direction of the sound, holding my gun in front of me and prepared to fire at the first sign of trouble.

The buzzing became louder and more apparent as I got closer to it. It had the sound of an old lullaby that has been passed down through the ages. I paused because of the melody's basic essence. Was this just one of the creatures' tricks? A trick to get into another trap?

In order to determine whether to advance or withdraw, I stopped and tried to determine the direction of the sound. The woods remained impenetrable and provided no new puzzles or hints. My entire being was tuned into that humming in the distance and was pulled to it like a moth to a flame.

Suddenly, the buzzing abruptly stopped. It left such a hole that I had to strain to hear even the tiniest sound of a whisper. However, nothing was there. My heartbeat served as the only indicator of the passing of time as I stood in the middle of a silent environment.

It's odd how loud silence can sometimes be. How it makes even the slightest sounds louder than they already are in your head. Each inhalation and exhalation of mine resounded loudly and raggedly into the abyss. Every sound, including the rustle of my clothing and the faint patter of my feet on the forest floor, was 10 times louder, adding to the overwhelming sense of loneliness.

Every branch squeak and leaf shuffle turned into a possible menace. My mind was tricked by the silence. A footstep behind me, was that so? Was that the quiet rustling of a garment upon the earth? Maybe it was simply the breeze. My imagination was out of control and conjured horrifying pictures of what might be hiding just out of view.

The seclusion was debilitating. The feeling of being suffocated in a big, silent vacuum was overwhelming. I had the sensation that the air itself had become thicker, squeezing in on all sides and suffocating me. The stillness weighed heavily and relentlessly on me.

Unease pricked at the surface of my skin, sending a shiver down my spine. I once again felt as though I was being observed. In this silence, every instinct shouted at me that I wasn't alone. However, I felt blind and exposed because there was no sound to direct me.

Being buried alive was how it felt. trapped beneath several layers of earth, the world above going on with no regard for your situation. A sense of helplessness nearly overcame me. Every worry and concern I had ever had were amplified in that eerie silence and vacuum, and they consumed me.

I had to proceed. It was impossible to remain motionless in this void. My every stride was a protest against the oppressive silence and a refusal to be sucked into the ominous abyss. I forced myself to put one foot in front of the other.

The change happened gradually and was initially hardly noticeable. My ears, in need of any sound to hear, grasped fervently to the slight rustling and quiet patter that erupted from the devouring silence. At first, it appeared to be one person's softly-fallen footsteps on the forest floor. But as the minutes grew longer, that peculiar rhythm became more prevalent.

It intensified, going from a lone shuffle to a cacophony of footfalls. They reverberated in all directions. The steps were moving in all directions—forward, behind, to the left, to the right—convergent but hidden from view. My heartbeat accelerated, and all of my nerve endings went into high alert as they sought to identify the source of the motions.

The footfalls had an unsettling air of deliberateness. Each move seemed meant to torture me or to trick me. These invisible beings were present, and I could feel their presence; even the slightest movement was accompanied by a threatening atmosphere. Even though the steps were never loud enough to be heard, they were definitely there.

They would vanish immediately after that. After the little respite, the quiet would return, becoming even more oppressive. I would strain my ears in a desperate attempt to hear the sounds again, even if they were accompanied by a sense of dread.

But just as I began to understand the pattern, the sounds would change once more. It wasn't just the footsteps, though. Low, guttural muttering could be heard echoing in the distance. whispers that contained hidden mysteries.

Even though there were no walls around me, I still felt hemmed in. trapped by unseen entities that appeared to enjoy playing this nefarious game of cat and mouse. The sounds eluded me more and more the harder I tried to identify their origin. The earth felt unstable, like if it might give way at any second and send me hurtling deeper into the dark recesses of the unknown.

Then, a finger tapped my shoulder.

Every instinct screaming to go screamed when I felt a swift touch on my shoulder. My torchlight immediately came back on, blinding me before I could respond. When my eyes finally adjusted, I was greeted by a very eerie image despite my efforts to squint against the sudden light.

They were arranged in a menacing semi-circle there, evenly spaced apart. There were about fifteen of them, all of whom were covered in voluminous cloaks that reached the ground and concealed their feet in any way. Because of their extreme darkness, the cloaks didn't reflect or have a sheen; instead, they appeared to absorb the torchlight. They had their hoods on, which obscured their features completely.

The fact that some had broad shoulders and others had smaller builds allowed me to recognize that they were human beings despite the bulky cloaks. They were the silent, immovable, and just by being there, they were displaying their power and possibly even their malice.

Even the nighttime wildlife seemed to have quieted down in respect for this gathering, as if they understood the power these humans had. The only sounds I could hear were my own rapid breathing and my heart's pounding with a vengeance.

I felt their eyes on me even though their faces were covered. I was obviously not in control of this situation; I was just a participant in a scripted performance.

I attempted to gather the strength to ask them, "Who...who are you?" as I opened my mouth, my voice trembled. With the weight of the stillness weighing down on me, my question hung in the air. The cloaked beings were motionless as statues.

The smell of rotting wood and moist earth combined with the foul odor of decaying remains of long-dead things to create an overpowering stench. I felt queasy from the smell, which seemed to creep into the very corners of my nostrils. I straightened my back, trying to find all the courage I could muster to fight the uneasy sensation and nausea that threatened to rise.

"What do you want?" Each syllable in my voice, which carried a mix of defiance and terror, was distinct and punctuated as it resounded through the silence.

The weight of the cloaked creatures' combined gazes pressed down on me for what seemed like an eternity. The forest was silent all around us, as though the universe was holding its breath while awaiting a response. It felt as though a wire had been drawn taut and was about to break.

The man in the middle of the semi-circle then moved forward very slightly. Even though there wasn't much movement, it was enough to cause me to experience new levels of dread. A leader or even a spokesperson for the group, this one action seemed to set them apart from the others.

A voice came from behind the hood of the vehicle. It lacked any clear male or female characteristics and had a chilly, metallic tone that made my skin crawl. "We are worshippers of the creature you saw"

The words of the hooded figure cut through the cold night air, landing heavily on my ears. I felt a chill run down my spine as I processed what he had just said. "Worshippers?" I whispered, my voice quaking with a mix of anger and fear.

"Yes," the hooded figure responded. The raspiness of his voice sent shivers through me. "We are the chosen ones, the devotees of the ancient entity that you have so carelessly stumbled upon."

He continued in an emotionless tone. "Our people have revered the ancient one who resides here for ages. Exactly the thing you and your pals had the misfortune of meeting. And he had asked for a sacrifice. Instead of one of you three who saw him. He picked Tessa's child"

Nothing could have prepared me for this revelation despite my best efforts to remember that horrible night's sights, noises, and palpable anxiety. My mind was racing as I searched for any semblance of logic. "Why Theo? " Why a helpless child? I demanded while trembling.

The leader, or at least I thought he was the leader, drew in closer, the shadows tricking my perception of his movements." It's an act of mercy. We shouldn't doubt the desires of the ancient one. We comply when it asks for a sacrifice. It selected the child out of charity for you three. The innocence and purity of a child have immense power.

My hold on my torch and shotgun tightened as a cold ran down my spine. My heart ached with a rage I had never experienced when I thought of Theo, the helpless infant. His fate had been predetermined by these hooded fanatics, blinded by their fervor for some primordial evil. I was also resolved not to give in to their demands.

"So, it's mercy to take an innocent child's life instead of ours?" I spat, my tone of voice indicating my rage.

"You trespassed on sacred ground, awakened what should have remained undisturbed," the commander retorted. There are repercussions. We don't anticipate you to comprehend.

I'd had enough of hearing. I was determined. "Where's Theo?" I commanded with a firm voice. "I won't ask again."

After a brief silence one of the hood figures unwrapped its cloak slightly revealing Theo.

My spirits briefly dropped when I saw Theo snugly wrapped up in the cloak. It was both a relief and a heartbreaking sight to see his small form, the smooth rise and fall of his chest, and his lovely, cherubic face in sleep. The dramatic contrast to the dire circumstances we were in was striking. Knowing he was still alive made me angry at them for daring to touch him as well as relieved. In the eerie glow, the greenish rash on his skin was more obvious, but other than that, he appeared unhurt.

I moved in closer while maintaining my focus on Theo, but the cloaked figure tightened the baby's hold, quietly reminding me of the threat the infant was facing.

I looked away from Theo when the leader said, "You cannot have him. You trespassed, and now you must pay. His future is decided."

"He's unharmed, "The cloaked figure with the child said, noticing my eyes locked on the child. It was a feminine voice. I could almost swear it was a familiar one

My voice cracked with emotion. "Give him to me," I demanded, my eyes never leaving the sight of Theo.

The leader chuckled dryly, "It's not that simple. The ritual has begun. Even if we handed him over to you now, the Ancient One will claim him, one way or another."

Desperation and fury intermingled inside me. "There must be something, some way to stop this. What do you want?"

"The Ancient One requires a sacrifice, as I've said." Another one of the cloaked figures said. It was a male voice this time.

I started to notice certain tones and inflections as they continued to chant, their voices melding into a melancholy song. Realization started to dawn as I strained my ears to distinguish between the several voices. The town's librarian, Mr. Anderson, could be distinguished by his raspy undertone in one voice. A different voice had the high, mellow pitch I had always associated with Miss Clara, the schoolteacher. What is going on here? Were they members of this ghastly cult?

As I tried to process this startling information, my thoughts raced. All my life, I had engaged with these people and knew them well. The possibility that they might be participating in something so ominous and evil was almost unbearable.

I whispered to myself, shaking my head in astonishment, "They can't be involved in this."

Internally, desperation tore at me. "Why are you doing this?" I yelled at the masked individuals, my voice filled with a mix of rage and disbelief.

However, they kept quiet as if I hadn't spoken anything at all, their voices unrelenting. Only the leader spoke in response, and his voice was so icy it sent chills down my spine. He said, "Sometimes, what's hidden in plain sight is the most terrifying truth of all."

Desperate to keep them engaged, I tried another tactic. "If your deity is so powerful," I said, voice trembling, "then why doesn't it show itself now? Why hide in the shadows and use you as pawns?" I was running on pure adrenaline, my mind racing as I tried to find an opening, a way to grab Theo and make a run for it.

There was a long, cold silence. Only the eerie whispers of the wind through the trees and the distant hoot of an owl broke the stillness.

Then, one of them stepped forward. The movement was slow, deliberate. "Our deity does not need to prove its existence to you," he said, his voice echoing in the stillness of the night. "We serve willingly, and through us, its will is done."

Another cloaked figure added, "It's not about proving. It's about believing. And we believe."

Their cryptic words sent chills down my spine. Were they truly so devoted to this mysterious entity that they'd kidnap an innocent child?

I took a deep breath, my eyes darting around, looking for an escape route. "Look," I began, trying to keep my voice steady, "whatever you believe in, whatever you think you're doing – it's not right. That child is innocent. He doesn't deserve whatever you have planned for him."

One of the figures whispered something to another, too soft for me to catch. The air grew colder, and I could see my breath fogging in front of me. My heart pounded loudly in my ears, each beat reminding me of the urgency of the situation.

The cloaked figure seemed upset as they stood coldly rooted to the ground glaring at me through their hooded frame. I could tell I made them upset. Maybe there could be a way out, I thought. But I wasn't going to leave without Theo.

Immediately, they unveiled their thorn-covered whips, which caused my eyes to widen in fear. My throat tightened in anxiety as I could feel the threat in the air.

All other sounds were muted as my heart beat faster than ever. It was quite horrifying to see the barbed whips in their hands. Each thorn looked more threatening than the previous as the pale moonlight glittered off its jagged surface. My frenetic cadence was echoed by Theo's small heartbeat as I squeezed him closer.

I rasped, "You don't have to do this," in an effort to gain some time and persuade them to see things rationally.

One of them growled, "Get out or face the wrath of the deity!" Every ounce of strength I had mustered was now quickly evaporating in the face of their overwhelming malevolence. The idea of those whips being used against me was agonizing. Each thorn on them appeared to be sharp enough to puncture skin and muscle.

I started to withdraw.

One of the veiled guys yelled, "We warned you. "You interfered where you shouldn't have. The almighty will not be kind to those who transgress!"

My thoughts were racing as I tried to grasp their threats and plan a way out. They could be heard whispering to one another, their voices tinged with a mixture of elation and rage. The thorns on their whips shone hauntingly in the dim night as they clinked menacingly.

"Go away now and never come back. The leader screamed, the whip trembling in his palm, "This is your only warning.

I assessed my chances with each stride backward. Clearly, the figures in cloaks were in the lead. I was encircled, outnumbered, and had no easy way to get out. And even if I did manage to escape, would I be able to outrun them while toting Theo?

I managed to squeeze out "You won't get away with this," while trying to project more assurance than I actually had. My voice trembled as I struggled with real fear.

My audacity appeared to amuse the figures. They produced a sinister laughing noise that made my blood chill. One of them gritted his teeth and gripped his whip tighter, "You're in no position to make threats," he growled.

But even as I was in a state of terror, an idea crossed my mind. These were people, most likely citizens of our town, not magical beings.

I took a deep breath, mustered all my courage, "This child is innocent. If you have any humanity left in you, any shred of conscience, let him go," I murmured in a voice that was remarkably steady.

Another protracted pause followed. The wind blowing through the trees and an owl's distant hoot were both audible to me. The figures in the cloaks appeared to be speaking inaudibly and possibly changing their minds. The leader spoke at last.

"Leave. And if you value the child's life, never speak of this night to anyone. Remember, we are always watching."

Immediately there was a long bang that pierced the air.

I jolted out of my paralyzed state when the sudden gunshot appeared to pierce the very fabric of the night. After the loud shot, the world temporarily went silent and my ears rang. I instinctively dove and pressed my body against the earth. The frenzied beats of my racing heart threatened to shut out all other sounds as they echoed in my ears.

I made an effort to process what had just occurred in the silence that followed. Was I wounded? I experienced no pain. I cautiously opened my eyes and looked about. The formerly terrifying shrouded figures held their ground but they were also startled. In response to the gunshot, some ducked, while others whirled around to look for the source.

I noticed a familiar face, hidden by the low light, as I cast a quick glance to my right. Tessa stood there, holding a shotgun with its barrel still smoking. She had a fierce cold look on her face as the smoke floated off her gun into the air

My tongue was filled with the icy, metallic taste of adrenaline as my mind rushed to process what was happening in front of me. I had many expectations, but seeing Tessa carrying a shotgun wasn't one of them. She had an incredible amount of fierceness and resolve, which was both inspirational and disturbing.

Seeing Tessa, like they were struck by lightning, every one of the cloaked figures scurried off into the dark abandoning the only lifeless one on the floor. It was the one with Theo, and it was the one Tessa shot.

I could hear infant Theo's anguished cries coming from beneath the thick cloth of the clothed figure, as we hastily drew near to the fallen hooded figure. Tessa quickly took Theo off the cloaked figure and quickly embraced him, attempting to quieten his startled cries with quiet reassurances and whispers. I was acutely conscious of how close we had come to losing him as Tessa cuddled him close, seeing his upset tiny hands punch and grab the air.

Tessa went closer, ejecting the spent cartridge from her shotgun, and rapidly reloading. Though her face was pale, her eyes were still ablaze with the fierce determination of a mother defending her kid.

Tessa used the butt of her gun to open the cloak of a figure that laid flat on the earth.

The understanding weighed heavy on my chest, and my heart was racing. It was Theo's babysitter.

The babysitter's once-vibrant face was now pale and dead, and her blank eyes were fixed unwaveringly into the darkness. My heart cruelly thudded against my ribs. Despite being dead, she had an expression of utter dread on her face, with her lips parted as if about to scream. The weight of what we had learned appeared to be weighing down on us, making the darkness of the night even more depressing.

Tessa said in an exasperated whisper, "I can't believe it," in a tight voice. Her eyes, which were filled with perplexity and rage.

With tears running down her face, Tessa screamed in a guttural tone that was equal parts outrage and despair. "She belonged to them! She turned on us!" We both felt terror and amazement as her voice resonated hauntingly around the cemetery.

I inhaled deeply and trembled as I tried to put the puzzle pieces together. The nanny had always appeared to be so dependable and considerate. We never suspected her of having any bad intentions despite the several times she looked after Theo. It was shocking to learn that she had connections to the masked individuals. Yet why? What was her relationship?

My thoughts were racing, making connections and concocting scenarios. Was she only an object in a larger game? Was she compelled to join this evil organization, or did she choose to do so?

Tessa crouched down next to the babysitter's body and reached out to touch her face with shaking fingers. She said, "Why?" with brokenness. "Why would you do this?"

Our only response was the dead silence of the cemetery, broken only by the faint whimpers of infant Theo and the far-off howls of nocturnal creatures. We were left with a puzzle that appeared to be even more complicated than before, as well as the unsettling impression that our problems were far from being solved.

I was startled out of my haze by the severity of the issue. "Tessa, we have to get going. Now!" I yelled while attempting to control my panic.

She gasped, looking warily into the darkness where the cloaked creatures had vanished, "They might regroup and come back."

We agreed by nodding, trembling at every shadow and tree rustling. Tessa turned to me as we drew closer to the cemetery's edge, her voice shaky but unwavering. She remarked, a mixture of terror and resolve in her eyes, "We're going to have to deal with this, Jason." "Until they achieve their goals, they won't stop. And I won't stop until I'm certain that my son is secure.

I pressed her hand while silently nodding in accord. For the sake of baby Theo and our own peace of mind, we would do whatever it took to confront these dreadful adversaries.

Tessa rapidly rose to her feet while still clutching Theo close to her breast. Neither the weight of the infant nor the shotgun in her hands seemed to slow her down in the slightest.

Every rustle and shadow that we encountered as we moved fast through the deep woodland sent chills down my spine. Our sole source of illumination was the moon, which cast unsettling, elongated shadows in our way. The occasional faint, far-off voice that appeared to travel on the wind to break the solitude shivered us to the core.

We continued, eager to put as much distance as we could between ourselves and the evil figures who prowled the cemetery. The darkness all around us appeared to go on forever, crushing us under the weight of our worries and the unknowable. Tessa's labored breathing next to me and Theo's quiet whimpers, who had gotten restless after catching wind of our concern, were audible.

Finally, the darkness was behind us as we emerged from the dense forest cover. We could see our car, which was parked close to the cemetery's entrance. Our breath came out in white puffs in the chilly air as we sprinted in its direction.

Thankfully Steve had been waiting in the car for us. We got in and suddenly a silence settled in.

I hastily bundled Tessa and the infant into the backseat as I yanked open the car door, finding no solace in the cold, metal handle. The only thing standing between us and the darkness that appeared to be closing in was the automobile, which served as our final line of defense.

With his eyes flashing in the faint light, Steven was pallid. The car wouldn't start once more, and he said, "Damn it!" with exasperation in his voice. Immediately, I started crying so loud. Theo's cries and the ignition's constant churn combined to create a chorus of agony within the car.

Tessa attempted to calm Theo while concealing her dread and tiredness on her face. The baby was crying despite her desperate coos, and she tried to comfort him. Every cry we made seemed to act like a beacon, attracting unwanted attention to us.

The graveyard was deserted outside. There was a deep, unnatural hush. The entire globe seemed to be holding its breath and waiting for something. The anxiety in the vehicle was obvious as my fingers grasped the edge of my seat.

Steven inhaled deeply as he attempted to revive the automobile once more. The engine stuttered and failed to start. The walls of the car started to feel more like a trap than a haven, and panic started to rise within me. I muttered, "Come on," mimicking Steven's earlier words, keeping a close eye on the rearview mirror for any activity.

The night was broken by Theo's sobbing. He sounded odd and urgent, as if he could hear things that we weren't able to. Tessa glanced up at Steven while her face was smeared with tears. She muttered, "We can't stay here," her voice trembling.

Steven had stern determination in his eyes. He answered, "I know," his voice rising with annoyance. He turned to face me and looked into my eyes. "We might need to get out of the automobile. If the next time it doesn't start...

His comments carried a heavy burden, and the inference was obvious. Giving up the automobile required facing the open graveyard and whatever lurked there. However, staying put was also not an option.

I firmly interjected, "We won't split up," stopping Steven in mid-sentence. "We stick together, no matter what."

Tessa nodded as she pulled Theo into her arms. "Agreed."

The silence outside was deafening. There was no wind rustling or insect chirping. There is nothing but our own heartbeats, which seem abnormally loud in the silence.

Steven made another attempt with one last, frantic twisting of the key. After a moment of hesitation and rumbling, the engine miraculously came to life. We all let out a sigh of relief at the same time.

However, before we could move an itch. I noticed something huge, looming at my peripheral eyes, by the window of the car. I turned to look immediately and it was the creature standing next to the window where Tessa was with Theo like it had been there all this while.

The entity's bright brilliance stood in stark contrast to the darkness of the night all around us. It was a form of bioluminescence, but it wasn't the reassuring blue-green variety that may be seen in some aquatic organisms. This had a ghostly brilliance surrounding it and was a spooky shade of dark purple.

The entity's ethereal, shadowy shape appeared to swirl and twist as if it were composed of smoke or another ethereal material that was not of this world. The silhouette reminded me of the swaying, reaching branches of a willow tree because it was human-like, tall—almost reaching the tops of the adjacent trees—and had extended limbs that appeared to taper to points.

It was overwhelmingly present. The air itself appeared to thicken and cool around it. Even the car's low hum seemed far away, almost drowned out by this being's throbbing aura.

My body's natural instincts shouted "danger!" Theo's piercing shrieks took on a new level of dread as if the infant could sense the villainy in the figure standing outside. Tessa held him even closer, protecting him with her body while her horrified gaze remained glued to the creature.

The car's interior was transformed into a vision straight out of a nightmare by the monster, which appeared to absorb the light itself. Its luminous glow projected distorted shadows over the vehicle.

Two dimly shining points of light, which might have been eyes, then emerged where one would anticipate a head to be and were intently staring at us. It appeared to be staring deeply into us as well as at us from the outside.

Its weighty stare almost physically pressed down on us, restricting our ability to breathe. I had a chilling dread that I had never experienced before. This was more than just terror; it was the knowledge that something ancient, potent, and wholly extraterrestrial was in the room.

Tessa said my name in a quivering whisper. I tried to soothe her as I turned to face her, but no words came. Both the beast outside and our terror had us in its grasp.

Though it appeared suddenly from the shadows, its presence was so strong and instantaneous that it seemed to be there the entire time. Its shape was lofty and menacing, posing with a sinister grace next to the car window. The entire thing exuded a strange brightness that stood out dramatically against the darkness of the surroundings. It was a chilly, bluish light that was nearly bioluminescent, resembling certain creatures living in the depths of the ocean. However, this was a harsh, unsettling, and intrusive glow rather than a gentle one.

The folds of the murky, shadowy shape concealed the entity's scarcely discernible features. In spite of this, you could make out hazy indications of its structure from the weak light it emitted. The way the light bounced and refracted off its form indicated fluidity, as if it were continuously altering, changing shape, and never remaining steady. It had an aura around it that I could feel was oppressive and heavy, and it gave me the chills.

Theo began to wail more loudly and desperately as if he could sense the threat this thing brought. Every breath we took seemed like we were taking in a mixture of the chilly mist and dread.

Our hearts were thumping loudly in our ears, and the silence within the car was palpable as we held our breath. Tessa tightly hugged Theo, her eyes wide with dread, unable to take her eyes off the ghost. Steve's knuckles were white as his hands squeezed around the steering wheel. We were entrapped and rendered helpless by the presence of the thing.

The creature's luminous glow appeared to pulse, with each pulse becoming brighter and more intense and throwing unsettling shadows that moved and flickered. All that was left was this thing, this dark sentinel that had emerged from the very depths of the night, as the world outside our car began to vanish.

The glow grew stronger at the tip of what appeared to be an arm as it was elevated. It emitted a low, humming sound that shook us to the core and threatened to breach the perilous partition separating reality from whatever realm this monster was from.

Time appeared to pass slowly. Every second seemed to last forever. It was clear that we and the thing were engaged in a game of intentions and wills. The distinction between reality and a nightmare was hazy at that time. The only things we knew for sure were the icy horror choking our chests and the eerie light of the creature, watching, inviting, and threatening.

Tessa's throat tore open as the entity's fingers encircled Theo, unleashing a primal, searing scream. The sound was amplified by the car's small interior, which caused it to resound and cover the entire nighttime area around us. A primal maternal urge propelled her hands to reach out and try to free her infant from the creature's grasp.

The struggle was fierce, terrifying and painful. Tessa's claws tried to get hold of the creature's eerie form by digging into it, but they were unable to penetrate its smoky essence. The creature's appearance was unstable and changed every time she appeared to get a grasp of it, making it impossible to hold onto. It was perplexing how the solid weight of Theo in its grasp contrasted so sharply with its own elusive, almost ethereal appearance.

Tessa's face distorted with the unadulterated emotion of a mother fighting for her kid, and her eyes were wild with horror and anguish. She threw every fiber of her being into the battle. She was straining against the monster, and I could hear her panting and hear her breaths coming in quick, sharp gasps. Even for a little moment, the thing seemed to be slowed by the sheer power of her resolve.

Steven and I were paralyzed for what felt like hours but was probably just seconds before we eventually moved. Steven reached out to Tessa in an effort to join the pull, and I raced in its direction, eager to offer any assistance I could. But before we could do anything, the beast managed to tear Theo free with a startling yank and fled into the night's shadows.

I'll never forget Tessa's screams as Theo was taken away, which were filled with deep pain. Every parent's worst nightmare was condensed into that one sound. Tessa's tear-streaked face and her hands still reaching into the space where Theo had been just seconds earlier in the aftermath of that battle would haunt my dreams for years to come.

Unable to stand to the sound, I got out of the car and chased it. I got my gun out and this time, shot at it.

While holding a gun that was still burning. The thing had stopped running and had focused solely on me at this point. It was the epitome of pure, dark malice. Around it, the darkness and silence appeared to have grown more oppressive and the night seemed to have grown longer.

I was still able to sense its eyes even though I couldn't see them. It felt as though they could see every worry and weakness in my soul, cutting right through. My body became utterly immobile under the weight of its imposing gaze, which made my feet seem like they were stuck to the ground.

The air around us appeared to become thick and almost suffocating due to the creature's presence. Every heartbeat was plainly audible to me as my body was racing, which stood out against the night's silence. Standing there, impasse-bound, neither of us moving for what seemed like an eternity.

I made an effort to summon what little courage I still had so that I could address the thing and get Theo back. However, the environment this creature was in seemed to sap my energy, leaving me speechless. Faced with such a powerful adversary, the shotgun, which had formerly been a source of confidence, felt little and even toy-like.

Knowing the vast power this thing held made me feel a chilling dread permeate into my bones. I was thinking in a terrifying maelstrom as each second it watched me felt like an hour. My thoughts became a cacophonous mess as I tried to sort through the images of the spooky dreams, the ominous atmosphere at the cemetery, and the shrouded men. I was ensnared by a force I couldn't understand at this very time, and I was trapped.

I saw a glimpse of motion blur out of the corner of my eye. Tessa attacked the beast with astonishing quickness as she was propelled by the ferocious determination only a mother could have. Theo was unflinchingly grasped by her outstretched hands. The being seemed surprised by her brazenness despite being intently focused on me.

The situation became more bizarre. However, it remained completely unchanged in attitude. It stayed motionless, its figure standing out starkly in contrast to the soft glow of the lunar night. I was the only subject of its undivided attention. I felt as though I was being sucked into its abyss, that I was being tested, that I was being dared to act.

But even in my frozen state of fear, there remained a simmering ember of rage. I felt a spark of defiance within me in response to this creature's arrogance in terrorizing us and stealing a child. I wasn't going to let this standoff conclude on its terms, even if it may have had the upper hand at this point.

Tessa's labored breathing broke the stillness, tightening her hold around Theo, but she never took her eyes off the monster. My paralyzed state was in sharp contrast to her courage and strong willpower.

It was easy to feel Tessa's uncontrollable wrath. I had never seen anything like it before—a combination of maternal instinct and untamed rage. She quickly drew her shotgun with one hand while pulling Theo close to her with the other. She fired directly at its face without any hesitation. The resounding sound broke the tense calm that had surrounded us.

Being taken off guard, the creature was knocked off balance and pushed backward against a nearby tombstone. It was clear how powerful Tessa's shot was. It attempted to stand up, but Tessa was unrelenting. With firm aim, she fired repeatedly. The beast was pushed deeper into the shadows with each gunshot that hit its target.

Its attempts to maintain control in the face of her assault failed. With each bullet, it lost stability, its shape trembling as if it were fighting for survival. Then, with one last, frantic lurch, it vanished, vanishing into the pitch-black night.

With the exception of our collective labored breathing as we tried to process what had just happened, the cemetery was silent once more. The threat appeared to have been temporarily avoided, but the night's horrors had left a permanent scar on our souls.

The car's engine noise filled the air and served as a siren, calling us to safety. Steven was sweating and his fingers were gripping the steering wheel with white knuckles as we drew nearer to the car. He screamed, his voice full of urgency, "Get in, NOW!" We virtually flung ourselves inside the doors as soon as we threw them open.

I turned to give a final glance in that direction as the tires squealed on the dirt road. The graveyard's eerie silhouette slowly dissipated into the distance as it was illuminated by the moon's gentle brightness. The shattered grave markers remained as mute witnesses to the carnage that had just taken place. The fractured stones where the thing had landed and the burned earth from Tessa's persistent firing were visible in the aftermath of our fight. It served as a somber reminder that what transpired this evening wasn't just a dream.

Steven dashed off, the trees fading into vague shapes as the wind roared by. While the outside world appeared to be moving at a rapid pace, time seemed to have slowed down within the car. Theo the baby was now quiet and comfortable in Tessa's arms, his gentle breathing in stark contrast to the rest of us' fast heartbeats. One of us would occasionally sneak a peek in the rearview mirror, half expecting to spot a shadowy figure trailing behind us, but there was never anything there.

Steven sped the car, trying desperately to get us away from the horrors we had just experienced. The tires squealed against the gravel. Tessa wasted no time in getting Theo close to her chest. Her eyes were still wide from the adrenaline and anxiety

Only the buzz of the engine and the steady thudding of our hearts broke the dense silence that pervaded the automobile. We were all deep in thought, trying to make sense of the horrible events of the previous night.

A sigh of relief could be heard across the entire vehicle as we increased the distance between us and that awful location. We were currently secure. However, this night would live on in our memory forever, serving as a terrible reminder of the darkness that lies just beyond the horizon of our comprehension.

The buzz of the motor and the soft rustle of the trees outside hardly ever broke the stillness inside the car. My mind raced, replaying each incident, and each whisper that now looked dubious. These individuals in the town who had comforted us with a word or a touch suddenly felt contaminated with distrust.

The thought sank in like a cold fog: perhaps the humans around us were the greater threat than the unidentified creatures in the cemetery. People we called friends or neighbors who we shared our lives with and saw every day. The idea terrified me. Was the safety we experienced after our escape merely a brief respite before being hurled back into the lion's den?

In the rearview mirror, I noticed Tessa's eyes moving. The same emotions that I was experiencing—fear, perplexity, and suspicion—were also there in them. Her arms held a calmly sleeping Baby Theo who was blissfully unaware of our internal struggle. His gentle snores served as a startling contrast to the tension in the car. But was he constantly in danger of dying in that town? Were all the well-wishers and worried citizens simply a part of a sinister plot?

Steven's knuckles turned white as he tightened his hold on the steering wheel. I could feel his internal struggle between turning around and returning to his familiar surroundings, or continuing on into the unknown. Had home changed into a haven for monsters with familiar faces, or was it even still home?

Our journey started to focus less on the distance we were traveling and more on the emotional and intellectual turmoil we were traversing. The evening had exposed a terrifying truth: sometimes monsters don't dwell in the depths of uncharted regions; instead, they may disguise themselves as people we can trust.

As I kept my eyes on the rearview mirror watching Tessa and baby Theo. I noticed something significant.

I blinked twice, ensuring that my eyes weren't deceiving me. The once prominent and sickly green rash, which had covered parts of Theo's body, had disappeared. It was as if it had never existed, leaving behind soft baby skin.

"Look, Tessa!" I said, pointing at Theo. Tessa, with her brows furrowed, carefully examined her baby. She gently pulled away the small red cloak that enveloped Theo and checked his neck, arms, and other areas that the rash had previously marred.

"It's gone," she whispered, her voice laced with a mix of disbelief and relief. "The rash... It's completely gone!"

The car's interior light illuminated her tear-streaked face, revealing a myriad of emotions – shock, relief, hope. Steven glanced over, his eyes widening in astonishment. For a brief moment, the tension that had gripped us all seemed to dissipate, replaced with a sigh of relief.

"Could it be that... when we defeated that creature, whatever curse or ailment it had cast on Theo was broken?" I pondered aloud.

Tessa remained quiet, she held Theo closer, pressing her lips against his forehead and pressed him closer to her chest.

"You know they are going to be back right?" Steve swallowed as he kept his eyes on the road, speaking to no one in particular. Tessa's eyes shifted from Theo to Steve and then I. She raised her gun up, cocked it and looked at me. 'I'll be waiting for them when they do."

The preceding several hours appeared to have passed in a nightmare fog, a never-ending maelstrom of horror that had threatened to swallow us all whole. However, as we drove further, a warm amber glow started to spread over the horizon, signifying the start of a new day.

Tendrils of sunlight, winding through the trees on either side of the road, were now progressively driving away the once-complete darkness that had been our world. Once oppressive and menacing in the dark, the tall, imposing shapes of the trees were already beginning to change. As their silhouettes started to soften and take on the dawn's burgeoning colors, they appeared friendly and welcoming.

The leaves of the trees, which had been shrouded in shadow, began to shimmer, each shade of green illuminating vividly as the sun's rays struck them. They made a calming rustling sound that was music to our ears as they slowly swung and danced to the morning breeze's beat.

The dark, ominous shadows were gone, replaced by gentler, shorter ones that stretched lazily across the road. They seemed lighthearted, which was a sharp contrast to the eerie people we had fled from only hours earlier.

The difference was not just apparent when I rolled down my window. The air was different now. There was now a sharp, energizing freshness in place of the oppressive, thick environment. It filled my lungs, expelling the last of the anxiety and uncertainty that had settled there. The scent of the breeze was energizing, carrying the scent of budding flowers, dew-kissed grass, and the distinct aroma of the earth waking to a new day.

The road seemed to get brighter and clearer as I looked forward. The surroundings were gradually regaining their color. Reds were more passionate, greens more rich, and blues more intense. Everything in the world, including ourselves, appeared to be given new vitality.

Tessa leaned forward while sitting in the rear seat and let the wind play with her hair. A small smile played across her lips as she closed her eyes and took in the warmth of the sun and the chill of the wind. Theo cooed softly while still in her arms, his little face gleaming with health from the morning's gentle light.

Despite still appearing shocked and exhausted from the experience, Steven couldn't help but smile a little as he looked around at the surroundings. He muttered, "It's beautiful," as if he were concerned that saying it aloud could disturb the peace of the moment.

It truly felt as though Mother Nature herself was attempting to calm our stressed nerves by enveloping us in a cocoon of serenity and beauty. A startling reminder that the most magnificent dawns always follow the longest, darkest nights.

I felt a sense of hope and gratitude as the miles passed and the sun kept rising, bathing the world in a golden tint. It was difficult to comprehend that we had been engaged in a conflict with unknown adversaries and powers beyond our knowledge only a few hours earlier given the stark difference.

The night's atrocities now seemed far away, almost strange, in the presence of this breathtaking panorama. Darkness and light, dread and serenity, despair and hope, all coexist in life, as the beauty of the dawn served as a sobering reminder. Which one we decide to concentrate on is all that is in question.

But things switched up when we arrived in town. The town, which had previously served as a safe haven for me, a place of fond memories from my youth, laughing, and camaraderie, suddenly seemed strange and dangerous. I couldn't help but sense a sneaky undertone as we drove through the well-known streets, which were dotted with ancient brick houses, mom-and-pop stores, and the little town square. The houses, which formerly seemed inviting with their white picket fences and well-kept gardens, now appeared more like facades concealing secrets.

Tessa's face was covered in anxiety as she held Theo closer to her bosom. She must have sensed the atmosphere's change as well. With a grim determination written on his face, Steven's grip on the steering wheel tightened and his knuckles turned white. No words were spoken, but we all sensed it: the community we once knew and loved had become a maze of mistrust and ambiguity.

Only the distant chimes of the town's old clock tower broke the oppressive calm that lingered in the air, making the streets appear smaller and the shadows darker. Every minute of that clock felt like a countdown, a signal that the threat was getting closer and time was running out.

Even the iconic features of the town, like the venerable fountain in the center of the plaza or the bell tower, which I had repeatedly scaled as a child, seemed tarnished. Every stone, brick, and nook contained a potential secret or buried truth that might suddenly emerge and startle us.

And as we passed through, attempting to return to routine and shake off the chilling effects of the previous night's events, I kept thinking that this town, these people, and the life I had known would never be the same again. The fundamental underpinnings of my universe had been shattered, and I felt as though I was a stranger in my own house.

Steve soon brought the car to a halt. His face contorted in a mix of frustration and realization. He looked at me, as if seeking validation, and I could tell we were all on the same page. The events of the night, the revelations, the uncanny familiarity of some of the cloaked figures; it was all too overwhelming, too close to home. Every pillar of trust we had built over the years had been shaken.

"Tess, we need to do something," Steve implored, his voice carrying a hint of desperation. "We can't just sit back and let these...these monsters roam free, not after what they did to Theo, not after what they could do to others."

Tessa took a deep breath, her face contorted with anguish. "I know, Steve," she whispered, her voice trembling. "I can't bear the thought of handing over our baby to someone who might be involved with them. What if they're everywhere? What if we're surrounded by them?"

The car was silent except for Theo's soft breathing in the backseat. The sheer gravity of our situation weighed heavily upon us. Trust, such a simple concept, had become a luxury we could no longer afford.

"I think," I began cautiously, "we need to be strategic about this. We need evidence, something concrete that the police can't dismiss or hide if they're involved. We should also consider reaching out to a journalist or someone in the media. The more eyes on this, the better."

Steve nodded, absorbing the weight of my words. "Yes, But first," he said, determined back in his voice, "we need to ensure Theo's safety. We need a place where he'll be safe, far from the reach of these...cultists."

Tessa looked up, her eyes filled with tears but also determination. "Then we fight. We fight for Theo, for our town, for everyone they've harmed. We uncover their secrets, expose them, and bring them to justice."

"Fight? What do you mean fight? Steve is right. We need somewhere safe for Theo and that will be out of this town. Its better you leave." I said.

The suggestion to leave hung in the air for a moment, heavy and thick. The car's interior seemed to grow smaller, the tension palpable as I waited for their reaction. The hum of the engine and the gentle rhythm of the day outside seemed to slow.

Finally, Steve broke the silence, his voice hesitant. "Leave? Just like that? This is our home, Jason. Our families, our lives, everything we've built is here."

I glanced at Tessa, searching her face for any indication of her thoughts. She away, her fingers playing nervously with Theo's tiny hand.

"But what if it's the only way to keep Theo safe?" I whispered, almost to myself. "I can't bear the thought of something happening to him. Not after everything."

For a moment there was a palpable silence in the car.

I cleared my throat, trying to find the right words. "I'm not saying it's a permanent solution, Steve. But maybe... just until we figure things out? Until we can be sure that Theo is safe? It might be worth considering."

Steve's hands gripped the steering wheel tighter, his knuckles turning white. "Run away? That's your solution? And what about the other kids, other families in this town? Do we just leave them to the mercy of this... this cult?"

My voice was gentle, but firm. "Steve, this isn't about running away. It's about ensuring your son's safety. If something happens to him. I don't know. Trust me on this, we need distance to think, to plan our next move."

The silence returned so I continued "Look, all I'm suggesting is a temporary retreat. Get out of town, let things cool off a bit, and then return when we have a solid plan. We need to be smart about this, strategic. And we can't do that if we're constantly looking over our shoulders."

Steve took a deep breath, letting it out slowly. The weight of our situation bore down on him. "Okay," he said, finally. "Okay, we'll consider it. But first, we need to find a safe place to stay today. And then, we'll decide."

Noticing the silence had returned again, I turned to Tessa and noticed she had been quiet throughout I and Steve's argument. Tessa lifted up her eyes from her child and turned to look at us with her gun still in her hand. Now that it was daylight, I could see her more clearly than I did in the graveyard.

"I'm not going anywhere." Tessa finally said.

I took a moment to look at Tessa, I was shocked by the ferocious intent in her voice. Tessa, who I used to know as a kind and soft-spoken person, had changed into a strong fighter who was prepared to defend herself and her own. It was a striking and admirable transformation.

A monument to the horror she had just been through, her hands were slightly trembling despite maintaining a tight grasp on the shotgun. She had never before appeared so determined, with her jaw set and her eyes blazing with a mix of rage and resolve.

"But Tessa, it's not safe," Steve said, his voice heaving with anxiety. "Not for Theo, not even for us."

With a sharp frown, Tessa interrupted him. "Steve, I'm done running. This is where we live all our lives. Theo was born here, and we intended to raise him there as well. Why are we supposed to leave? Why should we be the ones who have to live in continual fear?

"I understand, Tess," Steve said again. "However, it is no longer simply about us. Theo's security is at stake."

She inhaled deeply while maintaining her attention on Steve. "I cannot and will not continue to live a life of hiding. Steve, I'm sick and tired of being the victim. I won't allow them to take our child again when they already did it once. We must address this head-on.

I hesitated and was cautious with my words. "Tessa, a strategy is required if we are going to stay. Without understanding what to expect, we cannot just confront them."

She nodded slowly, her ferocious tenacity softened by a hint of softness. "I'm aware. But I'm over being afraid." she said, staring down at me with the ferocious determination in her eyes.

Steve sighed and rubbed his temples. He stretched out his hands to Tessa, held it tight and sighed, "Okay, we'll fight. On the other hand, we approach it wisely. Together, we complete it.

I couldn't help but be worried by their fortitude as I observed the two of them leaning on one another for support. They were prepared to stand tall and fight back an enemy we didn't understand or its followers in masks.

Tessa turned to look at me with tears in her eyes. "You think they stop at Theo? No they won't," she said as she wrapped her hands around her baby protectively. "Whatever, it is, I'm going to get to the bottom of it."

Tessa's words hung heavy in the car. The atmosphere was thick with tension, and the weight of her statement bore down on us. The silence stretched between us, punctuated only by the soft hum of the car's engine and the faint sounds of life outside. Her fierce determination, juxtaposed with the vulnerability in her eyes, painted a haunting picture of a mother ready to go to any lengths to protect her child.

I turned to face her, locking my gaze with hers. "Tessa," I began, my voice gentle yet firm, "I know how you feel. We're all scared. And I swear, we're going to do everything in our power to make sure Theo is safe. But we need to be smart about this."

She nodded, wiping away a tear that had started to roll down her cheek. "I just can't believe this is happening. Our own town, people we've known our whole lives, betraying us like this."

The pain in her voice was palpable. It felt like a blade slicing through the air. The realization of the depth of the betrayal we'd faced was hitting us hard. That our very neighbors could be part of something so dark and twisted was a bitter pill to swallow.

Tessa's eyes pierced into me, glistening with a combination of pain and resolve. She exuded a fierceness that I had never before noticed in her. A fierce protective instinct had taken the place of the fragility and fear I had seen earlier in the evening. Theo felt her tightening hold as if she were trying to protect him from the air around us.

"I won't let them hurt my baby," she muttered, her voice quivering a little." No one will ever touch him once more."

I gently nodded in agreement after realizing how steadfast she was. "Tessa, we'll get through this together," I said. "But we need to be smart about it."

As we spoke, I looked outside of the window and noticed the townspeople were up already, each going about their daily activities. I wondered who was who among these people and if they really were who they said they were. It was a scary thought.

Every face I came across seems to vanish into a haze of uncertainty and mistrust. I used to purchase pastries from Mrs. Whitman, the baker, every Sunday morning as she was setting up her stall. Was she just a regular baker, or did those sweet eyes conceal horrible secrets as well? Old Mr. Anderson, the town's librarian, was sweeping the steps leading up to the library. He always seemed to know just the right book to recommend. How many enigmas did he really understand?

Once sounding like music, the children's laughter on the streets now had a sinister undertone. Were their parents involved in this as well?

Were these little children being brainwashed into this evil world? I felt chills run down my spine at the idea.

At the main junction, I saw Officer Dan, the town's sheriff, controlling traffic. I experienced a wave of discomfort. Could there be a role for law enforcement? Were there any people we could really rely on? I used to fish with Officer Dan on the weekends, so the idea that he was a part of something so evil was difficult for me to accept.

Tessa tightened her grip on Theo as the car proceeded, and like me, she kept her eyes darting about. Her apprehension and stress were palpable to me. The town, which had once felt like a cozy, welcoming hug, now seemed to be closing in on him.

I returned my attention to Steve, who had a tightened jaw and appeared to be deep in contemplation. We could all feel the weight of our newly discovered truth. A reality where trust was a luxury we couldn't afford and where faces were masks. It would take everything we had to get through the intricate maze of shadows and secrets that had now taken over the gorgeous village we once called home.

I felt determination weigh heavily inside of me. I was aware that this wouldn't be simple, but I couldn't let it go. It was those voices. I couldn't dismiss the possibility that people I knew, had spoken to, and trusted would be complicit in such a nefarious and evil endeavor. What extent did this take? They either voluntarily participated or were being controlled. I had to learn more.

The town's librarian, Mr. Anderson, was well-known across the neighborhood. He was an elderly, feeble man who had watched several generations of the kids in our town grow up. He helped us on our scholastic travels with a kind heart and a patient hand. It was, to put it mildly, upsetting to think that he would be involved in something like this.

Miss Clara, on the other hand, was a young, vibrant woman who was constantly energized and enthusiastic about her work. She had a talent for bringing life to even the most dull topics. But now that I think back on it, there had been indications. Numerous seemingly unrelated details stood out, like her abrupt absences from school, her tendency to daydream during talks, and her unusually fervent interest in the town's past, notably its storied stories and legends.

I inhaled deeply and exhaled slowly. I had to travel the unpredictable and dangerous path that lay in front of me. not only for Theo's sake but also for the town as a whole. Whatever it was, this evil had been allowed to fester in our neighborhood for far too long. It was time to eliminate it, bring it into the open, and put an end to its tyranny.

But first, I needed to get additional knowledge, and I thought a decent place to start would be the library or a school where these people are. Both contained antiquated books, records, and documents that would provide some insight into what was taking place. I was hoping to find the solution to this enigma within those dingy pages.

I peered out the window as the car moved forward and observed the deserted homes, calm streets, and the silhouette of the town's church against the blue sky. Everything appeared foreboding, and every wind gust carried a secretive whisper. But I remained adamant. I vowed to do whatever it took to shield Tessa, Steve, Theo, and the rest of the town from this horror. I was all in because the stakes had never been higher.

I walked back to my house that morning, covered in dirt and sweat and all I wanted to was to take a bath.

As I stepped into my house, I started to feel increasingly uneasy while I was wandering around my home. My home's neat appearance was startlingly out of place. I've always been a little disorganized; it was almost like it was part of who I was. My living area was typically marked by books scattered across the coffee table, my jacket slung over the couch, and shoes dumped carelessly next to the door. However, everything was now tidy. Too tidy.

I entered the kitchen with caution as the hairs on the back of my neck stood up. Typical stack of dirty dishes? Gone. The counters? Spotless. The haphazard mugs I usually left around following my late-night caffeine fixes? arranged in the cabinets in a tidy manner.

I entered the bedroom, which had a strangely open door. I've always kept it shut. I carefully opened it and was greeted by another image of unnerving orderliness. The sheets were perfectly smooth and the bed was made. My disorganized clothing was carefully folded and set on the chair.

My spine began to tingle. Has anyone been here before? The entire set-up gave off the impression that it was intended to send me a subdued message or to disturb me. Who, though, would do this? Even more crucially, why? Was it another trick question from those figures in cloaks, or was it something else entirely?

Expecting to see yet another instance of disorganized chaos, I hurried to the restroom. But at least the toothpaste cap I always neglected to refill and the wet towel I'd left on the floor that morning were still there.

I took a big breath and realized I couldn't remain. Not when every nook and cranny of my own house felt contaminated by a presence. I hurriedly went to my bedroom, threw my clothes off on my bed and stepped into the bathroom for a quick warm shower.

When the water first rushed over my skin, it felt soothing. I shut my eyes and allowed the tranquil streams to wash away the dirt, the dread, and the memories of the previous night. I made an effort to picture a world in which everything had returned to normal and disturbing dreams and ominous figures in dark clothing were a thing of the past. I momentarily forgot the horrors I'd just been through as the rhythmic drumming of water droplets against the tiles seemed to surround me in safety.

I lathered up in soap and scrubbed layers of perspiration and grime off my body as the water cascaded over me. Both physically and emotionally, the evening's events had taken their toll. This was the basic purification I needed to feel like myself again.

But as the minutes passed, I started to detect a slight increase in the water's temperature. An initially soothing warmth started to change into an uncomfortable heat. The water resisted my attempts to turn the knob to a colder setting. The soft streams that had seemed soothing seconds earlier felt searing now.

As the heat increased, panic set in. I experienced a burning sensation on my skin and a sensation of being immersed in boiling water. I struggled with the shower controls in a desperate attempt to reach out, but it was ineffective. The water felt hotter than lava while obviously in the "cold" setting. Around me, the steam grew thicker, making it more difficult to see and breathe.

I didn't waste any more time and lunged for the shower curtain, shoving it aside, then leaped out, nearly tripping on the moist bathroom tiles. Red marks were beginning to appear on my body, and I could feel them.

As I jumped out of the bathroom. My eyes caught a dark shadow in the corner of his room. I walked in slowly into my room, careful to be sure I was seeing the right thing.

My heart was beating, so I cautiously moved in closer while squinting my eyes to see better in the poorly illuminated space. The shadow appeared to move and twist while stationary, almost as if it were mocking me. Every nerve in my body begged me to leave the room and run away, yet an odd fascination held me there. I had to understand.

The dark shadow's outline became more distinct as I drew near. It was only my shirt; it wasn't some frightening creature or another shrouded figure. Not just any shirt, though—the one I had earlier thrown on the bed. I tentatively reached out to touch it, but then I remembered. I threw it on the bed. I didn't hang it on the wall.

My thoughts were racing. Was I losing my memory or was there a visitor while I was in the shower? A cursory scan of the space revealed no further indications of disturbance. The window was properly locked, and my possessions appeared to be unharmed.

But I started to get a strange vibe. Who or what had been in the room if not me, as I didn't hang the shirt?

I picked up the shirt and threw it back on the bed after balling it up. I tried to slow down my pounding heart by taking a deep breath. I couldn't afford to indulge in crazy fantasies. The border between reality and fantasy seemed to be blurring just now, so I needed to be extra cautious.

I turned to look back at the wall and a horrifying scene unfolded in front of me. My eyes widened.

It was a blood-red statement on the wall were the words:

"You ARE NEXT!"

It was scribbled menacingly on the wall. My spine began to tingle. Each letter's strong, dark strokes gave the impression of slightly dripping, as though the message had just been painted. My stomach turned when I instantly detected the metallic odor of blood.

Fear overcame me. I stumbled back, my chest thumping furiously. I rapidly looked about the space, looking for any other alterations or potential threats. Everything appeared to be unharmed, but I had lost all faith.

The space seems to have lost all warmth at once. The inscription on the wall was vivid and blood-red, screaming danger. I tried to understand what was in front of me as I stood there for a brief moment while paralyzed.

"You ARE NEXT!"

Although the message was obvious, the motivation behind it gave me the chills.

As my mind raced, the color left my face. It was unsettling to think that someone had been in my room close enough to scribble this message without my knowledge. And it appeared that I was their newest target.

I moved in closer to examine the wall in an attempt to muster up some bravery. The fluid was brand-new and a little drippy.

But was that blood, really? Or was it just a nasty ruse to make me feel even worse? In any case, it was an outright threat, and I felt a surge of rage come over me.

I decided to take a picture as proof, so I took my phone off the side table. I noticed an unusual reflection as the camera flashed. A faint figure of a person standing outside could be seen through the glass behind me. I turned around with my heart racing but didn't find anything. There is only the quiet, deserted street outside.

I experienced a sense of constriction in the space and could detect the weight of ominous eyes on me. I threw some clothes on, gathered my necessities, and left the house as quickly as possible. I wasn't going to hang around to find out what they had in store for me next because whoever or whatever was responsible for this was nearby.

# Three

## CEREMONY, SACRIFICE, SALVATION

The silence in the chapel felt unsettling, like if a thick blanket were covering you and smothering you simultaneously. I was on one of the ancient wooden benches. I had been on the hard wood for too long, and my knees hurt, but I was afraid to get up. My hands were folded and my head was resting on them, which was resting on the back of the pew in front of me. I was worn out, my body collapsing from the constant terrors and restless nights.

I continued to mumble prayers, the words came out of my mouth in a stream that was constant and frantic. "Hallowed be the name of Our Father, who art in heaven." I stopped, swallowing forcefully, my throat itchy and dry. I clutched to the words like they were a lifeline, even though they seemed hollow. I had to think they were getting through.

The smell of incense filled the air, filling my nostrils and sinking in my lungs with its sweet, smoky flavor. The scent was well-known to me and had usually made me feel at ease, but now it was overbearing and nearly oppressive. The chapel exuded an ethereal serenity that made the hairs on the back of my neck stand on edge. It was almost unearthly. It was as if you were imprisoned in a dream, where everything seemed a little strange and surreal.

The area is filled with a kaleidoscope of hues from the stained glass windows that line the walls. With vibrant, dazzling detail, biblical images were brought to life in each window, telling a unique story. The one closest to me showed Christ's suffering at his crucifixion, carved into the glass. Shatters of deep blue and blood-red caught the light, illuminating the pews in an eerie glow. I discovered that I was fixating on the image of Christ, who had closed His eyes in endless agony. That agony reminded me that I wasn't alone in my suffering, which was a strange kind of consolation.

I tried to close my eyes and concentrate on the prayers. My mind was filled with dark, twisting things that were partially visible and partially imagined. They were there, waiting for a moment of weakness, and I could feel their evil presence closing in on me. My hands became more clenched, the knuckles going white. "Deliver us from evil." I said barely audible words in a whisper.

I felt a chill go down my spine and I made myself glance up. A gentle golden light enveloped the altar at the front of the church, with the candles flickering ever so slowly. It was supposed to be a reassuring sight, but today it seemed far away, almost unachievable. The saint statues that lined the walls appeared to be staring at me with unwavering eyes, calm expressions that were simultaneously accusing and peaceful. I couldn't get rid of the impression that they were evaluating me and were aware of my innermost secrets.

I moved on the pew uneasily, my muscles kicking up a fuss. The wooden planks pressed into my back, causing a persistent, dull pain that oddly enough I was glad of, It was something concrete, something substantial to concentrate on. I looked about the church, taking in the well-known features. The matching rows of pews stretched out in a flawless symmetry. The ceiling was tall and arched, appearing to reach the sky, with intersecting beams resembling the remains of a long-ago, dormant creature.

My eyes landed on the platform, where Father Michael was usually seen giving passionate sermons that echoed throughout the sanctuary. Except for me, the church was desolate tonight, and the pulpit was empty. It felt like both a comfort and a burden to be left alone. Nobody was there to witness my frailty or my anxiety, yet nobody was there to console me or promise me that everything would be well.

I inhaled deeply, the air in my lungs harsh and frigid. I had to gather my thoughts. I had to think that all of this was happening for a reason, that there was a reason I was suffering. To keep the darkness at bay, I had to believe in something. "Thy will be done, and thy kingdom come." The words came out as a frantic scream for assistance, a plea.

The shadows appeared to elongate as they crept across the ground in my direction. Their voices were like a sibilant hiss in the recesses of my thoughts, and I could almost hear them speaking. I attempted to silence the murmurs by shaking my head, but they only got louder and more persistent. Squeezing my eyes tight, I saw a tumbling, disorganized tangle of darkness behind my eyelids. "Give us our daily bread this day." The prayers were slipping through my fingers like sand, and I was losing my hold.

Once more, I opened my eyes and gazed at the crucifix situated above the altar. There hung the figure of Christ. My attention was drawn to His face and the pain that was inscribed there. In the middle of my chaos, I attempted to find some form of serenity and power from it. "Forgive us our trespasses, as we forgive those who trespass against us..." My words were nearly lost in the largeness of the chapel as my voice dwindled to a whisper.

The walls were illuminated by the streaming sunlight and the flickering candles, creating a macabre ballet of forms twisting and swirling. I was terrified and enthralled as I watched them. They moved with a purpose that eluded me, as if they had a life of their own. The murmurs intensified, a chorus of voices that got closer to overpowering me. I tried to ignore them by pressing my palms to my ears, but they persisted nonetheless.

"Lead us not into temptation." The words stuck in my throat as I gasped. The darkness drew nearer, weighing heavily on me. Their icy breath touched my skin, sending a shiver down my spine. "But protect us from evil." But I kept at it.

I felt as though the walls and roof of the cathedral were closing in on me. The hues of the stained glass windows blended together in an erratic swirl. I gripped the pew tightly, pressing my fingers into the wood. The murmurs intensified to an unbearable roar in my ears.

And then the cacophony stopped, as abruptly as it had started. The darkness withdrew, resolving into the church's corners. Again, the silence had returned to the air. I sighed in relief, my whole body quivering from weariness. With tears flowing down my face, I glanced up at the crucifix. I muttered, "Amen," trying to make myself heard over the large, empty room.

I remained there for a long while, feeling the silence envelop me in a shroud. Even though the church was deserted, I didn't feel alone. Something felt, something unseen, was present here. I had a glimmer of hope, a tiny flicker of light in the dark, but I wasn't sure if it was God or something else.

The church had evolved into my haven, the only place I could find any kind of comfort and relief from the unrelenting horror that had been plaguing me for the last several months. I could almost believe that I was secure here, that the horrors that awaited me outside couldn't penetrate these ancient stone walls, protected by the vigilant eyes of saints and angels.

Strange things had begun to happen to me again after seeing the bloodstained "YOU ARE NEXT" on my bedroom wall coupled with the trickling and the metallic smell blended well with the musty air in my room. Things were barely the same.

Even now, thinking about that evening still made me shudder. With a scream stuck in my throat, I staggered back and my legs gave way under me. I recall scurrying out the room, my heart thumping so intensely that it overpowered my ability to think clearly. I was unable to stay there. I couldn't be by myself.

At that point, I had to move to Tessa and Steve's place. When I showed up at their doorstep, terrified and with crazy eyes, stammering out the story of the gory message, they couldn't hold back, not after the terrible experience with those demon beasts that we had the night before. They offered me a place to stay and a safe sanctuary as they welcomed me in. They, too, had begun to notice odd, unpleasant things happening to them that made no sense. Together, we became entangled in this terrifyingly fantastical tale, with an evil power influencing our lives from the shadows.

Living with Tessa and Steve was a minor consolation. We attempted to make sense of the turmoil that had taken over our lives as we discussed our anxieties. But even with their backing, the fear pursued us, sneaky and unrelenting. Unusual sounds, shadows that moved on their own, and an increasing feeling of fear characterized our nights.

My sole haven in the middle of all this was the church. I could bow down in prayer here, finding comfort in the known customs and the reassuring silence. I could almost feel the church's presence, a serene glow that surrounded me like a shield. The colorful light from the stained glass windows, which featured vivid pictures of biblical scenes, gave a calming yet bizarre aura across the pews.

The constant coolness of the air within was a pleasant diversion from the unbearable heat of my worry. The aroma of incense and aged wood soothed my jaded senses. There was a sense of continuity and hope brought about by the flickering candles on the altar, their flames swirling and throwing soft shadows. I felt as though my nervousness was absorbed by the church's walls itself, leaving me with a shaky sense of tranquility.

Whenever they needed a break, Steve and Tessa would frequently accompany me here. In silence, we would sit together, each immersed in our own prayers and thoughts and seeking solace in the other's company.

Even with the little respites, I was constantly aware of my coming death. The graphic statement written on my wall served as a stark warning and an indication of far worse things to come.

I felt the weight of the world bearing down on me as I sat on the pew with my head bowed in prayer. The combination of fatigue, anxiety, and doubt made me feel as though I would lose my grip. However, in this hallowed area, I couldn't. Not yet.

During the weeks that followed the terrifying incidents that forced me to leave my house, I began to find the same serenity I found in the church with Tessa and Steve.

Their home soon became my haven; there, the warmth and laughter of their home hushed the whispers of the past and the darkness seemed less threatening. We were like a close-knit held together by the same objective: defending baby Theo and ourselves from whatever evil power had entered our life. Even on the worst days, Theo, who was growing to be a lively boy with infectious laughter, brightened our days.

Throughout the day, we strengthened the house and alternated in keeping an eye on one another. Steve transformed their house into a fortress by installing motion sensors and security cameras all over the property. Every night, we kept vigils to make sure that no area of the house remained unmonitored. I experienced a sense of safety and companionship during these times that I hadn't felt in months. Even with the impending danger, we took comfort in one another's company.

These were moments that seemed like heaven to me. The simple act of being surrounded by people who cared about me seemed to be keeping the nightmares and torments that had haunted me at bay. It seemed as though I had discovered a new family. Our relationship grew stronger with each meal we shared, each giggle, and each passionate talk.

This shaky calm was soon upended when Steve got a transfer out of town. It was a blow that none of us saw coming; it was quick and unexpected. Steve revealed the shocking information one evening when we were chatting about our plans for the following day in the living room. He had been working on the transfer for weeks, keeping me in the dark as he skillfully navigated the bureaucratic red tape. The room went quiet, shock and astonishment permeating the air when he eventually broke the news.

Steve clarified that he was taking advantage of a transfer that would allow him to further his career and give his family a brighter future. However, the timing could not be worse. We had just begun to feel confident and to think that we could handle whatever came our way as a team.

We were close to implementing our plans of confronting our suspect in town. We had our clue ready and we're going to produce sufficient evidence to hand to the police, ending this reign of terror once and for all.

I experienced a profound sensation of bereavement that moment. I had sensed something was off when he had been unusually quiet at dinner, pushing his food around his plate without really eating. When he finally broke the news, I felt a mixture of shock and betrayal. We had all been through so much together, and the thought of him leaving felt like a knife to the gut.

"What do you mean, you're leaving?" I asked, my voice sharp with disbelief. "We've been planning our defenses together, Steve. We've been through hell, and now you're just going to abandon us?"

Steve's face tightened, his jaw clenched. "Jason, it's not like that. This transfer is an opportunity for us. It's not just about me. It's about Tessa and our son. We can't keep living like this, constantly looking over our shoulders."

I couldn't believe what I was hearing. "You think moving away is going to solve everything? You think these... things won't follow you? We're safer together, Steve. We're stronger together."

The argument quickly escalated, voices rising and emotions flaring. Tessa tried to mediate, but the intensity of our disagreement drowned out her attempts to calm us down. We were both talking past each other, each too caught up in our own fears and frustrations to really listen.

Steve suddenly stood up, his chair scraping loudly against the ground. "Look, Jason," he said, turning to face me directly. His eyes were dark with determination and a hint of desperation. "We have a baby! A son! Who is wanted by a bunch of creeps we can't even identify in this goddamn town." He slammed his hands on the table, the sound reverberating through the room. "He deserves better. I want to protect my son."

The intensity of his words and the raw emotion behind them left me momentarily speechless. I could see the fear in his eyes, the fear of a father desperate to protect his child. It was a fear I could understand, even if I didn't agree with his decision.

Tessa, who had been standing off to the side, stepped forward. "Jason, I don't want to leave either," she said, her voice trembling with emotion. "But we have a son. I don't want to constantly be on edge, knowing he might be safe one moment and in danger the next. We have to think about what's best for him."

Her words hit me hard. I looked at Tessa, seeing the pain and fear etched on her face, and then back at Steve, whose resolve was unwavering. They were doing this for their child, and as much as I hated the idea of them leaving, I couldn't fault them for wanting to protect him.

The room fell into a heavy silence, the intensity of the argument hanging in the air like a thick fog. I took a deep breath, trying to steady myself. "I get it," I said finally, my voice subdued.

Steve's expression softened slightly, but his resolve didn't waver. "We'll stay in touch," he said. "We'll be there for each other, even if it's from a distance. But I have to do what's right for my family."

Tessa reached out and took my hand, her grip firm and reassuring. "We'll still be a team, Jason. We just need to be smart about this. We can't let our emotions cloud our judgment. Our son's safety has to come first."

I nodded, though the ache in my chest didn't lessen. "I understand," I said quietly. I wish I could tell them I didn't want to lose them and what we had.

"You're not losing us," Steve said as if he had just read my mind, his voice gentler now. "We're just making a change. We'll still be in this fight together, just in different ways."

Steve and Tessa's decision to leave was a turning point, a moment that marked the end of one chapter and the beginning of another. It wasn't an easy transition, but it was one I had to face all by myself.

The days appeared to fly by in a swirl of activities and feelings as Steve and Tessa's departure drew near. They had begun weeks in advance with packing, carefully going through their possessions. Tessa balanced the moving preparations with their son's demands. Amid the chaos, I made an effort to keep things as normal as possible by attending to our nightly vigils and according to the security precautions that Steve had painstakingly put in place. But the feeling of loss and uncertainty just grew stronger with every day that went by.

Steve made an effort to reassure me, promising to stay in touch and pay me a visit whenever he could. He tried to inject hope in a situation that was becoming more and more dire for me by talking about the opportunity the transfer would present for his family. His assurances, though sincere, sounded hollow to me. The situation was dire: I was losing all of my team members.

The day finally came for them to leave. I watched Steve load the last of his belongings into the car on the day of his departure, standing in the driveway. Tessa cuddled their son Theo, who was blissfully unaware of the gravity of the situation as he cooed. Steve gave me a strong hug, leaving a trail of silent thanks and regret. He repeated, his voice firm but a tinge of grief showing in his eyes. "Everything will be okay," he said. Tessa also returned the same gesture. I nodded, not knowing how to put into words how deeply I felt.

A knot formed in my throat as Steve drove off, the sound of his car disappearing into the distance. His leaving had left an emptiness that seemed to reverberate through the empty rooms of the house, and it was a deep sense of sorrow.

There has been an eerie silence since the morning after Steve and Tessa left. The absence of them left a yawning emptiness in the house that appeared to swallow all sounds. Overcoming my loneliness, I forced myself to follow our rituals that we had established. I felt the weight of isolation crashing down on me as I roamed the property's perimeter, updated our logs, and looked over the security cameras.

The house felt emptier than it had ever felt that night. I was sitting in the living room with a lot of questions and hidden anxieties, and the stillness was deafening. It felt like there were more shadows and darkness than I had ever experienced. I couldn't get rid of the idea that I was now more exposed, that the forces we were up against would see our vulnerability and take advantage of the chance to attack.

I made an effort to take comfort in our evening rituals, keeping up our watchfulness and the security precautions Steve had put in place. However, in his absence, there was a noticeable emptiness that none of us could ever fully replace. Despite her personal grief and the difficulties of moving into a new place, Tessa made a conscious effort to maintain contact. She kept in touch with me over the phone, giving me information on how they were adjusting to their new environment. Her voice was reassuring, reminding me that we were still a team.

Weeks passed, and I had a hard time adjusting to the new normal. It was as though the house had lost a significant portion of its soul. In an effort to maintain the sense of oneness we had previously enjoyed, I found myself withdrawing into recollections of our time together and reliving our talks and special moments.

Tessa's attempts to keep us in touch ended up becoming my lifeline. Her messages and phone conversations helped us stay connected even though we were physically apart by providing comfort and continuity in the face of uncertainty. Despite the distance between us, we found comfort in each other's company as we talked about everything and nothing at all.

Throughout it all, I clung to the hope that eventually, I would be able to fulfill Steve's ambition of leaving our community behind. I was full of longing and enthusiasm at the idea of joining them in their new life. I longed for a new beginning, an opportunity to rise above the ashes of the past and welcome a bright future.

But, I wasn't quite ready to go. Something held me bound to this godforsaken town, even with the pull of a new beginning with Steve, Tessa, and Theo. Perhaps it was the desperate attempt to comprehend the evil powers that had turned our lives upside down, or the longing for closure. Or maybe it was just a case of being stubborn and not wanting to give up the place that had been home. Since their departure, I've been quite busy with a lot of different things, all motivated by my need to find out what's going on in town.

The town itself has begun to shift as well. Not only did Steve and Tessa's departure leave an impression on me, but I also started to see other families packing up and moving out. The lively life that had once marked our community was only a shell of its former self as the formerly bustling streets got quieter. The town felt empty and more sinister than usual, as if an unseen force was shoving people away.

During a stroll in the neighborhood one afternoon, I noticed recognizable faces hidden beneath moving boxes and rental vehicles. Steve and Tessa's neighbors, Mr. and Mrs. Thompson, were packing their stuff into a van. Their three children who were usually so animated and chatty, stood silently by, holding onto their treasured toys. I looked at Mrs. Thompson, and for a split second, her face expressed the same perplexity and anxiety that I was experiencing. We gave each other a nod.

Over the next few days, I dug deeper to try to figure out why so many people were leaving. Talks with the surviving neighbors were reserved and hostile. People's eyes darted around, as if they thought danger would suddenly appear out of nowhere. The atmosphere of distrust and fear had replaced everything I was ever familiar with.

I started going to the local archives and poring over old municipal documents and newspapers, determined to find out the truth. Mrs. Edwards, the librarian, was one of the few people who hadn't packed up and departed. Her eyes were compassionate and she had a slight build, but she seemed to know everything. She gave me a knowing smile when I told her about my quest and showed me where the oldest documents were kept—in the rear of the library.

She whispered, "You're not the first to ask these questions, Jason," as she spoke quietly. "There have always been secrets in this town."

Days passed while I lost myself in the dusty archives for hours on end. I came up with articles concerning decades-old, inexplicable disappearances as well as spooky accounts of hauntings and unusual figure sightings in the town's surrounding woods.

The most unsettling find was an ancient diary concealed amidst the piles of abandoned literature. It belonged to a man who had resided in the town in the early 1900s. His journals described experiences he had had with eerie beings that resembled the ones we had encountered. He described customs and the efforts of the locals to stave off evil by making offerings and sacrifices. There was no mistaking the terror in his words, even if the last entry was smudged and almost unreadable. He talked about a darkness that will never go away from the community, a curse.

I experienced a revitalized feeling of intention, equipped with this fresh insight. I was unable to go just yet. Too many unanswered questions and loose ends remained. I had to know exactly how big of a problem we were facing. Perhaps, just perhaps, I could figure out how to stop the pattern and release the community from its troubled past.

I was watching the security camera footage one night when I noticed something that gave me the chills. A dark-cloaked figure standing at the boundary of the land. Even though it was hardly discernible, a shadow amid shadows, its presence could not be denied. It lingered for a few moments before vanishing into the darkness, and I froze, my heart thumping in my chest.

The figure's location was close to some bizarre markings that I discovered carved into the earth the next day. Though they were sloppily drawn, it was obvious what they meant to convey, a threat and a warning.

I experienced a rush of resolve in spite of the terror. This was no time for me to go. My nights were spent studying over the journal and attempting to comprehend its enigmatic contents, and my days were spent strengthening the house and erecting new traps and defenses.

Though the town had shrunk to a shell of its former self, its mysteries and history remained. I was resolved to reveal them and comprehend the gloom that had afflicted us for such a long time. I couldn't go until I confronted that darkness head-on and managed to free myself from its grip.

Something startled me back to the present and stopped my prayers. Startled, I peered around the church with my head up. It had been a quiet but clear sound, like a gentle shuffling or a whisper carried by an invisible wind. I looked around the vacant pews, trying to figure out what was causing the ruckus, my heart thumping in my chest.

The church was as silent as it had been when I had first walked in, but the silence had become heavy, as if a dark force had thickened the very air. The area was formerly filled with a calm, colorful brightness from the stained glass windows, but now it appeared as though they were casting long, ominous shadows. The vivid colors of the saints and angels appeared more sinister, almost frightening, as though they were observing me with disfavor or caution.

With my senses sharp and my muscles tight, I carefully got up from the pew. The sound reverberated in my head, enhancing the subsequent quietness. I walked down the aisle a few times, hesitantly, my feet scarcely making a sound on the aged wooden ground. I felt more uneasy because every ancient board's creak seemed to ricochet throughout the deserted cathedral.

"Hey?" I let out a quiet cry, my voice small and insignificant in the big room. There was just quiet, terrible silence that seemed to loom larger by the moment. The church's front altar loomed in the twilight, its crucifix creating a lengthy shadow that stretched across the ground. The whole building seemed to be holding its breath, as if something significant was about to occur.

I made a slow round while glancing around every nook and cranny. The pews, which had supported me in my prayers, suddenly appeared to be barriers, possible hiding spots for something invisible. It was difficult for me to breathe because of the heavy silence, and I got the uneasy feeling that someone was watching me.

I inhaled deeply, attempting to slow down my palpitating heart. Perhaps it was simply my imagination, exaggerated by the anxiety and tension that had become my daily companions.

I settled back on the pew and resumed my prayers.

It had been strangely quiet these past couple of days. There was an oppressive calm that seemed to engulf me from the inside out in place of the typical sensation of dread, the continual feeling of being watched, and the dangers hiding in the shadows. The town seemed to be holding its breath, anticipating anything to break the stillness.

I couldn't get rid of the notion that this quiet moment was only the beginning of a storm. It seemed as though the evil power that had tormented me  had only withdrawn to reappear stronger and deliver a more devastating blow because the silence was too perfect, too complete. The lack of the typical distractions did not calm my worries; on the contrary, it increased my level of anxiousness. The silence was oppressive, bearing down on me like a tangible burden.

There was an eerie silence in place of the usual creaks and groans that came with the old building shifting. The town's typical sounds, like the far-off buzz of traffic, neighbors chatting, and children laughing, had all but vanished. It appeared as though even the birds had left, their melodies replaced by a deafening quiet.

I discovered that I was aimlessly meandering around the home, trying to find some indication of movement or sound to break the silence. It felt like a pointless habit to monitor the security cameras and patrol the perimeter, which had once been reassuring. After the flag of the dark image which felt like a dream, there was nothing to observe or listen to. The images from the cameras showed nothing except silent homes and deserted streets; there was no indication that anyone was moving.

The toughest times were at night. It seemed as though the world had come to a complete stop because of the absolute silence. I used to lie in bed and listen for any sound, like a car driving away, a dog barking, or even my own heartbeat. However, nothing was present. As if the walls were closing in, the darkness seemed to enclose me, dense and unbreakable.

It was difficult to sleep. When I finally did fall asleep, the same oppressive silence that hounded my awake hours pervaded my dreams. My heart would be racing in my chest when I would wake up, and the silence would be like a leaden blanket. There was an engulfing silence all about me, an unseen force I was powerless to shake.

It seems that even the house had changed. There were no longer the typical creaks and groans, only a deathly calm.

In an attempt to break the spell of stillness, I sought to get in touch with Tessa. Steve was now distant as he had work and a different responsibility to worry about. I was never completely alone when I heard Tessa's voice, and her calls were like a lifeline. But the feeling of loneliness that had descended upon me was irreversible, even with her upbeat updates about Theo and their new existence.

I'd been struggling with depression and mental health problems for days, and they appeared determined to drown me. The stifling silence that had descended upon the town crept into my thoughts like a heavy, unmoving fog. More times than I can remember, I ended up in the hospital looking for some type of healing or a solution to the problem that was inside of me.

Various antidepressants were recommended by the doctors, but none of them seemed to work. Every medicine I took felt like a tiny concession, a last-ditch effort to reclaim some kind of normalcy. However, the gloom within me was sneaky; it encircled my ideas and smothered any glimmer of hope. My agony was partially eased by the meds, but it remained unresolved. The feeling of hopelessness persisted, like a big weight against my chest.

The days blended together in sticky sadness and a dull fog. Every morning, I would awaken with a sinking sensation in my stomach, dreading the hours that lay ahead. After serving as a haven, the house suddenly seemed like a jail. I felt more alone because the rooms were empty and the walls felt like they were closing in on me.

I made an effort to go through the motions, pushing myself to take a shower, eat, and take my medication. However, I had the impression that nothing was meaningful and that I was just going through the motions. The chores that used to feel like a regular were now like herculean struggles. I would frequently find myself retiring to my bed and pulling the covers over my head in a hopeless attempt to escape the crushing weight of my own thoughts since even the most basic tasks were exhausting.

Sleep was a torture and a haven. Whenever I did manage to get to sleep, I had terrifying, dark dreams. My heart would race when I would wake up in a cold sweat, and the stifling silence would seem even more terrible in the darkness. In my room, the silence seemed thicker and the shadows in the corners seemed to loom larger. It seemed like the evil that was hiding in the shadows was attempting to cripple me from the inside out.

The physicians would always ask the same questions over and over again when I visited the hospital. Yet their tone is a mix of real concern and clinical detachment. "How are you feeling today, Jason?" "Have you noticed any improvement with the new medication?" "Are you experiencing any side effects?" Though the words felt empty, I would respond as honestly as I could. The feeling of looming doom and the gnawing emptiness that hung over me like a dark cloud were beyond words.

I started to dread these visits since the bright lighting and immaculate rooms would just make me feel more hopeless.

During very difficult days, the idea of ending everything would nudge its way into my thoughts like a tempting whisper, promising relief from the agony. But I knew that I couldn't give up, even in my lowest points. I only needed the recollections of my mom, Tessa, Steve and tiny

Theo to stay connected to this world; they were like a thin thread that I grabbed onto for dear life.

Throughout the chilly void of my days, Tessa's calls briefly ceased. Perhaps she had other burdens to deal with. I couldn't blame her. I tried to reach out a couple times. Theo had been going through a number of phases and she had to be there for him.

When I was feeling more coherent. Sometimes I would drag myself outside in the hopes that the sunlight and fresh air would cheer me up. However, the town seemed abandoned, with its streets devoid of people.

I could tell evil was patient. Its goal was to exhaust me, to eat me from the inside out. As I sat on the pew, the noise persisted. The sound echoed through the quiet of the cathedral, making my heart race. The faint sound of rustling gave way to the sound of clear footsteps resonating against the old stone walls. With the hush that had descended upon the hallowed area, every step echoed like a drumbeat. The suffocating silence that had engulfed me strengthened its hold, making breathing difficult.

I strained to hear the footsteps and tried to figure out where they were coming from. The large, empty church allowed the sound to reverberate off the tall ceilings and stained glass windows. A drop of perspiration trickled down my temple as I became anxious about what or who might appear out of the darkness.

The footsteps became more deliberate and louder. My body tightened, every instinct telling me to go, yet I couldn't move from where I was. What had seemed like a consoling silence had taken on a sinister quality, as though the congregation was holding its breath in anticipation of the impending disclosure. Long, swaying shadows that appeared to dance in anticipation were created by the flickering candlelight.

The air thickened with the approaching footfall, the silence nearly oppressive. I scanned the dimly lit inside, looking for any indication of movement with my eyes. I could feel a heavy, unseen weight bearing down on me; it was strain. What had previously been a peaceful sanctuary was more like a set for a demonic play.

The footsteps abruptly stopped, just as they had begun. Deafening quiet ensued, a void that seemed to consume all sound. I forced myself to breathe while the silence weighed down on me almost physically. Time seemed to have stopped, immobilizing me for a minute in pure horror.

At last, a figure stepped into the faint light, emerging from the shadows. I gasped in recognition at the sight of the well-known face. It was Martin, a friend I had in middle school. A flood of relief swept over me, like if a thick blanket had been lifted. The stifling silence lifted. I released a breath I hadn't realized I'd been holding until my stiff muscles relaxed.

Martin's familiar features were a welcome sight in the eerie calm of the chapel, and his presence soothed my jangled nerves. There was a sensation of tranquility that replaced the suffocating atmosphere that had been weighing me down.

The church was no longer filled with the heavy silence that had descended upon it moments ago; instead, the air felt lighter and more permeable. A sense of normalcy was left behind as the sounds of Martin's footsteps faded into the distance. My heart began to relax, and the fear that had crept into my thoughts began to recede like a dark tide.

Martin was staring at me, and even though we didn't say anything, his presence told me a lot. It was then that I understood how much the silence had affected me, how my concerns had grown more intense because there was no human connection. The unexpected arrival of Martin was a lifeline that kept me from falling into despair.

The church no longer seemed so forbidding, but it had once seemed like a tomb. Instead of casting ominous shadows, the flickering candlelight now produced a cozy, welcoming glow. The windows with stained glass, which had formerly loomed large and menacing, now seemed to be telling tales of redemption and hope. The stifling quiet had vanished from the room with Martin's arrival, and in its place was a cozy, homey feeling.

There was hope, I could not help it, as I sat there and took in the sight of my old friend. The mere sight of a familiar face seemed to lessen the evil force that had looked so strong only moments before.

Martin was wearing a sleeveless top that emphasized his well-defined arms, which were both covered in a variety of tattoos that each had a backstory. His jeans fit his body perfectly, despite being robust and weathered. His typical nonchalant confidence was enhanced by the somewhat asymmetrical baseball cap perched atop his head. Martin's bluster was obvious and a sharp contrast to the stifling silence that had descended on the cathedral just seconds before.

With a casual gait, he strode across the room, his footsteps resonating off the stone walls and lending the otherwise quiet sanctuary a sense of life. His tattoos were accentuated by the flickering candlelight, giving the impression that they were dancing and changing with every step he took. Even with the baseball cap partially covering his face, there was a determined expression on his face that reminded me of the fearless friend I had known when we were younger.

His gaze swept the cathedral as he made his way down the aisle, taking in the ambience and emptiness that had so thoroughly scared me. He walked without faltering and showed no indication of the anxiety that had immobilized me. Martin's presence filled the cathedral with a force of nature, a jolt of vigor amid the deathly emptiness.

I watched him get closer, my heart rate calming down from its racing intensity. Martin's steady strides disturbed the suffocating silence that had appeared to magnify every creak and rustling. I was dragged back from the brink of my own worries by that sound, which anchored me. His typical arrogance was like a light in the darkness, so comforting and familiar.

Though he seemed out of place in the sacred, solemn environment of the cathedral, Martin's simple, casual outfit was ideal for him. The sleeveless shirt and pants reflected his carefree demeanor and his reluctance to live up to expectations.

Seated in the pew, I couldn't help but think back on how our lives had connected in the strangest ways as he got closer and the route that had brought him here.

Martin was unique from the beginning. He had always been drawn to the enigmatic and unfamiliar in middle school. Martin was enthralled with the paranormal, while the rest of us played computer games or went to sports. He would lose hours reading literature on old folklore, ghosts, and UFOs. His bedroom was crammed with oddities, crystals, and antique books that seemed more at home in a museum than a suburban house.

Martin was the target of many jokes throughout middle school because of his interests. Children can be nasty, and Martin was labeled as the "weird kid" because of his preoccupation with the paranormal. They would constantly make fun of his views and call him derogatory things. In one instance, the entire school laughed as he flinched in shock because someone had hidden a fake spider in his locker.

The bully eventually took a toll. Martin became more and more reclusive, immersing himself in his world of puzzles and novels. When we got to high school, he was hardly there because he thought he would be safer and happier away from the cruelty of his peers, so his mother made the decision to homeschool him. By making that choice, Martin was able to explore his fascination with the paranormal to a greater extent without fear of criticism or mockery from others.

While Martin was deep in his studies of the paranormal, the rest of us were getting ready for college and going to prom. He had complete support from his mother, who gave him all the tools he required to keep learning.

Martin turned his house into a haven and a fount of paranormal information. He gathered tools, books, and antiques from around the globe. He trained himself to use Ouija boards, dowsing rods, and other tools for paranormal communication. There was a subtle scent of herbs and incense in his house, and there were pictures and symbols of protection all over the walls.

Martin developed into something of an authority in his industry over time. In addition to writing articles for several paranormal journals, he helped people rid their homes of undesired ghosts and performed investigations. He became well-known and, instead of being the "strange kid," a respected member of the tiny but close-knit group of paranormal aficionados.

Martin and I maintained communication despite our growing distance from one another. I was impressed by his commitment and his steadfast faith in the afterlife. Even though I couldn't entirely comprehend his world, I was nonetheless moved by his boldness and devotion. It required a unique type of bravery to follow a road that was so frequently greeted with doubt and derision.

As I sat there in the church, I was thankful that Martin was there. He had conquered his personal demons and come out on top. He was someone I needed right now.

Martin strode down the aisle, his eyes darting over the stained glass window. I knew I had to get help from someone to combat these evil powers. I was mentally and emotionally spent as a result of the terrifying experiences and the ongoing sense of being pursued. To combat these invisible dangers, I needed allies, someone who could recognize the darkness that hid in the shadows and stand with me.

Martin would prove to be an invaluable ally because of his unwavering courage and competence in the paranormal, even though our paths had diverged since middle school. He had encountered comparable obstacles and triumphed over them. The terrible entities that plagued my life could only be faced with the knowledge and expertise he possessed.

My attempt at finding comfort in my Christian religion had been to take sanctuary in the church's well-known customs and prayers. I felt at ease for a while after that. I found momentary solace from the chaos both inside and around me in the church's sanctuary, the reassuring hymns, and the confidence of divine protection. Yet, It wasn't enough.

The demons and those who worshiped them were unwavering. Operating in secrecy, they could unleash surprise attacks that would leave a path of terror and hopelessness in their wake. They persisted like a malevolent shadow in spite of my prayers and efforts to deepen my faith; they would not be driven away by simple ceremony and verbalization.

I am a drowning man, while Martin's presence was like a lifeline. Accompanied by years of study and firsthand experience, he brought with him a pragmatic attitude. His own experiences with the paranormal were used to support my worries and doubts, rather than dispelling them. He was resolute and resilient, as seen by his tattoos, which served as emblems of his voyage and defiance of the unknown.

I felt like I had a new purpose as we revived our connection and formed an alliance. I had been alone with the terrible entities that had ruined my life for so long, we could face them head-on.

Our next steps were planned, notes were compared, and hours were spent talking about our experiences. Martin exposed me to tricks of the trade that provided some protection from evil spirits, such as protective rituals and symbols. We were able to safely traverse the perilous seas of the paranormal because of his extensive expertise and insightful advice.

As Martin bounced through the pew aisles, his playful demeanor brought a rare moment of levity to the heavy atmosphere that had weighed on me for so long. His casual irreverence toward the sacred surroundings was typical of him. It's definitely Martin-like to find humor even in the darkest of times.

"Talking to daddy Jesus again now, J," Martin quipped, a mischievous twinkle in his eyes as he addressed me by my childhood nickname. I couldn't help but smile at his antics, the tension in my shoulders easing slightly in response to his infectious energy.

I sighed deeply, rising from the pew and meeting Martin's gaze. "I just needed some guidance before taking this next big step, Mart. It's not an easy one," I admitted, my voice tinged with uncertainty and apprehension. The decision weighing on me was monumental, fraught with risks and unknowns.

Martin chuckled, his laughter filling the church like a welcome echo. "Well, if you're gonna ask someone for help for this, it shouldn't be Jesus," he teased, his tone light but laced with underlying seriousness.

Martin playfully patted me on the shoulder, I turned my gaze to the image of Jesus on the wall. The stained glass window depicted a serene figure, bathed in soft hues of blue and gold. The image had always brought me comfort, a reminder of faith and divine protection in times of need.

But now, as I stared at the depiction of Jesus, I found myself grappling with doubts. The challenges we were up against were not easily explained or resolved by traditional beliefs alone. The malevolent forces that had tormented me seemed impervious to prayers and supplications. I needed practical solutions, tangible defenses against the darkness that threatened to consume me.

Martin's presence beside me was reassuring. He understood my doubts and fears, yet he never wavered in his support. His unconventional approach to the paranormal had opened my eyes to new possibilities, to a world where faith and reason could coexist, where spiritual guidance could be supplemented by practical knowledge and experience.

I turned back to Martin, gratitude swelling within me. "Thanks for being here, Mart," I said sincerely, my voice low but filled with sincerity. "I don't know how I would navigate this without you."

Martin grinned, his expression softening with genuine warmth. "Hey, we're in this together, J. Whatever it takes, we'll figure it out," he reassured me, his eyes reflecting a determination that mirrored my own.

I stood there, facing the image of Jesus in the center of the pulpit. Martin clapped me on the shoulder once more as he turned to leave, stopping as he waited for me to catch up.

I glanced once more at the image of Jesus and I couldn't help but feel uneasy as I stood in front of the picture of Jesus on the crucifixion, illuminated by the church's stained glass window. Every aspect of his pain and anguish was captured in the eerie, lifelike portrayal. His face twisted in agony as his body, covered with blood and wounds, hung limply from the crudely hewn cross.

It was all too real, too vivid, the nails piercing his wrists and feet, the crown of thorns forced into his brow. When depicting the suffering of Jesus' last moments, the artist did not omit any details.

I couldn't get the thought out of my head that I didn't want to turn out looking like that when I stared at the picture. I had read about historical descriptions of the town's grim past in books, and those accounts had left me with vivid images of the cruelty of crucifixion. In those days, it was customary to offer sacrifices as a way to please supernatural beings or win the favor of evil spirits that were said to prowl the countryside.

They described bodies being set on fire, nails driven through flesh, and ritualistic beatings performed to please these evil entities. Superstition and terror characterized the town's past, when such horrific deeds were committed in the name of appeasement or protection. The idea of the anguish and suffering those poor folks went through chilled me to the bone.

Jesus' image hanging on the crucifixion brought the reality of human brutality, how people would go in order to exert control or dominance over others. Standing in front of it today, I couldn't help but get a feeling of dread, as though the crucified Christ was silently pleading with me on behalf of the previous tragedies of the town.

The church itself seemed to carry remnants of those gloomy days, with its aged stones and flickering lamps. The smell of incense mixed with the musty smell of old books and weathered wood filled the air. In the dark light, shadows danced around the walls, creating strange patterns that seemed to come to life.

Quickly, I wrenched my eyes away from the image, a knot of anxiety growing in my chest. Once a haven of comfort and safety, the familiarity of the church today seems tarnished by the weight of history and the enduring memory of previous tragedies. The dark secrets of the town were well hidden, yet they still crept through the gaps in the walls of the cathedral and made me think of the atrocities that had taken place here centuries before.

I followed Martin's and stepped out. The church doors swung shut behind me with a dull thud. The dull warmth of the chapel within stood in stark contrast to the crisp, cold air outside. It had grown dark quickly, bringing a gloomy tinge to everything. The sky overhead was a painting made up of ominous, dark clouds that held the possibility of rain. A shudder went down my spine and I wrapped my coat more around myself, finding comfort in its warmth.

Silently joining me, Martin was a comforting presence in the otherwise unpleasant atmosphere. We walked silently to his truck, which was parked close. In the last of the light, the car was a solid silhouette against the dark sky of the evening.

I got into the passenger seat of the truck as Martin opened it and felt the familiar comfort of the worn leather beneath me. The cabin's interior was softly illuminated, with the dashboard providing a mellow glow. As the truck came to life, Martin reached for the stereo and turned on the engine.

The truck's inside echoed with the strange notes of a haunting music that filled the air. The rock song had an ethereal yet ominous vibe that made you feel uneasy and eager. A melancholic tone permeated the dissonant harmony of the guitars, backed by a haunting vocal that seemed to reflect the evening's gloom.

The road opened up in front of us, dark vegetation and thick bushes bordering both sides. As the twilight wore on, the trees seemed to gather in around us, casting an eerie embrace over the road. The headlights broke through the darkness, bringing a sharp clarity to the meandering path ahead.

Inside the truck, the air was both tense and yet peaceful, as if we were both deep in meditation, trying to make sense of the day's disturbing occurrences. Our somber reflection was accompanied by an unsettling music whose mournful notes blended with the steady hum of the engine.

I peered out the window and watched as the scene passed by in a haze of subdued hues. The road meandered till it vanished into the dense woodland that bordered it. Shadows moved around the edges of my vision, reflecting the moods that were fluctuating inside of me.

Martin steadied his hands on the wheel and maneuvered the vehicle like a pro. He moved with a purpose, determined to make his way down the narrow path ahead, even with the unsettling soundtrack playing in the background.

With its heavy clouds full of impending rain, the sky overhead seemed ready to let go. Anticipation permeated the air, with the earthy aroma of damp vegetation blending with the scent of petrichor. It was a familiar aroma, one that spoke of purification and rejuvenation, yet tonight there was a hint of discomfort.

We continued driving in quiet, each absorbed in our own reverie. The road appeared to go on forever in front of us, a narrow strip of concrete slicing right through the middle of the woodland. With the exception of the sporadic glimmer of far-off lamps and the eerie illumination from passing cars, the blackness engulfed us.

The eerie music kept playing, its melancholic melody creating an emotional tapestry that reflected our journey's uncertainty. The melancholy of the evening was echoed by a haunting singing that accompanied the guitars reverberating around the cabin.

I looked at Martin and saw the crease in his forehead from concentration. His jaw was clenched in determination as he kept his eyes focused on the road ahead.

The road narrowed and the greenery got thicker as we continued driving into the night. With its old trees standing tall above us like menacing sentinels, the forest seemed to close in around us. The darkness was all-encompassing, drawing its arms around us as we continued forward.

From time to time, glimpses of wildlife racing across the road would appear in the headlights; a brief blur of fur and motion. There were invisible beings in the night, their existence sensed more strongly than seen in the growing darkness.

I returned my attention to the window and continued to observe the scenery as each mile went by. The truck's headlights carved a lonely trail through the night, illuminating the road ahead.

We had a plan and its weight lingered between us as we drove farther into the night, blending with the odd music that continued to play softly in the background.

With his undivided attention on the road ahead, Martin's knuckles were white against the steering wheel. I took a quick look at him and saw the resolve written all over his face. We had poured hours into planning, studying old books and practices that claimed to call spirits back from the afterlife.

The idea was simple but bold: we were going to try to call upon a spirit of the dead, someone who could make a goodwill appeal on my behalf to drive away the evil forces that had been tormenting me. We would force the spirit to reveal the identities of its worshippers—those who had plotted to unleash such horrors upon me—if it refused or proved recalcitrant.

Entering the supernatural worlds, where grave and unforeseen consequences could arise, was a risky endeavor. But I had moved past any reluctance or uncertainty. I had been plagued by the ghosts nonstop, feeling as though they were predators waiting to strike from the shadows of my existence. If calling upon a spirit was the sole means of obtaining the answers I sought, then that was acceptable.

The road spread out in front of us, headlamps piercing the night like a resolute beacon. With its old trees bending and swaying in silent communion with the night, the woodland murmured mysteries in the breeze. There was an unearthly intensity in the air outside, a tangible sensation of expectancy that reflected my own inner anguish.

Martin finally spoke, "We need to be prepared for anything," breaking the hush that had descended between us. He spoke in a serious although slightly nervous tone. "It is not something to be taken lightly when calling upon spirits. They might act erratically."

With a serious nod, I kept my eyes on the road ahead. I answered calmly, "I know," even though I was filled with a great deal of uncertainty. "I can't continue to live this way. I'm being consumed by the nightmares and the ongoing fear."

Martin's fists gripped the steering wheel tightly as his jaw tensed. "J, I understand," he said, momentarily meeting my gaze. "We must go cautiously. Human laws and reasoning have no power on spirits. Their terms of operation are their own."

With a heavy heart, I swallowed the truth of our strategy. We had studied old charms, rites, and incantations in an attempt to find a way to force a spirit to come forward and speak with us. It required a careful balancing act between decency and force, between begging for forgiveness and insisting on justice.

We drove along the narrow road while the truck trundled along, its tires pressing firmly against the pavement. With its thick underbrush creating sweeping shadows that swirled around the borders of our vision, the forest appeared to be closing in on us. I sneaked a peek at Martin, his features softly lit by the dashboard lights. His thoughts were concealed beneath a mask of intense focus, and his expression was inscrutable. But I was aware that he also struggled with uncertainties and anxieties beneath his composed appearance.

The truck continued to rumble, a lone ship crossing the surrounding sea of darkness. The journey ahead was unpredictable, full of curves and turns that reflected the intricacies of our personal lives. But with perseverance and unyielding will, Martin and I would take on whatever problems were ahead.

I closed my eyes for a moment, silently praying for protection and direction as the eerie soundtrack kept playing. The road opened up in front of us, a journey made clear by headlights and marked by an unspoken camaraderie and common goal.

The road wound into the center of the woodland and became farther and longer in front of us as the night grew darker. As the truck rolled along, Martin's hands remained solid on the steering wheel, and I sat next to him, my mind racing with a million ideas and anxieties.

My eyes strayed to the tattoos on Martin's arms. His skin was covered in sigils and symbols that had ancient power and served as wards against evil forces that wanted to harm us. In the past few days, he had led me through a number of protection rituals that combined invocations, holy plants, and incantations to keep the evil spirits that lurked in the shadows at bay.

In an attempt to defend myself, I had also resorted to extreme means. I had enrolled in online seminars taught by an African voodoo doctor, hoping to gain knowledge of powerful spells and alchemical mixtures in an attempt to combat the evil that was affecting me. The rites were intense and frequently disgusting, and the lessons had been hard. I had consumed bitter herbs, prepared foul-smelling mixtures, and gone through weakening, shaking purging sessions. However, I had persisted because I was determined to protect myself from the evil spirits' constant assault.

Even with the little calm I'd been able to achieve lately, seeing random strangers in the city suddenly made me feel uncomfortable. Every stranger I had met after that incident appeared to be a possible threat; their looks lingered for an excessive amount of time, and their actions were closely examined through the prism of paranoia that had crept into my thoughts.

Mr. Johnson, the tall high school teacher whose presence had become a disturbing obsession for me, was at the center of my suspicions. Though his height certainly resembled the people I had seen that fateful night at the gates of hell, it was more than simply his physical size that caught my attention. It was his voice, the way he carried himself, and the strange atmosphere that seemed to envelop him.

Mr. Johnson exuded confidence in every room he entered thanks to his towering stature. His eyes would always find me, staring at me for longer than needed with a sharp intensity that made me shudder. His voice had a remarkable tone as well, one that reminded me slightly of the voices I'd heard that eerie night amid the shadowy creatures dressed in dark robes.

He tried to be kind, as shown by the sporadic smiles that appeared when our eyes locked, yet there was a certain coldness about him. I noticed that his eyes remained icy and detached even when he smiled. Beneath that exterior of civility, there was a glimmer of something deeper, a venom that seemed to flicker in the depths of his sight.

The town eventually gave way to wide stretches of open road bordered by thick vegetation as Martin made his way through the meandering roadways. Above us, the sky was a tapestry of swirling clouds, with the countryside covered in deep shadows created by the waning light of evening. The creepy music Martin had selected kept playing in the background, its uncanny melodies highlighting the tension in the air between us.

I glanced over at Martin again. He was just as nervous as I was, but he kept his eyes fixed on the road ahead.

Martin finally spoke, "We need to tread carefully," breaking the silence that had descended between us. His voice was soft and somewhat warning. "Mr. Johnson may just be one piece of the puzzle, but if our suspicions hold true..."

With the inference obvious, he left the sentence hanging. If Mr. Johnson was indeed associated with the evil forces that had been torturing me, it may be dangerous to face him. However, it was a risk we had to take in order to break free from the web of deceit and evil that had ensnared me.

I agreed and nodded, my head buzzing with strategies and backup plans. "We'll tackle this with caution," I answered, maintaining a steady tone despite the internal conflict. "We need to gather more information from the spirit before we confront him directly."

Martin gave me a quick glance while expressing admiration in his eyes. With a tone of pride, he whispered, "J, you've come a long way." Martin nodded proudly "From the depths of despair to leading the charge against these... these dark forces."

I forced a little smile as appreciation for Martin's resolute support filled me.

The atmosphere in the vehicle remained tense but infused with an odd sense of purpose as we went down the winding road. With his eyes fixed on the road ahead, Martin's fingers tap in time to the eerie music that was playing menacingly in the background. I sat next to him, a plethora of feelings and concerns flying through my mind.

The road continued, its path lined by tall trees and thick foliage that created long shadows. The sky was covered with thick clouds that threatened to bring rain, and the night had completely darkened. With every mile we traveled toward our goal and the impending showdown, the atmosphere inside the vehicle grew more and more exciting.

Suddenly, Martin's voice rose above the stillness, his lips moving in time with a song that was on the radio. The song had a melancholic tune and mysterious, evocative lyrics that fit the spooky atmosphere of the evening. He sang with a raw intensity that made it sound as though he was putting our mission's core into every word.

With every mile that went by, the road ahead became less clear, and the headlights pierced the night like a lone beacon. The huge trees in the forest towered over us, creating lengthy shadows that swirled around the edges of my vision. The smell of earth and pine mixed with the subtle scent of the healing herbs that clung to my garments, filling the air.

"We're getting close," Martin said, jolting me out of my daydream and back into reality. His voice was low and hinting at expectation. "The clearing should be just up ahead."

As we got closer to our destination, my mind was racing and I nodded in silence. The clearing stood for a nexus, a location where the lines separating the material and spiritual realms would be sufficiently thin to allow our rite of summoning to take place. Even though it was a dangerous and uncertain enterprise, I knew we had to move on.

The truck's headlights lit up a little area of grass encircled by tall trees as we pulled into the clearing. There was an unearthly electricity in the air, a tangible sensation of expectation that reflected my inner anguish. After turning off the ignition, Martin stopped the truck and heard the engine purr.

We were enveloped in silence, interrupted only by the distant cry of an owl and the sound of leaves rustling in the wind. With the door open, I emerged onto the cold grass, feeling the soft ground beneath my feet. Martin came to join me, taking his time getting the bundle of ceremonial goods out of the truck's bed.

The house's outline emerged from the trees as we neared a curve in the road. It was Martin's mother's house, tucked in a remote area closer to the edge of the woodland. Even with the late hour and the foreboding surroundings, Martin's mood clearly changed. He appeared happy to be back in his familiar surroundings, which gave him a sense of security and comfort.

We were embraced by the chill of the night, which was only broken by the sporadic flashes of lightning in the clouds overhead and the faint illumination of far-off stars. The aroma of moist ground and pine mixed with the subtle scent of herbs that stuck to my garments, filling the air and serving as a reminder of the protective rites we had carried out earlier.

Martin did not waste any time. He ran toward the front door of the house, his gravel path-leading footsteps crunching softly as he approached the porch. With a voice that rang urgent and familiar, he approached the door and pounded loudly on it with his knuckles.

"Mama! I'm at home, get the door!" Martin's words drifted through the darkness, resonating softly against the home's walls. With a quick smile, he looked back at me and then picked up a rock from the porch to tap gently against the doorframe, which was his customary way of saying hello.

An uncomfortable serenity pervaded the air, a foreshadowing of the emotional upheaval and shocking discoveries that were in store for us.

The door opened after a little while, letting in the warm warmth of light that was seeping from within. Standing in the doorway, Martin's mother looked at her son with a mixture of relief and apprehension.

"Martin, my boy," she cried, a hint of maternal love in her voice. "You've arrived home! Come in now, hurry up. It's almost midnight.

With much anticipation, Martin entered the house and was embraced by his mother, who drew him in and provided him with warmth. Their chat, replete with assurances and murmurs that suggested a close bond between them, floated softly to where I stood.

I paused for a second, watching the loving reunion from outside. The image was familiar and comforting, yet I couldn't get rid of the nagging feeling of discomfort in the pit of my stomach. My sense of caution and mistrust had been heightened by the events of the past few days, as I realized that danger could be found in unexpected places.

Forcing myself to walk closer, I arrived at the porch where Martin had left the rock. Unconsciously, I picked it up and turned it over in my hands, looking across at the open doorway. As they made their way farther inside the home, Martin and his mother had vanished from view and their voices had become muffled.

The chilly night air shrouded me in a strange silence as I stood on the porch. My fingers traced the outline of the pouch secured at my side, where the reassuring weight of my gun nestled safely within. I had taken the precaution of hiding the gun under my jacket, ready for whatever was in store for us that evening.

Martin had vanished into the house's warmth behind me, with only the faintest sound of their words coming through the open doorway. I lingered for an extra second, taking careful note of my surroundings.

I gave Martin's house one more look over my shoulder before crossing the door. Soft lamplight filled the space, creating warm, dancing shadows on the walls. The smell of old wood and familiar spices filled the air, a welcome change from the ominous cloud hanging over us outside.

Martin's mother stepped close to the door with Martin's as if they came to get me. She looked to be an indifferent figure in her shabby pajamas that suggested she had had a restless night. Her silver hair was disheveled, and her expression still had hints of mild irritation mixed with drowsiness. She gave us a half-hearted look of interest, as if she had just woken up from a deep sleep and wasn't quite sure how to react.

"Martin, what on earth are you up to at this hour?" She muttered, a tinge of frustration in her voice. She turned to face me, and I gave her a courteous nod, but she was clearly not interested.

Martin said, "We have something important to discuss, mom," with a hint of urgency in his voice. With an air of both resolve and devotion, he drew nearer to his mother. "It's about what's been happening lately, and Jason here needs our help."

Martin's mother gave me a quick glance and her face softened somewhat as she heard my name. She moved aside and motioned for me to trail behind her inside the home.

"Come in then," she moaned. "But move quickly. I was about to get comfortable again."

I looked about, taking in the warm familiarity of Martin's childhood home as we followed her farther inside. The walls were covered in photographs that captured special occasions and events like family get-togethers, far-off trips, and Martin's early years captured in images of joy and purity. Despite the unusual nature of his interests, Martin and his mother had a strong relationship, as evidenced by the subtle hum of distant memories in the air.

We went into a modest sitting area with a faded sofa and comfortable armchairs glowing in the warm light of the lamp. With a tired sigh, Martin's mother sank onto one of the recliners and gazed at us with a mixture of interest and resignation, her posture easing slightly.

"Now then, what's all this about?" With a hint of doubt in her voice, she questioned. With her hands clasped in her lap, she looked hopefully from Martin to me.

With a carefree tone, Martin answered "We're going to summon a spirit to plead on Jason's behalf, to stop the forces that have been tormenting him."

Though a glint of worry darted in her gaze, his mother's eyebrows raised in surprise. She muttered, "Summoning spirits, Martin?" with a tone that was both skeptical and nervous. "You know I've never been comfortable with your... activities."

Martin gave a serious nod, his face full of sincerity. He argued, "I know, mom, but this is different." "We need to discover answers because Jason is in danger. We must discover who is responsible for everything."

I faced Martin's mother's stare and moved on, my resolve unwavering. "We think there are individuals in the town engaged in sinister rites," I clarified, maintaining a steady tone despite the gravity of what I was saying. "We want to confront them, but first, we need to understand their motives and their identities."

Martin's mother gave me an unreadable look. It was hard to tell how she looked with the warm dim lightening in the room. She whispered, "Jason, dear," speaking to me personally. Are you certain of this? It seems... risky."

I gave a nod, my expression determined. With a sincere response, "I have to do this," I said. "I can't continue to live in constant terror and worry about their next move. We must act now."

The room fell silent, the only sound coming from a nearby clock that was ticking slightly. Martin's mother observed us both closely, her expression a patchwork of contradictory feelings I could hardly put my finger on.

She sighed resignedly after a protracted moment, her shoulders lowering in grudging acceptance. "Very well," she said, a hint of resignation in her voice. "But swear to me that you'll use caution. Make me a promise that you won't act carelessly."

"We promise, mom," Martin said in his carefree tone and jetted up the stairs.

I nodded appreciatively, moved by the steadfast trust Martin's mother had shown in us in spite of her apparent misgivings. I truly said, "Thank you," feeling my heart soften at her act of confidence.

I trailed closely behind Martin as he bolted up the steps. The chaotic yet oddly fascinating scene that met my eyes as soon as I entered the room shocked me.

Martin's room was covered in a maze of eerie runes, sigils, and mysterious marks that covered almost every surface. The walls were covered in old-looking parchments with symbols written on them that had an unearthly force to it. Certain symbols were recognizable, taken from a variety of esoteric traditions: runes that resembled those in Norse mythology, intricately patterned circles, and pentagrams. Some were less well-known, with only Martin knowing their meanings and their origins remaining a mystery.

The space itself was compact and disorganized, with mounds of books scattered all over the ground and teetering on bookcases. With years of reference, the spines of the ancient tomes and contemporary works on paranormal phenomena caused the shelves to slump. Every possible surface was covered in crystals of all sizes and shapes, which caught the soft lamplight and reflected color prisms throughout the space.

A haphazard altar, complete with candles, incense burners, and carefully placed ritualistic artifacts, dominated one part of the room. In the middle was a little, worn statue of an ancient deity, surrounded by modest trinkets and offerings of dried herbs. There was a sense of reverence in the room as the flickering candlelight cast a beautiful, ethereal glow over the altar.

The bed itself was a mess of mismatched cushions and blankets, dreamcatchers and talismans dangling from the posts along the frame. With a joyful exuberance, Martin leaped over to it, his gestures suggesting a sense of comfort and familiarity in this world of the occult.

With a dramatic flourish, Martin flopped onto the bed and smiled, his eyes full of mischief. "Welcome to my humble abode," he said. "Sign off on the mess. I assure you that it's an organized pandemonium."

I took in the spectacle in front of me with a mix of fear and wonder. Martin's room served as a physical representation of his lifelong quest for knowledge and comprehension of the paranormal and a monument to his devotion to his trade.

The smell of incense lingered in the air, but there was also something stronger in the air, the stench of dirty laundry and the remains of fast food. There was a tangible energy in the space, even with the mess and the subtle musky smell hanging in the air, as though invisible forces were stirring just below the surface of awareness.

Martin's eyes glistened with excitement as he made passionate gestures throughout the space. With a lighthearted yet slightly arrogant tone, he asked, "See anything you like?" "I've spent years gathering these relics and symbols. Everybody has a unique power and tale to tell."

I scanned the symbols adorning the walls, which looked to be pulsating with dormant energy. I recognized a little wooden plaque with a symbol carved on it, a protective barrier against evil spirits with intentional, crisp lines. A tapestry nearby showed people engaged in an ageless struggle between light and darkness in a tale from ancient mythology.

"This one," Martin said, gesturing to a huge sheet of parchment bearing numerous elaborate markings, "is a binding spell." Its purpose is to contain and dispel negative energy.

I slowly nodded as I took in all the information and history that was entwined with each symbol and artifact. I was hesitant to delve further into the occult, but I felt confident in Martin's knowledge because he had spent years perfecting his abilities and comprehension of the paranormal.

A subtle intensity appeared to pulse through the room, a fusion of traditional knowledge and contemporary curiosity. Open books about ancient rituals and paranormal investigation were covered in diagrams and scrawled notes on a jumbled desk. Martin had probably spent many hours researching the unknown in this corner of the room, where the faint glow of a computer screen lit the space.

I was overcome with awe for Martin's commitment and fortitude in the face of the unexplainable as soon as I saw his room.

Martin sat up on the bed and looked at me soberly, his countenance growing serious. He said softly, "We'll carry out the summoning ceremony tonight. There are hazards, and it won't be simple."

Martin went on, his voice strong and determined, "But we'll be ready." "With your strength and my knowledge, we'll confront these forces together."

I returned Martin's stare with a nod of approval.

My gaze swept across the space, pausing on the ground near a painstakingly rendered image of the devil that was just waiting to be triggered. Only a faint red light broke through the blackness of the room, giving everything an unsettling sheen that added to the ominous atmosphere. There was a churning sensation in my gut as I felt the weight of the ceremony we were going to perform pushing down on me.

I sat down in the only chair I could find in the disorganized room and took a deep breath. The wooden frame of the old, creaky object groaning under my weight. My nostrils were overwhelmed with the stench of rotting food and dirty laundry, which made the space feel even smaller.

With a solemn expression, Martin, who had been frantically going through his belongings, turned to face me. "It's almost time," he stated in a steady, low voice. He gestured for me to get up and come along.

I got up, making the chair squeak in response. My chest constricted with anxiety, but I made an effort to ignore it by concentrating on the work at hand. With deliberate movements, Martin skillfully arranged everything for the ceremony. He started by lighting strategically positioned candles, which created dancing shadows on the walls with their flashing flames.

The space had an otherworldly feel to it because of the red light coming from the ceiling and the candlelight. In the faint light, the symbols on the walls and ground seemed to come to life. I observed as Martin continued to draw more lines on the ground, his movements deliberate and well-honed. He drew elaborate pathways in the chalk that connected to the devil's symbol, amplifying its potency.

Martin said, "These lines will help contain the energy," without taking his eyes off his job. "We need to make sure nothing escapes the circle once the summoning begins."

Feeling the seriousness of Martin's words, I nodded. I was aware that what we were going to accomplish posed a risk and that a single error may have disastrous results. My thoughts drifted back to all the rituals I had tried so many times in the last several days while Martin finished getting everything ready. Desperate to defend myself against the evil powers that tormented me, I have resorted to every tactic known to man.

I had consumed nasty mixtures, purchased online courses from questionable voodoo masters, and engaged in sorcerous practices that left me feeling weak and ill. And yet, in spite of everything I had tried, I felt helpless, like a little boat lost in a wild sea.

I was brought back to the present by Martin's voice. "Okay, we're almost ready." After arranging the final candle, he stood back to evaluate his efforts. With the symbols shining subtly in the candlelight, the room transformed into an intricate pattern of light and shadow.

My gaze went to the emblem of the devil on the ground. It was big and complicated, with angular, ominous lines. My spine tingled at the sight of it, but I forced myself to concentrate. Martin had reassured me that now was our finest opportunity to make an appeal to the spirits, to find a means to put an end to the suffering.

Martin reached up and raised a little, delicate dagger to the candlelight. He declared, "We need a drop of blood to activate the circle."

Even though I had anticipated this, the truth of it still unsettled me. I held out my hand, and Martin sliced a little hole in my palm, letting some blood trickle over the devil's symbol's center.

The symbol appeared to pulse with energy as the blood hit the ground; its lines briefly brightened before stabilizing into a dark, constant glow. Martin then added his own blood to the ceremony by making a similar incision on his own palm.

I inhaled deeply and stood up, allowing the room's stale, cold air to fill my lungs. Martin started preparing the space for the ceremony. He started by going to the pentagram's drawing in the middle of the space. He enhanced the complex pattern by drawing more lines and symbols around the margins with a deft touch. everything appeared as though he was creating a complicated network of magic and meaning with each stroke, giving everything weight and purpose.

Martin then reached into one of the jumbled shelves and pulled out a box of more candles. He arranged them around the pentagram in appropriate locations where the new lines met, designating their placements with smaller, nearly undetectable symbols carved into the ground. In the faint light, the smooth and shiny black and red wax of the candles shone brightly. He struck a match and lighted each one, the flames flashing to life and adding to the spooky atmosphere in the room.

Martin was whispering under his breath an incantation as the candles burned, a low, repetitive chant that seemed as though it was coming from the room's walls. The electromagnetic tension in the air caused the hairs on the back of my neck to stand up as it grew thicker.

I sensed the atmosphere change as I stood close to the door. The crimson glow appeared to be consuming the room's entire essence as it grew deeper and more obtrusive. On the walls, shadows danced in a hideous way, forming figures that twisted and twisted with a wicked delight.

Martin wore a mask of focus, but his eyes were glimmering with a strong purpose. He proceeded to a small, improvised shrine next to his bed, which was strewn with a variety of ritualistic objects, including crystals, bones, and jars containing strange liquids. From this collection, he picked out a knife with an elaborate handle etched with more of the bizarre symbols that decorated his room, and a small bottle filled with a dark substance.

Martin said, "Take this," and he gave me a tiny herb-filled pouch. "Throw this into the flame if a spirit shows up. It will tie it and force it to respond to our inquiries. If it doesn't then we are not dealing with a lesser spirit and most pay respect."

I gave a nod while holding the sack firmly in my palm. I was troubled by the fact that we were going to do this. We were about to call in a ghost, ask for help, or at least learn more about the evil powers that beset us. There was no margin for error because the stakes were so high.

Martin went back to the pentagram and stood in the middle of it. With a commanding power, he began to chant, raising the dagger and speaking louder than before. The markings on the ground appeared to shine from within, and the atmosphere pulsed with vitality.

He walked around the pentagram, dousing the candle flames with a concoction of powders and herbs. The concoction hissed each time it touched fire, shooting up bitter smoke that gave the room a strong, overpowering smell. My eyes began to water, and I resisted the need to cough so as not to disturb the gloomy solemnity of the rite.

With my heart racing, I observed as Martin's chorus intensified. The shadows were irregular and chaotic, the candles' flames flickering fiercely. I could only see the walls' twisting and warping in my peripheral vision as the room appeared to close in on itself.

Martin then gave one more, powerful blow, driving the dagger deep into the ground in the middle of the pentagram. The only sound in the room was the soft crackling of the candle flames as everything went silent.

There was silence for a minute. Anticipation hung thick in the air, and the stifling silence was nearly excruciating. Holding my breath, I waited, hoped, and wondered what would happen next.

The room's temperature abruptly dropped, causing a bitter coldness to permeate into my bones. The room was nearly dark as the red light flickered and faded.

The stillness became heavier and more suffocating than before. All sound appeared to vanish into oblivion, leaving just the sound of my heart thumping loudly in my ears. A chilly sweat appeared on my forehead, and I could feel my skin crawling with a sense of imminent disaster. The room's shadows appeared to be alive, writhing and twisting as if they were consuming the evil spirit that had taken over.

The silence was suddenly broken by a low, grating sound that sounded like metal scraping against stone. It was a dissonant, loud noise that made my teeth tense. An almost intolerable tension filled the room as the sound intensified. I cast a quick peek at Martin, but he was still chanting, his face a mask of focus, his eyes closed.

Abruptly the grating sound stopped, returning the room to that terrible silence. Breathing became difficult for me as if the air itself had been sucked out, leaving a void that bore down on me. The lights flickered, their flames leaping madly across the walls, creating shifting, hideous forms.

Martin's voice rose and fell in a haunting cadence, giving his chanting a new force. He extracted a bottle of dark liquid from a tiny leather pouch that was fastened to his waist. He poured the liquid quickly into the pentagram's center, where it splattered and smoked, sending a sickening smell that turned my stomach.

The stillness came back, heavier than before. I had the impression that I was looking into the emptiness from the edge of a massive chasm. Fear sent shivers down my spine and made the hairs on the back of my neck stand on end. The room's shadows appeared to draw closer together, engulfing the candles' meager light as the gloom grew deeper.

Something ancient and evil, something that observed us from beyond the edge of reality, seemed to be there in that silence. I was overcome with a primordial fear that would not go away when I felt its presence. I was aware that Martin's ritual had called something to the room, and that we were not alone.

The annoying noise was back, louder now, more persistent. The sound echoed through the house's very bones, appearing to originate from both nowhere and everywhere. Beneath the pentagram, the ground shook as the symbols emitted an awful light. Martin's voice cracked from the strain as his chanting reached a fever pitch.

And then the cacophony ended just as abruptly as it had started. After that, there was complete silence, a nothingness that engulfed every sound and left my heart beating in my ears. It was difficult to breathe because of the suffocating quiet, which seemed like a massive weight pressing down on my chest.

A faint, sickening glow flared from the dark liquid as it started to bubble and churn in the pentagram's center. The chillier the air got, and the unsettling light made my breath appear to be misting. With every instant that went by, the shadows in the room appeared to be pulsating with a demonic energy, becoming more twisted and deeper.

I could feel the fear eating at the corners of my mind, making my determination weaken. However, I was aware that we needed to finish this, that we had to.

I opened my mouth to say something, to break the oppressive silence that was suffocating me, but before I could utter a word, Martin's hand shot out and clamped over my mouth. His eyes were wide with a mix of fear and resolve, and he had a tight hold. I was instantly stopped short by the sight on his face—a damning, even frantic expression that suggested any sound may be lethal.

"Don't," he growled, his voice almost audible above a whisper. His stare was so intense that it made my heart skip a beat. Whatever was going on, it was much more than I could have ever anticipated.

Martin's hand slowly released my mouth and he signaled total silence with a finger to his lips. I nodded, swallowing hard to keep from speaking or even coughing, my throat dry. Tension was high in the air, and the stifling silence of the room made every sound seem louder.

With careful and steady movements, he made his way back to the center of the pentagram. The dark liquid kept churning and bubbling, the sickly glow pulsing in time with our hearts' silent pulses. Martin went on to light more candles, their flames creating strange, menacing-looking shadows that seemed to dance.

I watched, motionless, as he drew more symbols, each more complex and mysterious than the last, surrounding the pentagram. The smell of rotting food and dirty clothes permeated the room, combining with the sharp smoke from the candles and herbs. It was difficult to concentrate due to the sensory overload, but I made myself pay attention.

The utter silence made the smallest sound seem to reverberate indefinitely. The stifling silence made every sound—the rustle of clothes, the creak of the grounds, the sound of a breath—seem louder. An evil energy that appeared to be watching us with unseen eyes was becoming more and more present in the room, and I could sense it.

“We haven't summoned a lesser one, Jason.” Martin whispered and continued. With a low, repetitive murmur that matched the symbols on the walls and ground, Martin started chanting once more. The pentagram's dark liquid in the center started to change, brightening in color. A shiver ran down my spine as a basic horror gripped me. The area appeared to be transformed into a twisted nightmare as the shadows began to draw closer and press on my peripheral vision.

A deep, rumbling sound came from the pentagram's center just as I was about to give up on the quiet. I had never heard anything like it before—a deep, eerie growl that seemed to be vibrating through the air itself. The flames of the candles danced in the invisible breeze, creating strange patterns on the walls as they flicker erratically.

The roaring crept closer, and Martin's chanting became more frantic and loud. I noticed the tension on his countenance, as droplets of perspiration formed on his forehead. He was exerting all of his might and expertise to handle whatever was being called upon, straining himself to the breaking point.

The growl developed into a barrage of inhumane, guttural noises, each one more terrifying than the previous. The roar seemed to be vibrating the entire room, and the air itself was throbbing with a sinister intensity. I could feel my breath coming in short, shallow gasps and my heart thumping in my chest. Even though the terror was nearly unbearable, I knew I had to persevere.

And suddenly it stopped. Again.

The stillness seemed to engulf all sounds as it continued, as it was so dense and heavy. I could feel the intense tension in the room, my heart thumping like a drum inside my chest. The silence was suddenly broken by a voice. The voice seemed to reverberate through the walls themselves, coming from both nowhere and everywhere.

With a direct question, the voice said, "What is it that you seek?" It was resonating and deep, and it gave off an unsettling, otherworldly feeling that made my skin crawl.

I swung my head around, but I could not find where the voice was coming from. It seemed to emanate from every angle of the room, reverberating off the walls and casting a foreboding aura throughout. My gaze quickly shifted to Martin, who was standing quietly inside the pentagram with a determined expression on his face.

"We seek your help," Martin said, his voice steady and respectful. "Jason, this man is designated for sacrifice. We require your protection and we need to know why.

There was silence for a moment and soon a dark guttural laugher, a sarcastic, mocking sound that made my skin crawl. "I am aware of Jason's plight," it said. "He has been marked by forces that seek to use him in their dark rituals."

At the words, a shiver went through me. "Marked for sacrifice?" I said, trying not to cry out loud, but my voice was shaking. "Why? Why me?

The voice said, "You have been selected because you crossed a line." "You are one that is coveted by those who dwell in the shadows. Your fear, your despair, it makes you a perfect vessel for their dark intentions."

Martin moved forward and fixed his gaze on the pentagram's center. He enquired, "What can we do to stop this?" "How can we protect Jason from these forces?"

The voice trailed off, as though thinking. "Protection comes at a price," it said finally. "Are you willing to pay for it?"

Martin gave me a somber nod when I looked at him. "Yes," I replied. "Whatever it takes."

"Very well," the voice said. "There are rituals, ancient and powerful, that can shield you from those who seek to harm you. But these rituals require a sacrifice of their own."

"What sort of offering?" With a sinking heart, I asked.

"A part of your soul," the voice said. "In order to commit oneself to the guardianship of the spirits, you have to give something of yourself. It is an unbreakable tie that will alter you irrevocably."

I took a deep breath, feeling the decision's weight bearing down on me. "And in the event that I decline?" I enquired.

The voice answered, "Then you will continue to be vulnerable." "And those who pursue you will track you down, and they won't spare a thought."

There was quiet for a moment as the voice continued. It continued, its tone now more demanding. "But there is another way. The way is to appease the deity you have angered," it said, the words resonating with an eerie authority that left no room for doubt.

"How do I appease it?" I asked, my voice barely more than a whisper, the fear tightening around my chest.

The voice spoke in riddles and proverbs, each one more cryptic than the last. "The anger of the unseen can be soothed by the sacrifice of what is seen," it began. "A soul in turmoil must find solace in the act of giving. Blood ties the living to the dead, and only through blood can the wrongs be righted. The path is dark, and the way is fraught with danger. Remember, the shadows watch, and the price of ignorance is steep."

I exchanged a nervous glance with Martin, who seemed equally perplexed. "Can you be more specific?" Martin asked, trying to cut through the cryptic words.

The voice paused, then continued with more clarity. "You must return to the grave from which this all began. Under the cover of darkness, wear a cloak as black as the void. Bring with you one of your most prized possessions, something of great personal value. On this offering, sprinkle your own blood, for it is through this blood that the bond will be formed."

My heart sank as I realized what was being asked of me. The thought of spilling my own blood and offering something precious to me felt like a final, desperate act. But the voice wasn't finished.

"Once prepared, you must take this offering to the Gates of Hell. You know the place, where the boundary between worlds is thin. You must arrive at midnight, when the full moon is high. Only then will the deity consider your plea, and only then can the wrong be righted."

The weight of the instructions settled over me, a heavy, oppressive burden. I could feel the blood drain from my face, the enormity of the task almost too much to bear. Martin put a reassuring hand on my shoulder, grounding me in the moment.

"Jason, we can do this," he said, his voice steady despite the fear I saw in his eyes. "We'll prepare everything. You're not alone in this."

I nodded, trying to muster the courage I needed. "What if I…?" I began to speak, but Martin quickly moved to silence me, his hand firm on my mouth once again. "Shh," he whispered urgently. He then turned back toward the center of the pentagram, bowing low before the unseen presence.

"Great deity," Martin said, his voice reverent and humble, "we apologize for any transgressions. We seek only to make amends and find peace."

The oppressive silence that had enveloped the room seemed to lift slightly, as if the very air had shifted. The voice, once so commanding, fell silent, and a deep, profound stillness took its place. I let out a breath I hadn't realized I was holding, the tension in my chest easing just a fraction.

As the silence settled, I felt an overwhelming urge to voice my concerns. "Martin, I can't do this," I said, shaking my head vehemently. "There's no way I'm going back to that graveyard. It's too dangerous."

Martin's eyes were filled with a mix of determination and concern as he looked at me. "Jason, I understand you're scared. But this is the only way to break the curse. You heard what the voice said."

I shook my head again, more forcefully this time. "No, Martin. There has to be another way. I can't go back there. I just can't."

Martin stepped closer, his expression softening. "Jason, listen to me. I know this is terrifying. But the full moon is tomorrow night. We have a window of opportunity to set things right. If we don't do this now, who knows what will happen?"

I could feel the panic rising within me, my breath coming in short, shallow gasps. "But what if something goes wrong? What if we fail?"

Martin placed a reassuring hand on my shoulder, his grip firm and steady. "We won't fail. We'll prepare everything carefully. We have time to get ready, to make sure we do this right. I won't let anything happen to you. You're not alone in this."

I looked into Martin's eyes, searching for some semblance of hope. His unwavering resolve gave me a sliver of courage. "But what if..." I began, my voice trailing off as the fear threatened to overwhelm me again.

Martin's expression grew even more determined. "Jason, we've come this far. We can't turn back now. The full moon is tomorrow night. It's a sign, an opportunity we can't ignore. We'll take every precaution, and we'll do this together. I promise you, we'll get through it."

I took a deep, shaky breath, trying to steady my nerves. Martin was right—we had no other choice. If we didn't do this, the consequences would be dire. I knew that, deep down, but the fear still gnawed at me.

The abruptly resumed in the room, The voice replied with chilling finality, "Failure is not an option. Should you falter, the consequences will be dire. The spirits that hunt you will not rest until they have claimed what they seek. Your only hope lies in completing this task exactly as instructed."

The room seemed to grow darker, the shadows deeper and more menacing. I took a deep breath, trying to steady myself. "What do we need to do first?" I asked, turning to Martin.

Martin nodded, already thinking ahead. "We need to find a dark cloak, something that can obscure you completely. And we need to choose what you'll offer as your prized possession."

I thought about the items that mattered most to me, the things that held the deepest personal significance. My father's watch, an heirloom passed down through generations, came to mind. It was a symbol of my family, my history, and my connection to those who had come before me.

"My father's watch," I said, the words heavy with emotion. "I'll use that."

Martin nodded. "Good choice. It's significant and meaningful. Now, for the blood..."

I swallowed hard, the thought of cutting myself making me queasy. But I knew it was necessary. "I'll do it," I said, more to convince myself than anyone else.

Martin nodded, relief washing over his face. "I promise you, we'll be ready. We'll spend the entire day preparing, making sure we have everything we need. We'll figure out every detail, and we'll face this together."

We spent the next several hours discussing our plan, going over every possible scenario and what we would do in each case. Martin was meticulous, thinking of every potential problem and coming up with solutions. His thoroughness reassured me, calming my frayed nerves bit by bit.

"We'll need to gather some supplies," Martin said, making a list. "Candles, matches, a cloak for you, and of course, your father's watch. We need to find a knife that's sharp enough to draw blood but not cause serious harm. We'll also need to map out the route to the graveyard and the exact location of the Gates of Hell."

I nodded, feeling more focused now that we had a plan. "I'll get the watch and the cloak," I said. "Do you have a knife we can use?"

Martin nodded. "I have a hunting knife that should work. We'll also need to bring something to clean and bandage your hand after you cut yourself. We don't want any infections."

I nodded, feeling a hint of relief.

The next day dawned gray and overcast, a fitting backdrop for the task ahead. The weight of what I had to do pressed heavily on me, but amidst the fear and trepidation, there was an odd sense of peace. Perhaps this was the end of everything, of the terror that had haunted me, the nightmares that had become my reality. Maybe, just maybe, I could finally get back to my life without the looming threat of something unspeakable.

After a restless night, I decided to reach out to Steve and Tessa, the only people who had stuck by me through this nightmare. I sent them a text, explaining briefly what I was going to do.

"Hey guys, I know this sounds crazy, but I've angered some deity, and I have to appease it tonight. Going to the graveyard at midnight. Hopefully, this will be the end of it. Wish me luck."

I waited for a reply, staring at my phone screen until the text became blurry. No response came. Maybe they were busy, or maybe they thought I was joking. I couldn't blame them for either reaction. This whole situation felt like a bad horror movie.

With a sigh, I set my phone down and turned my attention to the table where I had laid out everything I needed. The black cloak, heavy and ominous, was neatly folded next to my father's watch, its worn leather strap and scratched face a testament to its long history. A box of my favorite shoes sat beside it, their polished surface catching the dim light.

In the center of the table was a small syringe filled with my own blood, we concluded using a dagger was practical enough and a syringe would do. Drawing it hadn't been easy. The sight of the needle and the thought of puncturing my own skin had made my stomach churn, but I had managed it. Now, the dark red liquid sat waiting, a vital component of the ritual that might save my life.

I felt a strange calm as I organized the items, checking and rechecking to make sure everything was in order. Martin's voice echoed in my mind, reminding me of each step we had planned. I couldn't afford to forget anything. One mistake could be fatal.

As I worked, a memory surfaced, my mother telling me stories about bravery and facing one's fears. She had always been my hero, a pillar of strength and wisdom. I wondered what she would think of all this. Would she believe me? Would she stand by my side as Martin did? I liked to think she would. Yet I couldn't bring myself to tell her. I didn't want her scared. This would be my fourth visit to that damn place.

The hours passed slowly, each tick of the clock amplifying the tension in my chest. I tried to distract myself by focusing on the preparations, but my thoughts kept drifting back to the texts I had sent. Steve and Tessa still hadn't replied. I hoped they were okay and that they'd understand why I had to do this.

My room's heavy curtains let in a meek stream of daylight that threw an uneven, murky light across the chaotic interior. It was a quiet morning, almost peaceful in its deceptiveness, as though the outside world had no idea of the chaos that was growing behind these four walls. I was sitting on my bed's edge, the black cloak weighing heavily on my lap as a subtle reminder of the work that still needed to be done.

I had been assembling everything I needed for the greater part of the morning. On the table were my father's watch, a box containing my beloved shoes, and a syringe that had my own blood. Each object had a great deal of personal meaning, and having them there just made the seriousness of what I was going to do all the more apparent.

Examining the garment, I did so with a sense of finality. The heavy, thick cloth absorbed light and exuded a sense of solemn intent. I adjusted it till it fit snugly over my shoulders and draped it over my shoulders. The cloak was designed to totally hide me and make me blend into the night's blackness, but it also gave the impression that it was a thin barrier protecting me from any unforeseen horrors.

My fingers grazed the cool metal of the gun I'd tucked inside the cloak as I fastened it. I wasn't gullible; I understood that the ceremony might not be enough to pacify whatever was waiting for me at the cemetery. I was worried about the voice that had spoken to us because of its vague directions and unnerving assurance. I wasn't going to go into this unprepared; there were just too many unknowns and variables.

I had made sure the gun was loaded and ready by carefully inspecting it. Its substantial weight provided comfort in an increasingly strange and dangerous world, serving as a concrete form of protection. I was aware that using a gun to combat otherworldly forces might seem pointless, but it was still preferable to feeling absolutely powerless.

I put several crucifixes inside a side pocket of the robe. Years ago, my mother had given them to me, adamant that with Jesus by my side, I could conquer all obstacles. I had struggled to believe for years, with the harsh truths of life wearing thin on my faith. But just now, I needed all the faith I could summon, facing the prospect of a confrontation with terrible forces beyond my comprehension. The crucifixes provided consolation and strength in this moment, connecting me to my mother's steadfast faith and my own history.

After making all the necessary arrangements, I reclined on the bed and gave myself a moment to relax. My mind was racing with ideas and feelings, fear and willpower battling it out for supremacy. The words of the voice reverberated in my head, serving as a continual reminder of the stakes. All I wanted was to be able to completely comprehend what I was getting into by asking more questions. However, time had been of the essence, and I now needed to proceed with the knowledge at hand.

Slowly, the minutes passed by, each seeming to go on forever. The walls of the room felt like they were pushing in on me, pressing me down with the weight of impending disaster. I made an effort to keep my attention on the activity at hand in order to prevent my thoughts from straying. However, it was challenging. The fear was a constant force that was eating away at me, threatening to break through my weak will.

I considered Steve and Tessa, but they haven't responded yet. I hoped they were secure and comprehended the necessity of my actions. I didn't want them to get caught in the crossfire if something went wrong tonight. This was my obligation and my load to bear. I needed to finish it.

The sun rose higher in the sky, but my room remained so dark that not much of its light could be seen. With each stride, the cloak fluttered about my ankles as I stood and paced. The weight of the gun kept me grounded and focused while serving as a constant reminder of the danger that lay ahead. I had to have faith in my ability to pull through and put an end to this horror permanently.

Suddenly, Tessa's call had come through, jolting me out of my thoughts. Her name flashed on the screen, and I hesitated for a moment before answering, my heart pounding in my chest.

"Hey, Tessa," I said, trying to keep my voice steady despite the nerves.

"Jason!" Her voice was filled with relief and worry. "Oh my God, where are you? What's going on? This whole thing sounds crazy. Are you okay?"

I took a deep breath, grateful to hear her concern. "I'm still at home," I replied. "I've been preparing for what's ahead tonight."

There was a brief pause on the line before Tessa spoke again, her voice tinged with worry. "Jason, I think this might be a trap. I mean, who knows what we're dealing with here? If anyone should be punished for angering some deity, it's me, not you."

I shook my head, even though she couldn't see me. "Tessa, don't blame yourself. This isn't your fault. I appreciate your concern, but I have to do this. I can't just sit back and let these things dictate my life."

"But Jason…" she started, her voice trailing off.

I interrupted gently, "How's the baby? Is everything okay?"

There was a soft sigh on the other end of the line. "The baby's never been better," Tessa replied, her voice warming slightly. "He's growing so fast. Steve's away at work, and I haven't had a chance to tell him about your text yet. He's going to be worried sick when he finds out."

"I'm sorry to put you all through this," I said sincerely.

"It's not your fault," Tessa replied firmly. "We're family, Jason. We stick together through thick and thin. If you're really going through with this, then I promise you, I'll be there to fight for you. We'll figure this out together."

I felt a wave of gratitude wash over me. "Thank you, Tessa. That means a lot."

There was a brief silence before Tessa spoke again, her tone softer. "Jason, I still think this is incredibly dangerous. Have you thought about what happens if this doesn't work? What if you make things worse?"

I nodded, even though she couldn't see me. "I know. But I can't let fear dictate my decisions anymore. I have to face this head-on. Besides, I'm not just interested in pacifying this deity. I want to understand these beings and the people who worship them. There's something bigger going on here, something we don't fully understand."

Tessa was quiet for a moment, processing my words. "I get it," she finally said. "Just promise me you'll be careful, okay? And keep me updated. I need to know you're safe."

"I will," I promised. "I'll call you as soon as it's over, I promise."

"Good," Tessa replied firmly. "And if anything goes wrong, you call me immediately. We'll come get you, no questions asked."

I smiled weakly, touched by her unwavering support. "Thanks, Tessa. I really appreciate it."

"You're welcome," she said softly. "Take care of yourself, Jason. And remember, we love you."

"I love you guys too," I replied, my voice thick with emotion.

We said our goodbyes, and I hung up the phone, feeling a strange mix of emotions. Tessa's concern had bolstered my spirits, but her words had also highlighted the gravity of what I was about to do. This wasn't just about me anymore, it was about my family, my friends, and the unknown forces that threatened us all.

I stood up and walked over to the table where the ritual items lay waiting. The cloak still draped over the chair, the gun hidden within its folds. My father's watch gleamed faintly in the dim light, a silent reminder of the generations that had come before me. I picked it up and held it in my palm, feeling its weight and history in my hand.

As I stared at the watch, memories flooded my mind—memories of my father's stories, of his strength and resilience in the face of adversity. He had always taught me to face my fears head-on, to never back down from a challenge. Now, more than ever, I needed to draw on that strength, to channel his courage and determination.

With a deep breath, I slipped the watch into the pocket of the cloak and checked the time. The hours were slipping away, bringing me closer to the appointed hour. There was still so much I didn't know, so many unanswered questions. But I couldn't afford to dwell on uncertainty now. I had made my decision, and I had to see it through.

I glanced at the crucifixes nestled in my pocket, their presence a source of comfort and reassurance.

The afternoon faded into evening, the room growing darker with each passing minute. I paced restlessly, my mind racing with thoughts of what lay ahead. The clock on the wall seemed to taunt me, its ticking a reminder of the relentless march of time.

Suddenly, there was a knock at the door, breaking the silence. I froze, my heart skipping a beat. Yet I knew who it was. I approached the door cautiously, my hand hovering over the handle. With a deep breath, I opened it.

Martin stood on the threshold, his expression a mix of concern and determination. "Jason," he said, "The earlier we get there the earlier we can get this over with." Martin scratched his hair looking at me with expectations.

I was grateful to see him, but I needed just a few moments to get my shit together. "Just a minute," I said and went back in

I looked at the wall clock, seeing the hands slowly turn to night. Time was running out, drawing me nearer to the decisive moment. In an attempt to quiet the storm inside of me, I closed my eyes and inhaled deeply. This needed to function. There was nothing else to do.

At last, the outside light started to diminish as the shadows lengthened. It was nearly time. I gathered my belongings and double-checked that everything was where it should be. Everything was there, prepared for the ritual, including the shoes, the blood syringe, and the watch. I felt the cloak's weight rest on my shoulders as I wrapped it firmly about me.

I moved toward the door as the last of the daylight faded. The quiet, chilly air was accompanied by an almost unbearable silence. I took time to appreciate my room's familiar surroundings and contemplated whether I would ever see it again. I took one more deep breath before venturing out into the night.

Martin was waiting for me, his face displaying a mixture of worry and resolve. His voice was firm but carried a hint of underlying stress as he inquired, "Ready?"

I felt the resolve inside me harden as I nodded. I answered, "Ready," using that word as a statement of intent.

Silently, we made our way to his truck as the darkness embraced us with its dark embrace.

Martin and I drove through the dim evening as the sky transformed into a deep, foreboding shade of indigo. The truck's stifling silence reflected the anxiety that had crept into my chest. The weight of the task ahead seemed even more palpable as each bump in the road appeared to startle my thoughts.

Upon departing from the well-known roads, I couldn't help but notice how different this drive was. The drive to the cemetery usually seemed to go on forever, with dread and anticipation building with every passing minute. But tonight, the drive felt unexpectedly short, as though time had suddenly sped up, pulling us relentlessly closer to our dismal destination.

The scene outside the window became a hazy patchwork of gloomy trees and empty streets. Only a faint glow remained after the sun had long since set behind the horizon. The truck's headlights sliced through the night, lighting the way ahead but not being able to chase away the nagging feeling of unease that stuck to me.

We had a quiet conversation on the drive. Martin had his head down and his jaw clenched into a straight line. His hands were clenched around the steering wheel, and his eyes darted to the rearview mirror as though he thought we were being followed by someone or something. My own thoughts were a jumbled mix of resolve, terror, and a strange detached feeling. It seemed as though a part of me was still astonished that we were actually taking this step and voluntarily moving toward the gates of hell, again. It felt like a dream I've had a thousand times now

Before long, the landmarks of the cemetery were visible, the towering gates were gone so I could tell we were near with the looming trees towering above the night sky. I felt a chill run down my spine at the sight of them. Shit was definitely real now. Martin brought the truck to a halt just outside the cemetery, the engine making a ticking sound as it cooled.

"Here we are," Martin softly whispered, breaking the silence that had descended between us. He gave me a quick glance, his gaze scouring mine for any hint of hesitancy.

I nodded after inhaling deeply. "Yeah, we're here."

With swift and precise motions, Martin leaped from the truck and surveyed his surroundings, searching for any indications of impending danger. I paused for a minute more, preparing myself for the impending event. The weight of the cloak on my shoulders and my objects of sacrifice bore down on me.

I got down from the truck carefully, and when I adjusted the cloak, it billowed gently around me. The smell of damp ground and rotting leaves assaulted my face when the chilly night air touched it. Through the trees, I could hear the discomforting soft sound of the wind rustling.

"You look dope, bro," Martin teased with a half-smile tugging at his lips. Even though his attempt at comedy didn't really lighten the mood, it was nonetheless appreciated.

I returned the favor with a meek smile "I look like I'm dressed for a Halloween gathering.

Martin laughed a little, but it hardly reached his eyes. "Ready?"

"As ready as I'll ever be," I replied, my voice steady despite the nerves that churned in my stomach.

We walked through the graveyard together. Passing through many tombstones. The familiar terrain took on an unsettling quality as the moonlight created sinister shadows.

We had to walk cautiously past overturned tombstones and gnarled roots that protruded from the ground like skeletal fingers because the graveyard's walkway was uneven and overgrown.

With the path ahead obscured by darkness, we moved toward the trees in the woods. As I moved, the sound of the cloak brushing against the ground made a faint whispering sound in the quiet.

The trees towered in front of us, their limbs extending like bony fingers. The mood grew more stuffy and darker as we descended farther into the woods. Only the occasional rustle of leaves or the distant screech of an owl disturbed the nearly oppressive calm.

With his flashlight piercing the obscurity, Martin took the lead. I trailed along closely, feeling the tension in the air sharpen my senses.

Martin continued forward, and I followed closely behind, walking with hesitation and uncertainty. He moved with his usual bravado, like we were just heading to a bar to grab a beer or something, rather than summoning a spirit in the middle of a graveyard that was haunted by demons. It was almost weird how casual he seemed considering the situation.

I had the unshakeable feeling that we were being watched as we strolled. My eyes raced around, looking for anything unusual, but nothing was visible in the shadows. Still, the feeling lingered, an itch at the back of my mind that would not go away. The atmosphere seemed to be electrified with an invisible force, brimming with excitement.

I couldn't contain my uneasiness and yelled, "Wait," to Martin. Where Martin's confidence was coming from eluded me. With a casual shrug, he looked back at me, his face momentarily lit by the flashlight's beam.

The cemetery was silent, and it felt oppressive, like a thick blanket covering me. Because of the unsettling silence that enveloped us, every step appeared to reverberate in the stillness. The smell of damp ground and rotting leaves filled the air, blending with another smell, something subtle, almost a metallic tang that made me shudder: The scent reminded me of the being who seemed to be waiting for me at the end of the road; it was the same one I had detected the last time I came here.

"Martin, are you sure about this?" My question was hardly audible above a whisper. The absolute stillness made talking seem like a transgression.

He came to a stop and looked back at me, his expression too dark to discern. "We've come this far, Jason. We can't back out now. Trust me, it's going to be okay."

Martin looked back again and chuckled. "Didn't you hear the spirit? The earlier we give the sacrifice, the better. 12:00 sharp, and we're done."

There was an eagerness in his voice that I didn't quite get. For him, this was an opportunity to go on an adventure and test his abilities and knowledge. But it was a desperate attempt on my part to put an end to the horror that had taken over my life. I could still clearly picture the beast from our previous encounter, its hideous shape rising out of the shadows. I swear, I wanted to turn back and go home at that very moment. Martin, though, was here for me and more excited than I could have imagined about this. I didn't want to let him down.

His words did little to release the knot of fear that was tightening in my chest. I nodded, convincing myself more than him, and we carried on.

The atmosphere grew more oppressive the farther we traveled. The silence got deeper as the shadows became darker. The sounds of the occasional twig snapping or leaves rustling beneath our feet felt abnormally loud, resonating in the silence like a gunshot. Every beat of my heart reminded me of the fear coursing through my veins. My heart pounded in my chest.

My mind was always racing with ideas of what was ahead as we strolled. The spirit had given clear instructions, but the ramifications were horrifying. It all seemed like a deranged nightmare, the thought of offering up something priceless, dousing it in my own blood, and taking it to the gates of hell at midnight. I had no option, though. This was the only way to calm the god, who had become enraged. The only thing that could have stopped the constant agony that had befallen me.

With a blood-curdling stare in its eyes, the full moon was looming over us. The moonlight's crimson glow gave everything an unsettling appearance, lighting our way and letting us see a little way into the woodland. The moonlight added to the bizarre ambiance of the night by casting long, twisting shadows that seemed to move and writhe with each step we took.

We could hear the sounds of the night closing in around us as we moved farther into the forest. The sounds of the leaves rustling, the occasional snap of a twig beneath my foot, and the distant hoot of an owl all mingled together to create an unsettling symphony. But then I started to hear other footsteps, like someone or something moving slightly out of sight. I glanced toward Martin in an attempt to find comfort as my skin prickled with terror.

Martin's gaze was fixed forward. I couldn't see his face but his body language exuded serenity and an unwavering sense of assurance. There was no sign of panic.

"Yeah, I sense some spirits here," Martin said in a steady, quiet voice. "These are by no means inferior ones. They are now staring at us right now so show some respect."

Even though his remarks made me shudder, I forced myself to continue walking. With every step we took, we ventured deeper into the heart of the forest. The silent oppression that had hung over the cemetery gave way to the soft sounds of the night forest, but the uneasy feeling of surveillance persisted. It appeared as though shadowy eyes were watching us from above, tracking everything we did.

There was a tiny, overgrown trail through the trees, with a tangled canopy of branches above us. Dappled patterns were created on the ground when the moonlight permeated the foliage. I could feel the moisture sticking to my skin because the air was damp and chilly. I could see movement every now and again out of the corner of my eye, but when I looked, nothing was there.

"Keep moving J. Take your focus off them."

Heart thumping in my chest, I nodded. The additional footsteps persisted. And I could tell the spirits Martin had felt were nearby, observing us with a malicious fascination.

I couldn't resist looking around to see if there was anything visible trailing us. Shapes appeared and vanished in an equally rapid manner as the shadows appeared to move and transform. The trees towered and gleaned, their limbs extending like bony hands.

Feeling like a shadow myself, I trailed closely after Martin's, my dark cloak snugly around me. The thick, cozy cloth provided a slight shield against the encroaching fear that could have easily overcome me. A package of my favorite shoes covered in blood, my sacrifice, trembled in my hands as I walked.

The feeling that we were being watched intensified as we ventured more into the woodland. It seemed as though shadowy eyes were monitoring us from behind, watching everything we did. With my pulse thumping in my chest, I nervously looked about, but I saw nothing. There was no way out of the darkness, and the moonlight revealed very little of our surroundings.

The moon's unsettling light was hardly enough to light our path as the shadows crept deeper underneath us.

Suddenly, Martin stopped dead in his steps, and I stopped right after him, a shiver running up my spine. A suffocating silence descended upon us, replacing the weird sounds of footsteps and rustling leaves that had once filled the forest. Martin was still, his head aimed ahead, his body stiff as if he had been immobilized.

My heart skipped a beat as my worry began to grow. "What's up, Mart?" I asked, attempting to maintain a steady tone. "Why are we stopping?"

There was no reply. Martin was eerily silent. I turned to see that the ghostly footsteps had stopped. The vast, dark woodland did not reveal any signs as to why Martin had frozen. I couldn't even tell where we were because we were basically in the middle of nowhere .

The stillness dragged on, every moment seeming to last forever. It appeared as though the shadows surrounding us were getting longer and more ominous, as though they were preparing to engulf us completely. I had enough of Martin's enigmatic silence.

"Mart!" I called once more, my voice resonating a little in the silence. He did not even flinch, nor did he move. He seemed not to have heard me at all though he was only a few feet away from me. I started to feel panicky as my thoughts started to race with all the possible outcomes. Was he under a spell? Has something been done to him by the spirits?

I anxiously searched my surroundings in the hopes of finding something, anything, to help me understand what was going on. A spectral glow appeared on the ground as moonlight seeped through the foliage.

The quiet felt oppressive. My terror increased as every sound I made seemed to reverberate in the void. My heart was beating like a drum inside my chest, and I was breathing quickly and shallowly. With a hint of urgency in my voice, I called Martin's name once more, but to no avail.

I hesitantly moved toward him and extended a quivering hand. "You know what, Mart, I'm just gonna drop this right here and be on my way back." Even to my own ears, my voice came off as timid and little. The offering I held in my hands seemed heavy, like a weight I didn't want to bear.

Martin said nothing at all, just staying motionless. A part of his face was lighted by the unsettling glow of the moon, underlining his intense, unwavering look. It appeared as though he was enthralled with something that only he could see, something both terrible and alluring at the same time.

I had a wave of annoyance and terror as the stifling darkness and silence closed in about me. It was getting too much for me. I considered abandoning him here, but my friendship with him prevented me from doing so. Now that he had come here for me, I could not let go of him.

"Okay, fine," I murmured in a tremulous voice. "I'll handle it on my own. We can leave when I make the sacrifice.

I put my blood-filled syringe and the package of my beloved properties on the ground. I shook my hands and tried to concentrate on the work at hand.

I was about to carry out what I believed was  the ceremony when I heard, barely audibly

"Stop." Martin said curtly. "Don't move." He commanded.

"What's this, Mart?" I asked, my heart skipping a beat at his icy tone.

"They are here. Not another word, J. Pay respect!" Martin's voice was low and tense, sending a chill down my spine. I stood still in the dark, gripping my sacrifice for dear life.

The forest around us seemed to close in, the trees looming like silent sentinels. The moon's light barely penetrated the thick canopy, casting eerie shadows on the ground. The air was thick with an oppressive, suffocating silence that threatened to swallow me whole. It was a silence so profound that it felt alive, a presence all its own.

My breath caught in my throat as I strained to listen, to discern any sign of what had so suddenly captured Martin's attention. The only sound was the pounding of my own heart, loud and insistent in my ears. Every rustle of leaves, every crack of a twig, sent my nerves on edge. I felt as though I was standing on the edge of a precipice, teetering dangerously close to the abyss.

I glanced at Martin, who remained rigidly still, his eyes fixed ahead with a look of intense concentration. His usual bravado was replaced with a seriousness that was almost frightening. He didn't look scared, but rather, focused and determined, as if he were communicating with unseen forces. The red of his shirt, with its giant silver skull, seemed to glow faintly in the dim light, giving him an almost spectral appearance.

"Mart," I whispered, my voice barely audible, "what's happening?"

"Shh," he hissed, not taking his eyes off the darkness ahead. "Pay respect, J. They're watching."

I swallowed hard, feeling the weight of his words settle heavily on my shoulders. I forced myself to remain still, my muscles tensed and ready to react to any sudden movement.

Suddenly, Martin slowly turned around. As he did, I saw an eerie glint in his eyes. "It's asking permission to possess me, J," he said, chuckling darkly. The gleam in his eyes was so unsettling I almost peed my pants.

"No, Mart. Don't fall for it!" I screamed, panic rising in my chest. I couldn't imagine what would happen to Martin if that evil thing got to him.

"Turn around," Martin said curtly.

I hesitated, my mind racing. This didn't feel like a request but a command, issued by someone or something with an authority far beyond Martin's usual bravado. Slowly, reluctantly, I turned around, my heart pounding in my chest.

As I completed the turn, I was met with a sight that sent chills down my spine.

And there they were, in front of me, the devotees of Satan. Their dark cloaks billowed softly in the night breeze as they stood in the horizontal perfect line. Their features were entirely hidden by their cloaks, giving them the appearance of ghostly figures rising from the shadows of the forest. Their presence emanated a tangible dissatisfaction, a quiet rage that lingered in the air like a storm cloud about to break, even if I was unable to see their expressions.

Every inch of the clearing was filled with an awful, horrible stench, and the atmosphere was oppressively thick. It smelled like rotting meat and decomposing plants combined with a harsh, sulfurous tang. It bit my nose and caused my stomach to turn, with a bile-like taste rising to the back of my throat.

The cloaks of the individuals blended in perfectly with the ambient darkness as they stood perfectly still. Their appearance was unearthly with just the occasional gleam of moonlight reflecting off their concealed eyes to indicate their presence. With their hands loosely coiled and ready to be unfurled at any time, each of them wielded a long and terrifying whip.

The only sounds in the deafening silence were the distant hoot of an owl and the sporadic rustle of leaves. The woodland appeared to be holding its breath, anticipating the occurrence of a heinous deed. The frenetic pace of my beating heart rang in my ears, adding to the unsettling silence all around me.

I could feel their eyes on me, penetrating deep into my soul with a ferocity that made my skin crawl, even though their faces were hidden. They seemed to be able to see right through me, past my outward appearance to my true nature. It felt incredibly disconcerting, like if a thousand cold digits were making patterns on my back.

The moonlight created shadows that appeared to twitch and writhe around them like a ghoulish ballet. It was difficult for me to tell where the cloaks ended and the darkness started because of the tricks that light and dark performed on my mind. It appeared as though the figures were somewhat solid and partially out of this world, as they moved and blurred at the borders.

I felt a chill go down my spine as a chilly breeze blew through the clearing and stirred the leaves. The rising feeling of dread was exacerbated by the chill in the air that seemed to penetrate into my bones. The stench intensified, becoming more overpowering and made breathing impossible.

Cold sweat appeared on my brow as I stood there, paralyzed by terror, and my hands shook as I gripped my sacrifice. The reality of the situation struck me like a ton of bricks. I was surrounded by powers that could completely destroy me—true evil that was beyond my comprehension.

"You came back!" one of them said, their voice a cold hiss that sent chills down my spine.

"Where are your friends?" another asked, the sneaky eeriness in their tone making my heart race even faster.

"I came to appease the deity," I quickly replied, my voice trembling despite my efforts to stay calm. "I realized I wronged you and want to make this right."

"What do you bring?" one of them demanded, their voice cutting through the oppressive silence like a knife.

I took the box and dropped the box right in front of them, hoping it would be enough. One of the cloaked figures rushed forward, their movements swift and almost inhumanly fluid. They checked the contents of the box, revealing it to the others. As they looked at each other, a wave of disbelief seemed to pass through them.

"There are only sprinkles of blood on it," one of them said, their voice dripping with disappointment and anger. "Where is the unborn child, the human heart, the flesh?" The voices echoed with an eerie credence, each word terrifying me further. I didn't know what to say.

"This was what I was told to bring," I stammered, my voice barely above a whisper. I felt a wave of nausea wash over me.

"By who?" Their deep, ominous voices growled like distant thunder. With my heart racing, I glanced back to Martin in the hopes of finding some comfort, but his look made me shiver. A hideous smile contorted his face, a sign of surrender to an invisible force that had taken hold of him.

He had been claimed by the dark entity that had hovered above us in the forest, entangling his will in its grasp. I looked around, feeling the weight of their combined attention bearing down on me, and fear tightened its hold on my neck. With measured and meticulous motions, they surrounded me, sending shivers down my spine with every step.

"Mart! Mart!" With desperation, I let forth a cry that reverberated across the silent night air. Martin, however, stayed still, his body stiff and unbending like a puppet they were controlling. My cries were met with an oppressive quiet, only broken by the damp earth beneath their feet and the rustle of their robes.

A basic instinct pushed me to run as the tension increased, to get away from these evil creatures before it was too late. But I was aware that there was no way to run from what was waiting for me in the middle of the forest, with the full moon and the evil spirits that hid in its shadows keeping a close eye on me.

The air grew even colder, and the silence that followed was suffocating. I felt like I was being crushed under the weight of their expectations, their anger. The oppressive atmosphere made it hard to breathe, and I could feel my heart pounding in my chest like a drum. My mind raced, trying to think of what to say, how to explain, but words failed me.

The figures seemed to grow taller, more menacing, as they stared at me. Their cloaks billowed slightly in the breeze, and the stench of decay grew stronger, making my stomach churn.

"You were given specific instructions," one of them said, their voice dripping with disdain. "This is not enough."

I swallowed hard, trying to find my voice. "I—I didn't know," I said, my voice shaking. "I was told this would be enough."

"Who told you?" another demanded, their voice sharp and accusing.

"The spirit," I replied, my voice barely audible. "It said this would appease the deity."

The silence stretched on, the oppressive atmosphere growing heavier with each passing second. The figures remained motionless, their eyes fixed on me. I could feel their anger, their disappointment, radiating from them like a physical force. My mind raced, trying to think of what to do, how to make this right.

One of them stepped forward, their movements slow and deliberate. "This is not enough," they repeated, their voice low and menacing. "You were supposed to bring the unborn child, the human heart, the flesh. This offering is an insult."

I felt a wave of panic wash over me. "I didn't know. I thought this would be enough. Please, give me another chance."

The figures remained silent, their eyes fixed on me. The oppressive silence pressed down on me, making it hard to breathe, hard to think. I could feel their anger, their disappointment, and it was crushing. I didn't know what to do, what to say. I felt utterly helpless, at the mercy of forces beyond my control.

"This was your only chance," one of them said, their voice cold and final. "There will be no more chances."

I realized with a dismal sensation that there was just one option remaining. I had to face whatever horror lay ahead of me, face the darkness head-on and hold onto hope that, in spite of everything, I may survive.

Quickly I brought out my gun and shot in the air. With a piercing crack, the gunshot tore through the strained air, breaking the serenity of the night.

I stood there with my gun in my hand and adrenaline pumping through my veins. The figures in hoods appeared unfazed. Even with their cloaks on, I could feel their eyes cutting right through me as they considered my next move with measured caution.

"You can make all the noise you want Jason, you can shout all you want," one of the cloaked figure said in a quiet, icy voice. "But your bullets will soon run out, and you'll have nowhere to go."

His remarks carried a dark assurance that made me realize how vulnerable I was in this dire circumstance. I tightened my jaw, determined not to give up in the face of insurmountable difficulties. "Cowards," I spit out, a hint of desperation and rage in my voice. "Show yourselves, take off your cloaks!" Even if this was my last moment, I needed to see who these people are.

The sound of an owl hooting in the distance and the rustle of leaves in the breeze broke the tense silence. The individuals in cloaks did not move, their wordless confrontation a sign of their unsettling determination. I was filled with a wave of fear and frustration, realizing that my defiance might not be sufficient to face them.

I noticed a glimmer of movement as the seconds passed by as though they were hours. With a leisurely motion, one of the figures moved forward and pulled down their hood. As the hood came off, moonlight seeped through the branches overhead, giving their features a soft glow.

At first, I swear I had never seen those faces before. These were strangers, perhaps from the next town. Their gazes were icy and aloof. Their faces were emaciated, the moonlight creating shadows that emphasized their sunken eyes and thin cheeks. They appeared to have lost all human warmth and compassion.

Then, my heart froze in my chest at what I witnessed next. I saw the faces I knew. Among them was Mr. Johnson, the high school teacher, his face as severe and menacing as ever. In the unsettling light, his towering, intimidating body appeared even more sinister. His eyes were icy, and I could feel my skin crawl as his lips twisted into a barely noticeable smile.

I then noticed a couple more well-known local faces. Mrs. Whitaker, the sweet old lady who was constantly baking cookies for the children in the neighborhood, stood looking grimly determined. There was an unnerving intensity in her formerly gentle eyes. There was also Mr. Hughes, the neighborhood mechanic who always offered assistance when someone's car broke down, his normally grease-stained hands now gripping a threatening-looking whip. Normally pleasant and humorous, his rough features now had a harshness about it that suggested terrible, deep secrets.

And at last, the most startling of all the revelations: Martin's mother. The sight of her standing there with her eyes fixed on mine made my breath catch in my throat. Although her demeanor was like the first time I saw her, like she had just woken up from a nap and did not give a damn about what was going on around her, there was a lack of curiosity in her eyes. There was no denying the seriousness of her presence. Her presence was a part of this, the same darkness that had been stalking me.

My bones ached with astonishment. Was this a ruse to trick me? Did Martin also know about this? Was he just another pawn in this bizarre game, or had he been letting me know all along that this was a trap?

With a rushing mind, I glanced back at Martin. He still had that unsettling, frozen look on his face, and his eyes were empty. His customary bluster and good humor vanished.

He appeared constipated as if his soul is being squeezed out of them. His complexion was clammy and looked incredibly pale. He had a stiff, stooped posture and his lips were tightened, his brows wrinkled, his jaw clenched in a strained attitude. There was an occasionally discernible lack of energy or slow motions, as though he was having difficulty moving or carrying himself.

His eyes appeared glazed over indicating that he was not quite present.

There was an aura of threat about the people I recognized from town, suddenly exposed as members of this evil sect. It appeared as though they were taking pleasure in my anxiety, thriving on the worry that was undoubtedly imprinted on my face. Their distinctiveness added to the strange misery of the scenario, and each of them had a distinct, unnerving presence.

A strange silence descended across the clearing as the final cloak was taken off. As the temperature dropped, a tangible feeling of fear descended upon me. My heart was thumping fiercely inside my chest, every beat resonating in the stifling silence. It felt like the shadows were getting closer to me as they grew thicker and deeper.

Then I noticed them: two luminous spheres glimmering behind the worshipers. Their otherworldly light pierced through the darkness as they shone with a malicious intensity. The thing started to come out of the shadows, and my breath caught in my throat.

It was big and powerful, its shape scarcely discernible yet ominously familiar. The body of the beast appeared to be composed entirely of darkness, a void that absorbed the surrounding light. It towered above us, a massive, stifling force that exuded hate and strength. Its strange energy began to thicken the air, as if it were pressing down on my very soul.

The most horrifying thing of all was its eyes. They were orbs of red and yellow that burnt with an ancient, unholy light, and they glowed with a scorching intensity. With a fury and greed that sent shivers down my spine, these eyes looked down at me from the heavens. The beast's stare was unavoidable; it was like a physical force that immobilized me.

"What are you?" I was barely able to speak in a whisper, my heart thumping loud enough to barely be heard. I could feel the anxiety creeping up on me, a chilling terror that was almost overwhelming.

Mr. Johnson took a step forward, a twisted smile taunting and mocking me. With a low, menacing voice, a tone full of derision and condescension, he remarked, "The one to receive your sacrifice." The darkness within his eyes appeared to radiate, mirroring the evil nature of the creature standing behind him.

With a chilling grace, the huge shape of the beast moved forward. It was hard to make out its shape because it seemed like the shadows themselves were living, moving and twisting all about it. But the sheer danger and force radiating from it was unmistakable. This was something much older and considerably more potent than a ghost or a demon.

The devotees dropped to their knees and bowed their heads in horror as the beast approached. A deep, rumbling growl filled the air, one that sounded as though it was vibrating through the ground under us. I was aware that I was in the midst of something genuinely wicked because I could feel it in my bones—a primitive, instinctive horror.

The closer it got, the more definite its form became. It easily towered over the highest trees due to its immense size. Thick black hide clothed its body, giving it an odd gloss that seemed to glitter.

I was staring at the eyes, though. Those piercing, evil eyes that appeared to see right into the core of my being. It was nearly intolerable to watch them as they were overcome with wrath and hunger. It took all of my strength to stay upright as I could sense the creature's wrath and desire for destruction radiating from those eyes.

I staggered backward. Fear and bewilderment were racing through my head as I frantically tried to figure out how to wake up from this nightmare. However, there was no way out. Here the beast was, and here it was for me.

That moment, Mart stumbled to the ground and began to convulse. His body contorted into strange shapes, and he let forth a horrible, guttural scream. He started throwing up, the sound of his vomiting filling the air as his eyes rolled back into his head. The smell was sickening, a sickly combination of blood and bile that turned my stomach. He lost control of his bowels a short while later, making the scene even more terrifying as he lay in his own squalor.

Mart's mother, her face a mask of panic and anguish, raced forward, seeing her son in such a dreadful position. "Mart! Mart, what's happening? What did you do to him?" Her voice broke with fear and agony as she yelled at no one in particular. She fell to her knees beside him, cleaning the blood and vomit off his face with the hem of her cloak while her hands trembled.

With a menacing light shining in its eyes, the beast towered over them. With their face still concealed by the shadows, one of the strangers wearing cloaks moved forward. The stranger growled, "Stay away from him!" with authority in their voice. "Your son is a seasoned vessel for the deity. Let it have its way."

With shocked and horrified eyes, Mart's mother remained still. She asked in a whisper, tears running down her cheeks, "A vessel? He's my son! He cannot put up with this."

The guy in the cloak remained still. "He has been chosen. It is his fate. Interference will only bring more suffering upon him—and upon you."

Mart was still convulsing, his shouts echoing through the darkness. Torn between her maternal instincts and the horror these people and this beast created, his mother gazed between him and the stranger. She was trembling as her hands hovered over him, yearning to help but being immobilized by the stranger's instruction.

The sound of the beast's low growl seemed to reverberate through the ground under us. Breathing became difficult as the odor of decay and sulfur filled the air. The believers stood motionless, staring at the scene that was being shown to them.

I watched in helpless horror, frozen in place. Mart's body kept twisted, his moans became ragged and weaker. His mother broke down in tears at this point, her hands gripping the hem of her cloak and her knuckles becoming white from stress. She pleaded, "Please," in a weak whisper. "Please, don't take my son."

The stranger did not avert his sight. "The rite needs to be finished. This is the divine will."

The creature released another low growl as its eyes brightened. Mart's back arched off the ground, his body going rigid as though some unseen force was drawing him upward. He suddenly wrenched his eyes open, wide and blinded by an awful, alien light.

His mother let out a shriek, her voice hoarse with pain. The man grabbed her wrist and pulled her back as she reached out to embrace him. "Avoid meddling!" they growled. "You will doom us all!"

Mart's mouth twitched, producing words that no human should ever pronounce, words that appeared to emanate from somewhere deep within him. His mother snatched her hands and ran back to him. The language echoed with dark power; it was rough and guttural, archaic. The exertion made his body tremble, and blood started to trickle from his nostrils, ears, and eyes.

Mart looked like life was draining out of his eyes, his gaze dull and unfocused. His chest heaved with labored breaths, and I feared he could die at any moment. His skin was pallid, almost gray, and his body lay in a twisted heap on the ground, soaked in his own blood and vomit. The stench was overwhelming, making it hard to breathe.

I tore my eyes away from Mart to look at the beast looming above us. Its eyes, glowing with a malevolent light, were fixed on me as if it was waiting for the perfect moment to strike. I felt its otherworldly energy pressing down on me, suffocating and menacing.

"What's this all about, Mr. Johnson? Why?" I shouted, my voice trembling with a mix of fear and anger.

Mr. Johnson turned slowly, joining the ranks of the other cloaked figures. His face was a mask of cruel satisfaction. "When you're dead, Jason, you'll find out at the gates of hell. We are the guardians of hell, here to bring the rule of our lord and his domination."

The words hung in the air, chilling me to my core. "You have defiled our god, and now our only judgment is death," Mr. Johnson said, his voice cold and final.

The cloaked figures closed in around me, forming a tight circle. Their faces, though partially hidden by their hoods, revealed expressions of grim determination. The air grew heavier, and the oppressive silence returned, broken only by Mart's ragged breathing.

Mart's mother knelt beside him, her tears falling onto his lifeless face. "Please, don't take him," she pleaded, her voice breaking. "He's just a boy. He doesn't deserve this."

Mr. Johnson ignored her, his eyes fixed on me with a cold, calculating gaze.

The beast let out a low growl, its eyes never leaving me. I could feel its hatred, its desire to consume me, to drag me down into the depths of hell. My heart pounded in my chest, and my mind raced, searching for a way out, a way to save Mart, to save myself.

The cloaked figures began to chant, their voices rising in a dark, malevolent harmony. The ground beneath us seemed to tremble, and the air was thick with the scent of sulfur and decay. The beast roared, its voice shaking the very earth, and I felt a surge of terror wash over me.

Mr. Johnson stepped forward, a twisted smile on his face. "This is the end, Jason. There is no escape. Embrace your fate, and perhaps our lord will show you mercy."

I took a step back, my mind racing. I couldn't let them win. I had to do something, anything, to stop this. But as the chanting grew louder and the beast's eyes bored into me, I felt my resolve waver.

Suddenly, the chanting stopped, and an eerie silence fell over the clearing. Suddenly, the creature let out a rumbling, savage cry that shook the surrounding trees in the forest. It was an overwhelming noise, a horrifying fusion of strength and rage that seemed like it was shaking my bones. I lifted my gun and fired at the beast, unwilling to lose up on life. The bullet went through its body, yet it appeared to have some effect because the beast paused and its luminous eyes narrowed.

I swiftly aimed my remaining shots toward one of the cloaked individuals that had his whip close in on me. I shot, and the person staggered back into the woods, holding onto his side. The others paused for a split second, glancing between the beast and the fallen figure.

But it was only a fleeting uncertainty. The other cloaked people gave a terrifying hiss as their whips cracked through the air and they pounced toward me. My gunshots reverberated through the forest as I fired at a few of them, but it was too late. With a lash, one of the whips tore through the air and into my shirt. My chest began to burn as the whip tore through my flesh, causing instantaneous and severe pain.

I staggered back, gripping the area of my chest where the whip had hit. My fingertips bled, and my nose filled with a metallic smell. Cloaked creatures closed in, their eyes unblinking and icy. I was struck again with a whip, this time across my back, and the blow knocked me to my knees.

With pain and despair clouding my eyes, I gazed up. With an uncanny silence, the beast stood erect and observed the spectacle with flaming eyes full of wicked satisfaction. With their whips ready to strike again, the cloaked creatures maneuvered around me. Their hate and rage were radiating from them, and I could feel the weight of their glances.

I pulled up my gun once more, trying to hit the closest figure in a desperate move. The sound of an empty room reverberated in the silence as I pulled the trigger. My ammunition ran out. My only weapon was now worthless, and panic shot through me. The shrouded man I had targeted smirked and moved closer, brandishing his whip.

"Is this how it ends?" My thoughts were racing with sorrow and terror. The whip dropped once again, slicing across my arm and making me scream in agony. The adrenaline that had kept me running was beginning to wear off, and I could feel my strength ebbing.

The figures in cloaks refused to budge. I was repeatedly lashed by their whips, and each blow hurt more than the last. I had trouble seeing as my vision became blurry.

With a taste of blood in my mouth, I lay there panting for air. With the sound of the beast's rumbling growl, I knew this was it. There was not a last-minute rescue, no escape. I would be sacrificed so that the beast and its adherents might have their way.

I tried to get up to my feet, but the pain caused my legs to buckle, causing me to stumble forward. My body rejected the movement, and my vision swam with stars and blackness. Another whip slashed across my head, and the crucifix dropped out of my pocket and clattered against the ground. My skull exploded with pain, and I felt a warm trickle of blood mix with the dirt and perspiration running down my cheeks.

The environment appeared to decelerate. I could hear the shrouded individuals' smug sneers, my breathless breaths, and the sickening thud of my heartbeat in my ears. Blood shot out of my nose, filling my mouth with its metallic flavor. Amid the turmoil and terror, I noticed a glimpse of hope: my mom's cross laying on the ground, despite every nerve in my body screaming in anguish.

I reached for it, shaking fingers grasping the cold, little sliver of metal like it was a lifeline. I was thinking of my mother when she said that everything could be overcome by faith. I needed all the faith I could get at the moment, even if I wasn't sure whether I believed it.

Perched precariously on the brink of unconsciousness, I mustered every last ounce of remaining strength. The beast's dark, scary figure loomed over me, its eyes glowing with hellish fire, even though my vision was blurry. I threw the crucifix at the beast in a desperate shout, throwing all of my fear, wrath, and defiance into that one throw.

The cross flew through the air, a little ray of light against the suffocating gloom. As it flew, spinning nonstop, it appeared as though time would never end. All around me, the cloaked beings halted, their actions stopping as they tracked its path. The only sound audible for a little period of time was the gentle whoosh of the crucifix piercing the atmosphere.

It hit the beast in the chest solidly. With a guttural cry of anguish and rage bursting from its throat, the beast recoiled. I could feel the oppressive energy around us waning as the intensity of its rage appeared to rock the ground beneath us.

The monstrous, luminous eyes of the beast flickered with a mixture of surprise and wrath. With a shiver, its huge figure staggered back. It projected a surge of dark energy that made the veiled figures around me reel. Its hold on the forest and its adherents appeared to loosen for a brief period of time.

I staggered backwards to meet with the ground, my head whirling, my peripheral vision growing darker. I knew I had to keep battling even though I wasn't sure what would happen next or if the cross had actually made an impact or had only enraged the beast even more. Though my wounds throbbed and my entire body ached, I felt a ray of hope when I saw the beast stumbling.

The figures in cloaks surrounding me wavered, their self-assurance dented. Their whip-grips loosened as they exchanged nervous looks. I saw the first traces of doubt appear in their eyes and a weakening of their determination. Reeling from the shock of the crucifix, the beast let out another roar, but this time it sounded less certain, less unbeatable.

"Is this all that you got?" My voice was raspy but defiant as I yelled. "Do you think you can shatter me? Do you think you could steal my soul?" With a furious and steady glare, I stared down the beast and its minions while spitting blood onto the ground.

The beast's eyes met mine, and for an instant I was afraid it might charge forward and swallow me up in its blackness. However, it stayed in one spot, its shape vacillating, its strength appearing to be lessened by my meek act of faith.

Mart moaned and moved a little, his face twisted in agony, still slumped on the ground. Trapped between her anxiety for her son and the cult's directives, his mother watched after him. The figures in cloaks appeared less confident, their solidarity breaking under this unanticipated rejection.

There was another roar in the jungle, a cry of sheer anguish this time. The beast gave me a menacing glance, its eyes blazing with rage and malice. I was breathing heavily and my strength was beginning to fail. My cross was nearby, glowing slightly in the unsettling moonlight, but I was too frail to get to it.

All of a sudden, there were gunshots everywhere, and then there was the distinct sound of sirens. The police sirens' piercing wails could be heard through the trees, getting closer and louder by the second. Police cars flashed their red and blue lights, flooding the forest in an instant.

The scene descended into chaos when cops descended upon it, their flashlights piercing the night and their voices yelling orders. They advanced on the cloaked individuals with their weapons drawn, encircling the area with military precision.

The followers of Satan, who had appeared so formidable and terrifying only seconds before, were now overcome with fear. They turned and fled for their life, seeking to get away from the approaching police enforcement as their black cloaks billowed behind them. I noticed the beast was suddenly nowhere to be found.

As the police closed in, some of them tackled the escaping believers to the ground, while others put handcuffs on their wrists. I watched in horror. The noises of battle, the groans and screams of the captured, and the police's yelled commands resounded throughout the woodland.

I noticed Mr. Johnson attempting to flee in the confusion, his terrified expression contorted. Two officers seized him, took him to the ground, and put him in a restraint. For a split second, his gaze came to meet mine, and I saw the understanding of his approaching demise flash across his face.

Despite the pain and fatigue that were about to overcome me, I made an effort to concentrate and maintain consciousness. I felt a glimmer of optimism

Seeing how damaged I was, one of the officers came running over to me. "How are you doing? His flashlight beam swept across me, exposing my bleeding face and tattered clothing. "Can you move?" he questioned frantically.

"I... I don't think so," I said, barely able to see him.

My head was hammering and my eyesight blurry, I spotted a familiar face approaching through the mayhem as I teetered on the verge of unconsciousness. It was Tessa, a worried expression on her face. Her terrified eyes widened as she hurried over to me.

"Are you okay, Jason?" Her voice broke through the din all around us as she screamed.

I tried to reply, but I could hardly raise my voice above a whisper. "Tessa... I... I think so," I was able to mumble. I had to use all of my might to keep my eyes open because the pain was so intense.

My vision was fuzzy, but I could see a lot of different things going on all around me. The demon worshippers who had scared us were being arrested by the hordes of police that were swarming the area. But the beast had vanished. It had disappeared into the night, leaving only a spooky silence and a light sulfur odor in its wake.

Mart lay motionless and lifeless on the ground. While his mother was shouting and attempting to reach him, the cops grabbed her and took her into custody while they raised Mart's bloated body and took it away. Her agonized screams blended with the officers' yells and orders in my ears.

"Mart..." My heart was hurting at the sight of my friend, I whispered. It was difficult to determine if he was unconscious or dead. His eyes were closed, and his face was pale.

Tessa knelt next to me and put her hands softly over my face. She begged, "Stay with me, Jason," as tears filled her eyes. You'll be alright, I promise. Help is here."

I made an effort to concentrate on her and find solace in her company. "Tessa... the crucifix..." I muttered, my mind jumbled and unfocused. It was lost in the confusion, but I remembered throwing it at the beast.

"I'll find it," she vowed, casting a furtive glance around. "Just hold on."

With stern and determined expressions, the paramedics arrived. They examined my wounds fast, their hands moving quickly to stabilize me. As they applied pressure to my wounds, I flinched because the agony was sudden and intense.

As one of them told Tessa, "He's in bad shape," "We need to get him to the hospital, fast."

With a quivering voice, Tessa answered, "Do whatever you have to do." Looking at me with worry coursing through her face "Just save him."

The officers retreated to get my stretcher. I had one last look at Mart before they put him on a stretcher. He was receiving care from a different team of paramedics, his body unconscious and limp. There was a profound, gnawing fear at the sight. I was unsure if he would survive this experience.

With a mixture of worry and anxiety on her face, Tessa hovered over me as I lay on the cold, hard ground, my body aching. "Can you please hear me, Jason?" She begged, her voice cutting through the fog that obscured my vision, "Stay with me!" My attempt to reply was unsuccessful as the oppressive blackness engulfed my words and surrounded me from every angle.

I saw it through the haze in my vision: the beast. It perched high up in the trees, its eyes glimmering with something menacing and malevolent. With an intensity that made me feel as though my entire soul was being drawn towards it, it peered down at me. The air became heavy and stuffy, making it difficult for me to breathe as though I were trying to do so through a small straw.

I felt a surge of dread sweep over me, stronger than anything I had ever felt, as the beast's gaze pierced into me. With its eyes promising nothing but misery and suffering, it seemed as though the beast was greeting me at the entrance to hell. My heart thumped loudly in my chest, resounding in my ears like a drum.

When Tessa saw that I was having seizures, she screamed out in a desperate attempt to get aid. "Please, someone help him!" Her voice sounded far away, muffled by the heavy oppression all about me. It seemed as though my limbs were no longer mine; they were heavy and unresponsive. I was immobile. Though I wanted to reach out to her and let her know that I was still here. I felt I had intangible barriers enclosing me and suffocating me.

My chest tightened, the sensation of suffocation grew worse, and I began to breathe in short, weak gasps. My mind raced as I battled the unseen force imprisoning me as panic crept in. It was similar to being imprisoned in a fever dream, with my ability to distinguish between nightmare and reality gradually fading. I attempted to scream and cry out for assistance, but nothing came out of my mouth.

The beast's stifling stare depleted my power and breath, making it feel like a tangible weight. The borders of my vision grew darker, a sly darkness that seemed to engulf me completely. My heart was slowing down, and I could feel the thuds become progressively softer. The voices and sounds faded into a far-off hum, and the world around me appeared to shrink.

I could still see Tessa's face in the midst of this oppressive blackness, her terrified eyes wide as she kept calling for assistance. Her presence was like a little, fluttering light in the searing darkness. I tried to concentrate on her and find strength in her tenacity, but the beast's unwavering stare and oppressive force pulled me further and further down the abyss.

The air was getting colder, the shadows were getting longer and closer, and every second seemed to drag on forever. I was entrapped, with walls of darkness closing in on me on all sides, preventing me from moving or breathing. My body erupted in violent convulsions, each one a last-ditch effort to escape the grip of the beast. However, it seemed to tighten its hold on me the more I fought.

Tessa's calls for assistance became more urgent, and her voice became a lifeline amid the oppressive darkness. "Hold on, Jason! She pleaded, "Please, hang on!," her hands firmly grasping mine despite her diminutive stature. My body wouldn't cooperate with my want to give her hand back and let her know that I was still struggling.

The creature's gaze never faltered, its evil light serving as a continual reminder of its dominance over me. It seemed to be enjoying my suffering and reveling in my powerlessness. My thoughts were racing, trying to figure out how to break free from the beast's stifling hold and the oppressive blackness that enveloped me.

The beast's stifling stare was more than just a sensation; it was a real force that was squeezing my life out of me. My soul was being wrung out, drop by drop, as if it were a damp cloth that had been twisted by invisible hands. I wanted to scream when I saw this devil face-to-face to let out the fear gnawing at my insides, but the sheer evil of what was in front of me hushed my voice.

My body was overcome with an odd, intense heat that made me feel as though I was in the middle of a raging fire. Sweat streamed down my cheeks, tingling my eyes and impairing my eyesight as it mixed with the blood from the cut on my skull. There was no way out of this nightmare; it was pure torture. I could feel myself falling farther and further into the chasm as the thick, sharp air burned into my lungs with every breath.

I opened my mouth to speak, to ask for assistance, but my throat tightened, preventing any sound from getting through. I felt a wave of panic go through me, my heart pounding as I fought the invisible bonds holding me captive. As I watched Tessa fade away, her agonized face came into focus. Her eyes were wide with terror and despair. Desperate to keep me connected to the living world, her palms gripped mine.

But I was reluctant to go. I was unable to let go. There ignited a spark of defiance somewhere deep within me. I begged and screamed as I struggled against the oppressive blackness, but nothing could be heard. I hung on to that tiny glimmer of defiance, not willing to let it go out, even though it looked like the world was closing in around me.

My thoughts were racing, with memories appearing one after the other quickly. Faces of family members, happy and sad times, all mixed together in a flurry of chaos. I was unable to part from them. I had to prevent this evil force from triumphing. I willed myself to escape the beast's grip by mustering all the strength I still had.

My skin felt like it was being burned from the inside out as the heat increased. My muscles seized as the pressure increased, causing me to thrash in agony. The scorching, vengeful eyes of the beast pierced me, promising misery for all eternity. However, I couldn't afford to succumb to my fears. For Tessa, for myself, and for everyone else who relied on me, I had to fight.

It felt like an interminable fight, with every second seeming to elapse into eternity. I clawed my way towards the light by pushing back against the darkness. There was a wordless roar of resistance echoing through my entire existence as my mind screamed. I could feel my awareness wavering, on the verge of collapse, but I would not allow it to go out.

I was on the forest ground, on the verge of unconsciousness, when Tessa abruptly reappeared, startling me back to reality. I saw her kneeling next to me through blurry eyesight, her expression resolute. She grasped my cross in her hands, which glinted in the dim moonlight. She put it around my neck with shaky hands, and when the cool metal fell against my flesh, a chill went down my spine.

I felt a rush of something I hadn't realized was lacking the minute the cross hit my chest. I felt a surge of vitality. A stream of strength and resolve suddenly poured from within me, like a dam had broken. I felt a sense of calm resolve replace the terrible weight that had been crushing me.

The cross seemed to be pulsating with strength. The darkness that had threatened to devour me was chased away by its presence, which gave me a fresh feeling of purpose. Feeling its comforting weight against my heart, I closed my eyes and concentrated on the warmth emanating from the crucifix.

All of a sudden, the atmosphere seemed to be bursting with vitality. The beast vanished into thin air, having stood over me with its menacing look. Its shape vanished in the breeze like smoke, leaving only the echo of its roars and a subtle sulfurous smell.

I felt a surge of peace wash through me. Like I was cocooned in a cocoon of tranquility.

My ears were filled with the gentle, comforting sound of Tessa's voice. Her words were a comfort to my tired soul: "You're safe now, Jason." Her hand was softly on my shoulder, bringing my sense of reality back into the residual fog of tiredness.

I inhaled steadily and deeply, letting the tranquility I had just discovered seep into my being. My head ached, but it was only a faint throb as the tightness in my muscles relaxed. I knew that Tessa's comforting presence and the cops were there to keep me safe.

I felt my mom's crucifix around my neck, comforting me, and reached up to touch it. It had been my savior, the spark that had pushed away the darkness that had tried to swallow me.

Predawn quietness shrouded the forest as hours passed in profound stillness. The faint owl's cry in the distance and the gentle rustle of leaves in the wind transformed into a calming lullaby that helped me release the last of my anxiety.

I remember waking up in the hospital the next day. My vision focused on someone sitting next to my bed; It was Tessa. She had been sitting next to me until I woke up.

She stood up and leaned in when she saw I was conscious "Are you okay? Do you feel any pain?"

"Yea…no. I feel sore but I should manage.

Tessa leaned in again and whispered "Hey look who you're sharing a room with." I looked over to my left and it was Martin! I looked back at Tessa and saw she was smiling. "I'll leave you two for a while" She stood up and left the room quietly.

I laid there and watched Martin for a while. He was breathing on his own but he was hooked up to a bunch of machines. Somehow, I knew he was going to pull through. I turned over on my back and took a deep breath. It was all finally over.

Then out of the corner of my right eye, I noticed a figure standing outside my hospital room door looking at me. I turned to focus on it, thinking it was Tessa. But to my horror, it was Dr. Sanders staring at me through the window of the door with the most horrifying crooked smile on his face. He stood there for a few minutes and then, he slowly turned around and left.

I realized at that moment that this will never end. The battle will always rage between good and evil.

# THE END